"Will you stay if I ask you to?

. . . I need you, Julie."

If she answered, he didn't hear. The throbbing of his own pulse drowned out any other sound as he gathered her once more in his arms and crushed her to him.

Del's hands found themselves seeking the fine silken tangle of her hair and then he buried his face in it. The fragrance intoxicated him.

He kissed her ear, letting his lips tug softly on the lobe until she sighed with mounting passion. He could tell she fought it. There was no reason to delay, to tease, to torment. One more kiss . . .

She opened her eyes and discovered the room had gone dark. Del laughed quietly, his breath warm against her neck.

She took a deep breath, and he was not unaware of the way her breasts pressed against him.

"Del?" she whis

"Yes?"

"Make love to r

Firefly

LINDA HILTON

PAGEANT BOOKS

♪

PAGEANT BOOKS
225 Park Avenue South
New York, New York 10003

Copyright © 1988 by Linda Hilton

Cover artwork by Morgan Kane

Printed in the U.S.A.

First Pageant Books printing: October, 1988

10 9 8 7 6 5 4 3 2 1

*For Doug,
who lights up all my days and nights;
and for Rachel and Kevin,
who are learning not to bug Mom
while she's writing.*

Firefly

Chapter One

✦ ✦ ✦ ✦

THE NOON SUN bleached everything a dusty white, from the cloudless June sky to the parched main street of Plato, in the Arizona Territory. Nothing moved in the heat, not the leaves on the few cottonwoods, not the flag atop the post office building at the far end of town. No one even left a horse tied in front of the Castle Saloon; two stray dogs lay sprawled in the shade under the sidewalk, their coats too dry and dusty to attract flies.

Simon McCrory lowered his ponderous frame to an unpainted wooden chair and tipped it back on two legs until his shoulder hit the front wall of his general store.

"Might just as well lock up and go home," he muttered to Lucas Carter.

Lucas spat a stream of brown tobacco juice, stirring up a puff of dust that hung in the motionless air.

"You had any customers today?" he asked Simon.

"You seen any since you been here?"

Lucas shook his head.

"I only been here since ten."

"Well, I didn't have none before ten neither," the storekeeper grumbled. "Too damn hot."

A movement in the street caught Simon's eye. He quickly recognized the figure and did not even move.

"Ain't too hot for Mr. Hollstrom's daughter to bring him his lunch. Lookit her. One of these days that girl's gonna get heat stroke or something."

Julie Hollstrom would have agreed with Simon had she heard him. She looked longingly at the restaurant across Main Street from Papa's telegraph office. He could have purchased his lunch there. But Mama insisted Julie cook a meal for her father every day and take it to his office rather than have him leave his post. Being the telegraph operator was an enormous responsibility, not one to be walked away from every time one needed a bit to fill one's stomach. Besides, as Mama never stopped reminding Julie, it wasn't wise to waste Papa's earnings. He had been lucky to find this job so soon after their arrival in the Arizona Territory.

Julie felt the perspiration beading on her forehead. She couldn't wipe it away, and by the time she reached the telegraph office, her eyes burned excruciatingly. The pain reminded her that she was the cause of the family's leaving Indiana for Minnesota, and Minnesota for Kansas, and Kansas for the Arizona Territory. And Julie remembered to feel properly penitent as she opened the door.

The staccato inside the airless office told her a message was coming in. Her father's still-inexpert hand could not tap out the code so quickly, but he seemed to have no trouble receiving and deciphering the clicks and clacks. Quietly, so she did not interrupt Wilhelm Hollstrom's concentration, Julie set the tray on his desk and began to lay out the silverware.

The tapping of the telegraph key stopped, and a few seconds later Wilhelm scrawled the last word on his paper.

"How is your mama today?" he asked in heavily accented English.

"She was in the parlor with her embroidery when I left. She said she might feel like taking a walk later this afternoon."

"That is good news. Perhaps she is beginning to regain her health. You go home to her and later you can come back for the dishes. I do not want her alone too long."

He never looked up from his meal, never thanked his daughter or complimented her on the food. But Julie did not expect the courtesies and therefore did not miss them. She pushed her wire-rimmed spectacles back up on her nose before they could fall off and then she walked out the door.

Relieved of the heavy tray, she strode more quickly down the empty street toward the small clapboard house at the opposite end of the town. Now she could wipe the sweat away before it blinded her. And she could see, over the rims of the still-sliding spectacles, that someone had joined the two men on the porch in front of the general store. Lucas Carter was an almost permanent fixture and Simon rarely stayed inside unless he had a customer, but Julie did not recognize the third man.

She felt his eyes on her and bitterly supposed he was just another busybody wondering why Wilhelm Hollstrom's daughter—no, those were ungrateful thoughts after all her father had done for her. The heat was making her think them. She straightened her tired shoulders and walked past the store with its three loiterers.

Delbert Morgan stared, but he didn't really see anything. His bleary green eyes rarely focused unless he forced them to, though when he was able to make out the feminine gender of the figure in the street, he did exert some effort to persuade the eyes to cooperate.

"Who's that?" he asked while he scratched his unshaven chin. The dark bristles were almost long enough to pull on; time to get a shave.

"Telegraph operator's daughter," Lucas informed him.

"Ed ain't got no daughter," Morgan argued, squinting determinedly.

"Ain't Ed's kid. Ed moved to Denver six weeks ago anyway."

"Oh, yeah, now I remember."

Lucas shook his head and spat again. Morgan tipped his battered, sweat-stained hat low over his eyes as he leaned back in the chair beside Simon. But he could still see the girl, the swish of her skirt a dark green against the pale dust of the street.

"I remember. Ed married that cousin of the preacher's and moved to Denver. When did the new guy, the one with the daughter, move to town?"

"Twenty-eighth of May. He's got a boy, too." Simon drew a deep breath and swore softly. "Aw, damn." He turned to Lucas and muttered, "I shouldn't've said that."

They both watched their companion for some reaction, but Morgan seemed not to have heard. "What's today?"

"Eighteenth of June. You want the year, too?" Lucas added with laconic sarcasm.

Morgan replied, "It was 1884 when I passed out in the Castle two nights ago, and I don't think I been drunk enough to see another year in."

The red-rimmed green eyes watched the girl open the gate on the once-white picket fence and walk up to the porch of her house. When she had disappeared inside its walls, Morgan pushed his hat farther down, to block out all light and sight. The sun made his head throb. The sun—and the memories of another afternoon almost six years ago when he had sat on this same porch in front of the general store and watched another woman walk down this same street.

A shout, or maybe it was a scream, pierced the somnolent silence. Simon McCrory jumped to his feet, and Lucas Carter stood up straight, his hand edging instantly toward the gun at his hip. Del Morgan didn't move a muscle.

"It's the Hollstrom girl," Simon observed.

"Runnin' like all hell was after her," Lucas added. "What you s'pose is the matter?"

"There, she's goin' to Doc Opper's place. Maybe somethin' happened to her ma."

"I saw Doc this morning," Lucas volunteered to his companions. "He was headed up to Steve Hollis's to see if his wife had that baby yet."

The green skirt settled about her ankles as Julie pounded furiously on the door and shouted the physician's name so loudly that the men in front of McCrory's could hear her quite plainly. Neither her shouts nor her repeated thumps on the door brought any response. Finally realizing no one was going to answer her summons, Julie turned uncertainly and headed for the only source of help she could find: the three men lounging on the porch of McCrory's General Store. Disregarding the heat, the sun, the dust, and propriety, she lifted her skirt and petticoat and ran.

Lucas spat just as Julie reached the steps. She ignored both the blob of brown spittle and the man who had jettisoned it.

She panted slightly, for she had run her fastest. And Julie Hollstrom did not run very often. Her mother forbade it.

"What's happened, Miss Hollstrom?" Simon asked.

"My mother has fallen and hurt her arm," Julie answered. "The doctor seems not to be at home, and I hoped perhaps you might recommend someone who can take his place in an emergency."

"Opper's the only doctor we got in Plato," Simon apologized sincerely. "Unless Del here wants to take a look."

Her eyes followed McCrory's gaze to the indolent figure. The suggestion that this creature might be of medical use refused to find credence in her mind. From four feet away, she could not mistake the odors emanating from his filthy form; whiskey, sweat, and horse manure were the least offensive. He had cocked his left ankle on his right knee, exposing the sole of a well-worn boot with a hole in it the size of a silver dollar. The hem of a denim trouser leg would have trailed frayed ends if they hadn't been matted together with dirt. The hat still didn't move.

"Hey, Del, you awake?" Simon asked cautiously.

"Yeah, I'm awake."

The angry rumble in that deep, slightly hoarse voice pushed Julie back half a step.

"The young lady here says her ma's been hurt and needs a doctor."

"Tell her wait till Opper gits back from Hollis's."

"Isn't there anyone else?" Julie begged. "I think the arm may be broken and—"

"Can she move it?" Morgan asked.

"I—I don't know. I told her not to. But there's a place where—"

"Is it swelling bad?"

"I couldn't tell. I was more concerned about—"

"How long ago did it happen?"

"Just now." She hesitated to go on, expecting to be interrupted again, but this time the slovenly stranger remained silent. "I had just opened the front door. She was halfway up the stairs and apparently turned when I came in. She lost her balance and fell. I tried to catch her, but it happened too fast."

"Is she conscious?"

"She was when I left."

"Then as long as there's no bones sticking through the skin, she'll be all right until Opper gets back and can look at her."

"But there *is* bone sticking through the skin. At least, I think there is. I kept trying to tell you that," she scolded tartly, "but you kept interrupting me."

When the stranger suddenly dropped his chair to all fours and pushed his hat back, Julie jumped.

"Oh, Christ," Morgan muttered. "I should never have sobered up."

He looked up, squinting against the brightness, and saw a tall, reed-thin creature staring at him with huge doe-brown eyes over the wire rims of spectacles about to slide off the end of a small, straight nose. He couldn't guess her age; she might have been a gangly fifteen-year-old or an unattractive spinster twice that. Someone had pulled her hair tightly to the back of her head in a knot the size of his fist. Almost as lumpy, too.

His eyes arrested Julie and halted her protest of his language. Their eerie green color was barred with black, making it difficult to tell just where iris met pupil, except for the flecks of gold that floated iridescently in the green. The intensity of his stare forced Julie to see beyond the bloodshot whites and the puffy lids to the extraordinary beauty of those eyes. That and the hint of sadness made her ignore the blatantly assessing character of his gaze.

"That kind of break needs immediate attention." He struggled to his feet, swaying unsteadily while he held on to the arm of the chair. "I don't know that I can do anything, but I'll have a look at it."

Julie's first thought as they began to walk toward her house was that if he fell or lost consciousness, she would have to leave him lying in the street. Though she was far from petite, she doubted the top of her head reached his shoulder. He was a big-boned man, not just tall, with broad shoulders that stooped a little under his filthy shirt. Only his unsteadiness prevented his long legs from quickly outdistancing even Julie's sturdy strides.

The smell of him, however, drove any appreciative thoughts from her mind. She doubted he had bathed in a month or more, and his clothes very likely had never known soap. He scratched repeatedly at his beard, probably to disrupt the noontime meal of the vermin happily domiciled there.

Halfway across the street he asked, "How old is your mother?"

"Forty-six, I think."

"And you've a brother. How old is he?"

Julie thought the man's voice choked, probably the effect of his unhealthy habits. He sniffed and rubbed the back of one callused hand under his nose.

"Willy's nine," Julie stated flatly and was glad they had reached the porch of her house. She held the door open for him and, without removing his hat, he walked inside.

Katharine Hollstrom sat crookedly on the bottom stair, leaning against the plain newel post. She was a small woman tending to plumpness, with a pile of dark brown hair twisted into a tidy, becoming knot on the top of her head. Her eyes slowly opened as Julie knelt on the floor beside her.

"I brought someone to help, Mama."

Morgan looked down at the two women, noticing only a faint resemblance.

"I, uh, I need a place to wash," he stammered. Old habits, though not indulged for years, refused to die.

"The kitchen is behind the dining room," Julie instructed, pointing him to the room on her left. "There's hot water in the reservoir and soap above the sink."

God, his hands shook so as he lathered them that the suds splattered on the wall and floor. And those hands embarrassed him with their filth and cuts and calluses and the blackened nail where he'd smashed his finger in a door out of sheer clumsiness. He hoped the girl was mistaken about her mother's arm, because he'd never be able to set a compound fracture with hands that couldn't hold on to a cake of soap. He couldn't even remember where he'd left his surgical instruments; he hadn't touched them in years. Maybe they were still in the bedroom he never entered, along with the memorabilia of an almost forgotten life.

He shook the water from his hands and dried them on a clean towel. They were steadier now, not still but at least he could probably hold a glass of whiskey without sloshing it all over himself. Whiskey. That's what he needed. A couple shots to steady his hands and quiet his stomach and ease the splitting ache behind his eyes. A quick glance around the kitchen revealed no welcome bottle, though Morgan did notice that the room was spotless, with copper and cast-iron utensils hung on hooks by the stove and a green checkered cloth on the table. The pain behind his eyes began to throb and burn.

Upon returning to the hallway, he swallowed heavily and told his patient, "First I want to move you somewhere more comfortable and with better light."

"The sofa in the parlor," Julie suggested. "I don't think she can walk farther than that."

"She won't have to."

Making it look easier than it actually was, Morgan lifted the injured woman into his arms. Her cry of pain might also have been a gasp of fright or disgust at being held by so unsavory a character, but before either she or her daughter could protest, Morgan had gently deposited Katharine on the black horsehair sofa and then retreated a step or two.

The bloodstain had been concealed in a fold of Katharine's sleeve. Unfortunately the girl had been correct. Morgan muttered an angry, silent prayer that Opper would come back in the next five minutes.

Firmly, Morgan told Julie without even looking at her, "The sleeve has to be cut away."

The sewing basket beside a chair yielded a pair of shears. Morgan took it from Julie's outstretched hand and carefully snipped away the pink linen fabric. A long sigh escaped him when he had exposed the wound. Blood oozed slowly from a long scrape, but there was no sign of protruding bone.

As Morgan's fingers lifted her arm and gently probed, Katharine drew in a breath and squeezed her eyes tightly shut. "It's broken for sure," Morgan announced even before he had finished his examination, "but not as badly as I thought it might be. This scratch was probably caused by a splinter on the stairs."

Katharine moaned as he found the break in the bone. The ends were out of alignment, not far but enough that he doubted the woman would be able to withstand the pain of having the break set. She was already near fainting.

He didn't take his eyes from the mother's pale, drawn face as he told her daughter, "I need a couple pieces of wood and strips of linen for a splint, plus some whiskey. She won't handle it without help."

"There's no whiskey in the house," Julie replied, wondering just who he thought needed the fortification of liquor. "I can find the other things, but Papa doesn't allow spirits."

"Then I'm afraid—"

He was cut short by shouting and fists pounding on the front door.

"Miss Hollstrom! Miss Hollstrom!"

Julie ran the few steps to the door and admitted the frantic, florid-faced old man with the black bag gripped in his left hand. He pushed past her rudely and stormed into the parlor.

"Simon told me you were here, Morgan," Horace Opper puffed. "You no good drunken bastard, you don't have any business tending this woman's injuries."

Horace drew up his portly figure to his full height of five and one half feet and faced the green-eyed interloper. Morgan just looked down his nose with as much disgust as he could muster; Opper seemed unruffled.

"Get out, Del Morgan. Go back to your bottle and leave the practice of medicine to sober physicians."

"Sober, true, but it's a good thing you didn't describe yourself as competent, Horace. You were washed up and out of date ten years ago." He scratched at his beard unconsciously again and closed the green eyes for a long second. When they opened he added, "By the way, she's got a displaced fracture of the left radius about three inches above the wrist."

Opper's red, fleshy face approached a brilliant crimson.

"I don't need you to diagnose my patients for me!"

As Julie watched in horrified disbelief, Morgan shrugged and backed off, then walked around the physician the way one would avoid horse droppings in the street. He came to a halt in front of her by the front door.

"That's five bucks for the consultation," he sneered. "Next time, wait for the old fool; don't take me away from my hangover and my bottle, okay, Miss Hollstrom?"

He held out his large, freshly scrubbed palm.

Five dollars was outrageous. Julie had some money in her apron pocket, a couple of silver dollars and some change, but not enough to make this charlatan's fee.

"This is all I have," she offered meekly. The coins jingled onto his hand, but he did not close his fingers over them.

He hadn't expected her to pay him anything. If she had kicked his worthless carcass out of her tidy little house, he would have shrugged and gone on his way, back to Simon's or the Castle. Three dollars and twenty-two cents would buy a day or two of oblivion, but somehow he couldn't take it from her. He dropped a fifty-cent piece into his shirt pocket before pressing the rest back into her slim hand. He could feel, if not see, the red roughness of that hand. Her mother's, in contrast, had been white and smooth and soft.

Then he walked outside into the blast-furnace heat of the afternoon, and he hoped those big brown eyes of hers weren't watching as he went.

Chapter Two

✦✦✦✦

KATHARINE HOLLSTROM SAT at the dining room table and smiled beatifically. Her left arm rested in its sling made of a torn bedsheet; her right hand lay patiently on her lap while Julie deftly cut a thick slice of roast pork into bite-sized pieces on Katharine's plate.

"I hate putting you to all this trouble, Julie," she apologized, just as she had at every meal for the past week. "Imagine, five more weeks of this!"

She raised the incapacitated arm and smiled again. Julie choked down a caustic retort. She took the bowl of mashed potatoes from her brother Willy and scooped a small serving beside the meat, then covered both with creamy gravy. A deep breath of that warm, rich aroma set her stomach to grumbling rather loudly, to Julie's acute embarrassment.

"Not too many green beans, dear," Katharine cautioned. "You know they don't agree with me."

Seated just around the corner of the table from Katharine, Hans Wallenmund grabbed the bowl the instant Julie set it down and quickly emptied the contents onto his own plate.

"Then that will be all the more for me," he exclaimed.

"Hans must be working very hard on his farm

16

to have such an appetite," Wilhelm observed
from the head of the table.

"And I do not cook so good as Julie," the
blond farmer replied. He added a mound of potatoes beside the beans.

When Julie had finished her mother's plate,
she walked around the table to her own place
opposite Hans. Her stomach growled again as
she sat down, but before she could put any food
on her plate, her father signaled for grace.

"Lord God our father, we ask a blessing upon
this bounty."

Julie bowed her head but did not quite close
her eyes while Wilhelm droned on. She could
almost see her reflection on the china's surface,
her glasses sliding slowly again, and bitter
thoughts filled her head. She hadn't eaten since
six o'clock that morning, and she had spent the
intervening hours—except the one at church—
slaving in the kitchen until she was exhausted as
well as famished. Now the green beans, fresh
from the straggly little garden, were gone; Hans
had poured nearly all the gravy on his heap of
mashed potatoes; and only one biscuit remained
of the dozen Julie had baked. She paid no attention to her father's prayer because all she could
think about was that biscuit, still warm in its
towel-lined basket. It was within her reach; if
she moved quickly at the end of the grace, she
would have it.

The biscuit became an obsession. The little
lump of flour, milk, and baking powder repre-

sented more than just a morsel of food to be
snatched before greedier hands grabbed it. Julie
fought the rebellion that smoldered in her, fed
by her gnawing hunger, but the feeling stub-
bornly refused to be suppressed. She wanted
that biscuit, wanted to smother it with fresh butter and wild honey, wanted to nibble at it and
savor the fluffy, doughy goodness that she herself had created.

"In the name of our Lord Jesus, amen."

Julie had listened for those words, and as soon
as they were uttered, her hand darted out and
her fingers closed around the object of all her
desire. She dropped the biscuit to her otherwise
empty plate and did her best to smother a tri-
umphant smile.

She plopped onto her plate the small serving
of mashed potatoes that clung to the spoon and
managed to scrape some gravy together. With a
slice of meat and a dish of applesauce, the meal
looked spare but sufficient, though Julie couldn't
help glancing at the green beans steaming on
Hans's full plate. She licked her lips despite her
efforts at control.

She did not have to exert the slightest effort,
however, to avoid looking at Hans Wallenmund.
Without looking up from her plate, she could
still see his smoothly handsome features, the
broad, strong nose, the wide blue eyes, the
square jaw, the blond hair from which a boyish
forelock tumbled. He wore a clean but unpressed
chambray shirt buttoned to his Adam's apple,
with black suspenders supporting his slightly

faded denim trousers. Hans dressed the same every Sunday when he came to Plato from his farm for dinner with the Hollstroms.

"I bought six more Holsteins this week," he informed his hosts. "No more little Jerseys."

He said it as if he were spitting out a piece of unchewable gristle.

"I get twice as much milk from a Holstein, and they don't have problems calving the way Jerseys do. The four I bought last year all dropped their calves with no help, but I had only three calves from my seven Jerseys—and I had to pull each one. Even so, I lost two calves and one cow."

"Such a loss!" Katharine exclaimed.

"With the Holsteins I can make up for it very quickly," Hans boasted, and he reached without asking for another slice of pork, his third. "Already every month I am making two hundred pounds more schmierkase."

At that point Julie stopped listening to the conversation. There was no excuse for this repeated bragging of the wealth and success of Hans Wallenmund. His farm, his crops, his livestock, his cheese, his barn, his house, even his new wagon had been verbally inventoried and spread out before her over the past three Sunday dinners. None of it appealed to her in the least, especially the thousands and thousands of pounds of cottage cheese.

Hans didn't appeal to her either. He was handsome enough, and he had money, though here in Plato there wasn't much to spend it on. His

manners weren't the best, but Julie had seen
worse. Lucas Carter, for instance, with his per-
petual chaw. Or that drunken lout Del Morgan
and his foul tongue.

She couldn't blame Hans for his lack of edu-
cation, though that was one of the points that
irritated her. Few of the farmers she had known
in Indiana or the other places the Hollstroms had
lived had been able to do much more than read
and write their own names. Hans at least could
print a legible letter and he knew enough arith-
metic to avoid being cheated when he sold his
precious cheese or bought another cow. But Katharine Hollstrom had raised Julie with a love for
literature and history, and Julie doubted Hans
would be the kind of husband with whom she
could share those interests—not that she expected to find such a man out in the wilderness
of the Arizona Territory any more than in the
frozen wastes of Minnesota or the wide golden
wheatfields of Kansas.

Hans pushed himself away from the table with
a loud belch, interrupting Julie's musings.

Katharine smiled indulgently and said, "I do
believe we're ready for dessert, dear."

Julie stared at her half-eaten meal. The potatoes were cold, the gravy congealed greasily.
She had barely touched her applesauce. The biscuit, however, was quite gone. She expected a
lecture from her father on this waste of good
food, but Wilhelm remained silent while she
gathered the plates and took them to the kitchen.

The pie on the windowsill fairly glowed in the

narrow band of sunlight. From the golden crust oozed lush red strawberry sauce, almost candied in the oven. Strawberries were Hans's favorite, and he had complimented her profusely last week for her unsurpassed handiwork. She had made this only at Katharine's insistence. The effort of preparing dinner was more than enough, and Julie easily could have done without the added work of baking a pie. Now she felt reluctant to share the splendid work of art. She hesitated before sliding her hand carefully under the pan and lifting the pie from the windowsill.

She *was* a good cook, she thought, smiling proudly to herself, no matter what anyone else said—or didn't say.

In the dining room, as she cut and served the pie, she said, "I have whipped cream in the cooler, and the coffee is hot on the stove. I'll fetch them in a minute."

Wilhelm took a healthy wedge of the pie, Willy demanded an equal portion despite his mother's protests that he would never be able to eat it all, and of course Hans took two, leaving barely a third of the pie. Julie cut what remained into two portions and gave one to her mother, then returned to the kitchen for the coffeepot and the bowl of whipped cream.

She didn't know why she resented everyone today. No one had ever helped her serve the meals, and there was no reason to expect any assistance now. Oh, they helped themselves when it came to filling their plates or garnishing their pie with whipped cream, but it was always

Julie who carried the dishes to and from the steaming kitchen, who served herself last, almost as though she were a servant relegated to the scullery—and the leftovers.

Maybe it was the weather. She had known heat like this in Kansas and even in Indiana, but rarely so early in the season and never so early in the day. Someone in church had said the thermometer at the post office registered ninety-two degrees at sunup.

And then to be forced to stand in the kitchen, with a pork roast sizzling in the oven of the monstrous cast-iron cookstove, and to bake a strawberry pie. Yes, it must be the heat that made her so angry that even when she was hungry enough to eat a horse, she could barely down a bird's portion.

She poured three cups of coffee, none for herself, and then Willy called for more lemonade.

The words of resistance hovered on the end of her tongue, daring her to spit them out. Willy had two perfectly healthy legs and two perfectly healthy arms. There was no reason he couldn't excuse himself from the table and refill his own glass from the pitcher in the cooler. Instead, he held the empty glass out to his sister.

By the time Julie had done her brother's bidding and returned to the dining room, Hans had helped himself to the last of the whipped cream—which she really didn't care about—and the last slice of strawberry pie—which she did.

* * *

It was too hot to walk far, but Julie consented to stroll with Hans for a while after she had finished washing, drying, and putting away the dishes. She would have done just about anything to get out of that kitchen for a while.

At the north edge of Plato, where the street began its rise to the mountains, the cottonwoods grew thick along an icy, snow-fed stream. Here there was some respite from the sweltering sun, from the glare and the breathless heat, but not from the internal fire. Julie fumed with each step she took, though she kept a smile on her lips.

"I still can hardly believe you are here, Julie," Hans said quietly as they passed the church and the iron-fenced cemetery. His accent had thickened as the volume of his voice dropped. She strained both to hear and to understand him. "Soon I will have what I have waited so long for."

Julie swallowed hard and glanced down to the dust at her feet. She had expected this conversation last Sunday, but Hans had been too enthusiastic over the breeding of his precious cows and had not broached the subject. Now he had nothing to distract him from his purpose.

"I have spoken to your papa, Julie. He says we should wait and see how things are, now that you have come to Arizona. It has been a long time, and he thinks we might not feel the same as we did then."

She wanted to run but knew he would stop her, and she did not think she could bear his touch. His emotional declarations could do no harm, and the presence of a solitary mourner in the graveyard assured her that Hans would only plead his case, nothing more.

"My feelings haven't changed, Julie, except maybe they are stronger. I think we should get married very soon, so I can take you to the farm and—"

"Sssshhh," she whispered, raising a finger to her lips and nodding her head in the direction of the man who knelt by one of the graves, his back to the couple under the trees. Hans bowed his head with a crimson blush, but Julie had to refrain from letting out a long sigh of relief. She had already heard quite enough.

Hans, however, had much more to say.

"I have thought of this for so long that I do not want any more time to pass. I have dreamed of us, Julie, of you and me making the farm something to be proud of to pass on to our sons the way my father could not do for me."

In his enthusiasm, Hans had raised his voice again, despite Julie's repeated cautions, and this last statement carried to the man in the cemetery. He rose, anger in his movement, and turned to face the people who had disturbed his communion.

Now Julie blushed. In the dappled shade and from a distance of perhaps fifteen yards, she could not possibly see his eyes, but she didn't need to see them to remember their eerie green and the way Del Morgan could level them at her. He stared only for a moment, no more than a handful of long seconds, and then he returned to his contemplation of a grave Julie could see was carefully tended, with a lovely red rosebush blooming riotously beside a small headstone.

That stare had sufficiently cowed Hans as well. The burly farmer backed a step or two away from Julie and said nothing. She took advantage of the opportunity to whisper, "I think we should go back. We've disturbed that gentleman." She ignored the blatant inappropriateness of applying the term to Morgan. "And Mama may need me."

She tried to ignore the guilt she felt at using her mother's injury, toward which she held a mounting resentment, as an excuse to escape Hans's attentions, but it was much easier to imagine Del Morgan a gentleman than to clear her conscience.

Guilty feelings or not, she continued in the same vein.

"I could not even think of leaving Mama until her arm is healed and she can handle some of the housework."

"That is only five more weeks. She said so herself. Surely you could speak to your papa and at least start to make some plans for the wedding," Hans said in an almost whining tone.

Julie turned to walk toward home. She didn't particularly want to go back there, back to waiting on her mother and listening to her father, but neither did she wish to spend any more time with Hans. Especially not with Del Morgan around to watch her with his leering green eyes.

"I will think about it," she told Hans, feeling

her spectacles starting to slide again. "But you must remember that my mother is not well and she needs me to help her. And I owe my parents much more than I can ever repay. It would not be right for me to walk out on them suddenly. I must not be ungrateful or put any more burdens on them."

As Julie pushed her glasses back up to the bridge of her nose, Hans mumbled an apology.

"I have been unfair," he said as they stopped just outside the fence enclosing the Hollstroms' yard. "But it is six years since I first spoke to your papa about our marrying, and that is a long time to wait for a wife. Promise me it will not have been in vain."

Julie remained silent for a dozen heartbeats or more, trying to devise a promise that could be honorably broken. There had never been a formal betrothal all those years ago in Minnesota. Julie had given Hans no promise then and she had no intention of doing so now.

"I will abide by my father's wishes," she told him finally. "I will do what is best for all of us."

It was a weak vow, one she worried he would easily see through, but Hans seemed happy to accept it. With a clumsy flourish, he took both her hands in his and clasped them tightly. A broad grin lit his face, and Julie thought he intended to dance with her right there in the street. She glanced quickly to see if anyone in her own house or those nearby might be watching, but all the windows were curtained against the heat.

When Hans planted a wet kiss on her cheek, Julie resisted the urge to wipe it off, not with her hand but with a handkerchief or the corner of her apron.

"Now I am happy," he sang, reluctantly releasing her hands. "You talk to your papa, and next Sunday, when I come for dinner, we will have it all decided. Good-bye, Julie!"

He looked as though he might give her another kiss, but he only smiled, with a bright blush on his cheeks. Twice he turned as he walked in the direction of the hotel and waved to her, and Julie forced herself to wave back the second time, but with little enthusiasm.

She passed through the open gate and walked up the steps to the porch, never realizing she had wiped her hands vigorously on her skirt before Hans was even out of sight. Nor did she see Del Morgan walk through the cemetery gate and shut it quietly behind him.

He squinted in the sudden brightness and quickly clapped his beaten hat to his head. His knee hurt from a small stone he had knelt on in the graveyard, and he rubbed the sore spot with a relatively clean hand. Other aches were not so easily disposed of, like the one that stung his eyes and another that tightened in his chest. Much as he disliked sitting home with no other companion than a full bottle of cheap whiskey, he had no choice. The Castle was closed on Sunday, and none of his drinking cronies allowed him in their homes.

He watched the girl, noted the way she rubbed

her hands against her skirt as though to rid them of something unpleasant or dirty. Then he let his gaze follow the blond, heavily built farmer who had disturbed the cemetery's solitude with his outburst. Morgan shook his head. Hans passed the hotel and walked into the narrow alley between the Olympia House and the boardwalked shops of Plato, and if Julie Hollström didn't know where her future husband was headed, Del Morgan did.

Chapter Three

✦✦✦✦

JULIE HEFTED THE big wicker laundry basket to her hip and trudged toward the house. Her spectacles slipped; she pushed them back where they belonged and sighed with Monday morning weariness.

But the morning was almost over. The kitchen smelled of fresh bread, frying sausage, and potato pancakes. Julie dropped the basket onto the table and hurried to check her father's lunch. The sausage had just browned and the potato pancakes, set over to the side of the stove, were barely golden on the underside. It hadn't been easy to do the laundry, bake bread, and wait on

Mama, but Julie had accomplished it all and had managed not to burn her father's lunch.

She fixed the usual tray with silverware wrapped in a napkin, a coffee cup, and a small pot of freshly brewed coffee. She wondered how he could drink the stuff on a day like this. Already she had downed four or five glasses of water and still felt thirsty.

As soon as she delivered Wilhelm's meal, she could come home to her own lunch. Katharine had breakfasted late and was back asleep, and Willy had gone fishing with some of his friends. Julie dared to hope she might sit down and eat her meal undisturbed—if the heat left her any appetite.

Not that there wouldn't be plenty of work waiting for her after lunch. Her bed and Willy's needed to be made with these clean sheets, and she hadn't even started the dusting, a daily ritual in this land of arid winds and clouds of fine grit. Of course she'd have dishes to wash and supper to cook. If Willy brought home a mess of fish, she'd scale and gut them before she fried them nice and crisp for tonight's meal.

But she wasn't sure the luxury of fresh fish was worth the gruesome task of preparing them. It would be much better if he came home empty-handed. Then there'd be no gory dressing of the catch, as well as no congratulations. If he was successful, Willy would be praised for enticing a stupid fish to swallow a dead cricket and thereby impale itself on the hook, while the lightly seasoned breading with which Julie coated those fish would be taken for granted and not a single word of praise would ever come her way. Besides, she wanted that brand-new fishing pole to fail.

She picked up Wilhelm's lunch tray and pushed her jealousy of the fishing pole out of her mind. She had envied Willy his possessions before and she probably would do so again quite frequently in the future, so there was no sense ruminating about it now when work waited.

The dining room was as cool, on the shaded north side of the house, as the kitchen was steaming, but Julie walked quickly through to the front door and out to the porch. She blinked to adjust her eyes to the brightness of noon sun on white dust, and then she stepped sturdily down the stairs and toward the street. Just as she kicked the gate open, the boys came running.

"Julie, Julie, Julie!" Willy wailed. His short legs pumped unsteadily as he charged through the trees behind the cemetery. "Help me, Julie!"

She saw the blood first, the smeared red streaks that covered nearly all one side of his face and the spatters that had turned brown with dust on his white shirt. From the healthy sound of his cries and the way he ran, she took immediate reassurance that his injury could not be life-threatening, but the amount of blood frightened her. She set her father's lunch tray on the ground. Quickly she ran to Willy, scooped him up in her arms, and carried him, still screaming, into the house.

"Clancy, go find Dr. Opper," she ordered Simon McCrory's youngest son when he and his companion gathered on the porch to peer through the screen door. "If you can't find him, get that Mr. Morgan. I'm sure your father will know where he is."

"Yes, ma'am, Miss Julie. C'mon, Donnie, we'll go get Doc."

She heard their bare feet slap on the wooden steps and pound in the dust before they ran up to Opper's house two doors away. Relieved that the boys could carry out simple instructions, she began a closer examination of Willy's wound.

He lay on the sofa, moaning softly, his eyes squeezed as tightly shut as he could get them. There was blood everywhere, more than she had thought, and it still trickled steadily from the cut above his eyebrow.

"Willy, I'm going to the kitchen for water and a rag to clean this with. Just lie still and I'll be back in a minute, all right?"

"Am I gonna die?" he whined.

"Not hardly, but I think you may need some stitches."

That was the wrong thing to say. The boy set up a wild keening and rolled about on the sofa, getting bloodstains all over it.

She tried to settle him and calm his fears, but to no avail, and the bleeding didn't stop. She had to clean him up and see just how much damage had been done by the fishhook still embedded in the skin. Thankful that she had plenty of hot water from the morning's laundry, she filled a basin from the reservoir and grabbed a

clean towel from the laundry basket. Willy
started fresh moaning the instant she knelt on
the floor beside him.

"Put your hand down and let me see it," she
ordered gently, prying his cupped fingers away
from the cut. "Maybe it won't need stitches after
all, but I can't tell until I get it cleaned up."

That seemed to calm him, and he took his
hand away. Using the utmost care not to disturb
the implement, Julie dabbed as close to the fishhook as possible with a damp corner of the cotton towel.

The point had entered at the inside edge of the
right eyebrow and then had been pulled upward
diagonally to leave a jagged gash more than an
inch long. Head wounds always bled worse than
anything else and invariably looked worse than
they were, but Julie knew this was not just a
scratch, as the wound on her mother's arm had
been. Stitches would be necessary, probably five
or six from the looks of it, and even then there'd
be a scar.

"Am I gonna need stitches?" Willy asked, still
moaning but with less real pain in his voice.

"We'll have to wait until the doctor gets here
and let him make that decision."

She got from her knees to her feet and had
taken a couple steps toward the door when she
heard the voices approach. The children's were
unmistakable.

"It's really horrible," Donnie Kincheloe said
with all the drama of an eight-year-old, putting

excessive emphasis on the last word. "I think he took his whole eye right out of his head."

"Oh, he didn't neither," the McCrory boy insisted. "He just got blood all over hisself."

"We'll see, we'll see," the physician grunted, his own voice strained and breathless.

Horace Opper came to the foot of the porch stairs and stopped. Watching him from the doorway, Julie was struck by the man's age. He looked so much older than he had just a week ago, when he had puffed and panted his way through setting her mother's broken arm. Now he gasped, and he could hardly open his eyes.

"Another accident, Miss Julie?" he asked. He put one foot on the bottom step and hoisted himself upward.

"Willy's caught a fishhook in his eyebrow."

It seemed to take Opper forever to reach the door, and then he leaned against the frame, neither in nor out of the house.

"I practically ran all the way from Nellie's." He panted and pulled out an already soiled handkerchief to wipe his dripping face and the deep creases of his neck. Julie turned away, half sickened by the glimpse of his filthy, sweat-stained collar. "Oh, beg pardon, Miss Julie. I oughtn't to speak of that place, I know. Probably oughtn't even to go there myself, but one of the girls got beat up a bit the other night, and Nellie pays me to take care of them. I can't afford to turn away a patient who pays."

"I—I told you I'd pay you some every week

until it was taken care of. I have a dollar to give you today right here in my pocket."

The physician tried to laugh, but the sound turned to a wheeze and his face purpled.

"I don't worry about you, Miss Julie. I know your pa'll pay me as soon as he can. Now, let's see this young man with the fishhook in his eye."

Opper pushed himself away from the doorframe and went into the parlor where Willy waited. Julie followed, and as she passed the stairway she saw her mother at the top, her face registering the grogginess of one just wakened from sound sleep.

"Is something wrong, Julie?" Katharine asked sleepily.

Julie glanced from Willy, who was terrified and still very bloodstained on the parlor sofa, to her mother. Julie climbed the stairs quickly but without panic and put one arm around Katharine's shoulders before she explained what had happened.

"Willy's been hurt, Mama, but it's nothing serious. He'll be fine in no time," she said softly. "The doctor's here and will take care of him."

Katharine seemed to lose some of her strength and slumped a bit, but Julie held on to her and gently guided her back to her room and the bed she had just left. Katharine must not see Willy as he was now, panicky and covered with his own blood. She wasn't the sort of woman to take things like that easily, and with the victim her only son, it was best to keep her away until the doctor had finished.

"It wasn't your fault, was it, Julie?" Katharine asked.

"Of course not! I was here at home, and he was out fishing with the McCrory boy and Donnie Kincheloe. I was on my way to—"

Willy's shrieks of terror and pain cut her off and she was out the bedroom door and down the stairs like a coyote after a rabbit. For the second time in less than half an hour, she completely forgot her father's lunch.

When she saw the cause for Willy's cries, she reacted instinctively, without any thought at all.

Horace Opper, breathing in heavy gasps, sat on the edge of the sofa with Willy pressed against the back cushions. One of the physician's pudgy hands held the boy's wrists flat on his stomach, so that only Willy's head and legs were really free to move. The doctor's free hand held a large threaded needle and was poised to strike the boy's pale face.

"For the love of— Whatever are you doing, sir?" Julie demanded. "Are you planning to beat him or sew his wound?"

She grabbed at that threatening arm and caught a handful of woolen coat cuff, enough of a hold to bring the arm and the terrifying needle down. Willy did not stop his struggles, though some of his hysteria subsided.

"Then you sit on him," Opper grunted, "so I

can get these stitches in. The little hellion won't hold still."

"He's hurting me, Julie," Willy whined, but there was more fear than petulance in his tone now. "And he's gonna poke that big needle into my head."

The needle was indeed huge, as big as the one Julie used to darn socks. And the fishhook was still stuck in his flesh.

"Have you nothing smaller?" Julie asked.

"Smaller? I had a hell of a time getting this one threaded. Now here, you hold his hands and his head while I sit on his legs so we can get this done and over with."

Opper's hand shook uncontrollably, and the image flashed into Julie's brain of the old man's hand missing its mark and poking the enormous needle into the boy's eye. The end of the cut was barely half an inch from the eye itself, and even a slight slip could spell disaster. She hadn't been to blame for the accident, but Julie would never be able to rid herself of guilt if she didn't stop this man at once.

"Dr. Opper, sir, I think perhaps you had best leave this to me," she told him as sternly as she could. Her knees shivered under her petticoats, and her palms began to perspire from something other than the midday heat.

Opper snorted angrily but did not get up from the sofa.

"Do as I say, girl, and we'll have this done. You called me in, so settle down and get to work."

Her heart pounded. Horace Opper was a figure of some considerable authority, and Julie remembered all the times she had gone against authority and suffered for it. Defying the doctor was something she could not do without careful consideration of the situation and a lot of courage.

"I called you in, and I can send you away. Please, I was wrong to have bothered you for something so minor as this little scratch. You may return to whatever you were interrupted at, and I will take care of my brother."

She heard the thudding of her heart in her throat and heard the nervous knocking of her knees, but she did not hear the footsteps on the porch or the slight squeak of the screen door as it opened.

"What is going on here, Julie?" Wilhelm asked. "Where is my lunch?"

If she had been unsure of herself and frightened when she ordered the doctor out of the house, Julie trembled with real terror when she faced her father. It didn't matter that she was a full inch taller than Wilhelm; she felt as small as one of the spiders she squashed under her foot in the kitchen or the privy, and every bit as defenseless.

"Willy's been hurt, Papa."

Wilhelm's face paled, then reddened, but he did not waste time venting anger. He rushed past his daughter into the parlor and knelt beside his son. Willy's tears returned full force.

"*Gott in Himmel*, he's bleeding to death!" the

father thundered. "Do something, *Herr Doktor*. You must stop this bleeding!"

"I was just preparing to do that, Mr. Hollstrom. Your daughter here seemed to think she could do it better herself, but I think this requires professional treatment."

Julie sickened. It wasn't just the thought of those quaking hands holding the needle that curdled her empty stomach; there was a glint of greed in the old man's eyes, and a smile of avarice on his puffy lips. Worse yet, she knew exactly what she had to do, and the very thought of searching for Del Morgan brought an unpleasant taste to Julie's mouth.

The McCrory boy and his companion had settled themselves on the top step of the Hollstroms' porch to await the outcome of the medical drama within, and Julie turned to them for what assistance she could get.

"When I sent you for the doctor," she asked patiently, "did you happen to locate Mr. Morgan? I know it took you a long while and I thought maybe . . ."

She had trouble finding the right word, but it didn't matter. Clancy McCrory answered quickly.

"Del's over at the Castle. I seen him go in this morning, just before we went fishin', and he don't never come out till they carry him out or he runs outta money." He paused, then asked, "You want me to go get him?"

"No, I'll do it myself."

Willy's cries, loud and clear in the still, sultry air, sped her feet toward the saloon that dominated the west side of Main Street.

The Castle stood by itself, a long, two-story building with an extra story added to the false front that had been built to resemble the owner's idea of a medieval castle. Julie lifted her skirt delicately as she climbed the four wooden steps to the front porch that ran the length of the building. She wiped her palms on her apron and took a deep breath, then pushed one side of the swinging door open and walked into the Castle.

The sudden gloom left her lost and disoriented, but she was instantly aware that the noise of men's voices and women's laughter had suddenly ceased. A bottle clinked on the rim of a glass, and there was a soft thud as the bottle was set down, but only a deathly silence followed.

"I—I'm looking for Mr. Morgan," she said softly, her fear of her father's wrath overcoming all others. "I was informed he might be found here."

Someone laughed, a woman perhaps, then a masculine voice called from some dark corner of this cavern, "Hey, Del, ya got a young lady lookin' fer ya. Are ya here, or should I tell her yer gone?"

Laughter broke out everywhere, and Julie felt as though a thousand voices rose in ridicule. Her stomach turned over at least twice, but the thought of Wilhelm's fury if anything happened to his son kept her feet rooted to her spot just inside the door. At least Morgan was here; she wouldn't have to repeat her humiliating plea elsewhere.

"Yeah, I'm here," growled a figure slumped at the corner table. He reached for the bottle in front of him and took a hearty swig before asking, "Who wants me and why?"

Aware of the eyes that watched her, Julie approached with all the confidence she could muster. Even this drunk, Morgan couldn't be worse than Opper was sober.

"I need you, Mr. Morgan," she stated plainly. "My brother's been hurt."

"Oh, it's your brother now. Last week your mother falls down the stairs and this week your brother has—?" He tipped the bottle up again and didn't look at anything else while he waited for her to finish his question for him and answer it.

"He's caught a fishhook in his forehead and the cut needs stitches."

"Don't you know how to thread a needle?" Morgan asked her sarcastically after he had set the bottle down. "Or can't you find old Horace again?"

The man was stinking drunk, and even if he had been sober, she couldn't tell him the truth in front of all these other people. Not the whole truth.

"Yes, I found Dr. Opper. He is—well, he is unable to perform the job satisfactorily."

Morgan laughed.

"And you think I can?"

He wasn't quite drunk enough to ignore the girl; he wished desperately that he was. He didn't like the feeling her stare stirred in his guts. Maybe if he had been more drunk he could have spit some filthy excuses at her and have gone back to his bottle, but the obscenities stuck in his throat. And the girl kept staring at him.

She swallowed and rehearsed her plea once more. Then she let the words out, emphasizing each word in rapid succession.

"He is a little boy in a great deal of pain and he is very frightened. I would appreciate any help you can give me."

She could hear her father's words if he had witnessed that pleading tone. *Hollstroms do not beg*, he would have scolded her. *A Hollstrom should order others to do his bidding, not the other way around*. But Julie had far more experience following orders than giving them, and now she hardly knew how to act. All she knew was that she had to have Del Morgan's assistance.

The queasy feeling in his stomach had little to do with the quart or so of whiskey Morgan had swallowed since nine o'clock. He was used to the humiliation, the laughs when he stumbled, the snickers behind his back when he dragged himself home or collapsed halfway there. He wasn't sure he was ready to face Horace Opper again. Besides, he had turned tail last week, had slunk away like a whipped cur and had let the old quack take care of the woman. He'd need a lot more courage than what was left in his bottle to stand up to the old fart again.

But last week the patient had been an adult. A child was different. Could he put a young life in the old man's hands? And the girl, so trusting, so pleading, and so obviously frightened. Of what? Morgan asked himself. Of me? Of the charming, civilized patrons of this elegant establishment? Or of something else?

Sheer willpower got him to his feet in a single, more or less steady lurch, and he sidled around the table toward the girl, without that last swallow of whiskey.

Willy's screams had brought several of the neighbors to their porches, and three more boys had joined Clancy and Donnie on the Hollstroms' steps. They all watched silently, expectantly, as Julie and Del Morgan strode past them and into the house.

The needle had so far not touched Willy's cut. Wilhelm Hollstrom knelt awkwardly on the sofa, his square strong hands clamped on either side of Willy's head, while Horace Opper lay sprawled on Willy's chest. But even that brute strength wasn't enough to halt the boy's thrashings. Opper hadn't even removed the fishhook. The gash was slightly longer now, and the trickle of blood continued. There were spatters of it on the wall above the sofa back, on Wilhelm's shirt and face, and even on the faded floral carpet.

"He's going to die, Julie," Katharine wailed

from her chair by the window. "My baby's going to die! Julie, Julie, do something so Willy doesn't die!"

Still standing next to Morgan in the doorway, Julie looked up at him and whispered almost sarcastically, "You had best see that Willy doesn't die." Then, realizing she had let her irritation and impatience show when she most wanted not to, she added in a calmer tone, "I'll take care of my mother; you do the mending."

He made no move to do anything at all. The sight of the boy stunned him, froze him where he stood in the doorway arch between foyer and parlor. He had to choke down the nausea raised by the blood and the child's frightened face.

The boy must be eight or nine, though he was small for his age. Built like his mother, Morgan decided, and he'll end up on the paunchy side like her, too. His hair was somewhere between her brown and the father's dull blond, his eyes a bright blue. But the delicate, almost feminine features and the slightly pouting mouth were inherited from the female side; there was nothing soft at all about his father's features. And the boy was indeed terrified.

"God help me," Morgan prayed under his breath as he took the first faltering step into the parlor.

"Get the hell out of here, Morgan," Opper hissed, threatening the younger man with the black-threaded needle. "We're busy."

"I can see that. Busy, but you haven't accomplished much."

Opper looked up, and Willy took the opportunity to plant a solid kick in the old man's side. Horace grunted, then slapped the boy hard in the face. Blood sprayed freely, and Willy let out a furious shriek of pain and anger.

Morgan's hand was a bit unsteady, but his grip held like a bear trap on Opper's flabby upper arm. With the gentleness that only comes from strength, he pulled the wheezing physician off the boy and shoved him out of the way.

"What do you think you are doing?" Wilhelm sputtered. "Who are you? My son's life is at stake; he needs the doctor."

"His life is hardly endangered by a fishhook, unless he's a trout, but I don't think his rib cage will sustain the weight of this overstuffed flounder much longer."

Julie had never heard such a commingling of emotions in so few words. Morgan was angry, that was clear, but he seemed almost to be fighting back tears, and there was more than a trace of the black, bitter hatred Julie knew could only be turned toward oneself. She had felt it often enough. And yet he could still turn up a wry smile at the cleverness of his own metaphors as he knelt by the sofa and placed gentle, trembling fingers on Willy's forehead.

"It's going to be all right, son," he crooned. "Miss Hollstrom, would you get me some wet cloths so I can clean up this mess, and then we'll see just how much sewing we need to do."

Willy stiffened, but he didn't fight. Even Wilhelm seemed subdued by the drunkard's speech. With quiet reigning once again in the parlor, Julie scampered to the kitchen to refill the basin with warm water and bring fresh towels.

When Julie walked back into the parlor, Morgan was saying to Wilhelm, "Take her upstairs and keep her quiet. Give her some whiskey or wine to settle her down."

Wilhelm drew himself up and spouted, "I do not keep spirits in this house."

"Then go out and get some," Morgan ordered. "I need some to clean this wound and your wife needs something to help her sleep."

Julie took the basin and towels to Morgan and knelt beside him, well aware of the man's unwashed odor but more concerned about Willy, who now lay calm but pale on the sofa.

"Here, you can wash your hands in this and I'll get fresh for Willy," she suggested as she set the basin on the floor between her and Morgan.

She had thought she would simply get up and fetch another basin from the kitchen. She had no intentions of looking at Morgan, because she remembered those eyes and didn't want them examining her, as though she were the patient. But when she got to her feet, she looked down and saw him gazing up at her with those strange green eyes.

Horace Opper broke the trance.

"I'll see you in court, Morgan," the doctor panted from where he sat on the floor, his back propped against a maroon mohair chair. His face was nearly the same color. "You can't practice medicine, and you can't attack a licensed physician like that and get away with it."

"Horace, if you ever were licensed, which I doubt, it had to have been because some official was drunker than I've ever been." He reached for a dry towel after washing his hands and then turned to Wilhelm, who still stood beside Katharine's chair. "I thought I told you to get that woman out of here. I don't want her fainting on me, or worse, getting hysterical again. I can only handle one patient at a time." Then, to himself, "And I'm not even sure about that right now."

Julie heard him, but she ignored the remark and instead directed her comments to her father.

"Mr. Morgan is right, Papa. I can help with Willy; you take Mama to her room and stay with her. I'll send one of the boys for the whiskey."

"*You* will take care of your mama, and I will see that this drunken pig leaves my house," Wilhelm answered her. He stood between the two women, Julie standing firm, Katharine white-faced and limp on her chair. "Then Dr. Opper and I will see to Willy's wound."

"No!" Willy howled. "He'll poke me with that big needle, and I'll die!"

Before Julie could return to her brother's side, a rough, callused hand touched the boy's forehead and the wild crying stopped almost instantly.

"No big needles, I promise," Morgan soothed. "I can't promise it won't hurt, but I'll do everything I can to make it hurt as little as possible. How about if I promise some strawberry ice cream afterwards? Or do you like chocolate better?"

"Chocolate," Willy replied. "Julie likes strawberry."

It took longer than any of them expected, thanks in part to Wilhelm's frequent interruptions and to a fishhook that had to be cut out. That meant more bleeding and two extra stitches, none of which Willy took with much fortitude. Julie held his hand and let him give vent to all his pain, while Morgan waited patiently, his own brow as sweaty as the boy's and his face almost as white under its unshaven tan.

No one noticed when Horace Opper left. Wilhelm, despite repeated orders, did not leave the parlor any longer than was necessary to escort his wife to her room and pour her a glass of sherry. He stood in the archway between parlor and foyer, arms folded across his barrel chest, blue eyes trained coldly on the man and woman and boy. Julie shivered more than once when she caught that icy stare, but Morgan never turned away from his task.

The black sutures wandered almost two inches from the inner edge of the eyebrow upward in a diagonal. There'd be a scar, no doubt about it, but at least the bleeding was stopped.

Julie began to pick up the damp, bloodied towels and cloths that littered the floor. It gave her something to do while she thanked Morgan.

"I greatly appreciate your coming here this afternoon. I know you didn't want to, but I'm glad you did," she whispered.

"Yeah, well, you're welcome," he stammered. He recalled the way he had left her last week, demanding that exorbitant fee. She probably expected him to ask three or four times that much now that he had actually done something. "Uh, I think I'd better be going, Miss Hollstrom. He'll be all right now. The stitches might draw and itch in a few days. See if you can't keep him from pulling them out for a week or so and then just let Horace take them out. I think he can handle that."

He couldn't remember making a speech that long in years and quickly bit his lip to keep from blabbing even more. Besides, now that the job was done, all the quivery feeling returned to his stomach. If he was going to lose its contents, he'd rather do it at the Castle or at home, not in front of the girl who had for some strange reason trusted him.

"I must owe you something for what you did here today," she said. "I can't pay you right now, but I'll try to get you something as soon as I can."

Oh, God, the nausea was worse now that he was on his feet.

"Let Willy sleep as long as he wants; it's the best thing for him. I'll, uh, I'll stop by tomorrow and get him that ice cream."

Without another word, he turned and bolted for the door, pushing Wilhelm out of his way and slamming the screen door back on its hinges in his flight.

He made it to the stairs before the first convulsion hit him. He controlled it only long enough to charge down the stairs and then lose his balance. The sunlight and the heat and the frayed ends of all his nerves combined to topple him in the dust as the bitter taste flooded upward.

There was dust in his nostrils, and the bright red and white of flowers danced in front of his dizzy eyes. His whole body curled fetally as his stomach emptied itself on the ground. The red and white petunias turned to bloodstained petticoats in the tormented vision of his memory.

Chapter Four
✦ ✦ ✦ ✦

THE NIGHTMARE LINGERED even after he was certain he had wakened. There was light on the other side of his matted eyelids, and he thought he smelled bacon frying. But the aroma brought back the nausea and that was part of the nightmare, so he couldn't be truly sure of anything.

Had he slept, or had he just been unconscious all that time? He didn't know. Vaguely he was aware that he lay on something hard and relatively smooth, just as he vaguely remembered collapsing in the girl's flowerbed and throwing up his liquid breakfast. He had almost reached the memory of sewing the boy's forehead back together, an essential part of the nightmare, when his head cleared enough that he heard voices and could actually understand the words.

"You mean he just died?" A child's voice, it sounded like the boy's.

"Apparently."

"Well, who found him? I mean, how did they find out he was dead? And where did he die?"

"Mr. McCrory found him early this morning in the alley behind his store."

"How'd you find out about him?"

There was a clattering and the tapping of an eggshell on the edge of a skillet, followed by the unmistakable sizzle.

"Mrs. McCrory came over earlier, before you were awake, and told me. The funeral is to be this afternoon."

"How come so soon? When Mr. Callahan died they had that big wake for him, with all the—"

"That was in Minnesota, Willy, and here they just can't wait that long. Besides, Mr. Callahan was Irish, and it's a custom with the Irish to do that."

Morgan struggled with his eyes, tried to open them and wondered if perhaps they were held shut with coins, maybe even silver dollars from Julie Hollstrom's apron pocket. No, he seemed able to move his limbs, though with a great deal of stiffness and plenty of pain, too, so he didn't think he was the person scheduled for burial this afternoon.

He rolled onto his back and discovered a small pillow. He eased it under the back of his neck and then rubbed his eyes, feeling the rough granules that stuck his lashes together finally loosen. After a few tentative flutters, he opened his eyes and struggled to focus them.

Despite the pain it brought, the blinding morning sunlight was one of the most beautiful things Del Morgan had ever seen in all his thirty-four years. His head pounded, his eyes felt as though they were being slowly burned from their sockets, his hip and shoulder joints practically squeaked with aching stiffness, his belly growled with hunger he knew he didn't dare satisfy right away or he'd lose whatever he ate, and his mouth tasted as if some old buzzard had dragged a piece of carrion in there and left it. Yet he was so relieved just to be alive that he smiled and then stretched with a loud yawn.

He realized he hadn't felt this good about being alive for years, though he felt so lousy that he didn't care to wonder why he felt so good.

He lay to one side of the Hollstroms' porch, and the pillow under his head was a well-worn cushion from one of the old wicker chairs at the other side of the porch. He was indulging in another yawn and stretch and wondering where the nearest privy was when the screen door opened.

If there hadn't been a railing to the porch, he

would have tumbled into the petunias again, but he was not going to lie down while Julie Hollstrom came out with his breakfast. He clutched the turned pillar with numb fingers and prayed that the world would stop spinning quite so recklessly, but at least he was on his feet before the door had closed behind her.

"Look, Miss Hollstrom, I—"

"I thought I heard you waking up out here," she interrupted rudely. "Do you take anything in your coffee?"

"No, but I—"

"And would you prefer strawberry preserves or orange marmalade on your toast?"

"Strawberry, but you don't—"

"I hope you don't mind, but I only fixed you some toast and coffee; I didn't think you'd be up to much more after the way you felt yesterday." She walked past him and set the tray on the railing, then pulled one of the wicker chairs closer to him. "Why don't you sit down while you eat?"

Well, did you really expect her to invite you into her kitchen for breakfast? he asked himself caustically. It ought to be enough she's feeding you here on her front porch, instead of calling someone to drag you home and out of her sight.

So he did as he was told and sat down on the chair that still had its cushion and let Julie set the tray on his lap before she uncovered the plate of lightly buttered toast. The slices had been cut

into neat little triangles, and there were two
dishes of jam, one red and one yellow to match
the color of their contents. Morgan stared, then
picked up the knife and began to spread strawberry jam on one slice of toast. He was about to
pop the morsel into his mouth when he suddenly realized where he was and what he was
doing.

"Look, Miss Hollstrom—"

"No, you look, Mr. Morgan."

She was a tall girl, as he remembered from last
week, and he rather enjoyed looking up at her,
even if he was about to receive a lecture.

"I won't flatter you by telling you how you
miraculously saved my brother's life. We both
know he was in very little real danger."

She wore a dress of faded green calico with
that ever-present apron tied around her waist.
Morgan noticed it was a small waist, and he
turned back to his toast.

"*He* sure thought he was a goner."

"Be that as it may, I still want to thank you for
the help you gave me. My parents are inordi-
nately fond of Willy, and I confess I would rather
have had the blame for any disaster fall on your
head than on mine."

"So all I was was a scapegoat?"

"If I thought that, I wouldn't have told you.
No, I wanted to thank you for doing a much
better job than I could have done, and certainly
better than poor Dr. Opper."

"*Poor* Dr. Opper? Hell, Horace rakes in more

than I ever did, and he does less for it, too. I'd
hardly call that old quack *poor*."

He crammed the toast into his mouth and
chewed furiously.

"Well, you needn't worry about him anymore. Dr. Opper is dead."

Morgan choked. If he had had any more in his
mouth, he probably would have choked to
death.

"Horace is dead?"

"As the proverbial doornail. Mr. McCrory
found him lying in the alley behind the general
store. Apparently he just died."

"People don't just die, Miss Hollstrom. Probably his heart gave out, or he had a stroke. He
didn't look too good yesterday afternoon, but I
sure didn't think he'd give up the ghost this
quick."

He sipped the fresh hot coffee slowly, careful
not to burn his mouth, and mused on the passing of Horace Opper, a man he had never liked
but never really gave a whole lot of thought to.

"Shall I pour you some more coffee?" Julie
asked, breaking into his thoughts.

"No, thanks." Then he looked up at her suspiciously. "Just what is it you want from me? I'm
a drunk, Miss Hollstrom, and it was only sheer
luck I wasn't out cold when you came looking
for me yesterday. You have Sid Ackerman and
his card game to thank for that, not me."

"I didn't go around asking questions about
you, so you can rest easy on that," she began.

"But I've been around enough doctors to know one when I see him."

"All right, so I was a doctor," he snapped back. "I'm not anymore, haven't been for a long time."

"Well, you see, my mother and brother are not exactly in the best of health."

"They both looked pretty damned healthy to me."

"Looks can be deceiving," she shot at him tartly.

"Yes, they can. For instance, why do you wear those ridiculous spectacles? Every time I've seen you, they've been about to fall off the end of your nose, and you're always looking at people over the top of them."

Julie knew she had blushed red from her collar to the roots of her hair. She had to turn her back to him to push the glasses up to the bridge of her nose, though she knew they wouldn't stay there very long.

She stammered, "That . . . that isn't what we have to discuss here this morning."

"I didn't know we had *anything* to discuss."

He tried to tell himself that the only reason he listened to this garbage was because he was hungry and this was the best breakfast he'd had in years.

"What we have to discuss is you resuming your duties as a physician."

"*What?*"

"I am prepared to assist with your rehabilitation and—"

"And what if I'm not prepared to be rehabilitated?" he fired back at her, so sharply that she hopped a step away from him. "I happen to like being drunk. It's a hell of a lot better than being sober when . . ."

His voice lost its fire almost immediately, and he turned those penetrating green eyes away. No matter how good the breakfast, he couldn't stay there any longer. Controlling his temper only so he didn't sweep the tray and its contents to the porch, he set the tray on the railing and got to his feet. Now he was taller than the girl, and though he had intended to use that to his advantage, he discovered he didn't like the frightened look that came into those eyes of hers.

"Good day, Miss Hollstrom," was all he said before he strode down the stairs and out toward the street.

The cemetery, with its shivering cottonwoods, was a welcome relief after the stifling conditions inside the church. Reverend Wintergarden kept the service mercifully short, extolling the late doctor's virtues in as few words as decently possible, but even with all the windows and the front door open, the church quickly became an oven when packed with townspeople in the middle of the afternoon. The service began at two o'clock, and before half-past the preacher issued the order to have the casket removed to the cemetery for burial.

Julie sat with Willy and Katharine in the next-to-front pew and didn't notice until they rose to depart that Del Morgan had not attended. She hadn't really expected him to; he was probably down at the saloon. She shook him out of her thoughts and ushered Willy ahead of her toward the door.

The grave had been dug in a corner of the churchyard where there was little shade, but Julie herded her mother and brother toward the back of the crowd and thereby found a cooler place under one of the trees. She had been surprised when Katharine expressed a wish to attend the funeral, but she had not argued. And Katharine seemed to be bearing up quite well, considering she had had so much excitement the day before and hadn't even had a nap all day today. That in itself was unusual.

With fans and folded pieces of paper fluttering to provide some breeze on this still afternoon, the mourners gathered quietly while the Reverend Wintergarden intoned the familiar service. He was halfway through it when Julie caught something out the corner of her eye, some movement at the edge of the crowd. She dared to chance a peek and saw Del Morgan shoving people out of his way.

What nerve! He had scolded her and Hans that Sunday evening for disturbing him, so what did he think he was doing now? And she had thought to reform him. He was better off drunk and disreputable.

Horace Opper was laid to rest with no family but the town of Plato to mourn him, and they dispersed rather quickly when the token spade of dirt had been tossed into the open grave. Julie linked her mother's arm through her own and then clasped her brother's hand to keep him from running off in his good clothes.

The rosebush caught her attention, though she hadn't looked for it and had in fact almost forgotten it. It wasn't the blaze of red blossoms that she remembered, either, for only two or three half-faded blooms still hung on the canes. Julie peered over the rims of her glasses and saw the damage done when rough, greedy hands had pulled the lovely flowers off.

While contemplating that destruction, she saw the name cut into the polished granite marker.

"Amalia Morgan, born April 12, 1851, innocent victim of violence August 3, 1878. Beloved wife of Delbert, mother of their son Jason, who lies with his mother now and for all eternity."

Chapter Five

✦✦✦✦✦

BY WEDNESDAY AFTERNOON, Willy's stitches were driving him crazy—and Julie, too. As if the boy's complaints about the injury itself weren't enough, he continually asked when he was going to get the ice cream Morgan had promised and then failed to deliver.

"You ought to go find him, Julie, and make him buy me my ice cream," he told her while he watched her flour the chicken she intended to fry for supper. "He did promise and he oughtn't to make promises and then not keep them."

With the back of her hand she pushed her glasses up again and dipped another piece of chicken in the egg-and-milk batter.

"He promised me ice cream, too, Willy, and you don't hear me whining about it, do you?"

"Well, but you don't count. You're a grownup, and it's all right to break promises to grownups."

Katharine walked into the room just then, but she did not provide a diversion from this unpleasant topic. Though coming down a different path, she reached the same junction.

"Julie, dear, I simply cannot get rid of this headache." She wiped the back of her right hand across her forehead dramatically. "I have taken the last spoonful of that elixir poor Dr. Opper gave me, and now I am in pain again."

"As soon as I finish here, Mama, I'll go ask the marshal to open Dr. Opper's house and I'll see if I can find anything," Julie said, sighing. This morning it had been a stomach potion, and last night a sleeping powder, neither of which had been located. "Do you know what it looked like or tasted like? Did he give it a name?"

Katharine turned her eyes toward the ceiling and thought for a long while.

"It tasted rather like burnt sugar," she answered slowly. "Or was that the sleeping powder? No, the sleeping powder tasted like lemon, and the stomach potion was very bitter. Yes, the headache elixir tasted like burnt sugar, I'm positive."

She smiled triumphantly. Julie sighed again and wiped her floury hands on her apron.

"I'll go find the marshal, but I don't think we'll have any better luck this time. The doctor never labeled any of his bottles, and I really wonder that he didn't kill anyone with the wrong mixture. They all look alike."

"Oh, dear."

Katharine sat down at the table beside Willy and her smile melted away.

"Do you think it might be unsafe, even if you found something that tasted like burnt sugar?"

"Possibly. I'm not a doctor, Mama, and I don't know anything about the medicines Dr. Opper gave you."

Except that they cost nearly every cent we could spare from Papa's wages and none of them really did any good, she said to herself.

Again Katharine sank into thought, this time staring at the checkered tablecloth.

"Do you suppose that Mr. Morgan could help you?" she suggested. "He did say he was a doctor once, didn't he? Why don't you go find him and ask him if he'd help you look for my medicines."

Julie groaned. She knew exactly what would come next. Already Willy's pout had turned to a wide grin.

"And then you could ask him about my ice cream, too," the boy reminded her.

Julie went to McCrory's first, where Simon and his ever-present companion sat on the porch. Lucas waited until she had climbed the steps before he spat.

"As a matter of fact, I haven't seen Del all day, Miss Hollstrom," Simon answered. "I was busy unloading wagons this morning, though, so I might've missed him. Did you try over at the Castle?"

"I'd prefer to avoid the place if I can."

"Can't say as I blame you. Not exactly the place for a young lady like yourself."

"Is there somewhere else I might look for him?"

Lucas shifted his weight to his other foot and spat again. Then he drawled, "He might be to home, ya know. He got pretty drunk last night after them folks took all the flowers off'n his Amy's grave."

"I could hardly go looking for him at his house."

Simon offered a solution.

"Winnie Upshaw sort of keeps house for him, and I just seen her go over to the post office. You could ask her if he's home and then maybe she could go with you if he is."

"I'm afraid I don't know Miss Upshaw."

Lucas volunteered, "Can't miss her. 'Bout as high as my pocket, and 'bout as big around as Simon's cracker barrel. Talks all the time, too, and don't say nothin'."

That description was accurate to a fault. Miss Upshaw lacked a good two inches of being five feet tall. There was a slight indentation at her waist, but otherwise she did indeed resemble the cracker barrel in the middle of McCrory's General Store, especially as she wore a brown calico dress just the color of aged wood. And Julie heard the nonstop voice well before she walked into the post office and found the expected figure standing at the window.

"Now, you promise me that letter'll go out on tomorrow's stage to Yuma, right, Mr. Nisely? I don't want anything to happen to delay it, because my sister in San Francisco always worries if she doesn't hear from me faithfully every month. She thinks I'm out here in some wilderness with Apaches surrounding me and coyotes howling at my door." She halted only briefly to turn and see who had come into the post office. "Oh, hello, Miss Hollstrom. How's your little brother? I saw him come running through the trees there Monday afternoon, and he certainly—"

"He's just fine now," Julie interrupted. She wondered how long the woman would have gone on if she hadn't broken into the steady stream of chatter.

"Well, that's good. Of course, Dr. Morgan always was a one with children. Why, I remember when Dennis McCrory broke his leg falling out of the livery stable loft that Halloween night when him and those horrible Sanderson boys—"

"Do you happen to know where I might find Dr. Morgan now?" Julie interrupted again. She must assert herself or run the risk of listening to Winnie Upshaw for an hour or more. "I was told he might be at home, but I wanted to make certain first, before I disturbed him."

"He's home, all right!" Winnie said, laughing. Her voice was bright, almost childish. "I stopped by there on my way here and he was still asleep. Last night, though, well, he was roaring in there until almost dawn, and I can't say as I blame him. Of course, most of those people who stole the roses were new folks to town, ones who weren't here when Amy Morgan was killed. But still, it ain't right to go pickin' flowers off somebody else's grave."

Julie hesitated despite the break in Winnie's conversation.

"If he's still asleep, then perhaps I'd best wait."

"What did you want him for, anyway? Somebody else get hurt?"

Julie wished she hadn't taken off her apron, for it would have given her something to twist her hands in. She felt awkward here in the post office with Mr. Nisely listening carefully to her every word.

"It's about some medication Dr. Opper had given my mother," she muttered.

Winnie laughed again.

"You'd better not call old Horace's concoctions medication in Dr. Morgan's presence! Come on. You and me'll go wake him up and see what he has to say. Don't worry," she said, turning toward the door and taking Julie's arm in a firm grasp. "He won't bite, though he barks a lot."

Del Morgan's house was set back from the street down a short lane, just past the Olympia House and almost directly across Main Street from the late Dr. Opper's house and office. Unlike nearly all the other buildings in Plato, Morgan's house was built of adobe, not timber, and the dull brown color blended well with the dusty surroundings. Flourishing vines shaded the west-facing porch; someone obviously watered and tended the plants carefully, for there were no others like them in Plato. Even Julie's rows of petunias seemed pathetic in comparison, and she wondered, remembering the rosebush in the cemetery, if Morgan himself did all the watering and weeding.

The house seemed larger than its neighbors, too, but Julie noticed as she and Winnie walked up to it that it had only a partial second floor, with stairs leading up the outside to a rooftop patio.

"Mr. Morgan lives *here*?" Julie asked. This was hardly the sort of place she had expected the derelict physician to inhabit.

"Used to belong to an old Mexican, Don Ricardo de Santanero. When Dr. Morgan came in 'seventy-one or 'seventy-two, Don Ricardo was his first patient. He must've done something for the old guy, because when Don Ricardo died about a year later, he left everything to Dr. Morgan and Amy. Had a regular will, all legal and proper, signed by lawyers and witnesses and everything."

The two women, one tall and slim and hesitant, the other short and round and bold, mounted the single step to the porch and faced a handsomely carved door with a rounded top, quite unlike anything Julie had seen before. Winnie didn't knock; she pounded with her fists, both of them. When no one answered, she simply turned the latch and walked in.

"Is that you, Winnie?"

Julie didn't enter the house, but Winnie had thrown the door open wide. Peering in cautiously, Julie saw a dim foyer from which a railed staircase rose to a small balcony. Del Morgan leaned over the banister, his body a shadow against a whitewashed wall.

"Yes, it's me," Winnie replied cheerfully. "I brought Miss Hollstrom with me. She was lookin' for you and I told her you were here. She didn't want to come by herself, so I came with her."

"What the hell do you want now?" Morgan bellowed. "Your daddy stub his toe or something?"

No man had ever made her feel so childish. Her father filled her with a sense of guilt and inadequacy, but this man made her want to cry and run away. Or scream. Or hit something, preferably some part of his anatomy. There he was, no doubt leering down at her from that balcony, ready to burst into laughter when she told him she'd come for his assistance in locating a headache powder.

"Well, what did you want me for?" he yelled again.

"My mother has a headache." She knew he probably hadn't heard her, for she'd kept her voice low, but the simple absurdity of the situation sent blood rushing to her cheeks.

"What? Do you expect me to hear your little mousy squeaks all the way up here?"

Julie turned to Winnie in panic.

"Oh, Miss Upshaw, I'm so sorry I troubled you, but I really think I've made a mistake," she apologized in a voice as quiet as before. "I shouldn't have made you bother him, and I hope he won't—"

She was cut off when his booted footsteps pounded slowly down the stairs.

"Go on home, Winnie," he ordered quietly. "I'll holler if I need you."

Still chuckling to herself, Winnie Upshaw skipped past Julie. Julie wanted to follow her, but there was something so terrifying in the way Morgan looked at her that now she couldn't move in the opposite direction either.

He filled the doorway, one hand reaching up to the top of the rounded frame while he crossed one foot over the other so the toe of his boot rested right in the corner. Sometime since Monday afternoon he had gotten a shave, but already the black stubble shaded his cheeks and chin and jaw again.

"Are you going to tell me what you came here and woke me up out of a sound sleep for? It isn't often I actually sleep, and I really hate to be disturbed unless it's for a damned good reason. You do have one, don't you?"

If he had simply been angry, Julie could have found the courage to run away from him, or even to tell him the truth. But to have him stare at her, with his green eyes like river ice in the middle of winter, unnerved her.

"I told you before that my mother's health is not good. She was under Dr. Opper's care and he had given her a headache remedy. She has taken the last of it and wondered if you could help me go through his effects and possibly locate some more of this . . . compound."

"If I did, I'd probably throw it in Cold Creek here and hope it didn't kill the fish."

She didn't laugh. He wished she would. She had a nice mouth, not too wide, and the lips were a little thin, but he thought she might actually be pretty if she smiled. And there went the glasses, sliding down her nose again. She didn't seem to notice and just went on staring at him over the tops.

"Please, Dr. Morgan, I do not—"

"Don't call me that, Miss Hollstrom. I let Winnie get away with it, but no one else."

A small spark of fire blazed in his eyes, but the ice quickly dowsed it and cold returned.

"I'm sorry. But you don't understand my position. My mother is a very sick woman. If I can't find some way to relieve her suffering . . ."

She could not have put it into words, much less uttered those words to him.

He looked down at himself, at the faded denims, the dilapidated boots, the shirt that needed laundering and patching and two buttons replaced. He had shaved yesterday, fully intending to go to Horace's funeral, but in the end he had chickened out and sat home. Only when it was too late to go into the crowded church did he venture to the graveyard, and there he had witnessed the desecration of the roses. He hadn't been so filled with fury in almost six years.

"I'm sorry, Miss Hollstrom, but I can't help you. You saw what happened the other day; that's what I've become, and I can't go back to what I was before. Eventually there'll be another doctor in Plato, and your mother can get her headache medicine from him. Now, go on home and brew her a nice cup of tea or some cold lemonade and for God's sake, leave me alone."

The ache in that gentle plea and the knowledge of what caused that ache helped Julie stand her ground. She would have gone if he had raised his voice or if he had simply turned around and slammed the door, but she had known that same desperate pain herself, and for an even longer time.

"If you won't help my mother, would you at least keep your promise to Willy and get him his ice cream?"

The knot in his chest tightened. He couldn't count the empty promises he had made and broken over the years, never giving them a thought afterwards. But no one had ever called him to task for them, either.

"Not today, Miss Hollstrom. I don't think I'd be very good company today. But we could meet tomorrow afternoon at McCrory's and have regular sundaes, all right?"

"It would be better if you just came to our house and took Willy," she stammered, turning her gaze downward again. She could make sure Katharine was in attendance, so there would be no quarrel with her father.

Morgan was about to tell her that he would be happy to, though he couldn't figure out why he would want to give her that kind of answer. Before the first word was out of his mouth, a man on horseback had just turned off the main street and thundered recklessly down the narrow lane. In the dust and with the sun in his unshaded eyes, Morgan couldn't identify the rider, but the man's furious ride boded ill news.

Julie coughed on the dust but still heard the stranger's impassioned plea.

"Del Morgan? You probably don't remember me; I'm Steve Hollis. Bought the old Chernicky place north of here. My wife's havin' a baby and Doc Opper's been keepin' an eye on her, so I come to town to tell him it's time, and they tell me he dropped dead yesterday."

"I can't help you, Hollis," Morgan croaked in a voice barely audible. Under the bluish shadow of beard his face was white, and his eyes glazed, then glittered, and he blinked as though to hold back tears.

"You can't mean it?" Julie whispered to him.

He looked at her, at those eyes enormous with shock, at those lips he had thought too thin, now parted in disbelief. She couldn't know what went through his mind now. If she had, she wouldn't ask this of him. But she didn't know, and she was asking.

"Is your wife alone?" he asked Hollis, the voice louder now but not any steadier.

"Grace Fulton's with her."

"Grace will take care of her. She's got six kids of her own and delivered a helluva lot more, so she knows what to do." Oh, God, but he needed a drink now, and there wasn't a drop in the house. Just as there hadn't been any last night when he'd been so furious about the roses and didn't even have the money for a bottle at the Castle.

Why the hell did Opper have to die like that?

Morgan ran his fingers through his hair and tried to think. Hollis wasn't the type of man to show fear, but he was plainly terrified. Morgan couldn't send him away alone.

"Okay, Mr. Hollis. I want you to go back home. I'll get my things together and ride out as soon as I can. I know the place. You go home and stay with your wife."

"I got your word you'll be there?" Hollis asked doubtfully.

"My word."

The man tipped his hat and wheeled the horse back down the lane, raising another massive cloud of dust.

Chapter Six

◆◆◆◆◆

"WELL, DON'T JUST stand there," Morgan told Julie. "Go get Winnie and find out where the hell she hid my instruments. And tell Bert—that's her nephew—to go down to the livery and saddle a couple of horses. Sam for me and probably Woody'll do for you. You ride much?"

She collected all her scattered thoughts and replaced her sliding spectacles. Squaring her shoulders, she faced him with firm determination.

"Mr. Morgan, I will ask Miss Upshaw where she has hidden your instruments, whether in hell or anywhere else, and I will ask her nephew to hire a horse for you, but you certainly don't expect me to come with you!"

"Why not?" The normal color came back to his face, though his eyes still sparkled a bit too brightly. He resumed that lazy stance in the doorway. "You said yesterday you were, if I may quote you, prepared to see to my rehabilitation. Apparently you weren't very prepared at all or else you wished to do it from a polite and safe distance."

"I don't see how my accompanying you on an errand of mercy can—"

"Look, Julie, are you gonna help me or not? Peg Hollis might very well die if you stand here arguing. And you'd better get word to your mother that her headache is going to be around for a while. We may not get back until sometime tomorrow."

The argument with Katharine lasted just as long as it took Julie to fetch a shawl and a pair of gloves and to give final instructions for supper.

"I'm going, Mama, because the woman may

die if I don't," she explained, wondering if it was really a lie.

"But what will I tell your father? This Mr. Morgan is so . . ."

"So unsavory, Mama? Yes, I suppose he is, but he is also a doctor. He said he might be able to find something for your headaches, but he has to see to Mrs. Hollis first." Pacify her, Julie thought, play on her own needs.

"How come I can't go with you?" Willy asked.

"Because it isn't a place for children," his mother explained. "It isn't as though Julie is going visiting, you understand."

And yet as she dashed out of the house and ran toward Morgan's, Julie felt as excited as if she were going to a party.

Steve Hollis's ranch lay some four miles north of Plato in a shallow valley. Morgan pointed out the log and stone house as soon as they had crested the last hill. It was a small building, single storied, with a porch at one end. Chickens pecked in the yard until scattered by the horses, and a barking dog bounded up to greet them.

The woman in the doorway must be Grace Fulton, Julie guessed. Iron-haired and built as sturdily as many of the men in Plato, she looked at the visitors with cautious eyes.

"You sober, Morgan?" she called before they had dismounted.

"Yes, ma'am. And alive, which is more'n you can say for Horace."

She didn't appear to approve of his humor, but she backed up enough to let him enter. Julie followed.

"Who's she?"

"Julie Hollstrom. I'm training her to be my nurse."

Grace Fulton snorted.

"What happened to Winnie Upshaw?"

But by the time she finished that question, Morgan had already passed through the main room of the house to the bedroom where Steve Hollis stood guard.

"We lost one last year," the rancher said quietly. "She wants this one real bad."

Julie sank to the bench at the kitchen table and stared at the cup of coffee in front of her. She was too tired even to pick it up. The clock on the mantel chimed softly eleven times. Morgan Julian Hollis was an hour old.

"I seen breech births before," Grace Fulton commented, "but never one like that, with the cord around the neck."

Steve Hollis poured another tin mug full of coffee and held it out to Morgan. He took it and blew gently as he wrapped his fingers around it. Even though he braced his elbows on the table, his fingers still shook.

He sipped the scalding coffee and said, "Your wife's a good, healthy young woman and I don't see any reason why she shouldn't be up and around very soon. Just remember to take good care of her and that baby, and watch for any signs of fever. If anything goes wrong, you come get me, okay?"

The young rancher nodded gravely.

Morgan set his cup down as he got to his feet and shook the man's extended hand. It was a queer feeling to stand up and not sway or feel like the floor was made of pudding.

"Thanks, Morgan."

"You're welcome. You coming, Miss Hollstrom?"

Grace jumped from her chair and put a hand on the girl's weary shoulder, but she addressed her words to Morgan.

"You can't mean to ride all the way back to town now. This poor girl will fall right out of the saddle, if her horse don't stumble in the dark and throw her first."

Julie smiled weakly. The thought of that long ride when she was so utterly exhausted was terrifying, but more so was the thought of arriving home in the morning.

"Miss Hollstrom is needed at home," Morgan explained. "Her mother isn't well." He pulled her shawl from the wall rack where someone had hung it earlier and draped it around her shoulders. "Here, you'll need this now that it's cooled off. Got your gloves?"

"Yes, here in my pocket."

Reaching for them, she felt something else in the pocket of her skirt and for a single instant she panicked. When had she taken the glasses off and put them there? Had anyone noticed? Had she even had them on when she arrived, or had she taken them off on the ride up here? It was too late to worry about it now, and she wouldn't need them in the dark.

And the night wasn't so dark after all. A brilliant yellow moon rode low in the eastern sky, almost full, and bright as a lantern. Julie's eyes had adjusted to it by the time she unhitched Woody and let Morgan boost her onto the animal's back. Shadows of mesquite and cactus stood out eerily in the pale light, and the skittering of nocturnal birds and animals set Julie's nerves on edge. But at least she was awake and alert.

After they had passed that first hill and were out of sight of the little ranchstead, Morgan said, "I must say, you surprised me, Miss Hollstrom. You held up pretty good."

"Thank you, I think. I mean, that was a compliment, wasn't it?"

He chuckled.

"I'm sorry, Mr. Morgan, but I'm very tired, and I guess I'm not thinking very straight. I'm probably not speaking very straight, either."

"You're doing fine. And yes, it was a compliment."

When was the last time he had paid a woman a compliment? He must be out of practice, if she didn't recognize it. Or maybe she's out of practice, he thought. Probably doesn't get too many compliments, a tall girl like her with that hair pulled back and those glasses.

He looked at her, riding next to him.

"What happened to your spectacles?"

"What? Oh, well, I . . . I took them off when we left so I wouldn't lose them if I fell asleep."

She held her breath and prayed that he wouldn't go on—but he did.

"No, you didn't have them on all evening. In fact, I don't remember you having them on since we got to Hollis's place."

She had one more chance, a slim one, but she took it.

"Of course I did. You just don't remember, because you were busy with Mrs. Hollis."

"No, I remember perfectly."

He was tempted to rein in Sam and question the girl out here where she'd be scared to death and would tell him anything, but he let the horse plod on toward home. He didn't want Julie Hollstrom afraid of him.

Not after tonight.

So he dropped the subject abruptly and went on to something else.

"I kind of enjoyed tonight, myself," he said quietly. "It's been a long time since I helped deliver a baby, saw the way a woman looks when she holds him for the first time. I kinda missed it."

"All you need to do is go back to the work you left. It's waiting for you."

"It wouldn't be quite that easy. I'd need some help."

"Someone to keep you rehabilitated?"

"No, more than that. Well, that too, but before I—when I was practicing before, I always had a nurse, someone to lend an extra hand and calm people down in emergencies when I wasn't right there."

It was painful to talk about it even in such an oblique way. Julie heard it in the lowering of his voice and saw it in the way he turned his face away from her. She wondered if he had ever talked about it to anyone.

"What about Miss Upshaw?"

"Winnie? Winnie faints when she pricks her finger with a darning needle."

"But I thought when Grace Fulton mentioned her that—"

"Winnie is a dreamer. She comes over and cleans my house once in a while and she pretends she's my nurse and we are saving lives by the thousands. She was fourteen when . . . when I stopped practicing medicine, and I think she had it in the back of her mind to bring me back to it someday."

"Oh."

"What, is that guilt I hear?"

She lifted her eyes from her hands to look at him and saw that he was smiling at her.

He had a nice smile, she decided, if a little bit crooked, and there was warmth in the way his eyes crinkled at the corners. If he shaved regularly and had some of that shaggy hair cut, he might be quite a handsome man. A bath wouldn't hurt, either.

"I just feel rather sad that Miss Upshaw, after all her dreams, couldn't have been the one to do it," Julie said. "I mean, I'm a newcomer, and I feel I've taken a prize someone else has been trying for."

"Well, you haven't saved me yet, Miss New Girl in Town. And we aren't far from town now, so you'd better put those spectacles of yours back on before somebody else notices you took them off. Vanity can put some pretty big obstacles in your path to trip over, too."

So that's what he thought! Rather arrogant of him to presume she'd removed the things because she wanted to appear more attractive to him. But it was probably less dangerous that way. If she went to work for him, she would simply have to be more careful.

But working for him was a terribly big "if" right now. Katharine might be persuaded because she needed a doctor's care, and that need was Julie's leverage. Katharine had already consented to tonight's errand, and with surprisingly little protest, as Julie recalled with a puzzled frown. In fact, Katharine had hardly argued at all. But of course, Wilhelm had not been home at the time.

Wilhelm was a different matter entirely.

Chapter Seven

✦✦✦✦✦

MORGAN SAID GOOD night to Julie while he walked her to the porch of the darkened house. Odd, he thought, that no one had left a light for her. He waited an extra minute or two after she had gone inside, just in case there was an argument, but the house remained as silent as it was dark.

He took the horses back to the livery stable, where he woke Gus and then helped the old Swede put the animals to bed. Tired in body but not ready for sleep himself, Morgan began the long walk back to the other end of town.

Main Street was bright compared to the track up to Hollises'. Light spilled from the Castle's wide windows, and the saloon was noisy, too, even this late. Fred's piano plinked away and raucous voices raised in what passed for song.

The temptation brought Morgan up short. He stopped and stood in the middle of Main Street.

Two days of sobriety. He couldn't remember when he had last gone that long without the comforting oblivion. And tonight he needed it. He had delivered a baby—a living, kicking, nuzzling little mite who curled into the comfort of his mother's embrace. It was a scene he'd never forget, and one he couldn't bear to remember.

He turned away from the saloon's enticement and headed home again, with a smile of self-satisfaction. It hadn't been an easy delivery, but he had managed to save both mother and child. He didn't know what made him insist the Hollstrom girl come with him, except maybe to pay her back for all the grief she had given him lately, but in the end he had been pleased with her.

And hell, she wasn't a girl any more than he was a stripling boy. She was a woman, a quiet and strong woman who on more than one occasion in his sometimes patchy memory had done what needed to be done. And she made everything seem more normal, more like it had been with Amy.

He pushed the front door open and dropped the black bag to the floor. Leaning back until the portal latched, he smiled at the lamp Winnie had left in the parlor window. No doubt she had filled a big basin of water for him in the kitchen, too.

He stripped off the filthy shirt and managed in the process to skitter another button across the floor. The garment was beyond salvage anyway; he ripped it in half and tossed the pieces on top of the cold stove. The pants landed there, too, though the worn denim resisted his efforts to separate one leg from the other. He would have disposed of the boots as well, but they had to serve one more day at least.

"You ought to be in bed," he told himself aloud, "not trying to take a bath in a dishpan." He dipped each arm in the tepid water and reached for the cake of soap.

He couldn't rinse the soap completely off when there was soon more of it in the water than on him. Without bothering to cover any of his nakedness, he walked out the kitchen door and crossed the yard to the creek. The gravelly soil hurt his feet, but with some help from the risen moon he avoided any stray cactus spines. Well aware of the temperature of Cold Creek, he took a deep breath and placed one foot in the gurgling stream.

By the time he had washed the last of Winnie's homemade soap from his body, he ached and shivered. But he felt clean, and revitalized. He brushed droplets of icy water from the hair on his chest and then shook his head like a dog.

He found towels enough to dry his skin and hair, then walked through the house to the stairs, stopping in the parlor to take the lamp with him. He couldn't remember if there was one in the closed second bedroom upstairs.

There was, on the table beside the bed, but the wick looked old and frayed and the oil was nearly gone, so he set the lamp he had brought beside it and then walked to the wardrobe. He didn't look at the bed. He knew it was shrouded in sheets, the folds dark with the accumulated dust of six years.

The dark walnut wardrobe was carved in an intricate pattern reminiscent of Old Spain. The key in the lock turned easily. The tarnished silver hinges swung with only a slight squeak. Morgan stood for a moment and stared at the empty half of the wardrobe, letting the memories fill him. The party dresses, the apricot satin ballgown she had worn the night of their engagement party, the blouses she had so lovingly stitched and embroidered and tucked. And that nightgown of layer after layer of lace. All were gone now, though he could see them as if they still hung neatly just after she had put everything away.

His own shirts and trousers hung on his side, as dull and unexciting as Amy's had been bright and gay. Of course, there was that pair of red suspenders she had bought him for Christmas one year. He opened the single shallow drawer in the bottom of the wardrobe and found them, along with a pair of gold cufflinks and a mismated pair of socks.

He took down a white shirt, dingy even in this poor light. He'd have Winnie wash it for him in the morning, and with a pair of black trousers and a coat, he'd be a long way toward looking respectable again. If they fit. He drew on the shirt, enjoying the feel of crisp linen after how many years of chambray and threadbare flannel. He had lost a little weight since he last wore this shirt, but that was better than gaining a paunch. He tried on the pants with a bit of hope that they, too, would fit reasonably well.

"I'll need to pull in my belt a notch or two to hold them up"—he laughed in the empty room—"but I'll be damned if I'll wear those red suspenders!"

The sheets on his bed smelled of sweat and stale whiskey, but he blew out the lamp and collapsed on them. He would get word to Winnie in the morning that he wanted the house cleaned thoroughly along with his laundry.

He rolled onto his back and stared at the ceiling. So many plans, so many things to do. Tomorrow he would have to wire Denver or Santa Fe for medical supplies, and find some books in order to get caught up on the last six years' medical advances. No sense being as out of date as Horace always had been.

But before that, he had some shopping to do. New boots and a decent hat were first on the list. Then a trip to the barbershop for a haircut and shave. When he stopped at the haberdashery for the hat, he'd ask Mr. Farnum about alterations to his present wardrobe. It would be a while before Morgan could afford new clothes, but these would suffice for a while if they were taken in.

If he was going to let the Hollstrom girl make a doctor out of him again, he might just as well look the part.

For the first few hours of that restless night, Julie lay on her bed and dutifully tried to sleep. But too many thoughts rampaged through her head, all shouting and fighting for supremacy. Before there was even a hint of gray in the sky, she had left the wrinkled sheets and stood by the window facing the black western sky with its spangled stars already paling around the moon.

She remembered how joyful Mrs. Hollis had looked in her exhaustion when the ordeal was

over and she held her new son in her arms.
There had been no such euphoria when Katharine Hollstrom was delivered of Willy nearly
nine years ago, and the memory of that night
with all its horrors came back to haunt Julie. She
thanked Providence there was no tree in the
silvered backyard under her window, especially
no oak tree with wide-spreading branches that
made such a convenient gallows. Death and new
life. How strangely they had come together that
night.

Now there had been death and new life again.
Horace Opper had died and Morgan Julian
Hollis had been born. Julie wondered if those
events would change her life as much as when a
drifter named Ted Sheen had lost his life at the
end of a rope and a fragile infant named William
Shakespeare Hollstrom had come squalling into
the world.

And then there was Del Morgan. He stole into
Julie's thoughts no matter what other subject
had momentarily claimed her attention. What
right did she have to speak to him as she had, to
demand he return to whatever his former life
had been? She knew too little about his wife's
death. Winnie Upshaw had said something
about Amy Morgan being killed, and Julie resolved to seek out the ebullient Miss Upshaw to
learn the rest of the details. Knowing the cause
of the man's grief might help her in her crusade.

She tried to make herself believe Morgan's rehabilitation was her only interest in the man.
She used Katharine and Willy as excuses to urge

him to take up his profession again, but such tactics didn't fool her and she knew they would never fool her father. He had no more forgotten Ted Sheen than she had.

Which brought her back to the question of why Wilhelm hadn't waited for her until she and Morgan returned. It must have been long past midnight, and yet the house was dark and everyone had seemed asleep. Julie was so certain Wilhelm had heard her come in that she waited a long time before she ventured to remove her sweaty, dusty clothes and don a cool nightgown. As the hours passed and still nothing happened, she became more and more afraid of what would happen come morning.

But nothing happened then, either. Wilhelm said nothing to her, nor did Katharine, except to complain rather more than usual about her headache. Willy went off after breakfast to find Clancy without even asking Julie the details of her adventure—which was exactly the way she saw it as she busied herself with the dishes and then baked a batch of sugar cookies.

Katharine sat in the parlor with the latest *Saturday Evening Post*. Her occasional moans floated through the house, and twice she came into the kitchen to look for something to settle her stomach. Julie sympathized all she could, but she had no remedy for either that complaint or the headache.

The last sheet of cookies had just come from the oven when Katharine made a third foray.

"I don't know how much longer I can bear this," she groaned. "After your father comes home for lunch, I'm afraid I shall have to—"

"Papa's coming home for lunch?"

He never did that. Never.

"Yes, didn't he tell you? Oh, no, I don't think he did. I think he wanted me to tell you." She sat down at the table and helped herself to a cookie from the barrel-shaped jar. "I'm afraid he's not very happy about what you did yesterday."

Julie slipped the spatula under a row of cookies on the sheet and lifted them to the wire rack to cool.

"I didn't think he would be. But Mama, it isn't what he thinks. Dr. Morgan *did* need me, and there wasn't anyone else," she insisted.

"The chicken burned a little," Katharine told her. "I had to lie down on the sofa for a while, and the chicken burned. And I put too much honey on the carrots."

The accusation was clear. Wilhelm had complained of the poorly prepared meal. Had Julie been home, his supper would have been perfect. She shook her head. Wilhelm complained when she wasn't there, but he never complimented her when she was.

What would happen when she told him Morgan had asked her to work for him? If she accepted, it would mean changes in the Hollstrom household. Just the matter of turning the cooking over to Katharine was enough to assure Julie of her father's refusal.

She had known from the start that the venture was doomed, but she hadn't wanted to accept it. Even now she fought against it.

"Mama, I don't mean to sound ungrateful," she began, "but I think it's time—who can that be?"

The light tapping on the front door was almost inaudible. Settling her spectacles back on the bridge of her nose where they belonged, she walked to the foyer and pulled the door open.

"Good morning, Miss Hollstrom."

"Dr. Morgan?"

She tried to hold back the title he had forbidden, but he looked so deserving of it, standing there still smelling faintly of shaving soap, shampoo, and bay rum. He slid the brim of a new, low-crowned hat through his fingers nervously and peered through the screen. Julie knew he probably could barely see her, for the hallway was dark and he'd just come out of the sunlight.

"I came to see if you and Master Willy were free for that ice cream I promised."

"Oh, I'm sorry, really I am. Willy's with Clancy McCrory right now, and in a few minutes my father will be home for lunch." She felt like a fool, sending him away like this. He had gone to a great deal of effort and expense to change from yesterday's derelict to the well-dressed, clean-shaven gentleman at her door this morning.

Despite her words, he seemed undeterred.

"Perhaps this afternoon?" he asked. "I have

some business of my own at McCrory's. We could meet there at, say, two o'clock?"

He could see her better now, though the screen still blurred her features somewhat. He thought for an instant that perhaps she was about to agree to meet him, by the brief smile, but then anger puckered her brow.

He mumbled, "It's all right, Miss Hollstrom. I understand." He felt like a complete ass. He had just turned to leave when the reason for her scowl clumped up the stairs behind him.

"Off my porch, Morgan," Wilhelm growled, pointing a finger toward the street. "I will deal with you later."

"Papa, please."

"You go in and leave this to me." Now he shook the finger at his daughter. "I don't want you—"

"Well, hello, Dr. Morgan!" Katharine sang behind Julie. She hardly sounded like a woman with a throbbing head and a churning stomach.

"Good morning, Mrs. Hollstrom."

"It isn't morning anymore, Dr. Morgan. It's five minutes after twelve. Have you had lunch?"

"Katharine, this is not the time—"

"Oh, nonsense. We have plenty for one more, don't we, Julie?"

Julie felt trapped between her insistent mother and her obstinate father. Wilhelm shoved his way past Morgan, but he stood on the threshold, neither in nor out of the house. And Julie couldn't move out of his way.

Julie could see Morgan clearly now, and he seemed to hide a sympathetic smile when he said, "I don't want to put you to any trouble, Mrs. Hollstrom."

"No trouble at all, Dr. Morgan." Katharine reached past Julie to take her husband's arm. "Come on in, Wilhelm, and don't block the entrance."

Without bothering to plead her useless arm as an excuse not to offer some assistance in the kitchen, Katharine led the gentlemen into the parlor while Julie gathered lunch. Julie found a platter of leftover chicken and discovered it wasn't burnt as badly as Katharine had let on. Then she took a pint jar of corn from the pantry and dumped the contents into a pan with a lump of butter to heat while she sliced bread.

Though she worked frantically, Julie couldn't keep her mind off that image of Del Morgan as he walked through her front door. He looked so different that she had trouble recalling the man who had brought her home last night. Instead of faded denims he wore a pair of black trousers, plain but of good quality. The tattered plaid shirt was replaced by one of clean white linen, over which he wore a black coat open just enough to reveal a blue waistcoat and a heavy gold watch chain. She wondered if the black boots were new enough to hurt his feet and hoped that they didn't.

Julie had boiled some eggs this morning and now quickly deviled them, then filled a bowl with applesauce. She carried these to the dining room and began to set the table.

Katharine talked, but no one listened. Wilhelm glowered, and Morgan watched the girl in the dining room. She was quick and efficient and graceful despite her haste. And so thin. It was no wonder he had missed the resemblance between mother and daughter. Katharine was as plump as a spoiled cat. Julie only had hints of the dimples in her mother's cheeks.

When she finally called the others in to eat, Julie felt exhausted. And out of place. Katharine, as always, looked as if she had just come from the parlor and the *Saturday Evening Post*. Papa wore his usual office clothes, and Morgan in his new incarnation put Julie's old calico dress and scuffed shoes to shame. She pushed at a loose strand of hair and resituated her glasses, but that wasn't enough to make her feel comfortable when he came to hold her chair for her. She blushed hotly.

He moved to the chair Katharine had indicated for him and sat down. As Julie picked up the platter of chicken and passed it to him, he noticed how thin, how fragile her wrists were. He could almost see the bones through the skin.

"I'm afraid I didn't apologize for making you miss your supper last night," he said, letting his eyes draw hers. He slid the serving fork under a plump breast half and placed it on her plate. "How about a wing, too?"

"No, no thank you," she stammered. She knew Wilhelm was glaring at her.

She got up to help her mother, but even that did not save her. Morgan returned the favor, dishing a healthy spoonful of buttered corn onto Julie's plate, then spreading butter and jam onto a thick slice of bread for her.

"You'll need plenty of strength if you intend to be my nurse," he said without looking at her. "It isn't easy work, and if you don't put a little meat on those bones, you'll waste away to nothing in no time."

"My daughter is not going to work for you, Morgan," Wilhelm interjected. "She works here, in her own home, taking care of her own family."

Morgan buttered a slice of bread for himself and bit back the words. A woman's "own" family is her husband and children, he thought, not her mother and brother.

"But, Wilhelm, think how much more help Julie could be if she learned something about medicine," Katharine suggested.

Julie stared briefly at her mother, unable to believe that Katharine had sided with her in direct opposition to Wilhelm.

"And who will do the work here?" he asked. "You are too ill, and until the arm is mended, you can do nothing anyway."

Satisfied that the issue was therefore ended, Wilhelm leaned back in his chair for grace.

"Perhaps Dr. Morgan would like to do the honors," Katharine hinted sweetly.

For the first time since Wilhelm's arrival, Julie saw Morgan's composure slip. He regained it quickly, however, and murmured a short, simple prayer that, if it didn't measure up to Wilhelm's long-winded standards, it got them eating quickly. And back to the conversation.

"Did you tell your folks about last night?" Morgan asked Julie.

With her mouth full, she had to shake her head. That loosened her spectacles, and she pushed them up again.

"Well, let me tell you," Morgan began, taking advantage of her inability to speak for herself. "She was marvelous, especially when you consider the circumstances. With formal training, she'd be another Florence Nightingale. I know Horace got along without a nurse, and I don't know how he did it, but even ten years ago there was a doctor in Yuma—or maybe it was Prescott, I don't remember which—who offered fifteen dollars a week for a qualified woman."

Julie brought her head up so suddenly the glasses fell completely off. Luckily, they landed on her lap rather than in her corn.

"Fifteen dollars a week?" she gasped.

"Whoa! I hope you don't think I could pay that kind of money! I might be able to manage seven and a half to start, plus free medical care, of course."

He looked at Julie, but he hardly saw her. His attention was focused on her father. Had the tactic worked? Was Wilhelm greedy enough, or did his cruelty outweigh his avarice?

Morgan realized too late that he had underestimated the man's pride.

"I do not send my daughter out to work!" Wilhelm thundered, rising half out of his chair. "And I take no charity." Again the finger waved sternly, then pointed toward the door. "Out, drunkard! You want to trade? All right, I will trade. You saved my son, so I fed you lunch. We are even, now, no?"

"Wilhelm, please," Katharine begged. She reached across the table for him, but he was too far away. "Sit down and eat your lunch. This shouting gives me a—"

"You always have a headache, whether I shout or not!"

It happened very quickly, but Julie was neither surprised nor angry. Katharine got shakily to her feet and, before anyone could reach her, softly and silently collapsed in a dead faint on the floor.

Chapter Eight

✦✦✦✦✦

KATHARINE HOLLSTROM KEPT her smile to herself as she let Julie tie the sash of her dressing gown around her waist. For a few moments Katharine had been worried, but now that the examination was over, she felt perfectly confident.

At Morgan's request, Julie left the bedroom and closed the door. Curious as she was, she would never dream of listening, and Katharine had counted on that as well. That and the fact that Morgan himself, for all his faults, was a man of honor and integrity. He would never betray a confidence.

Neither would he lie.

"You're perfectly healthy, Mrs. Hollstrom, except for the arm, of course."

"Am I? Then how do you account for my dreadful headaches?"

He shrugged.

"Maybe a lack of exercise and fresh air. Maybe your stays are too tight."

She laughed just a little. "I suppose that accounts for the stomach trouble, too?" she added.

"It could."

"And the sleeplessness?"

He look her straight in the eye and told her, "Maybe you've got a guilty conscience."

"Maybe I do. And now that you've given me your diagnosis, what's the treatment?"

She sat propped up against a huge fluffy pillow, a rather attractive woman of forty-six years who didn't look her age. Most women lied in the other direction.

"It depends."

"On what?"

"On how much of my advice the patient will follow."

"Have no fear, Dr. Morgan, I'll follow all your advice. I am as eager to be cured as you."

"I see."

Morgan leaned against the closed door and studied her, noting the almost cocky hint of a smile, the sparkle in the eyes that were so like Julie's, the tilt to her head. He wanted desperately to know what was going on inside that head right now, though he doubted he'd like it.

"You have only two children, correct?" he asked.

"Yes. Julie is twenty-six, and Willy almost nine."

"A long time in between."

She shrugged, but the smile didn't change.

"And none since?"

"I was not a young woman when Willy was born, and I nearly died. We felt it best not to risk having any more."

"You and your husband do not indulge in marital relations." He stated it without embarrassment and without query.

"Not since Willy's birth."

Her voice altered slightly. A defiance tinged it, and her words had a ring of finality about them.

Morgan understood completely. This woman loathed her husband.

"My suggested treatment will be very simple. I'm going to prescribe a tonic to be taken daily. If it is to have any effect at all, you will have to adjust yourself to the climate. Those stays must be loosened, and you need more exercise. A little light housework wouldn't hurt."

Katharine nodded her approval.

"Would you estimate that by the time this thing"—she raised the splinted arm—"is healed, I'll be well enough for my daughter to take on some duties outside the home?"

"I see no reason why she couldn't do so right now."

He waited for her next comment, but she slipped into what seemed serious contemplation. No doubt she's deciding whether to give up the indentured servant who waits on her hand and foot or to take advantage of an opportunity to rid herself of an unwanted daughter, Morgan thought. Perhaps the father had something to do with it, something that lay beneath Katharine's undisguised hatred of her husband. Morgan did not sense the same emotion when Katharine spoke of Julie. Here there was concern, not hostility.

"If Julie were to go to work for you, Dr. Morgan, there's her reputation to consider."

"I didn't ask her to wear red satin dresses and black feathers and get up on a bar and sing."

"No, of course not, and I suppose nursing is a very honorable profession."

"Damn right it is."

"But I am remembering your own reputation. One would hardly describe it as illustrious. No mother wants to hand her child, especially her daughter, over to a man of less than honest intentions. I would hate to see her chances ruined by an association with someone whose habits might reflect poorly on her."

Chances for what? he almost asked her. Marriage? To whom? Not counting the scattered miners and prospectors, there were exactly four eligible men in Plato: Lucas Carter; Bern Hicks; Mr. Nisely the postmaster, who was older than Julie's father; and Skip the smith's apprentice, who was barely eighteen and had a face full of pimples. Oh, and the blond farmer who wanted so badly to get married that he had to sneak into Nellie's every time he said good night to Julie.

"I would be a fool if I tried to deny what I've been for the past few years, Mrs. Hollstrom."

When he drew himself up like that, Katharine thought, he looked much younger, stronger. He lost that kicked-puppy look, though she wasn't at all sure she wanted him to. At least not so soon.

"Let me be blunt, to a point," Katharine began. They laughed at her unintentional contradiction, yet there was a cold, serious bitterness even in the laughter, and no humor. "We both want the same thing, which is for Julie to assist you. Our motives are probably quite different—but not necessarily—so let it suffice for now that we desire the same end result."

He nodded but said nothing.

"And we know that we have an obstacle, namely my husband. Now, it so happens that I know how he can be manipulated."

"Not many women would confess to that."

"Well, I do simply because I do not have many opportunities. Wilhelm has very few weaknesses. He doesn't drink or chase women or gamble. His vice is money."

She fell to a whisper, as though revealing a dread secret.

"Wilhelm is a very methodical man when it comes to his greed. He is not the usual penny-wise, pound-foolish miser. I, on the other hand, am a fairly foolish woman with no head for finances. But when I see a chance to get my own way, I take it. I see such a chance now."

The woman's selfishness brought a bad taste to his mouth, one he tried to spit out with angry words.

"Did it ever occur to you to ask your daughter's opinion first?"

"I don't really think I need to do that, Mr. Morgan," Katharine replied in that same sweet voice. "We both know the way she looked when she left this house yesterday afternoon. The girl was positively beaming."

Morgan's craving for a drink increased with every step he took. Laughter from the Castle beckoned him to join in the companionship of oblivion. He had money for it, too, though these last few dollars were intended to pay for the telegrams. Even if he decided not to spend it all on whiskey, he could certainly use a shot or two of courage.

He felt a trickle of sweat slide down his spine until it encountered a place where his shirt already stuck to his skin. He knew it wasn't just the blistering sun that drew the perspiration like his life's blood from his pores. He was terrified.

Reaching in his pocket for the list of items he had to order, he shut his eyes to the sight of the welcoming saloon door. He needed all his wits about him if he was going to keep his story straight and persuade Hollstrom to let the girl go. Morgan wasn't used to lying, or at least not consciously so, and he wondered just how much of the truth he could get away with.

And when it was over, when he walked out of the telegraph office and left an angry but believing Wilhelm Hollstrom behind, Morgan's thirst had at least tripled. He licked dry lips and swallowed convulsively as he put one foot in front of the other toward the row of boardwalked shops that ended at McCrory's General Store. Once his boots touched wood, he felt as if he could breathe again, as though he had been drowning and finally broke through to the surface.

There was no ice cream parlor in Plato, but Simon usually kept some in the store. There was a short counter and a couple of chairs that could be supplemented with stools or barrels. When Morgan entered the store, he saw Julie waiting, her back to him, with Willy seated on the chair beside her.

"Julie, Julie, Mr. Morgan's here!" the boy shouted.

Julie gave Morgan a smile as he pulled up a three-legged stool and sat at Willy's other side. He removed his hat and wiped his forehead with a handkerchief from his pocket, but before he could make any further statement on the weather, Ada McCrory waddled up to wait on them.

"Del Morgan? Is it really you?" She placed her fleshy hands on the counter and leaned forward to get a closer look at him, revealing a good deal more flesh as she did so. "I heard someone say this morning that—"

"Have you got any chocolate ice cream?" he interrupted to avoid her inquisition.

"A bit, not much. Is it true you—"

"And how about some strawberry?"

"Simon and the boys made some last night and there's a little left, I think."

He turned to Julie, noticing that she had changed her dress for a navy blue skirt and a blouse the color of sweet cream butter. "Which would you prefer, Miss Hollstrom?"

"Strawberry would be fine," she said quietly.

"Good, and I'll have—"

"You'll have vanilla, Del Morgan, 'cause that's all I got left. No butter rum today."

She set three small bowls on the counter and then served up the ice cream. Julie's portion was somewhat larger than the others, as though Ada had noticed the girl's painful thinness, too. Willy didn't wait for permission; he dove noisily into his quickly melting treat.

Morgan spooned the cold sweetness slowly, savoring the shiver. As hard as he tried not to watch Julie, he couldn't keep his eyes from straying in her direction and watching her over Willy's bent head. The boy smacked greedily, and Morgan quelled an urge to scold him, only to have Julie do it a few seconds later.

"Willy, mind your manners!" she admonished sharply. "Don't slurp."

"I can't help it. It's melting."

"Then just eat it faster," she suggested.

The faster, the better, Morgan thought. Then go out and play so I can talk to your sister alone.

But even when Willy had finished, there was Ada to contend with. A customer took her attention for a while, but almost as soon as Willy had dashed outside, Simon's wife returned, full of questions.

Morgan didn't have the time to waste satisfying her curiosity. And he doubted Julie would consent to go anywhere else with him. Already he sensed her nervousness.

"Ada, have you any of those fancy Cuban cheroots?" he asked before the heavy woman had a chance to speak.

"Sure. You want one?"

"Give me a couple. And some matches."

If he was going to do without the comfort of his whiskey, he would at least be able to smoke.

As Ada waddled off, he took the opportunity to watch Julie, knowing she was aware of his study.

She, too, let the pleasure linger, enjoying each mouthful of berry-flavored goodness. He couldn't help but compare this scene to others, to one night in particular that stood out in his memory suddenly stronger than all others. Perhaps watching another woman's delight in the cold refreshment made the image come so clearly, but whatever the cause, he saw it all again as though it were yesterday.

Amy St. Rogers in a ruffled blue dress was a picture of summer ecstasy. She had sat in her father's buggy with a blue parasol to shade her face while she watched Del play shortstop in a Friday night sandlot baseball game. He'd had a good game, three hits including a home run. He was hot and he was tired and he was so dusty he felt the sand grate in his joints. But he was happy, too.

After the game was over, they all piled into Peter Eiseley's wagon, Del and Ship McCullough and Tom Barrows and the girls who always came to watch them play, even Amy this time. She had never consented to ride on the wagon with them before, and when they went into Grandpa Barrows's ice cream parlor, she led Del to a table by themselves. He hardly tasted the ice cream that night because his eyes feasted on Amy St. Rogers, her laughing dark eyes, the curls of lustrous auburn hair that snuggled against her neck under the edge of her blue bonnet, her lips wet and sweet with buttered pecan ice cream, her favorite.

He didn't notice when Ada returned with the cheroots. When Julie set down her spoon and wiped her mouth daintily on a handkerchief, he took his eyes from her for a moment and there lay the cheroots beside his empty bowl.

Now it was his turn to feel nervous. Breaking this news wasn't going to be easy, but it was better done and out of the way. "I had a long talk with your father just before I came here. I had a little difficulty persuading him to try my methods."

"He is a stubborn man."

"So I discovered. But he is very concerned about your mother's health. Since nothing the other doctors have tried has worked, I suggested it was time to try a different technique.

"You see, the more your mother rests, the more she needs to rest. Well, I intend to turn that right around. The more exercise she gets, the more she will need. And we are going to start tomorrow."

The combination of hopefulness and weariness that filled Julie's eyes touched something inside him. No doubt she had been through so much of this already that she didn't care. He wanted her to care, wanted her to hope. And he wanted to take those spectacles off her nose to see if he was right about her being more than almost pretty.

He swallowed thickly and took a puff on his cheroot.

"Tomorrow morning I want you to turn over

some of your chores to your mother. She can dust, can't she?"

Julie nodded, and within a few minutes they had made a list of several tasks Katharine could take on. Then, when she regained the use of the injured arm, she would tackle the heavier chores.

"Can you teach her how to cook?" Morgan asked.

"She knows how. She used to do it all the time before Willy was born."

So the boy's birth had indeed been the turning point. Morgan found some of his suspicions confirmed, but other new ones were raised. And he wondered why Julie had begun to lose her enthusiasm and turn surly.

Best to broach the subject now rather than let her stew.

"Miss Hollstrom," he said quietly, "is something wrong?"

"I'm fine. Please, go on."

He'd used the wrong strategy. Once warned that he might pry, she had her defenses up. He would have to get her to lower them.

"In time I think your mother will recover fully. There should be no reason why she can't take on her normal responsibilities for her family. It isn't going to come overnight; changes of this magnitude never do."

Had she been home, in her own house, Julie would have run up to her room and sobbed. She caught a corner of her lower lip between her teeth and tugged on it to still the trembling. But her efforts to control the tears left her tongue free, and before she could stop them, the words poured out.

"And just what am I supposed to do when they don't need me anymore?"

Chapter Nine

+ + + +

"I THOUGHT YOU were going to come work for me."

Then Julie whispered, "You still want me to?"

"Of course I want you to." Later, if necessary, he would tell her how much he needed someone with her strength, her calm.

"Is it really all right with Papa?"

"He agreed, but only with certain conditions."

"Such as?"

"I didn't like his terms. I agreed to them only because he didn't leave me any other choice." That stetched the truth a bit, but not very much.

"Did he leave *me* any choice?"

"Not much. I'll pay you eight dollars a week, but five of it goes to him. He said it was to pay off an old debt."

What kind of debts do children owe their parents? What kind of parents demand payment?

Why does your father hate you? he wanted to ask.
"What else?"

"He wants you available to take care of your
mother if the treatment doesn't work."

"That much at least is reasonable. And I do
owe them."

"Look, I was prepared to offer you ten, so that
still leaves you five dollars every Friday. If you
want, I'll give him the extra two bucks, and pay
your debt off that much sooner."

He never meant to be so forward, especially in
plain sight of Ada McCrory, but he couldn't help
taking one of Julie's hands in his. It lay limply, as
though she didn't know what to do, and slowly
he let his own fingers slide across the back of it.
He could almost count the bones, for there was
little flesh under the skin. He touched a knuckle
covered with a rough scab where she'd hurt herself somehow, and when he turned the palm
upward, he saw an almost-healed cut undoubt-
edly made by a kitchen knife.

He didn't dare go farther, up to her wrist
where the bones were almost visible, or to the
shoulders so painfully thin under her blouse.

"Are those terms acceptable, Miss Hollstrom?"

She heard his voice, but his touch over-
whelmed all her other senses. She no longer felt
the close afternoon heat or smelled the sharp
tobacco smoke. The sticky sweetness left on her
tongue by the ice cream disappeared, and a
warm dryness replaced it. She knew, in some
shadowy corner of her mind, that she was star-

ing over his shoulder toward the front window, where Ada was displaying a bolt of blue calico to Estelle Kincheloe, but Julie's eyes saw nothing. Morgan's fingers, gently stroking across her palm, were all that existed.

"Miss Hollstrom, are you all right?"

His voice, raised and sharp, broke through her spell. Her hand lay on the counter; his were on his knees as he leaned toward her.

"Yes, yes, I'm fine. Did you just ask me something?"

"I did." His voice dropped again. "I asked if those terms were acceptable."

"Yes, I suppose so," she mumbled, folding her hands in her lap again. "I'm sorry, I wasn't paying attention."

"No, Miss Hollstrom, I'm the one to apologize. This isn't something to be discussed over ice cream in the general store."

But where? And when? "Look, I have a lot of things to do this afternoon," he continued. "I'm going to talk to the marshal about opening Horace's house so I can sift through the wreckage and see if there isn't something of value to be salvaged. Would you care to come and help me?"

Morgan and Julie spent the rest of Thursday afternoon cleaning the small house Horace Opper had lived in and used as his office. They made so little progress that when Julie returned to the house Friday morning, she could hardly see any difference.

Katharine did not volunteer to help, nor was she asked, but when Julie returned to her own house to fix lunch, Katharine agreed to take Wilhelm's to him. How she was to carry the heavy tray presented a problem until Del suggested a picnic basket. Horace, it turned out, had one he wouldn't be using.

Saturday was much the same, except that now progress could be seen. The front parlor, which was to become the waiting room, had been thoroughly cleaned. The floor shone with a fresh waxing, the window sparkled after its first washing in several years, the two small tables had been dusted and outfitted with periodicals bearing the current year's date. Katharine checked all of the magazines to make sure she hadn't missed anything of interest.

Late on Saturday afternoon, the first patient arrived. The two companions who brought him in explained they were prospectors working a small mine in the mountains north of town. A shoring beam had given way, crushing their partner's right leg.

"We spent hours diggin' him out," the shorter of the two men explained. They hadn't given their names, but the taller one addressed the patient and apparently forgot some of his caution.

"It's gonna be awright, Louie. We found ya a doc, an' he's gonna fix ya right up."

Julie saw no signs of such confidence in himself when Morgan got his first look at the injury.

He helped carry Louie on his improvised stretcher to the room designated as the surgery, though it hardly looked the part. The enameled table was clean, but the counters were still littered with assorted instruments, spools of ordinary sewing thread alongside surgical gut, rolls of gauze, and sundry items of dubious use and value. The last thing Morgan wanted was to perform a major operation under these conditions.

Julie stood in the doorway and waited for instructions. She discovered her hands were clammy, and the sight of so much blood had done queer things to her stomach.

Morgan didn't seem to notice her.

"All right, gentlemen, we've got him settled now, so you go on into the other room and let us get to work," he told Louie's friends. Then he signaled to Julie. "Close the door," he whispered.

She did as she was told, then remained by the door, not daring to venture any closer.

"Is he still alive?" she whispered back.

"Unconscious, but alive. I'm afraid you're about to have your first lesson in surgery."

"You have to operate to set his leg?"

He reached for a pair of shears tangled with other implements Julie didn't recognize.

"I don't think I can set it," he told her, snipping away at the bloodied trouser leg. "This leg is going to have to come off."

She felt the blood drain from her cheeks and chin. A queer numbness remained.

"Are you all right?" Morgan asked.

She nodded. This wasn't what she had expected. Delivering babies and sewing cuts wasn't very difficult at all, but an amputation required more fortitude than Julie thought she had.

"Don't be afraid to tell me if you feel sick or start to faint. You wouldn't be the first one."

She didn't altogether lose consciousness, but she came close. And she did have to run out back one time to be sick.

When it was over and Louie had been moved to a cot hastily set up in what had been Horace's dining room, Morgan calmly walked alone to the small unpainted building behind the house and followed Julie's example. He had struggled for hours against a nameless fear, wishing a thousand times that Horace Opper hadn't dropped dead in McCrory's alley. Wiping sweat from his eyes and spitting the last of the foul taste from his mouth, he cursed the woman who had brought him to this situation.

"Damn you, Julie Hollstrom," he hissed in the near darkness. "Why didn't you leave me alone? Who appointed you to sainthood? And why the hell do you have to drag me with you?"

Aware that she expected him back, he straightened and ran his fingers through his sweat-damp hair. He couldn't indulge in this kind of self-pity when he had a patient to watch.

Katharine complained of a headache Saturday after supper, so Julie stayed home while Morgan watched Louie through the night. Louie's two nameless friends volunteered to share the vigil.

Winnie Upshaw brought a pot of coffee around nine o'clock. She offered him supper and he felt guilty telling her Julie had already brought him sauerkraut and sausage.

Every hour he took Louie's temperature, watching it rise steadily as infection settled into the miner's old, tired, battered body. Morgan began to doubt Louie would ever learn he'd lost the leg.

Julie arrived sometime between dark and dawn, when it was possible to move through the house without a lamp and not stumble. She brought a skillet of fluffy scrambled eggs flavored with ham and peppers, a platter of crisp bacon, warm buttered toast, and fresh coffee.

The aroma brought a weak but sincere smile to Morgan's face.

"A true angel of mercy," he said, taking a plate from the basket over her arm.

He looked awful. In a way, he looked worse than when she'd first seen him. Blood, sweat, and the ever-present dust stained his once clean white shirt. Dark hollows shadowed his cheeks, with weary circles of almost the same color under his eyes.

"I think you had better eat this and then get yourself some sleep, Dr. Morgan."

A yawn prevented any protest.

"Aren't you going to have some of this? There's enough here for the both of us and then some." He dished up some eggs and took a couple slices of bacon.

"I've already eaten. How is Louie? Any better?"

Morgan shook his head.

"I told his friends a coupla hours ago that I didn't think he was going to make it."

"Oh, no. I'm so sorry. You tried so hard."

He shrugged.

"It happens. He was an old man who didn't take very good care of himself, and he had lost a lot of blood."

He took a clean cup from the basket and handed it to Julie. She filled it with steaming coffee, never once thinking of all the times she had performed the task before.

"Thanks," he breathed after the first scalding gulp.

"If you don't need me for anything else, I have to go home and get ready for church." She took a step toward the door, then stopped. What she was about to do required a great deal of thought, more than she had time for right now, so she took a deep breath and let it out slowly with words she could hardly believe she was saying. "Would you like to come for dinner later? We eat about one o'clock, and I'm fixing roast beef."

Chapter Ten

✦✦✦✦✦

THE REVEREND MR. WINTERGARDEN was not usually given to short sermons, and he remained true to form that morning. There were those in the congregation who dozed quietly while he indulged his enthusiasm for a particularly obscure passage in Revelations, and there were others who paid rapt if confused attention. Julie did neither. She prayed.

She prayed for the life of the injured miner, then prayed for forgiveness because she had asked for the man's life out of selfishness. She wanted the glory of saving his life for Morgan. The man needed the victory.

At her left, Willy fidgeted impatiently. She asked for strength in dealing with him, which she knew would be more and more difficult the less time she had to spend with him.

She glanced down the pew to Wilhelm. Stern as always, he stared intently at the preacher. Wilhelm paid no attention to his son or daughter, but that was hardly unusual.

Julie did not pray for him.

She prayed for Del Morgan until tears came to her eyes at the memory of the grave just outside the church. She had not had time in the past few days to talk to Winnie Upshaw about Amalia Morgan's death, and she could not talk to Morgan himself about it, not yet. He was still too much a stranger to her.

When the last hymn had been sung and Reverend Wintergarden gave his benediction, Julie slid past Katharine as unobtrusively as possible and headed for the side door, to hurry home ahead of the rest of her family.

She couldn't avoid walking past the grave, nor could she keep from looking at the rosebush.

The damaged canes had been pruned carefully to conceal the worst wounds, and a single fresh blossom had just barely opened its fragrant petals, vibrant red in the summer sunshine. Julie had no idea when Morgan found time to tend the flower, but obviously he had not neglected this special duty.

She turned her gaze and footsteps toward home and encountered a familiar figure square in her path, waiting for her.

"Good morning, Hans," she greeted stiffly.

"Good morning, Julie."

"I missed you in church," she lied, feeling horribly guilty. She hadn't once thought of him, much less missed him.

"I was busy at the farm."

He looked as he always looked, his hair a week longer, his shirt as clean and wrinkled as ever.

As they walked through the open gate of the churchyard and crossed the empty street, Julie tried not to think about the confrontation to come. She struggled to keep her mind on Hans, who had dared to take her elbow when they reached the private precincts of the Hollstroms' yard. He was saying something about a calf being turned the wrong way.

"Like a breech birth in a woman?" she suddenly asked, taking an interest that obviously surprised Hans.

"I . . . I don't know about women. I only know cows and horses and sheep," he stammered.

"I watched a baby being born the other night," she told him, forgetting his grip on her arm. "It—I mean he—was turned the wrong way, too. Dr. Morgan had to pull him out, and he said the baby would have died if I hadn't been there to help. I helped deliver him, and Mrs. Hollis named him after me."

She had been excited, even telling him so briefly about her experience, but the excitement died quickly. There was no matching joy in Hans's blue eyes, only cold disapproval.

"Women do not speak of such things," he told her through tightly clenched teeth. He let go her elbow with a gesture of distaste. "Go in the house and fix dinner. I will wait here for your papa and mama."

There was plenty of work in the kitchen to keep her mind off the coming debacle, but the harder Julie worked, the more she thought about Morgan and Hans. Morgan might not accept the invitation, which would solve a great number of difficulties, but she did not wish for that solution. She was peeling potatoes to lay around the roast when she first admitted how badly she wanted him to come.

But where would she seat him? In the past, she had put Hans on one side of the table, with herself and Willy on the other. Wilhelm and Katharine occupied opposite ends. But should she put Dr. Morgan beside Hans, and if so, which of them would sit directly opposite her? Or, considering his position as a hopeful future husband, did Hans rate the place beside Julie, with Willy next to Morgan? She certainly couldn't put Morgan at her side and Hans opposite.

With the roast and potatoes in the oven, she shook her head clear of etiquette problems and began the cake.

Applesauce and cinnamon scented the entire kitchen. After pouring the batter—of which she'd had more than enough sample tastes to be sure it was perfect—into the pan, Julie stood back from the oven just to drink in the delicious smell. A light tapping on the back door brought her out of her reverie.

The look in his green eyes told her all she needed to know.

"When?" she asked, wiping her hands on her apron and sliding her glasses back up.

"Half an hour ago."

She pushed the screen door open to admit him to the kitchen. He sat down at the table, unmindful of the bowls and measuring cups and mixing spoons that littered the checkered cloth. A long reddish streak of cinnamon lay under his forearm.

"I knew there wasn't much hope when they brought him in, but when he made it through the night, I thought maybe he had a chance."

He spoke calmly, either hiding his disappointment or not yet feeling it. After a long silence Julie walked up behind him and lay one hand on a weary shoulder. It shuddered with his sigh.

"You did what you could," she said. "Sometimes you just can't do anything more. At least you tried."

"Yeah, at least I tried."

Her lower lip trembled; she bit it to hold it still and tried not to let her hand shake. But it wasn't sorrow that sent nervous quivers up and down her arm.

She had touched him to give him comfort, but that touch brought something else to her. A few days ago that hand had lain passive while he caressed it, chasing all coherent thought from her. Now she touched him, and the effect was as startling as it was different. For now she was as much aware of her surroundings and circumstances as she was of the hard muscle beneath her fingers. Only a layer of linen shirt separated her palm from the warm skin of his shoulder, but the spark arced that tiny distance and current hummed along the wires of her nerves. Her heart beat as unevenly as the dots and dashes of the telegraph code.

He must have had a few hours sleep, though she couldn't guess where, for his hair was mussed and flattened on one side and his cheek, under its black stubble, bore a crease, as though he had lain on a wrinkled pillow. His rest had not been enough to erase the bluish circles under his eyes.

"Is there anything I can do?"

He shook his head.

"His friends plan to take him back to the mine to bury him. I sent one of them to the church to get Wintergarden; they wanted somebody to say a few words over Louie first." Morgan fell silent and drew a deep breath.

Oh, God, Julie, don't touch me like that, he groaned inwardly. Amy used to do that, and then she'd rub my shoulders and my neck and my back and she'd take all the pain away. She'd tell me I had done my best and I couldn't do more than that.

But Julie's hand remained still, and Morgan did not move away.

"You should get some sleep," she suggested quietly. "Go home and rest, and I'll bring your dinner to you later this afternoon."

She felt guilty again, taking advantage of his exhaustion to escape an uncomfortable situation. Yet he obviously needed the rest, and maybe he hadn't intended to come for dinner after all.

"You don't need to go to all that trouble. I can go over to Daneggar's or the Castle—"

"No!"

Her half-shouted forbiddance startled them both. Julie felt her cheeks burn, and she quickly drew her hand away from his shoulder.

"It's Sunday, and the restaurant is closed," she said, struggling not to stammer. "And I don't want you going anywhere near the saloon. Besides, I invited you to join us, and I'll be highly insulted if you go elsewhere."

"Thanks, but I think not. You're right. I'm tired and I need some decent sleep." He stood up, carefully keeping his back to her. "I'll stop and ask Winnie to cook something for me. I'd forgotten Daneggar's is closed today. I guess I kind of lost track of the time."

"There's no need to bother Winnie. I've got more than enough here for all of us, even with Hans. So if you won't come for dinner, at least let me bring some to you."

Yes, that was the best way to do it. She was safely out of the predicament by his own agreement, without resorting to the slightest falsehood. And she'd kept him away from the saloon, too.

He heard her little sigh of relief only because he had been holding his breath ever since she uttered that name. So the blond farmer was the reason she'd allowed him to back out of her invitation. Must be she didn't want her catch to get any wrong ideas about her and the town drunk, even if Morgan did pride himself more than he probably ought to on the fact that he hadn't had a drink since—good heavens—since Monday. Almost a week.

He put on a smile and then turned to face her. "Your roast beef sure smells a lot more appetizing than Winnie's chili. And that's applesauce cake you're baking, isn't it."

He inhaled deeply and let his eyes fall closed

with the enjoyment of that spicy, warm aroma that brought back a thousand memories.

"Do you like applesauce cake?"

"Better'n chocolate." He sighed. "Mom used to bake a cake almost every morning in the winter, when we were in school, and when she made applesauce cake, we'd have the whole thing eaten as soon as we got home."

He chuckled, recalling those days so long ago and so far away, and before he could say another word, Julie made up his mind for him.

"Then if you want fresh, still-warm cake for dessert, I suggest you get yourself right home to bed so you can get at least a little sleep before dinner."

The adobe house was cool and quiet when Morgan entered. It did not stay that way for long.

He built up a hearty fire in the stove, then filled two heavy cast-iron cauldrons at the pump just outside the back door. Next time he'd remember to keep the cauldrons on the roof where the sun would warm them so he'd have hot water for his bath any time he wanted it.

He stripped off the clothes he had dozed in when he lay down on the sofa in Opper's waiting room. No, it was his waiting room now, difficult as the change was to believe. Had he really gone almost a week without a taste of whiskey? He laughed, amused at himself for so easily falling into the girl's hands.

Dressed only in his underwear, he dropped his dirty laundry into the basket by the door and then went upstairs to bed. Winnie had aired the mattress and pillows as well as washed the sheets. He liked Winnie and hated to take advantage of her infatuation; he'd find a way to repay her tomorrow.

Settling his weary body in bed, he wondered sarcastically if anyone had ever taken advantage of the determined Miss Julie Hollstrom.

She had certainly manipulated him right to where she wanted him. He almost wondered if she hadn't somehow arranged Opper's demise and then Peg Hollis's labor. No, even Julie Hollstrom couldn't bring those things to order, but it sure as hell was fortuitous that the old man dropped dead when he did. And Lord knew her family, if no one else, took plenty advantage of her. They treated her like a slave.

Morgan pounded a fist into the pillow and rolled over on his side. He reminded himself not to get carried away. Julie couldn't have been responsible for the events of the past week. They were perfectly normal. In fact, there had been fewer emergencies than when he first came to Plato twelve years ago. Someone had estimated a thousand prospectors staked small, private claims in those mountains. Anything that even vaguely hinted at attempted claim-jumping was often instantly countered with a gun. How many bullets had he and Amy pulled out of shoulders and thighs and hips and ribs? This past week had been quiet in comparison.

Morgan yawned and stretched lazily, then settled more comfortably under the cool sheet. Miss Julie Hollstrom thought she was going to push him around, did she. Well, he'd show her a thing or two about manipulation. She had so carefully let it slip that Hans, the oafish, over-sexed farmboy, was coming to dinner, too. But if she thought that little hint would keep Del Morgan away from applesauce cake, she had another thing coming.

He couldn't figure out why she had invited him in the first place if she knew Hans would be there. And she obviously didn't want to take advantage of Morgan's offers to get a meal elsewhere. He tried to reconcile the conniving Julie Hollstrom who had talked him into going out to the Hollises' with the fragile Julie Hollstrom who wore those old faded dresses while her mother— but it was too much to think about now. He was too tired, another, longer yawn reminded him.

Julie was stirring the gravy when Morgan knocked on the front door. She couldn't see him from the kitchen, but she knew it could be no one else, for Hans and her parents already occupied the parlor. And no one ever called on the Hollstroms unless invited.

Wilhelm answered the door, and Julie could hear his subdued greeting. He had protested when she told him she had invited the doctor, but Katharine had expressed pleasure in the idea of a new guest. It was her wish, therefore, that Wilhelm granted, not his daughter's. When Julie walked into the parlor a few minutes later to announce that dinner was on the table, she could feel the tension in the air.

Hans frowned as he took the chair Katharine indicated, the one near Wilhelm. He clearly was not pleased with the addition to the party.

"And you, Dr. Morgan, please, sit here beside me," Katharine said, flashing him one of her most enticing smiles. "Willy, you sit down there by Hans, and watch your manners."

That put Julie next to her brother and directly across from Morgan—and as far away from Hans as she could be.

"Mama, don't you think—"

"Why, Julie, dear, how lovely the table looks," Katharine interrupted, as though she hadn't heard Julie's quiet protest.

"Thank you, Mama," she murmured. She knew it was too late to do anything now, for Morgan had already moved to hold Katharine's chair for her.

Julie pulled her own chair out and sat down. She didn't look at Hans but knew he was staring at her. If she could have, she would have taken her plate and retreated to the kitchen.

"That roast looks delicious," Morgan commented, lifting the platter and helping himself to a juicy pink slice of meat. "This is probably the last time you'll be fixing a heavy Sunday dinner like this, I expect, with the summer heat coming on. Mrs. Hollstrom, would you care for a more well-done piece?"

"Oh, no, I like it rare," Katharine said, smiling back.

He selected a generous slice and, after she nodded her approval, he placed it on her plate. Then he passed the platter to Julie, who took it without meeting his eyes. Not even over the edge of her glasses.

"If you think it's hot in that kitchen now, just wait another month or so," Morgan continued as he took the bowl of potatoes Hans handed to him. "And how many of these lovely crisp potatoes, Mrs. Hollstrom?"

"I think only two, although they do look awfully tempting, don't they?" Katharine purred right back at him.

"Then I'll give you an extra."

The exchange of pleasantries between Katharine and Morgan resumed with the peas, then the biscuits and butter, and again when the gravy came around. No one else, not even Willy, said a single word.

Morgan was again invited to ask the blessing on the meal, and this time he did so gracefully, intoning a short but moving prayer that held a ring of tradition. Julie's curiosity about it was stifled by the continuing anger in Hans's unnaturally composed features. But Katharine had no such restraints. While Julie picked up the knife and fork to cut the food on Katharine's plate, Katharine indulged her own inquisitiveness.

"My, what a lovely grace, Dr. Morgan. Is it some special prayer from your childhood, perhaps?"

"It's a poor translation, Mrs. Hollstrom. My father was a deacon in his church before he left Wales, so we had plenty of prayers in Welsh when I was growing up."

"The Welsh are very musical people, too, aren't they. I once knew a singer in New York named Thomas Pritchard who was Welsh."

Katharine's head tilted back just a little, as though she were calling up old, pleasant memories. Julie recognized the glow that came into her eyes and knew the warning from Wilhelm could not be far behind.

"Are you originally from New York, Mrs. Hollstrom?" Morgan asked.

She was about to answer when her husband stopped her with a request for more butter.

"Your food is getting cold," he reminded her as if she were a child.

Katharine brought her eyes to bear on her husband but kept her smile when she told Morgan, "Yes, I was born in New York."

Julie choked, not intentionally, on a piece of beef. The discomfort was easily outweighed by the relief she felt at drawing some of the attention from her mother.

The incident seemed to bring an end to conversation completely, and everyone settled down to enjoy the delicious meal Julie had prepared. Morgan's occasional compliments brought blushes to her cheeks—just another reason for her to keep her eyes downward. She knew he was looking at her, waiting to see her reaction, and she wouldn't give it to him, certainly not with Hans watching for the same thing.

No decent woman invited two single men to dinner at the same time. If one happened to be her fiancé, well, that made matters even worse. Julie felt the shame of her stupidity turn her cheeks more scarlet than Morgan's praises had done, and she wanted desperately to excuse herself from the table and hide in her room.

How often had her father, either with angry words or angrier glances, reminded her that she never was and never would be a decent woman? Hadn't her elopement with Ted Sheen proven that?

Chapter Eleven

✦ ✦ ✦ ✦

KATHARINE OFFERED TO help with the dishes while the gentlemen retired to the parlor after dessert. The last thing Julie wanted was company in the kitchen, but she dared not displease her mother.

"You just start washing these things, dear,

and I'll bring the rest of the plates," Katharine suggested. "My, but that really was a very nice meal you fixed for Dr. Morgan."

Julie's protest had to wait. Katharine had no sooner uttered those words than she strolled back to the dining room for another handful of silverware. Julie couldn't call after her for fear the men in the parlor might hear.

But when Katharine returned to the kitchen, her daughter had a retort fully prepared.

"I did not fix that for Dr. Morgan, Mama," she insisted.

"Didn't you? But I thought sure, when he thanked you for the applesauce cake, that you had—"

"No, Mama. I swear, I planned to bake that cake before I knew anything about it being his favorite."

Katharine dropped the knives and forks into the pan of hot soapy water with a small splash.

"Then how fortunate you made such a good guess."

"Why do you consider it so fortunate that I pleased Dr. Morgan with my choice of dessert?"

"Well, isn't that what you wanted to do?"

"No! I mean, yes, of course I wanted to please him, but, Mama, you make it sound as though I set out to do it in some special sort of way."

"Didn't you?"

On that note, Katharine smiled and escaped again, leaving Julie with her hands in hot water.

There was no one to blame for the disaster of this Sunday dinner but Julie Hollstrom.

She took a stack of plates from Katharine and slid them into the dishwater.

"Mama, I think it is time to start thinking about the future," Julie said quietly.

"Yes, I think so, too. Dr. Morgan is right. It really is getting too hot for you to be doing so much cooking. Do you suppose you could ask that Miss Upshaw how she gets by during the summer? I never gave anything like that much thought."

"Please, Mama, that isn't what I meant. I meant about Hans and me."

"Hans?" Katharine stopped halfway to the dining room and turned around. Her forehead wrinkled in a confused frown. "Has he spoken to your father?"

"He said he had last week. He has waited a long time, Mama, and so have I."

"Then he can wait a little longer."

Julie nearly dropped a coffee cup at the spit of anger in her mother's usually placid voice.

"For heaven's sake, Julie, you can't go off to that ranch of his and leave me here with this broken arm." There, now the more familiar whine had returned. "And we don't know yet how effective Dr. Morgan's treatment will be."

"I'd say it's been very effective so far." This was the first time Katharine had volunteered to help with any form of housework in months.

"That may be, but I'm still far from fit to take

over all the household duties you've handled so capably for me."

Why not add that it's been nine years since I started, Julie thought uncharitably.

"And who would take care of Willy?" Katharine continued.

"Willy is quite capable of taking care of himself. He doesn't need someone to spoon his food into his mouth or change his clothes for him anymore."

Julie had to calm herself when she realized how furiously she was wiping the dishes clean. It was just luck that kept her from dropping the platter and breaking it to smithereens.

"Mama, I don't ask for much, but please, I need—"

Katharine propped her left wrist on her hip and sternly faced her daughter.

"Just the other day you asked to work for Dr. Morgan. If you off and marry Hans, what will the doctor do for a nurse?"

Morgan waited a decent interval after Hans returned from the privy, then excused himself for the same purpose. He was surprised to find Hans waiting for him when he emerged.

"I would have some words with you, Dr. Morgan."

Morgan only nodded, deciding to say nothing until he had heard what Wallenmund had to say first.

"You know Julie and I are almost betrothed."

Another nod, as calm as the first.

"I am going to talk to her papa today to set a date for the wedding."

"Fine. Congratulations."

He hoped that wasn't the reaction Hans was looking for.

"Then you will leave her alone and not try to change her mind?"

"Of course."

"But she is going to work for you, no? And you will see her every day while I am out at my farm and only see her on Sundays."

Morgan pulled a cheroot from his inner pocket and placed it carefully between his teeth. If his words sounded stilted or unnatural, let the blame lie on the cigar rather than on feelings he hadn't expected and didn't understand.

"Look, Hans, I'm not out to take your girl away from you, if that's what you're worried about." He tried to sound reassuring but didn't think he accomplished it at all, by the way Wallenmund looked at him. "I didn't ask for any of this. When my wife died six years ago all I wanted to do was forget, and for six years I came pretty close to it. Now, through absolutely no fault of my own, I've been dragged back into being a physician, one of the most agonizingly frustrating professions in the world. That problem is enough trouble for one man without trying to court a woman already engaged to someone else."

"Then I have your promise she will marry me as planned."

Was the man serious? Apparently he was, because he put no question mark at the end of that statement.

Morgan sighed impatiently. "I have nothing to do with it. I can't promise things for someone else. If Miss Hollstrom has said she'll marry you, then that's her business, not mine. I'll lose a damn good nurse, more than likely, but there's nothing I can do about that, either."

"She won't work for you after we are married," Hans insisted. He drew himself up a little taller, but he still lacked several inches of Morgan's rangy height. "She will be my wife and work in my home."

I don't doubt that, Morgan mused bitterly.

He was hot, standing in the sun, and there were more pleasant places for conversation, even unpleasant conversation, than the side of an outhouse. But when he made a move to walk toward the house, he found Hans blocking his departure.

"I am not finished yet, Dr. Morgan."

"I see that."

"You do not know Julie as I know her. I know her weakness and how it almost ruined her life."

A man's past—or a woman's—was a private thing in the Arizona Territory. Too many people wanted it that way. Del Morgan found himself one of them.

Morgan bit off the end of the cheroot and spat it out. He watched where it landed, the little wisp of dust rising and then settling. He almost expected the tobacco to catch fire and smoulder in the piercing sunlight.

"Let's leave Miss Hollstrom's past out of this discussion. If she wants me to know about it, let her tell me, all right?"

Somewhat awkwardly, Hans agreed, but not without a few final words.

"You are a man without a wife, Dr. Morgan, and you will spend many hours with Julie every day. It would be easy for you to take advantage of such a—"

"Damn it, you fool!" Morgan turned away from the youth and stared up toward the blinding sun. If the discarded stub of cigar hadn't kindled, his temper had. "I don't want the girl, Hans. I have no use for her, except as a nurse. Why can't you leave it at that?"

"All men have needs."

Morgan's fist raised, not threatening Hans but poised to strike the bleached wall of the outhouse.

He had watched a man die today, and he had had little sleep. Exhaustion and frustration ate away at his nerves, leaving them raw and painful and more sensitive than he could stand. Slowly he lowered his hand until it hung tensely at his side and he turned to face Hans once more.

Morgan said in a strained, angry voice, "Six years of cheap whiskey takes away a man's need. I don't want your girl, Wallenmund."

A kind of horror spread across Hans's features, and he backed up a step.

Morgan made a sound that might have been a laugh, but if it was, it was full of bitterness.

"Impotence isn't contagious," he assured Hans. "You needn't fear failure with the girls at Nellie's tonight."

But Hans, for whatever reason, seemed unable to remain in Morgan's presence a second longer. He turned without another word and started toward the house. Morgan didn't watch him; he kept his eyes on the dusty bare soil at his feet until he heard the back screen door squeak open and then shut.

When Hans had announced he wished to speak privately with the doctor, Julie hadn't worried. However, when both men remained outside longer than she thought either of them would find comfortable, she insisted to herself she was doing nothing but checking to make sure they were all right.

She hadn't intentionally listened while she looked out the kitchen window, and she hadn't heard all their conversation. Only Morgan's tensely whispered words came on the scorching breeze that stirred the curtains. Hans's back was to the house; Julie neither heard him nor saw his facial expressions. She could read every bit of Morgan's pain in his.

If she had found them engaged in a rolling, tumbling brawl, she would have been less surprised than at this horrible revelation.

She knew exactly what Morgan was talking about.

She tried to tell herself she had been worried about some of his motives and what their working so closely together would develop into. This news should have reassured her, but oddly it worried her even more. It wasn't a lie, of that she was sure. Morgan, whatever else he may be, wasn't a liar; and no man would admit such a thing about himself unless it were true.

She ducked into the pantry the instant she saw Hans turn and head for the house. Until he walked through the kitchen and on into the parlor, she didn't dare to breathe. She did not wonder that Morgan hadn't followed.

When Julie peeked out the window, Morgan was walking slowly toward the house. His shoulders seemed more stooped, his steps more weary, and he hesitated at the bottom of the stairs as though to rest before a long climb. Julie caught her breath. She filled the kettle and set it on the stove for tea.

When Morgan came into the kitchen, quietly and without letting the door slam, Julie jumped. She turned to face him, remembering somehow to put a smile on her face first.

"Mama suggested some tea," she said, knowing how banal such a statement sounded. "Would you care for some?"

He shook his head.

"You're gonna kill yourself if you don't stop behaving like this was New York or Ohio or wherever it is you folks came from. You can't keep cooking all summer, not here, not in this heat. Draw your mother a glass of cold water or make her some lemonade," he snapped.

She shrank from his anger until, an instant later, she realized she was not the intended target. But before she could say anything—though she had thought of nothing appropriate to say—Morgan apologized.

"I think I'd better take my leave now and go home. I could use some sleep, and after yesterday and this morning, I don't suppose I'm very good company."

"I'm sorry to have kept you so long, but I'm glad you came for dinner." More banal small talk, when she wanted to say something entirely different.

"I am, too." He smiled and said sincerely, "Thank you, Julie. You really are a very good cook, and I enjoyed the meal immensely. It was worth losing a little bit of sleep for. But I meant what I said. If you're going to stay in Arizona, you have to get used to a different way of doing things."

For a moment, or two or three, there was silence, then he said good-bye to her in the same quiet tone before he left her and walked into the parlor. Julie could not follow him, not with the enormous lump in her throat. She heard him bid her parents and Willy and Hans farewell, all the usual polite phrases of a departing guest. Finally she managed to get away from the kitchen long enough to see him out the door.

"I'll see you tomorrow morning, won't I, Miss Hollstrom?"

How could he smile? she wondered. But she answered, "I have laundry to do first. I might be late, maybe not until noon or even after."

"That's all right. Just come when you can. Good afternoon, Miss Hollstrom, and thanks again."

He touched his hat before he turned and walked down the stairs of the porch. Julie watched him as long as she dared, then escaped to the kitchen once more. When the tea was ready and she could find no other excuse to avoid the parlor and its occupants, she straightened her shoulders and made up her mind to be as brave as he had been. Only then did she notice that her cheeks were wet. She wiped the tears on her sleeve.

Morgan stopped at Opper's—he couldn't get used to the idea that the house and its contents were his—and tidied up a few things before heading home. He stopped at the cemetery only briefly, long enough to note the new blossom and to tell Amy about the miner. He apologized for the brevity of his visit, saying that he was so tired he could hardly keep his eyes open, and promised to come again during the week and stay longer.

He wondered if Julie and her betrothed would stroll under the cottonwoods again this Sunday but decided not to wait to find out. He hadn't told Amy about Julie or about taking up his practice again or even about Horace's death. There were a lot of things he wanted to talk to her about, but they would all have to wait. He did not want to be seen by the girl and her lover.

Winnie was busy with the flowers when he arrived. Before she had a chance to start one of her endless streams of chatter, he sent her home, knowing full well that he was rude and unthinking. Poor Winnie couldn't know or understand all that he had been through today, and none of it was her fault. But he couldn't stand the thought of her invariable cheeriness. Despite his abominable lack of manners, she bid him a pleasant evening and strolled, whistling, back to her sister's house.

He draped his clothes fairly neatly over the back of a chair in his bedroom, then lay down on the bed. He had set the bottle on the table beside the lamp. In the afternoon dimness, he could just barely see the difference in color where the amber liquid filled the brown glass bottle's slender neck. He had found it in a cupboard in Opper's kitchen and had ignored its temptation all these days. Even last night, when he had sweated and worried and cursed and cried, he had practically forgotten the bottle.

He didn't know exactly when he had remembered. Maybe when he told Wallenmund about his disability. Or maybe not until he saw the way Julie looked at him in the kitchen. She must have heard his confession.

The first swallow seared his tongue and lips and throat and brought tears to his eyes. He should have known better than to gulp fine scotch, but when the agony passed, he repeated his foolishness. This time the pain moderated, and the warmth concentrated in his belly. He lay back, eyes closed as he savored the glow, and held the bottle balanced on his naked chest. The cool glass felt soothing there.

He didn't bother to deceive himself that the liquor was to relax him so he could sleep. Oblivion, the old familiar forgetfulness, was what he wanted. A week of sobriety hadn't changed anything, hadn't dulled any of the pain or made it any easier to bear. It hadn't made him a better doctor or saved any more of his patients from death and suffering. It hadn't even made him a man again.

The level of whiskey dropped. Everything felt satisfactorily fuzzy, and his eyes no longer focused clearly. The doorway wavered between sunshine and shadow, or maybe his eyes just slowly opened and closed. He knew they were wet, but he also knew he didn't feel so bad about crying when he was drunk.

Chapter Twelve

✦✦✦✦✦

WITH UNWILLING BUT welcome help from Willy, Julie had finished the laundry and the dishes and was able to leave the house shortly before eleven. She expected to find the front door to the doctor's office open, but to her surprise it was closed and locked as well.

She walked with calm, unhurried determination across the street and down the lane, past Winnie Upshaw's sister's house, and up the single step to the weathered planks of the flower-shaded porch.

If in the past few days she had become somewhat relaxed in his company, all her previous anxiety returned the moment she stepped onto the porch of the adobe house. Since the afternoon Steve Hollis had ridden up with his urgent message, Julie had not come this close to Morgan's house.

She raised a lightly clasped fist but then could not bring her knuckles down on that lovely but forbidding door.

Who might be watching her, and what might they be thinking? Surely everyone in Plato knew by now that she had gone to work for Morgan, that he had given up his old ways and was once again practicing medicine. There was no reason for Julie to drop her hand to her side and hide that little fist under her apron. Her reason for being here, she told herself over and over, was just as respectable.

If my intentions are so respectable, I'd look guilty if I retreated, she scolded herself.

She lifted her hand again and rapped so sharply that the iron-hard old oak hurt her knuckles. Instinctively she put the sorest into her mouth and gently sucked on it.

There was no response to her summons. She knocked again, this time making certain she pounded on a smooth, uncarved section of the door. Although no one answered her entreaty, the door had not been latched securely, and this heartier pounding jarred it open slightly.

"Dr. Morgan?" she called in a voice hardly above a whisper and surely nowhere near as loud as her knock. If he hadn't heard that, he could hardly have heard her call.

Something had to be wrong. Julie swallowed all her protests and pushed the door inward. The hinges made no sound, and a breath of cool air sighed out into her face, beckoning her inside.

She felt her pulse in her throat as it leapt against the tight collar of her dress, and she wiped her hands on her skirt. That was the only movement she could make, paralyzed as she was with fear.

An agonized groan from upstairs added, if that were possible, to her terror. Someone was in mortal agony, she knew, and that person could only be Morgan. Forgetting all other fears,

Julie dashed up the dark staircase toward the source of that moan.

He was in mortal agony, all right. Seated on the edge of the bed, with a corner of the sheet draped across his thighs, he rested his elbows on his knees and his head on his hands. Julie saw the empty bottle, tipped on its side in a pool of its contents, and she knew the man was in no danger. Except possibly from her own outrage.

He looked up, alerted by her gasp of disapproval and disappointment.

"Morning," he said, with no attempt whatsoever to smile.

He couldn't distinguish colors, for the room was too dim and his eyes too hazy, but he knew her dress was dark, with a prim little white collar. The light that seeped in around the shutters reflected off her glasses where they hovered on the tip of her nose. He didn't have to see to know that; they always teetered on the brink of disaster. He laughed, then gripped the sides of his head as the pain echoed between his ears.

"You deserve it, you miserable . . ." But she couldn't think of a word to call him.

"Oh, I know that. I just forgot how rotten it feels, that's all. I never used to get really sober enough to feel good and hung over like this." The ringing stopped, and he tipped his head back again, trying to adjust his vision.

"Do you know what time it is?" she asked.

"Nope. I was going to set the alarm for eight, but I guess I forgot." He reached for the little brass clock on the table. "I guess I forgot to wind the clock, too. It says quarter to four."

Some of Julie's anger gave way to common sense while he talked, and she realized with new horror that she was standing in the doorway to the man's bedroom, that he was sitting on his bed completely undressed. In fact, she supposed there was nothing under that corner of wrinkled sheet but Del Morgan. She immediately turned her back and pressed her fingers to her burning cheeks.

He took advantage of her modesty, which he was conscious enough now to notice. He grabbed his trousers from the chair and quickly stepped into them, then dragged the crumpled shirt over his arms. Barefoot, he stepped into the sticky puddle of spilled scotch and swore.

The word was one Julie knew existed but had never heard uttered with such casual obscenity.

"Dr. Morgan, please!"

He chuckled, even though it made his head hurt.

"Sorry," he apologized with the same casualness. "I'm not used to waking up with ladies in my bedroom."

"I'm not *in* your bedroom," Julie retorted, feeling her cheeks catch fire once more.

"Well, you're damned close to it." He came up behind her, but she didn't move. "What time is it, anyway?"

"A little past eleven o'clock. And must you stand so close to me?"

"When you're blocking my door, yes."

She jumped out of his way.

"Thank you." He sidled past her into the hallway and headed for the stairs. "I don't suppose you fixed my breakfast or heated my shaving water, did you."

"I most certainly did not," Julie snorted. "I'm your nurse, not your . . . your wife."

She drew in a sharp breath, but of course by then the words were already out and beyond recall.

"I'm sorry," she quickly apologized.

He stood at the bottom of the stairs and hung one hand over the banister. Very slowly he raised his head and looked at her. His steady gaze burned like a brand.

"I'll just bet you are," he said softly.

"I *am* sorry," she called, following him down the stairs and through the house. "I was angry and I said something I wouldn't have if I hadn't been so furious with you."

"You were furious? What the hell for?"

"Because you were drunk again."

"Haven't I got a right to a drink or two now and then? Even a doctor is entitled to a glass of whiskey." A glass, maybe, but not a whole bottle, and Morgan knew that as well as she.

"Yes, I agree, and after yesterday I should have realized that you'd be tired and want to sleep late."

She stopped in the arched entrance between the parlor and the kitchen. Morgan tossed a handful of kindling in the stove and struck a match on the top. He moved too quickly and the tiny flame went out before he could touch it to the shavings and torn paper. He swore again, using slightly less offensive terms but muttering them quite clearly.

Julie suspected he was trying to anger her further and she wasn't about to take his bait.

The second match flared and the kindling caught instantly. After adding a few small sticks from the woodbox, Morgan straightened and spun to face the girl.

"After yesterday it's a wonder I got up at all."

"I know it must be terribly frustrating to spend so much time and effort on a man only to have him die, but surely after all this time you must be somewhat accustomed to it."

She knew she had once again said the most wrong thing possible. His eyes told her, their green turning to black and the little spots of gold catching fire like the crackling tinder in the stove.

"I don't ever get accustomed to death, Miss Hollstrom. The man who does doesn't deserve to practice medicine." He took a step toward her, his eyes rendering her immobile. "It is because I can't get used to it that I opened that bottle of scotch last night, a bottle that I might add I got from Horace's bedroom. He may have treated himself to more expensive liquor than I could afford, but he was no teetotaler, believe me."

He stood so close now that she could look up and see each black whisker on his chin. His bare toes just touched the hem of her skirt. Yet try as she would, and she did, she couldn't back away from him. She knew he would only follow her.

"I do believe you," she whispered.

Just as abruptly as he had stormed toward her, he retreated, leaving her breathless and gasping.

After lifting the coffeepot from the stove and feeling it full, he took it to the back door and tossed the contents into the yard. Julie heard him take the pump handle and jerk it up and down several times before the water splashed out. When he came in again, his pant cuffs were wet. He left dark footprints on the tile.

"If you'll just tell me where the key to the office is, I'll get it and leave you to your breakfast," Julie said in as calm a voice as she could command at that moment.

He didn't turn from his task of measuring coffee into the pot.

"It's in my coat pocket. Upstairs in the bedroom, on the back of the chair."

"Thank you," she mumbled as she finally regained the use of her legs and left him.

If she had thought for half a second before scurrying out of the kitchen, she wouldn't have had the nerve to enter his bedroom, but now she was there, and there was nothing to do but find the key and get out of his house.

In the semidarkness Julie fumbled through each of the many pockets until she found the key. She dropped it into her own pocket and then put the coat back exactly the way she had

found it. It should have been hung up; it would
be wrinkled when he put it on again. But that
wasn't any of her concern, she told herself
sharply. She was, as she had said earlier, his
nurse, not his wife.

She walked over to the toppled bottle and
picked it up. If she had had a wet rag, she would
have mopped up the sticky spill, but saving
Morgan from injury on the bottle, which he
might have tripped over in the dark, was
enough. She set it on the table beside his bed.

The photograph lay in a worn cardboard
frame, and even as Julie reached for it, she knew
she shouldn't. Though her eyes had adjusted to
the shadowy light and she removed the annoy-
ing spectacles, she could see very little, but even
a little was enough. More than enough.

No doubt he had stared at that picture while
he drank last night. It was a wedding portrait,
the bride smiling radiantly in her satin dress and
filmy veil. Her hand, which displayed a new
gold band, covered her husband's, resting pro-
tectively on her shoulder.

Julie might have hated another woman who
looked like Amy Morgan, or at the very least
been painfully envious. Even in this small portrait, viewed in miserably inadequate light, the
woman's beauty could not be missed. Dark hair
was swept up in a mass of curls that tumbled
around her face. She had lovely hands, small
with elegant fingers, and her eyes fairly sparkled
on the paper. Julie knew the smile that flickered

on Amy's lips, restrained for the portrait, was as genuine and fresh as the roses that lay on her lap.

Julie carefully put the picture back where she had found it and turned to leave the room. She had just reached the door when Morgan appeared at the head of the stairs.

"Did you find it?" he asked.

"Did I— Oh, the key. Yes, I found it," she stammered, uncomfortably aware of the little lump in her throat.

"You were up here so long I thought maybe I had put it somewhere else and you couldn't find it." He went back down the stairs, but halfway to the bottom he stopped suddenly and turned. Julie, following, nearly ran into him.

Looking down at him was a thousand times more disturbing than looking up at him. She tried to back away, tripped on the stair and her skirt, and sat down painfully and humiliatingly on the top step. Morgan didn't move, not to prevent her fall or to help her to her feet again.

He stared blatantly at her face.

Aware of his scrutiny, Julie touched quivering fingertips to her cheeks and asked, "What's wrong?"

His eyes roved her features anxiously, but his voice carried no emotion.

"You've lost your glasses again, and you've been crying."

She turned a deeper crimson, but by then Morgan had rushed past her and couldn't see.

Julie scrambled to her feet and dashed down

three or four of the stairs before she stopped. If she went home without the glasses, there would be too many explanations, not only of how she'd lost the spectacles but of why she couldn't seem to stop crying. Slowly, she remounted the stairs.

She waited in the doorway and watched him. He must have felt her gaze, for he spun around almost instantly, and she saw he was holding both her forgotten spectacles and the portrait.

He threw the glasses at her. She caught them easily, relieved that they were neither broken nor bent, but she did not put them on.

"I don't know which makes me more angry, that you lied to me or that you were spying on me."

"I wasn't spying," Julie protested. "I didn't want you to fall on the bottle and get hurt, so I picked it up and—"

"And there was my wife's picture, so you thought you'd just look at it a while."

"She's very lovely." Tears flooded the great round brown eyes. "I'm sorry, really I am. I didn't mean any harm."

He lifted the photograph and let it bring back the memory of that day. No tears came to his eyes.

"That's what they said when that kid shot her. 'He didn't mean any harm.' "

Julie's knees melted, then solidified again as she grabbed the doorframe for support. She doubted Morgan would have noticed if she fell.

"Please," she begged, trying to bring him out of his gloomy memories. With the spectacles

once more in her possession, she could have fled
the house and gone home, but there remained
still her tears to be explained. And she could not
have left Morgan alone.

"You want to know about her, don't you,
Julie."

"Yes," she admitted, too numb to think
straight. Then she stammered, "No, please,
don't talk now. I'm sorry, for everything. For
coming here, for looking at her picture, for lying
about the glasses. I'll leave, and I won't come
back, and I—"

"Stop it!"

His free hand gripped her shoulder firmly,
though she wasn't aware of having approached
him until that instant. She must have walked
toward him while she babbled her frantic apology, for Morgan hadn't moved from his place by
the table and Julie now stood directly in front of
him.

Tears dripped down her cheeks and a warm
longing grew inside her. She wanted to comfort
him, to hold him in her arms and console him for
the loss that left such pain in his eyes. And she
wanted to be held, too, to feel more than just his
hand on her shoulder. Other needs, other
wants, could not be so clearly defined, but she
felt them and recognized them just the same. As
forbidden as they were, she could not deny
them.

Angrily, as though he had seen those shame-
ful desires in her brimming eyes, Morgan shoved
her away from him. She fell back a step or two

and buried her face in her hands as the silent tears changed to sobs.

"Damn it, Julie!" he shouted. "I want to go back to the way it was, back to forgetting, back to all the nothingness." He looked about him for something to throw, not at her but just to feel the satisfaction of destroying something. There was only the whiskey bottle.

"Yesterday was our wedding anniversary," he went on. "Twelve years ago, on the first day of July, Miss Amalia St. Rogers and Dr. Delbert Morgan were united in holy matrimony. Adam St. Rogers was one of the most powerful and wealthy men in Cincinnati. Still is. Banker, industrialist, war hero, manipulator of politics and politicians throughout the state of Ohio. And yet he let his only daughter marry me. He gave her away proudly to the son of a Welsh coal miner."

"But she loved you, didn't she?"

"Yes, she did. And I loved her." He stared down at the portrait again and shook his head. "Or at least I thought I did. But how can a man love a woman and then bring her out to a place like this to die? I should have stayed in Cincinnati, let her father put me in some silly office in the bank, and Amy would still be alive, still be happy." He sighed, but none of the anger left him. He picked up the whiskey bottle and flung it across the room.

Glass shattered and sparkled, but neither the man nor the woman moved. When the last little twinkling had faded, Julie turned to leave.

"No!" Morgan shouted at her.

She froze.

"You wanted to hear this; now you're going to listen. And look at me when I'm speaking to you!"

Julie was thankful for the thick adobe walls. If this had been an ordinary frame house like her father's, every word of this conversation would have gone through the walls. Here, the secrets remained.

"Amy died out in the street, right in front of your house. Some miners had just come into town after hitting a big strike and they were celebrating, dancing, shooting, not hurting anything. But some fool kid on the stage thought it was a holdup. They said he thought he would be a hero and save the town from the robbers. He shot twice. One of those shots hit Amy."

"No, no more," Julie pleaded. "I can't stand it, and neither can you."

"Can't I?" he asked, his voice gentle now and quiet. "I've been standing it every day, every second, for damn near six years. I was sitting in front of McCrory's, waiting for her, watching her come toward me. She just crumpled like a puppet whose strings have been cut. I ran to her, even though I knew I couldn't do anything. I don't think—and I've prayed a million times that I was right—that she felt anything. I'm sure she was dead before she fell."

Pain and memories of her own welled up in Julie's chest and spilled over with a harsh cry. She could see the street, the dust, and the sun, and Amy Morgan lying in her blood with her husband kneeling beside her.

He was warm and he was strong and he was shaking when Julie's arms went around him, drawing him into an embrace she could not prevent. Where his shirt gaped unbuttoned, her cheek rested against his bare chest, the dark hairs coarse and irritating on her skin. But she felt only the essence of the man, not the small elements.

"Amy was eight months pregnant when she died. I carried her to the surgery myself, not trusting anyone else, and I tried for two days to save the baby I had taken from her body. I couldn't even go to her funeral because I was trying to keep that tiny bit of her alive; but in the end I failed. I buried him myself. I opened up her coffin and put him in her arms."

Chapter Thirteen

✦ ✦ ✦ ✦

HE COULD NOT weep. All the tears were spent long ago. Only the sharp pain remained, and even it seemed to have lessened.

He held her, not remembering when his arms had circled around her slender body and drawn her to him. He rested his gaunt, rough cheek against the smooth silk of her hair. He felt no stirring of forgotten emotions, no rising of lost hungers, only the warm comfort of the girl's nearness and her tears on his chest.

For whom do you cry, Julie? he wanted to ask, but he knew no words would come from his constricted throat.

When her sobs subsided and her tears slowed to a mere trickle, he loosened his embrace and gently freed himself from hers. He shivered, deprived of her warmth.

"I never told anyone before," he said. "And I thought you knew."

She shook her head slowly. "I wanted to ask you, but I didn't want to pry."

Her voice, like her embrace, was soft, and kind, and comforting. When she looked at him, which she did only cautiously, he saw how deep the pain ran in her eyes. Tears had darkened her lashes and stuck them together in long, thin triangles above and below those brown eyes that reminded him so much of a terrified deer. Yet Julie Hollstrom hadn't run away.

He wondered again what she was so afraid of.

He lifted a hand with intentions of wiping away the last tear that slid down her cheek, but he thought better of it.

"You go downstairs and pour us both some coffee while I get dressed a bit more decently," he suggested. "Then we'll go over to Horace's and get to work, all right?"

In the kitchen, Julie found cups and saucers

and poured the black bitter coffee into them. It was far too hot to drink, but the act of holding the cup and blowing gently on the mirrorlike surface calmed her.

She could think clearly now, without clouds of memory to obscure her rationality.

Morgan walked quietly into the kitchen and poured himself a cup of coffee. Standing across the table from Julie, he told her, "They say that sorrow shared is sorrow halved. Maybe I needed to tell someone. Maybe I should have done it a long time ago."

She didn't answer, having no words to match her feelings. And she wished he wouldn't talk about it.

"I feel better now, Julie. I don't think there will be a repetition of last night."

The old prospector's death, the revelation Morgan had been forced to give Hans, the lack of sleep, and all on the anniversary of his wedding. No, that combination would hardly come again, Julie knew.

"And I intend to see that it doesn't," she resolved, sticking an extra firmness into her tone. She swallowed the last few drops of coffee and set the cup down with a thump. "I believe we've been here long enough. We have work to do."

"Yes, we do." Now he felt just as awkward as she did when they faced each other across the table. "Oh, here, I almost forgot." He pulled her spectacles from his pocket. "You must have dropped them again. I found them on the floor."

He handed them to her, but it was a moment

before she could bring herself to reach for them. With the table between her and Morgan, however, Julie withstood the shock brought by the simple touch of his fingers on the palm of her hand as he dropped the glasses onto it.

They kept themselves occupied and out of each other's way for most of the day. Julie concentrated her efforts on the kitchen, which Horace had used rarely but had never cleaned, and Morgan set himself to the obnoxious task of sorting the late Dr. Opper's collection of unlabeled bottles, boxes, and jars of medicaments. An empty nail keg was used for the discards, which far outnumbered the supplies Morgan deemed fit for use.

On her hands and knees, with a bucket of hot, soapy water and a stiff-bristled brush, Julie listened to the muttered curses and snorts of disgust that accompanied the crash of glass containers into the keg. Morgan had clearly lost himself in his work and his mind was on it entirely, whereas hers kept wandering despite her most strenuous efforts at control.

"What a mess you've gotten yourself into now, Julie Hollstrom," she scolded with her teeth clenched tightly together.

She scrubbed at a particularly nasty spot until the substance—something totally beyond recognition—came loose from the floor and could be picked up and dropped into the bucket. She moved over a foot or two, half afraid she would wear a hole right through the floor with the force of her scrubbing. Half panting from the exertion, she swept the back of a wet hand across her forehead. Her hair had come loose from its tight coil at the back of her neck and now a thick braid hung over one shoulder to trail a bedraggled end in the dirty soapy water on the floor. Sweat dripped off the end of her nose.

The glasses slid back down as soon as she had pushed them up, and her worries gave her no rest. At least this time Julie knew it wasn't entirely her own fault. Katharine had gone out of her way to be friendly with the doctor, and it was she, not Julie, who had begged that Julie be allowed to accept Morgan's offer of employment.

Julie felt a prickle of apprehension down her back as she resumed a rhythmic circular scrubbing and whispered, "He's a doctor, and Mama's concerned about her health, that's all. Nothing more. She didn't really mean to push me from the frying pan into the fire."

When the spectacles she had just put back on slid instantly down her nose and nearly fell off, she shoved them into an apron pocket so furiously that she tore the edge of the pocket.

"What fire are you talking about?" Morgan asked.

Startled, Julie turned and tried to get up at the same time. She was in too awkward a position to do so gracefully, and being in that position too long had left her back and leg muscles painfully cramped. She became tangled in her wet skirt and petticoats and ended up sitting flat on the wet floor, her feet spraddled and her face beet red.

"Oh, I . . . I was just . . . talking to myself," she stammered.

"Glad I'm not the only one. Although most of my comments were for the late and less-lamented-than-ever Horace Opper."

His green eyes left their momentary inspection of the figure on the floor and examined the work she had done. Julie struggled to her feet, successfully this time, and tried to smooth some of the wrinkles from her skirt, though she knew it would take much more than that to make her presentable.

"Uh, we seem to have a problem here, Miss Hollstrom."

Her head snapped up.

"A problem? What problem?"

A sizable expanse of wet kitchen floor separated them, for which Julie was immeasurably grateful. Having Morgan something slightly less than five feet away from her was not enough to keep her palms from sweating and her knees, half numb after kneeling so long, from quivering weakly.

"Well," Morgan went on in a slow, teasing drawl, "I have this barrel of garbage to dump down the privy and I can't get to the back door."

"Can't you just take it out the front and walk around the house?"

"Of course I can, but what are *you* going to do?"

But by the time he had uttered those words, Julie had realized what a stupid thing she had done. She stood in a corner, with wet floor completely surrounding her. The nearest escape was two or three long strides to the back door. And the floor was slipperiest there, with the risk of falling greatest.

"I haven't rinsed and waxed it yet," she informed him. "We can walk across it with no damage."

"Are you sure? I don't want you to get hurt."

"I won't."

She took the first step, carefully placing her foot where there was the least chance of slipping, but Morgan's shouted "Wait!" stopped her.

"Can you see?" he asked. "Where have you put those glasses to now?"

"Ouch!" she cried, withdrawing a hand that quickly dripped very bright drops down the front of her skirt and onto her clean floor.

Ignoring the little puddles, Morgan crossed the room in a few easy strides and took her hand in his.

"Come into the other room," he urged. "The light is terrible in here; I can't see a thing. What in heaven's name have you done?"

What she had done was very clear. The spectacles were now nothing but a few pieces of twisted gold wire and a thousand shards of broken glass.

"You must have broken them when you stumbled getting up," Morgan observed as he dumped the contents of her apron pocket onto the table in the surgery. "But then, you don't really need them, do you."

"No, I don't," Julie admitted. She was over her humiliation enough to be frightened again.

She sat on a plain wooden chair beside the enameled table and rested her hand on the cold surface while Morgan adjusted a lamp with a small reflecting mirror so that the light concentrated on the injury. The bleeding had already stopped from the two tiny stabs in the end of her third finger. Morgan pulled his stool in front of her and sat down. He had a pair of tweezers close at hand.

"I don't see any other slivers," he announced. "It's a wonder you didn't cut your knee."

"Then may I leave?"

"Leave?" he echoed. "Why?"

"It's late. I need to go home and fix supper."

"Let me put a plaster on that first. And some iodine. I don't want it getting infected, and after being on that floor all day, you've probably got a Mongol horde of germs on your hands."

But she jerked her hand away and said, "I can take care of it at home. Please, let me go."

He was tempted to accede to her wishes. She could be awfully moody and stubborn at times. But he had bared his soul to her this morning, and he decided now it was time for her to do the same. Obviously she disliked his touch, for she had drawn away from him as though burned just now, and he remembered how horrified she had looked the other day in McCrory's when he had held her hand. Maybe she had had a bad experience with a man before.

"It's not even half past three," he argued. "You have plenty of time to fix supper, if you use some common sense and fix something appropriate to the climate. Besides, I want to show you the proper way to bandage a minor laceration."

"What for?"

He reached behind him for a bottle of tincture of iodine.

"There may be times when you'll have to handle little emergencies on your own. Here, give me your hand again and let me show you."

She bit her lip, not against the pain but against the more torturous sensations caused by his touch. As he bent his head over the wounded finger, which didn't hurt at all, Julie felt an insane desire to slide the fingers of her other hand into his hair. The tousled curls, dark with a few stray strands of gray, tempted her, so comfortably within her reach. She knew how they'd feel, soft and silky and springy to her touch.

Why, oh why couldn't he go back to being the wretch he had been two weeks ago? Why couldn't he still be dirty and drunk and disreputable, instead of this highly desirable man who was holding her hand and dabbing it gently with iodine?

She jerked at the sudden sting.

It brought her back to reality.

"Keep it out of water, if you can, for a day or two," Morgan ordered as he wrapped a sticking plaster around it. "You may have to ask your brother to help with the dishes."

Julie stared at the white bandage.

"I didn't think it was all that serious."

"I just don't want to take any chances. I can't afford to lose you."

For all his seriousness, he gave her a smile. The wound wasn't anything to worry about, not really, but he liked the idea of making someone else pamper her for a change.

"What about the rest of the floor?" she asked. "And don't tell me you'll just have Miss Upshaw finish it. I won't have you taking advantage of her."

"Then I suppose I'll have to do it myself. Will you show me how?"

He smiled again, this time with pleasure at having made her laugh. She was quite a sight in her dirty wet clothes, with that thick rope of braid hanging down her back and streaks of grime like war paint on her face. When she laughed, he forgot all that. He saw only the glow in her eyes, the pink curve of her lips, the lift of her delicate chin.

He wiped the thought of kissing her out of his head. When it tried to sneak back, Willy's shouts from the waiting room chased it safely away. The boy had come to have his stitches removed.

*   *   *

"What do you mean you aren't going to re-place them?" Wilhelm bellowed. Katharine shushed him with a finger to her lips, but he waved her gesture aside. "Such a decision is not yours to make."

Julie had fully expected this outburst when she told her father about the eyeglasses. She sighed, partly with exhaustion and partly with relief. She had had to wait until after Willy was safely tucked in bed before braving this discussion, and by then she was more than ready for sleep herself.

"Papa, I don't need them. I can see perfectly without them, and they only get in the way."

"That is no excuse. Your mama and I decided long ago that they were necessary. Tomorrow you will purchase new ones."

Wilhelm leaned back in his chair and picked up the newspaper.

"I won't. Besides, Dr. Morgan knows I don't need them, so if you think—"

The newspaper snapped down.

"Wilhelm, please," Katharine begged. "Don't wake Willy."

That, Julie calmly told herself, was the straw that broke the camel's back.

"Of course!" she shouted. "Don't wake Willy! Never mind what happens to Julie, so long as you don't wake Willy!" She saw a pained look come across Katharine's face but ignored it. She knew her mother too well. "For once, just once, you're going to listen to me, and to hell with Willy!"

She got to her feet and faced her father. She was shaking and flatly refused to listen to anything that resembled better judgment, but the consequences of her actions could hardly be worse than the consequences of inaction.

"I am not going to wear those ridiculous glasses anymore," she announced firmly, her voice far steadier than her knees. "I don't need them, and there is no way you can make me wear them. If I did, Dr. Morgan would only want to know why, since he knows I can see perfectly without them, and I don't suppose you want me to tell him the truth. Now, if you'll excuse me, I'm going to bed."

She stormed out of the parlor, but at the bottom of the stairs Wilhelm caught her, grabbing her by the arm so harshly that she knew there would be bruises.

"You think you can fool me," he hissed under his breath, "but I am not fooled. For once you are the fool. Go ahead and flaunt yourself at that man, but it will do you no more good than it did before. And Morgan is less of a man than the horse thief or any of the others."

"I am not the child I was nine years ago, Papa. The dreams I had then died a long time ago. And if they hadn't, Dr. Morgan would be the last man to answer them. He's still in love with his wife, and even without the precious eyeglasses, I would never be able to replace her. I have too much self-respect to try."

She pulled her arm free of her father's grasp,

though she heard the soft tearing of worn fabric as he held on to the sleeve of her dress a second too long. It didn't matter; she would have left the man's presence even if he had ripped the garment to shreds. By the time she reached the top of the stairs and stormed into her own room, the tears were hot on her cheeks. She slammed the door as loudly as she could, but it drew no angry retort from her father or complaint from Willy in the next room.

She had lied. Guilt brought the tears, not only for the lie but for the shame of the truth.

In the dark of her bedroom Julie fought against the words. To speak them in her heart was bad enough, but if they came to her lips, however silently, she would never again be able to deny them. Yet keeping them inside only added to the pain.

And the pain demanded release. Involuntarily, her voice no louder than the breeze at the uncurtained window, Julie whispered, "I love you, Del Morgan."

Chapter Fourteen

✦✦✦✦✦

THE WORD *IF*, Julie decided, aptly characterized the rest of that week. As she went through each exhausting but satisfying day, the litany of circumstances chanted through her brain.

If she had not broken the spectacles, she would not have fought with her father.

If she had not fought with Wilhelm, she would not have admitted to herself that she was in love with Morgan.

If she had not admitted to her emotions, she would have told Morgan about her promise to Hans.

If Morgan had known she was all but formally engaged, he might have gone ahead and found someone else to work for him, thus releasing Julie from her torment.

When she came to that part of the sequence, she felt a cold chill, for she knew that if Morgan had terminated their working relationship, she would have gone insane.

Although loving Morgan when she knew he would never return her feelings made her ache inside, Julie also loved her work. She quickly got over the initial queasiness of surgery, and when Paddy McCrory, Clancy's fourteen-year-old brother, blew off three fingers on the Fourth of July, Julie's hands were as steady as Morgan's during the operation. Two days later, he let her wield the needle herself, and she sewed Jack

Brohagen's cut elbow with a row of fine, neat stitches. The bartender twisted his arm to look at the work and grinned.

"Next time I lean on a broken bottle, I'll make sure Miss Hollstrom does the mending. Looks just like embroidery!"

She had blushed—that was one habit she couldn't seem to break—but with pride rather than embarrassment.

If she had not taken pride in her work, Morgan would not have teased her about it for the rest of the afternoon.

"They really were nice stitches, weren't they," she commented while they cleaned the surgery.

"Oh, not bad. I've seen better."

"You haven't either! They were all exactly the same length and spaced exactly the same distance apart."

Morgan leaned against the doorframe and folded his arms across his chest.

"I remember an old bachelor doctor back in Cincinnati who did real embroidery on his patients. On a cut like Jack's, old Sam'l Wooden did featherstitching so pretty that people hated to take it out. He did a lot of work during the war, Union Army, of course, and he had a different stitch for each different kind of wound. Satin stitch for amputations, french knots for bullet holes."

She knew he was lying, by the smile and the twinkle in his eyes.

"Don't be silly," she retorted. "You can't sew things together with french knots."

"You can't?"

His feigned disbelief was so guiltily exaggerated that Julie started to giggle.

"You don't even know what a french knot is," she accused. "Now, if you had asked, I might have been able to put Mr. Brohagen's elbow back together with satin stitches, but not french knots!"

"Well, Dr. Sam'l Wooden could!"

"He couldn't!" Julie insisted, caught up in the game. "It just isn't possible. Here, I'll show you."

Morgan tried to stop her, but Julie wouldn't let him. Now it was her turn to tease, and she intended to see it through to the end.

"Men always think they know everything," she harped while she gathered the items she needed. "And they think that when they don't know everything, they can still bluff a woman into believing that they do. Men never bother to remember that there are certain things women know more about."

"Like french knots."

"Exactly." She got out the needles and thread they had just put away. "I am going to demonstrate just how impossible it is to suture a wound like Mr. Brohagen's with french knots."

"All right, all right." Morgan laughed, taking up the spool of heavy black silk and replacing it on the cupboard shelf. "I believe you. My word, Julie, I was only teasing."

She smiled, but not directly at him.

"I know that. I'm teaching you not to."

"Can't I just apologize?"

Julie shook her head. She had the needle threaded and only needed some strips of cotton bandage material to sew together. There were rolls of it on the top shelf, which she could reach with only a little stretch.

If Morgan had been standing six inches to his left, he would not have blocked her reach, and her sleeve would not have caught on the nail sticking out from the edge of the cupboard door. In the single split instant it took her to realize she had snagged the sleeve, the fabric was already torn.

Her gasp of surprise and dismay brought concern from Morgan, who could not see the damage.

"Are you hurt?"

"No, I've just—"

If she had moved out of his way more quickly, he would have seen nothing and suspected nothing. But the clumsy haste in which she clasped the torn edges of cloth together wasn't enough. The tear gapped to reveal bruises, faded now to a purplish yellow but still dark enough for a doctor's eyes to see.

Morgan pried her fingers from her sleeve without a word. When the rip fell open, his initial guess was confirmed. The marks of four fingers and a thumb stood out too clearly to be mistaken.

All the laughter and teasing fled.

"Who did this?"

"My father."

"Why?"

"He wanted me to do something that I didn't want to do and I was too tired to argue with him. I was going to my room, and he stopped me."

"Did he hit you?"

"No."

He believed her. And after the first shock of seeing the bruises, he realized they were not serious. But on her fair skin, they had seemed monstrous.

"What did he want you to do that you refused?"

He had no right to ask, but if he didn't, he wouldn't be able to live with himself. He had tried not to think about what went on in that house when Julie was away from him, because he reasoned that her life could not be as bad as his distrust of her father made him imagine. Perhaps the truth was worse yet.

She told him about the eyeglasses and her stubborn refusal to purchase another pair.

"If you don't need them, why does he want you to wear them?" He was beginning to think the whole family was crazy. Katharine lied about her health, Willy was spoiled like a rich widow's dog, and now Wilhelm the miser expected his daughter to buy glasses she didn't need.

"He thinks the spectacles will make me less attractive to men."

Morgan laughed just once; then, when he saw the look on her face just before she turned away, he apologized.

"I'm sorry. I didn't mean that the way it sounded."

He curled an index finger under her chin and tilted it a fraction of an inch higher.

No boisterous nine-year-old interrupted him this time. He kissed her very softly, feeling her fright in the quiver of her lips as he touched them. But she did not pull away.

And he did not apologize.

The kiss was not mentioned Saturday morning. Julie, either out of exhaustion or shock, had slept well the night before; Morgan, she was sure, had not. At least he looked as though he had not. But she had no time to question him, nor he her, because the office was filled with patients almost as soon as Morgan unlocked the door.

Winnie brought coffee at ten-thirty; they had no time to drink it before Katharine arrived with lunch from Daneggar's two hours later. Julie urged Morgan to eat, which led to an argument, but in the end it didn't matter. Lunch waited, as did the man with the boil on his face and the woman with the swollen ankle. Marshal Ted Phillips brought in a gunshot victim.

Ted Phillips was a beefy man who carried his paunch proudly. He stood as tall as Morgan, maybe an inch taller, but was twice as wide. The man he supported nearly matched him in size.

"Tried to jump a claim," Phillips explained as he dragged the barely conscious patient into the surgery. Julie was still cleaning up from the last case, Donnie Kincheloe's stubborn nosebleed. "Says a couple of old coots shot him before he could tell 'em he was lost, not tryin' to steal their mine. I got a feelin' it was them same two that brought in the old man who died last week."

Morgan took the injured man's feet and helped Phillips hoist him onto the table. Blood stained a dirty shirt of indeterminable color; the man had been shot at least three times that Julie could see.

Phillips leaned forward as Julie began cutting the stained shirt away from the wound.

"You think he'll make it?"

"Hard to tell," Morgan said as he poured ether onto a cloth and handed it to Julie. She placed it gently over the man's nose and mouth. He struggled just a bit, but he was already too close to unconsciousness to fight the anesthetic long. "Depends on how much damage there is inside. Was he on the horse when you found him?"

"Nope, he was sitting in the shade, restin'. Got back on, though, by hisself. Rode pretty good most of the way, but o' course I didn't rush him. Still, it's prob'ly close to two, three miles from town where I found him."

"Well, just let us get to work on him, Ted, and I'll do the best I can."

The marshal nodded, tipped his hat to Julie with a bloodstained hand, and backed out. The room had seemed noisy with his bulky presence; now that he had gone, the silence deepened.

"There are three shots, but four wounds,"

Morgan observed as he rolled his sleeves past
his elbows. "The one just below the ribs is a
flesh wound; it can wait. The one in the right
thigh is probably the worst. I'll bet you a five-
dollar gold piece the bullet is stuck in the femur."

"Is that bad?"

Her voice wasn't shy and quivery anymore.

"Yeah, it's bad. The guy's got legs like tree
trunks; I'm gonna have a hell of a time finding
that slug."

His first task was to staunch as much of the
bleeding as possible. The shoulder wounds
quickly saturated the cotton cloths Julie had put
on them.

"Get fresh ones, and then hold your hand
here." He put his own finger on a spot where
the pulse beat strongly. "It cuts off the circulation and gives the blood a chance to clot. I'm
going to do the same with the leg."

It would have been easier to work with the
man's pants off, but instead Morgan just cut
away the leg. They were ruined anyway, with
that ragged hole where the bullet had gone
through.

Morgan took a wide leather band, not unlike a
belt, and slipped it around the top of the thigh,
right where the hip joint drew the muscles in.
When he tightened the tourniquet, the flow of
fresh blood ceased almost instantly.

"There, that will hold the leg while we figure
out what to do about this shoulder," Morgan
said in a voice reminiscent of a schoolteacher.
While Julie placed a pile of towels and a basin of

warm water at hand, he gingerly poked the area around the wound with a finger. The patient showed no response at all. Morgan picked up a towel, dipped it and wrung it out, then began washing the mutilated flesh. "I don't want that tourniquet on too long, so I'm going to work as fast as I can."

The bullet that had gone through the shoulder had hit and chipped the shoulder blade. Closing the entrance wound was relatively easy, but the gaping hole on the man's back and the removal of the fragments of bone took time, and patience, and a steady hand. Julie watched in amazement as Morgan worked. After each piece of bone dropped into the waiting glass dish, the physician placed a bloody hand on his patient's neck, then nodded with unemotional satisfaction when he found his pulse still strong.

"I think that's the last of them." He let the forceps fall off his fingers and clatter to the metal tabletop. "Keep your hand on that spot while I cauterize and then you can close this wound. I've got to get at that leg."

Morgan took a damp towel and wiped his hands on it as he walked around the table to the other side and the naked, bluish leg. With the blood wiped away, the wound appeared nothing more than a neat little hole. Morgan slid one long finger into it. Blood welled up around his hand, but it did not gush, nor did it look fresh. Some of it had already clotted.

He wiped his hand again, then reached for the glass tray of instruments.

"I found the slug, just barely touched it with the tip of my finger. It's in the bone deep."

Julie watched calmly as his strong fingers gripped the forceps again and inserted the blades into the man's flesh. No hesitation, no trembling, just the assurance of a man doing what he knew was necessary.

"What are his chances?" Julie asked.

Morgan shrugged. He had the instrument in as far as he could get it and still maneuver.

"Fair. Maybe a little less. If I were a gambler, I wouldn't put much money on him."

He was fighting death again, even though he knew the odds were not in his favor.

Julie heard the sound of metal on metal. Morgan wasted no time congratulating himself, because a second later the blades of the forceps snapped together, empty. He swore.

"One more try. If I don't get it then, I'll cut to it."

Julie held her breath even as she drew a gut-threaded needle through shoulder muscles. And she prayed. Not just that this attempt to remove the bullet was successful, but that this patient would live. He might very well be a claim jumper, a thief, the very wickedest of wicked men, but his life seemed suddenly very precious.

She let her own work wait a moment while she took a dry towel from the pile and wiped it across Morgan's forehead. In the small closed room the air was stifling, and Morgan's hands were otherwise occupied. It was the least she could do.

"I've got hold of it again," he breathed, snapping the instrument's handles together. "Keep your fingers crossed."

He pulled with slow, steady force, not daring to wiggle the forceps even to dislodge the dollop of lead. The muscles and tendons of his wrist and forearms corded with the strain of maintaining that pressure. A single stout jerk might have brought the misshapen projectile out easily, or it might have slipped the forceps off with another disappointing snap. Julie crossed her fingers and prayed again.

"I think it's coming," Morgan said through clenched teeth. "Can you wipe my forehead again? Thanks."

She used the towel to push back the lock of hair that had fallen over his brow. Sweat dripped down his temples, and she wiped that away, too.

He nearly fell backward when the bullet finally gave and came free, but even then he did not so much as smile in celebration until he had examined the forceps and verified that they did indeed hold the flattened slug. After a single deep breath that was probably meant to be a sigh of relief, he removed the bullet from the forceps and reinserted the instrument into the wound.

"I want to make sure there aren't any slivers of bone or other pieces of lead that I missed," he explained. "Then we'll sew him up and wait to see if he survives."

Julie lost track of the time. She had heard

voices in the other room occasionally, but not for quite a while. She thought she recalled hearing the door open and several pairs of footsteps descend the porch stairs, but she couldn't be sure and it seemed quite some time had passed since then.

They worked silently, each aware of the tension that filled the room, the desperation, the fear, the hope. And when they had finished, almost at the same time, they dropped bloody needles to the tabletop and sighed wearily.

Morgan was the first to speak, his voice drained and emotionless.

"Can you pour me some of that coffee?"

"But it's hours old!"

"It's also wet, and I'm thirsty."

The coffeepot Winnie had brought that morning sat on the counter by the single window, which faced the backyard. When Julie turned to pour the cold, stale coffee, she could not help but see the glorious vermilion sunset that silhouetted the mountains under the faint twinkle of the evening star. The sun was gone; only its glow remained.

Morgan drank the bitter coffee in almost a single gulp, then made a face at the taste.

"*Gawd!* Remind me never to do that again."

"I'll try. Did you know it's almost dark outside?"

He looked over his shoulder at the window. The scarlet had even in those few seconds deepened to crimson, and that would not last long.

"I'm not surprised. If you want, you can go home and I'll finish up here. You look exhausted."

She smiled weakly.

"So do you. Besides, you'll need someone to help sit up with him, won't you?"

Morgan shook his head.

"If Ted's not still out there waiting, I'll bring him from the office so he can help. You go on home and get some sleep. Ted and I can carry this guy into the other room, and I've got a decent chair there now to sleep on."

"A decent chair to sleep on?" she echoed. "Are you trying to be a martyr?"

"No, just a typical frontier physician. It won't be the first time, believe me."

Julie began to gather up discarded towels and rags that had been dropped carelessly to the floor. Without looking at Morgan, she scolded him as firmly as she would have Willy. "I don't know when was the last time you slept on a chair, but I do know it is definitely the last time. You've worked too hard today, and whether you intend to admit it or not, you didn't get much sleep last night, if any. You can't continue without sleep and expect to work your best."

With a rueful little chuckle and a gentle shake of his head, Morgan bent to help Julie clean up the mess. She could be marvelous, this Julie Hollstrom, when she wanted to be. Hanging on his every word one minute and ordering him around like a sergeant-major the next. And all this with a man lying on the table, bloodied and barely alive.

"First I'm going to clean up, or we won't be able to stand this place come morning," she said.

He watched her, and he did not have the strength to order her away. Not tonight.

She carried the instruments and gory cloths to the kitchen, where all was nearly dark. After she had dropped the towels and rags into a bucket of cold water by the door, she struck a match and lit a lamp on the table.

There were two empty buckets on the back porch by the pump, Horace's one convenience. Once outside, Julie thanked the late physician for the laziness that made him put down a new well close to the house. She also paused, for just a moment, to inhale the peace of the summer night.

What a lovely night it was, with just the last fading glimmer of blue crowning the mountains and the dark velvet sky sprinkled with stars. In the clear desert air, they seemed closer than ever, almost near enough to touch. Crickets scraped their tuneless violins, an owl hooted like a staccato bassoon, and a soft breeze sang in the distant cottonwoods like fairy fingers on a harp. Though the air was warm, Julie shivered with a chill after the steamy confines of the surgery.

Or maybe something else sent that shiver through her.

She clasped her arms about her for a moment while she stared up at the stars. She knew the Great Bear and found him, but Orion had not risen yet, the only other constellation she could recognize. Failing to locate any other familiar patterns in the pinpricks of twinkling light, she bent to fill the buckets and take them back to the kitchen.

She found Morgan with his arms in a shallow basin, scrubbing them with a cloth as bloodied as any soaking in the other bucket.

"Here," Julie offered as she set a bucket on the table. "This may be cold, but at least it's clean. It will be a while before I have hot water; the stove's cold, too."

"Don't bother lighting it now." He accepted her offer and dunked his arms up to his elbows in the fresh water. "As soon as I get the worst of this off, I'll get Ted to come sit with this guy, and then I'll go home to clean up. I've got plenty of hot water on the roof."

"On the roof?" She handed him a towel and a tumbler of icy water to drink.

"Sure. The sun warms it. Saves on firewood, too." He finished with the towel and tossed it back to her, then gulped down every drop of water. "You keep an eye on our hairy gentleman in there, and I'll get Ted." A slightly crooked grin crinkled his eyes as he added, "You might want to clean up a bit yourself."

Then he rolled down his sleeves and headed for the front door.

Less than ten minutes later, when Julie had barely finished rinsing the last of the patient's blood from her own hands and was wringing out the towels that would need washing in the morning, Morgan's footsteps mounted the porch again, alone.

"Where's the marshal?" she asked.

"Sawing wood that'll never burn." At the puzzled look in her eyes, he explained with a weary smile, "Ted's asleep, snoring like a two-man saw. Even if I got him over here, he'd be back in dreamland before I got out the door."

A yawn, the fourth since he'd left the marshal's office, sneaked up on him. He tried, more or less successfully, to stifle it.

"You won't last much longer," Julie told him. "If you won't go home and leave me here with Harry, at least lie down on the sofa. I'll bring you an extra blanket from home and a pillow, if you need them."

"All right, all right." He stretched, too. "We've got to get Harry into the other room and on the bed first. But as soon as we get any sign that he's coming to, you wake me and get yourself home."

Julie nodded. Morgan might have noticed her lack of sincerity, but he was in the midst of yet another yawn.

Moving their patient was no easy task. Morgan took the man's shoulders, and Julie settled herself between Harry's knees with her arms clamped about his thighs. Very carefully, they maneuvered him out of the surgery and into the single-bed infirmary, converted from Horace's dining room. Harry groaned, but did not fully regain consciousness. Dressed only in his ruined one-legged pants and his boots, he lay like a fallen tree.

Slightly out of breath from his exertions, Morgan walked up to Julie and extended his hand. At first she hardly knew how to react, then slipped her own into it and let her fingers clasp his.

"I still wouldn't put good money on it, but I think he might make it," Morgan conceded in a cautious whisper. "We done good, Miss Hollstrom."

She felt awkward, unaccustomed to such praise and less accustomed to the sensations his touch aroused. She wanted to jerk her hand away, to break the circuit and stop the flow of current, and yet she was held by a force far, far stronger than his grip.

"You did most of the work, Dr. Morgan. I just tried to help and stay out of your way."

He shook his head firmly.

"No, that's not true. I couldn't have got him this far alone. I needed you, Julie, and I'm damn glad you were there."

He was tired clear through to his marrow. And he was sufficiently hopeful of Harry's survival to consider some minor celebration in order. But when he kissed Julie, it was simply because he wanted to, not because he was too exhausted to know what he was doing or because he was elated over his success.

She let him pull her closer; she did not fight or try to push herself away. And when his lips came down softly on hers, she did not turn her head. He was gentle, as she had known he would be, and not demanding. Her eyelids drifted down.

Chapter Fifteen
✦ ✦ ✦ ✦

JULIE HEARD THE nagging little voice that warned her she was going too far, but the sweet pleasure of Morgan's kiss set her heart to singing. His arms went around her, curling her into an embrace she fit so perfectly she might have been made exclusively for him and no other to hold. As he lifted a hand to cup the back of her head, she let her own arms encircle him, and the bond was complete.

His lips were firm, his mouth cool from a long drink of icy water. He demanded no response, but the slightest hint of his hunger, the barest pressure of desire, and her lips parted tentatively. Delightful shivers spread through her whole body, and though she instinctively suspected they were the mere prelude to further pleasures, Julie had no idea what her own part should be. She hesitated only an instant, but it was enough to alert Morgan to the danger.

With a sigh, he sealed the kiss and released

her still trembling lips. Her eyes remained closed, and she did not lift her back-tilted head. He did not mind holding it a little longer.

He kissed her nose, just the tip of it where those silly spectacles had always rested. She panted slightly, breathing through flared nostrils and barely parted lips. A wild pulse beat in the hollow of her throat and at her temple, where he placed yet another kiss on a strand of sweat-damp silver silk that had come free from her carefully twisted braid. He was just about to brush his lips against a shuttered eyelid when it fluttered open.

Her cheeks turned the most succulent shade of scarlet, then paled as her eyes widened. Slowly she drew away from him, until his hands slid from her shoulders down her back and came to rest lightly just above her hips. He knew by the quivering of her body beneath his palms that she was ready to run. The terrified doe poised for flight.

He must not let her go—not yet.

He took his hands away but replaced them gently atop her own, still clinging tightly to his shirttails. He covered the little fists, then pried them loose and held them chastely in the narrow open space between their tensed bodies.

"Go home, Julie," he ordered, unaware until he opened his mouth that his voice was hoarse and his words unsteady. "We're both of us tired, and I don't think we really know what we're doing. Tomorrow is Sunday, a day of rest. We need it."

She backed away finally, letting her hands fall

from his only when neither of them could reach
without straining. Then her eyes fell, too, and
her shoulders slumped with something more
than ordinary weariness.

No one had seen them, no one need ever
know what had happened, and yet Morgan
couldn't help but think that Julie walked away
from him with a terrible burden of guilt on her
slender shoulders.

At the precise instant that Julie turned the
handle and opened the door to leave the room,
Harry stirred, drawing Morgan's attention.
Though it took him only a few seconds to determine that the patient was still far from regaining
consciousness, when he turned again, she was
gone. The quiet latching of the front door told
him she had left the house.

Julie walked down the steps and out to the
street, to enter her own yard by the gate. She did
not hurry, for she needed every second she
could find to settle her emotions and compose
her features. A light burned in the parlor; someone waited up for her, and she could not let
either her mother or her father see her in this
state.

The noise from the Castle drifted down the
street, but it did not cover the sudden angry
voices coming from much nearer than the saloon. Halfway home, Julie stopped and turned
in the direction of the voices, one male, one
female.

They stood in the edge of the lantern's pale
glow, silhouettes against the general store's
blank north wall. Another step or two and they
would have been in the alley between the main
block of commercial buildings and the detached bulk of the Olympia House. Julie
strained to hear the words they spoke, but
now her ears were attuned to every night
sound—the crickets, the owls, the piano at the
Castle—and the argument was not nearly as
loud as it had been.

The woman, identifiable by her ankle- and
calf-revealing skirt, let out a little shriek after
some low, rumbling words from the man, whose
shadow she partially blocked. Julie would have
gone on, having ascertained that the disputants
were only one of the girls from Nellie's and a
customer, but the sharp crack of flesh on flesh
and the woman's louder cry this time halted her
steps.

The man grabbed the woman's arm and tried
to drag her down the alley that led toward Nellie's establishment. He slipped almost completely into the invisibility of the buildings'
shadows. As Julie hesitated between confront-
ing them herself and going for Morgan's help,
the girl in the short green dress broke free and
ran toward the Castle. The man cursed, a single
word, then went after her. His legs were longer
and he was unhampered by high-heeled shoes
in a street of thick dust. In three long strides he
had caught her.

He had also walked through the bright pool of light from the lantern.

Julie put a horrified hand to her mouth to stifle her gasp. She could not be mistaken; no one else had that tousled golden hair, that strong, broad physique, that purposeful gait. Yet she stared unbelieving as Hans returned through the lamplight, dragging the girl with him.

Julie stumbled through the house, her mind blank except for that image of Hans with the nameless prostitute. Though the lamp burned in the parlor, no one had waited up. Julie promised a special prayer of thanks for that; she could not have faced anyone after the shocks of that evening.

She collapsed onto her bed after she had forced herself through the rituals of removing skirt and blouse and underthings and slipping a nightdress over her head, of unplaiting and brushing her hair prior to rebraiding it for the night. Her arms ached, but the pain in her heart was worse, much worse.

Last Sunday, when she had so accidentally discovered that Morgan did not and could not want her, she had reluctantly allowed Hans to speak to her father. She had not told Morgan. She should have. Though no specific wedding date had been set, Wilhelm had agreed that autumn, when Hans had most of his work finished and before the busy spring calving season arrived, would be a good time for the marriage to take place. This would give ample time for the negotiations on Julie's dowry, a tradition both men insisted upon even though neither of them had any intention of returning to most other Old Country ways. And it would allow time for the less important aspects of the union, the things Julie needed to take care of: a wedding gown, trousseau, and acquisition of such items as she would need to set up housekeeping as Hans's wife.

She was too exhausted to dwell on it now, but though she fell asleep almost instantly, the thought remained with her and troubled her dreams. When she wakened not many minutes into the pinkness of dawn, the same worries nagged at her.

Hans wanted her; he had assured her of that every time they met since her arrival in Plato. He was not a man to declare his emotions in simple terms, but surely his insistence upon a wedding at the earliest possible date was proof of his desire for her. And he was respectable, something Morgan might or might not be two weeks or two years or two decades into the future.

After dressing quickly and quietly in the cool of her room, Julie slipped downstairs to begin breakfast. Already the morning promised more heat, but she knew mere sunlight could not match the burning torment in her soul.

She took her place in church with the rest of her family, joined, somewhat to her surprise, by Hans. Knowing that she could not confront him there and then, she forced herself to put on a smile to greet him. He did not immediately return it.

Nothing that the Reverend Wintergarden said penetrated her thoughts. She sang the hymns distractedly, losing her place more than once. She didn't even try to follow the sermon; she sank into her own world of hopes and dreams and nightmares and horrors and disappointments.

Hans who wanted her and had slapped the girl in the green dress. Hans who kissed her so clumsily and then blushed. Morgan and his cool, gentle kiss. Morgan and his fiery outburst as he confessed his debility to Hans. Ted Sheen, the man who had promised her so much. Lieutenant McWilliams, the soldier who had asked her for so much. Del Morgan, who had lost as much as she had, or maybe even more. Or maybe he simply had had more to lose.

After the benediction, she ducked out the side door as usual and fairly ran through the graveyard. She did not glance in the direction of Amy Morgan's grave, where the roses were a profusion of scarlet blushes now.

The churchyard gate was closed, but it took Julie only a few seconds to lift the bar and swing the portal open. When she turned to close it again, Hans was no more than four or five steps behind her.

"I'll walk you home, Julie," he said sternly with no joy or even hint of happiness.

She could not refuse his company.

She made certain no one else was within hearing and then she confronted him. The gate formed a barrier between them, one she intended to keep in position.

"I need to talk to you, Hans," she said. She could not meet his eyes, but she did not let her voice quaver at all. "I saw you last night with . . . with that girl from Nellie's. You hit her, and I want to know why."

He coughed, glanced around nervously, then tried to push the gate open. Julie held it firmly closed.

"I paid her for something and then she refused to give it to me, but it is not something for you to talk about. It is a man's thing. You must not even know about it."

"But I *do* know about it. Is it the first time, or do you always—"

"I said we do not talk about it. Now, come, we will go to your house and wait for your mama and papa. What is for dinner today?"

He tried again to force the gate, and he was stronger than she. She had no choice but to step out of his way or risk injury. Hans, she suddenly realized, would not hesitate to hurt her. He had hurt at least one woman before.

With the gate no longer a shield, Julie could merely back away from Hans, but he took her arm and began to lead her in the direction of her father's house.

"I want an answer," she demanded, jerking her elbow out of his grasp. "I will talk about it, and if not to you, then I will tell my father."

Hans took her arm again, holding too firmly

for her to escape without making a scene—and they were now in the middle of the street, with a crowd outside the church door to watch them.

"It is something a man must do," he hissed. "The women at that place are paid to do what men need. I paid her, too, but she would not go with me. A man must have what . . . what a man needs so he can be a man."

They had reached the gate to the Hollstroms' yard. Hans opened it with his free hand and pushed Julie through. Had she not seen Willy racing up behind them, she would have given full rein to her anger.

Willy captured Hans's attention with a display of his scar, thus allowing Julie to escape to the sanctuary of the kitchen. The smell of a savory stew bubbling on the stove brought her back to life from her momentary sojourn into hell.

She had not invited Morgan for dinner. Last night she had been in no state even to speak to him, much less encourage further contact. When she walked out of the office, she had had no idea what she would discover; she could not have foreseen the horror she felt even now at Hans's explanation. Stirring the rich gravy in which chunks of beef and carrots and potatoes and onions swam, she wondered if she would have invited Morgan had she seen him in church. He had not attended, though she did not know if he had gone home to sleep or if he was still watching his patient at the office.

Katharine came into the kitchen with a last little echo of laughter. Julie did not turn from her work, and in fact stirred the stew more vigorously.

"Dinner smells simply marvelous, dear. Is Dr. Morgan joining us again?"

Julie noted how carefully her mother's voice dropped for that question, as though she asked it in a kind of conspiratorial confidence.

"No, Mama, I didn't invite him."

"Oh." Was that disappointment Julie heard in her mother's voice? Perhaps not, for Katharine quickly changed the subject and returned to a normal tone. "I see Hans is all spruced up. That talk he had with your father must have put him in a regular courting mood."

Julie wanted to scream. She closed her eyes to still her temper, but she opened them quickly when Katharine came up beside her. She took the long spoon from her daughter's hand and sipped the stew herself.

"It tastes every bit as good as it smells, too. Will it be ready soon?"

"No, not for quite a while. The meat is not near done, and the potatoes are hard as rocks yet."

"Good. Then I shall have time for a little nap. I feel one of those terrible headaches coming on."

Katharine raised a hand to her temple and pressed slightly.

"But, Mama, you haven't had a headache since you started taking the new medicine from Dr. Morgan."

Julie set the spoon down and finally faced her mother with genuine concern. If Morgan's treatments didn't work, then she'd never be free of Katharine and Wilhelm and Willy.

"Well, you know he said it would take time. And I've been so busy this week, with you spending so much time with him. Perhaps I just overdid myself too soon. I'm sure a little nap and a sip of his medicine will help considerably."

She swept out of the room without another word to Julie, gave her excuses to the two men in the parlor, and climbed the stairs. Julie heard the bedroom door close, but though she listened carefully for the squeak of her mother's bedsprings, the sound never came.

Harry slept through the night, allowing Morgan fitful rest of his own. The sun was well up before either man stirred. Harry's first feeble groans brought Morgan instantly to his bare feet and racing into the other room.

"Don't try to get up," he cautioned the still-groggy victim. "Tell me what you want and I'll get it for you."

"Where the hell am I? And what the hell happened to me?"

"You were shot, three times. I spent most of yesterday taking one bullet out of your leg and sewing up the holes from the others."

Harry slowly explored the bandages, coming eventually to the painful area of the shoulder wound itself.

"It come out the back, too?" he asked, unable to reach that far.

Morgan nodded even while he rubbed his eyes and yawned. His stomach growled almost as loudly.

"How 'bout my leg? You have to cut it off?" He couldn't reach past the bandages that shrouded the upper half of his thigh.

"No, it's still there, and likely to be for a good long time. But you'll be laid up for a week or so at least."

"Aw, shit!"

The big body went angrily limp.

"I gotta file my claim in Prescott before the end of the week or I lose it to my ex-partner's wife."

Morgan pulled up a chair and sat down, placing his hand on Harry's broad forehead. There was no sign of fever.

"Well, today's only Sunday. Maybe by Thursday you'll be recovered enough to get on the stage to Prescott. If you take it easy until then, that is. You want some breakfast?"

That idea seemed to cheer the invalid.

"Yeah. 'Bout two dozen eggs over easy, a whole slab o' bacon, ten pounds o' potatoes, and a gallon o' coffee. And gimme the coffee first."

"I'll be back in a few minutes," Morgan said while he pulled on his socks and boots. "I've got a neighbor who does my cooking, so I'll go order up some breakfast."

"I hope she's a good cook, and fast."

After straightening up his appearance as much as possible, Morgan saw to other, more immediate needs of his patient, then went to find Winnie.

He crossed the street just as the preacher, his voice carrying through the open doorway, called upon the congregation to rise for the closing hymn. Winnie would be there still, as well as Julie and her family. Morgan refused to think about her. He hurried to his own house, quickly wrote out a note for Winnie that he slid under her door, and then was about to return to Harry. But he remembered that church would be letting out just then, with the townspeople milling about outside the door and in the street. He could not face them yet. Maybe in a week or two. He especially did not want to see Julie.

He walked upstairs and out onto the rooftop, where his two cauldrons of water sat in the early-morning sunlight. The night had been warm; the water was sufficiently heated for washing and would take only a few minutes to heat for shaving. He might as well make himself presentable while he waited for the Sunday morning crowd to disperse.

The house was cool, much cooler than the sunny patio outside the second floor. Morgan stripped off his shirt and washed right there. He liked the invigorating warmth that followed a morning scrub, and the soft early breeze provided a much gentler towel than one washed in Winnie's homemade soap. While he splashed the suds off, he let his gaze wander to the stream

of townsfolk coming from the church. He swore
to himself he wasn't watching for her.

But he saw her nonetheless, alerted by the
bright sun on the pale coronet of her hair. She
had done the braids differently this morning,
winding them around the top of her head like a
tiara rather than in a simple knot at the back of
her neck. Her dress was a dark blue calico, not
nearly as faded as most she wore, but the color
did not suit her at all. On Amy, with her dark
auburn hair and jewel-bright eyes, such a dress
would have looked quaintly becoming. On Julie,
it made her look every inch the drudge she was.

Yet when he saw the figure in the dark suit
join her at the cemetery gate, Morgan thought
only of how pretty Julie's face had been in the
lamplight of the surgery when she concentrated
all her efforts on saving a man's life. He recognized Hans and wondered immediately why the
farmer had suddenly shown up in something
other than his work clothes.

Morgan picked up the bucket he had filled
with his shaving water and stormed back into
the upper hallway, slamming the oaken door
behind him. He had seen Julie submit to Hans's
taking her elbow to lead her home; he did not
see her throw that hand off.

Katharine's headache did not go away. She
did not come down for dinner and merely picked
at the servings brought up on a tray for her. For
once, Julie came close to enjoying waiting on her

mother; it kept her away from Hans, who had announced immediately after Wilhelm's grace that he intended to begin making wedding plans.

Though Julie had no appetite herself, she knew she had gone too long without food and forced herself to eat. She tasted nothing. The slow-cooked stew might as well have been warmed-up mud, and the crumbly, sweet corn-bread stuck drily to the roof of her mouth. But her thoughts of Morgan reminded her of her promise to him to take better care of herself.

But for what? She remembered the way he pushed her from him last night after that moment of sweet insanity. The disgust in his voice when he sent her home could not have been clearer. Yes, they had been tired, and yes, they had been elated over Harry's survival. But it hadn't taken Morgan long to realize Julie wasn't the wife he had once shared such victories with. She wasn't Amy and never would be.

Julie started to choke on a piece of meat but quickly washed it down with a sip of lemonade. Hans looked across the table at her, but almost immediately he returned to his food. He, too, ate in silence, except for infrequent statements about his plans for the future. When neither Julie nor Wilhelm responded to his ideas, he returned to his meal. Julie suspected that if he had spoken a single word directly to her, she would have burst into tears and run from the room, possibly even from the house.

She washed the dishes without assistance, tak

ing her time to delay joining the men in the parlor. She desperately wanted to know how Harry was and even contemplated a brief escape from the kitchen to visit the doctor and find out. But she knew it wasn't curiosity about Harry alone that prompted her thoughts.

It was impossible not to hear Hans's half of the conversation in the parlor. Wilhelm could, when he so wished, keep his voice down. Hans could not, and the more excited he was, the louder his voice became. He was excited now.

"I will need a new barn before winter, too. I have more cows this year than last, and I will need space for the heifers born this spring."

Wilhelm mumbled something too quietly for Julie to hear, but she wondered, while her father spoke, what Hans needed with another barn. Hadn't he bragged just a few weeks ago about how large and clean and spacious his current barn was? Hadn't he told her he built it much bigger than his present herd needed because he was counting on the increase? Maybe he had, or maybe she had misunderstood him. She rarely paid close attention to him; maybe he had only been speaking of plans then, too.

"The house is plenty big, but I don't have so much furniture for myself, so I will have to buy more when I have a wife. She must have a nice place to work, a new stove, curtains, a big dining room table for all our sons."

Julie warned herself sternly: All farmers want

sons to help with the labor; I mustn't hold that against him.

But when she tried to argue that even Del Morgan had wanted his son, she found an ache tightening in the back of her throat. Morgan hadn't wanted sons to work in his fields and tend his livestock: he wanted that baby because it was something he and his wife had created out of love. Hans, Julie suspected, would never understand that. She swallowed the lump and started drying plates.

Katharine called from the top of the stairs just as Julie finished cleaning the kitchen. She wanted a pitcher of fresh water.

"And could you help me out of this dress? I just don't think I'm going to feel well enough to join your father and our guest this afternoon. My headache isn't getting any better. Do you think you ought to bring Dr. Morgan here to see if he can do anything?"

Although the bed was turned down, Katharine hadn't been in it. She had sat in her little chair by the window, and when she noticed how Julie stared accusingly in that direction, Katharine gave a weak smile and an easy alibi.

"It's so much cooler by the window, you know. I get so warm lying down and I wear my poor hand out with that fan."

Julie could not deny that there was a breeze, unusual as it was to come out of the east. And though it wasn't cool, it did stir the air enough to be more comfortable than lying on a feather-bed.

"I'll see if I can find him. I'm not sure he's at the office; he may have gone home, depending on how Harry is."

"Harry? Is that the poor man who was shot so badly? I didn't know you had learned his name."

Julie unfastened the long row of buttons down the front of her mother's blouse.

"We haven't learned his real name, but we had to call him something. He has such very hairy legs that 'Harry' seemed quite natural."

"Is Dr. Morgan confident of his survival?"

"Relatively." Julie pulled the sleeve over the splinted arm, then loosened the stays while Katharine unbuttoned and stepped out of her skirt. Thinking of Morgan's confidence brought back the memory of that celebration kiss last night. Bittersweet. Julie knew the meaning now.

"Well, I do hope he can spare a few minutes away from this hairy Harry to come see me," Katharine added as she lay down on the bed. "Of course, you mustn't tell your father what you just told me. I mean, about the man's legs. Good heavens!"

Julie heard very little of her mother's last words. She had gone back to the window to close the shade and make the room dark for Katharine to rest better, and she had seen the view from the window. Only from the odd angle of Katharine's chair could she see across the

street and down the little lane to the adobe house
with the patio on the roof.

Chapter Sixteen
✦ ✦ ✦ ✦

KATHARINE FELT SUFFICIENTLY recovered, after Morgan prescribed a mild sedative Sunday evening,
to help Julie with the laundry and baking Monday morning. Though the chores still weren't
done until almost one o'clock in the afternoon,
Julie had time to dash over to the clinic shortly
after nine to check on Harry.

"To begin with," Morgan told her, "his real
name is Thaddeus Burton, he has a legitimate
claim to a mine just beyond where Louie's
friends shot him, and he's doing damn fine. I
hope to keep him in bed another day or two, if
possible, but I doubt he'll stay put past tomorrow afternoon. He's already pestering me about
crutches."

They sat in the kitchen over cups of inky coffee, Morgan looking far better than he had last
evening. Perhaps he had taken a dose of the
sedative himself.

"How's your mother today?" he asked when
Julie had sat in stony silence for a long while.

She hadn't even sipped at her coffee, though he knew he had made it much too strong for her. "Did she sleep well?"

"Just fine, she says. She helped me with the laundry this morning, if that's any indication."

He nodded and drained his cup.

"I think her diagnosis last night was pretty accurate," he commented, getting up to refill the mug. "She's going too fast, trying to do too much before she's really ready. She has to take it easier and not expect so much of herself."

He peered over the rim of the cup at Julie and wondered what her reaction to that news would be. It was not what he had expected.

She took a deep breath as though striving for patience and then let it out with a long, slow sigh. He hated it when her shoulders slumped like that and her features seemed to sag with defeat.

"I'll try to be more helpful," she said. "I blame myself partly for her relapse, because I've taken such advantage of her this past week. I won't do it again, I promise."

She got up to leave, having barely touched her coffee. He could see the weight of guilt she bore even for that simple sin. And who was she to worry about taking advantage? He wanted to throw his cup on the floor in anger, but it was the floor that Julie had so patiently scrubbed and kept so spotless; he would not add to her burden.

Yet hadn't he already added to it with his lies? Katharine's headache last night was no more real than any of her other complaints, and the sedative he had given her was nothing but a combination of vinegar, sugar, and enough of Horace's scotch to make it taste like medicine. The cure was as phony as the ailment. But Julie's guilt was genuine—and wholly without cause.

He hated these lies and wondered where the truth was hidden, how deeply it might be buried.

"Don't go yet, Julie, unless you have to. I need to talk to you about a few things."

She turned slowly, but did not move away from the door.

"Please sit down, or do you have something urgent to get back to?" he asked.

She shook her head.

"No, not for a while. The dough is rising, and I have no more room on the clothesline just now until some of the other laundry is dry."

"Good. Then we can talk."

He told himself he wasn't going to add to the stack of lies he'd already told. He was merely seeking another route to the truth.

"To begin with, you shouldn't be baking bread in this kind of weather. Ask Mrs. Alvarez to show you how to make flour tortillas or something, but you've got to learn you can't cook the way you did in Minnesota, for heaven's sake."

"But my father—"

"Damn your father, Julie. When it's over a hundred degrees outside, you can't fire up an iron cookstove to bake bread without risking your health."

"I'm sorry," she apologized like an unjustly chastised child.

Morgan drew back and calmed his anger.

"No, Julie, I'm the one who's sorry. I didn't mean to yell at you like that, though I did mean what I said. But it's really your mother I wanted to talk about."

"Mama?"

"Don't panic; she's doing fine, better in fact than I had expected." That much at least was true. He hadn't thought Katharine would shed her old habits so quickly. "But I need some additional information on her medical history to determine what course the treatment should take now."

"I thought you had asked her all the questions you needed."

"I did, I did; but sometimes it helps to get another person's viewpoint. We don't always tell the whole truth about ourselves, you know."

All the blood drained from her face, and her heart stopped beating for a second or two. He couldn't know, she assured herself. He's just a doctor asking perfectly normal questions. He can't know everything; he can't.

"You said your mother went into this decline, for lack of a better term, after Willy was born. That would have been when you were seventeen, right?"

"Yes. I had just turned seventeen. My birthday is the end of July; Willy was born the end of August."

"Then you were old enough to remember

most of the details. Was there any problem with your mother's pregnancy? Did she have a great deal of illness, morning sickness, was she confined to bed for any reason?"

"No, not that I remember. Papa worked in a bank then, and we lived on the edge of town, but Mama used to walk to the post office almost every day, and it was half a mile or more."

Some color came back to her cheeks, though they remained pale. Something he said had frightened her. Whatever it was that brought that look of terror to her eyes every now and then was connected to her mother, and quite possibly to Willy, too. Morgan recalled, in a quick few seconds, the times he had thought the relationship was just a bit odd. Now he was certain of it. When he mentioned Willy's birth, the girl had gasped and turned white as a sheet.

"Then if her pregnancy was normal, did she have difficulty in the delivery?"

"I don't know. I wasn't there when he was born. I just know that he wasn't due until October and he came early. Mama was sick for several weeks afterward. I helped to take care of her, but Papa had the doctor in almost every day, for her and for Willy."

She rolled the hem of her apron around her finger, then unrolled it. Morgan knew she would not meet his gaze, though he kept it trained carefully on her. She was worse at lying than he, and he was terrible.

But he wasn't accomplishing anything either, except to make her squirm, and he didn't want to do that. He didn't dare pry any further. Old habits were hard to break; in Cincinnati one knew everything about everyone, but in Arizona one didn't know and one didn't ask. He'd been in Arizona too long.

And the question that hung in his mind now was one he simply could not bring himself to ask, not of her.

"Well, that doesn't help me much, but it's a start. Thanks, Julie."

She could have left then, but she remained by the back door, still twisting her apron around her finger. Instead of divulging a part of the secret he knew she had to be keeping, she merely offered him lunch.

"I have some stew left over from yesterday, more than we'll eat. Would you like me to bring some over for you and Mr. Burton, or is Miss Upshaw planning to provide your meals today?"

"No, Winnie's busy at the house today. I hadn't given much thought to lunch. I'm sure Mr. Burton would be happy to have some of your stew, and I know I would. That includes some of that fresh bread I warned you about, doesn't it?"

He was teasing, very gently, but his smile soon brought hers out of hiding.

"If I get myself back to work, some fresh butter for it as well." She laughed.

Her laughter did not last, however, for as soon as she had left his kitchen, her thoughts and fears returned. By the time she reached her own porch, her forehead was creased with worry.

If Morgan knew about her and Ted, then Hans must have told him. No one else could have. Katharine knew, of course, and Wilhelm, but they were as sworn to secrecy as Julie herself, for the same reasons. Willy had never been told, but Hans knew, and Hans, as Julie knew only too well, was cruel enough to expose her. Cruel enough, her conscience tried to reason, but why would he do it? She could come up with no reason and finally forced herself to accept Morgan's curiosity about Willy's birth as nothing more than what he had said.

The dough was ready for the oven, and when she had set the loaves in to bake, Julie took the last of the laundry outside. She took down what was dry and hung up what was wet, but she could not get the nagging fear out of her mind.

Morgan knew something. Or at least he held some very strong suspicions. Julie hadn't missed his hesitation or his caution in the way he phrased his few queries. He was clearly looking for something other than just her mother's medical history. Was it something about Julie herself? And why would he care?

Del Morgan still mourned his wife and still loved her as he had when she was alive. As for that kiss Saturday night, it was nothing but an overflow of good feeling at having saved a man's life. If he had wanted—but she refused to follow that line of thought.

Katharine, who had not been in the kitchen when Julie returned from Morgan's, now sat at the table with a cup of fresh tea. And the mail.

She must have walked to the post office, something she had not done, not alone, in the last nine years.

"A letter from Uncle Max, in German of course," Katharine said. "*Godey's*, with at least three dresses I want."

Julie shrugged. She had more imporant things to worry about than a letter from her father's uncle and a fashion magazine. She quickly forgot them both and tended to her chores. There was butter to churn from the cream Hans had brought her yesterday, and ironing, which she hated only slightly less than scrubbing floors. Beds needed to be made, though Katharine had already done the dusting.

When Julie sat down at the table to begin churning, Katharine had resumed her page by page perusal of the new *Godey's*. The pages turned in accompaniment to the rhythm of the churn.

"You ought to think about your wedding dress soon," Katharine remarked lazily. "If you want something elaborate, you'd best get started. Working for Dr. Morgan doesn't leave you much time to sew."

"I wasn't planning to have an extravagant gown, Mama. The weather will still be warm, so I thought perhaps just a simple summer dress in white muslin, with some lace maybe."

"That would be nice. I'm sure Hans won't mind. He'll be happy just to see the long wait over."

"Yes, I'm sure he will," Julie agreed, thinking

of the woman from Nellie's. Then she remembered why she had gone to see Morgan in the morning.

Katharine continued to chatter, about dresses and accessories, about hats and shoes and gloves, about lace and ribbons and all the things a mother should discuss with a daughter about to become a bride. But Julie hardly heard. She didn't want to hear. The more her mother talked about the coming event, the more Julie wanted to call it off. She could not help reliving that horrible scene of a man striking a woman and dragging her away. Julie felt almost as if she had been the one slapped in the alley and so rudely possessed. So strong was the anger she felt rising within her that she found relief when Wilhelm walked up the steps for lunch.

When lunch was over, she washed the dishes with Willy's help, then finished the beds and excused herself to join Morgan. She did not notice, in her haste, how her mother smiled when she watched her daughter snatch off her apron, smooth back a few loose strands of hair, and dash out the front door. It was a smile of almost complete satisfaction, of self-congratulation, of triumph.

Thaddeus Burton sat propped up in bed, his chest and belly covered by a voluminous nightshirt. Morgan settled a legged tray over the man's lap and then Julie placed the plate of stew and several slices of bread on the invalid's table.

Burton drew in a long, deep breath.

"Sure smells good, Miss Hollstrom. Been a long time since I ate this kinda food."

He looked pale, faded like washed-out flannel, but his appetite was good, and his sense of humor intact.

"Just take it easy," Morgan cautioned. "This'll build up your strength and maybe we can have you up and out of bed tonight."

"I sure hope so. I gotta get to Prescott Friday." He took a big spoonful of stew, chewed it with the enjoyment of a man who had only eggs and soup yesterday, then smiled broadly at Julie.

"Tastes even better'n it smells. And I guess I gotta thank you along with the doc here for savin' my hide."

She blushed, but didn't stammer when she told him, "I'm really just an extra pair of hands. Dr. Morgan tells me what to do, and I follow his orders. But you're quite welcome, Mr. Burton, both for the help I rendered the other night and for the stew."

While Burton ate, Morgan led Julie into the kitchen, where he had made fresh coffee, weaker than usual. When he offered her a cup, she took it and actually drank some.

"What are we going to do today?" she asked. "I can start cleaning the upstairs, if you like."

"I think we can let that go another day or two. Besides, I have other tasks for you today that won't wear you to a nub." He had seen the laundry she had done that morning, and he knew the washing wasn't the worst of it. "I got a load of supplies in on this morning's stage, so you can put them away for me. Do you know how to check items received against the list that I ordered?"

"Yes, but then what? Surely that won't take all afternoon."

"It won't. I'm sure we'll have a few callers, too. And you can help me put my sign back up."

"Your sign?"

"Winnie found my old shingle last week and had it spruced up for me. I was going to have it up to surprise you, but I got busy this morning with Mr. Burton and with another small emergency."

"Was it serious? Why didn't you call me?" Julie asked, worried that something might have gone wrong.

Morgan bit his tongue, angry that he had let that information out. He hadn't intended to tell her at all, which was precisely why he hadn't sent Nellie for her when the brassy-haired madame brought in the girl with the black eye and swollen lip.

"It wasn't anything I couldn't handle on my own. I knew you were busy yourself."

He felt relieved when she didn't press him for details. Nellie had lied, saying the girl had fallen down the stairs that morning. The cut on her lip was half healed, and an eye doesn't blacken in a matter of hours. She'd been beaten up by a customer, probably Saturday night. Nellie, knowing Morgan was busy with the shot-up stranger, must have waited until Monday.

He shouldn't have kept the information from Julie, he told himself. She'd soon see enough of the girls. And Julie Hollstrom didn't seem the type who needed much protection from the cruder aspects of life. Burton's half-naked body hadn't shocked her sensibilities. But it wasn't the impropriety of Maude's profession that kept Morgan from discussing the case. It was what he knew about Hans Wallenmund.

He was about to change the subject entirely when Burton called from the other room to announce he had finished his lunch and wanted some more.

Morgan got up, gesturing to Julie to remain seated and drink her coffee. He took the tray and dishes from his patient while explaining that he didn't want the man overdoing it yet. He promised as much as Burton could eat for supper, but one serving of lunch was enough.

"Well, you tell that Miss Hollstrom she sure is a damn fine cook." Burton's voice carried through the house, as though he wanted Julie to hear for herself. She smiled privately at his compliment and tried desperately, but as unsuccessfully as ever, not to blush. But she soon learned that his voice boomed naturally. Even when he dropped it to what he called a whisper, she heard every word.

"Hey, doc, before ya go, kin I ask somethin'? I ain't meaning to pry, but I couldn't help seein' that little girl that come in this morning. Did somebody do that to her?"

Morgan, in the doorway with his back to the

hall, said something too quietly for Julie to understand. She thought from the tone of his voice that he reassured his patient there was nothing to worry about, or to worry about his own injuries before someone else's.

"Well, like I said, I was just wonderin'. I know I look like a big mean bugger, but there ain't nothin' makes me madder'n seein' a girl, even one like her, git beat up by a man. If you say she just fell, well, I'll believe you. She sure looked terrible, though."

A thousand explanations for Thaddeus Burton's words came to Julie, but she rejected them all. Maybe she hadn't had on a green dress this morning, but the patient with the small emergency must have been the girl Hans hit outside the general store Saturday night. Recalling the incident, Julie doubted a single slap had done the damage Burton had seen; Hans must have beaten her later, in the privacy of her room at Nellie's establishment. Julie felt that pain herself, and the helpless horror of the girl forced to submit.

Morgan carried the tray to the kitchen and set it on the table.

"Do you want to do these dishes now, before they dry, or let them go for a while?" he asked.

"I'll just run them home and take care of them now. I left the dishwater for them, anyway."

But as she stacked the silverware on the plate and reached for the cup, Julie's fingers trembled. Burton's big voice, so full of concern, echoed in her ears, and her eyes could see nothing but those shadowed figures in the pale yellow light of Simon McCrory's porch lantern. The cup, containing a mouthful of stale coffee, slipped from her hand and shattered on the floor.

Julie's nerves shattered with it. She gave a little cry of surprise, then fell to her knees. She picked up the scattered pieces of pottery, keeping her head down to be sure Morgan wouldn't see her uncontrollable tears until she could stop them—somehow.

"How clumsy of me!" She managed to laugh as Morgan handed her a towel to blot up the spill. She rattled the remnants of the cup in her hand to cover the sound of a sniffle.

Oh, God, she *had* been crying. He saw the droplets on her lashes now. But the brave face she presented to him told him she did not want her weakness acknowledged by anyone but herself.

In her normal tone of voice she said, "I couldn't help but hear what Mr. Burton said about the little girl. Was she hurt badly?"

Thaddeus had indeed said "little girl," though both he and Morgan knew he hadn't meant a child. The physician was relieved to find such a convenient falsehood come to his rescue. He took the fragments of coffee cup from Julie's hand and dumped them into the nail keg by the back door, then helped her to her feet again. There was a stain of coffee at the knee of her skirt.

"She'll be fine, Julie. I said it was a small thing. She cut her lip and blackened her eye, that's all."

Julie didn't seem very relieved. Her brow remained puckered, and her eyes, though they didn't turn away from him, seemed still to be asking questions.

Something told him he needed to bring her back to reality from some curiously distant thoughts. "Aren't you going to take these dishes to wash them?" he asked gently.

"In a few minutes. Please, Dr. Morgan, I need to talk to you. I know you'll tell me I should ask questions like these of my mother, but I can't. She wouldn't give me answers; she'd just tell me . . . well, she wouldn't give me the kind of answers you can. You're a doctor."

The rambling gave away her nervousness. She sat at the table and linked her fingers around her coffee cup, barely half full. Morgan, afraid he'd be called to task for his lie, busied himself refilling his own and then stood discreetly against the oak cupboard, three or four feet away from the table.

Pieces of a very unattractive jigsaw puzzle began to come together in his mind. The girl's dislike for men, her parents' insistence that she be made to look as unattractive as possible, her constant burden of guilt and responsibility, her almost maternal concern for Willy when he was hurt, her lack of the usual modesty when Peg Hollis delivered. And now her breakdown over the discovery that one of Nellie's soiled doves had been beaten up by a customer. Morgan didn't delude himself any longer. Julie had heard Burton's comments and interpreted them correctly. Morgan would only be hurting her further himself if he continued to lie.

"I'll do my best, Julie. Ask me anything you like. I'll give you the most honest answer I can, and if I don't know the answer, I'll tell you so."

She swallowed some coffee, then looked at him.

"Can Mr. Burton hear us?" she whispered.

"No, I closed the doors, and he'll be asleep soon anyway. I gave him a light sedative in his coffee, and he was yawning before he finished your lunch." That seemed to reassure her, but Morgan went one step further. "And whatever you tell me I'll keep in strictest confidence. You needn't worry that I'll tell anyone, not even your parents."

"I didn't think you would."

How trusting her eyes were then, as wide as they had been before in fear but open now and believing as they met his. She didn't smile, but for almost the first time since he had met her, Morgan thought she looked hopeful.

Chapter Seventeen

❖❖❖❖

"I MEANT TO tell you last week, but we were so busy," Julie began. She forced the words to come slowly, calmly.

"Tell me what?"

"My father has given his permission for Hans to marry me." She added quickly, "No date has been set for the wedding, because Papa wants to wait to see how Mama responds to your treatment. He seems pleased with her progress so far, but of course it's really too early to tell much, isn't it?"

"Much too soon." It was a prayer as much as an agreement.

"I'm sure the wedding won't be scheduled sooner than October, when Hans is finished with his harvest. Do you suppose you'll be able to tell about Mama by then? That's three months away."

Morgan remained wary. Not once had Julie referred to the wedding as hers or even "ours." And there was no excitement in her proclamation. How could a woman, even one as sensible and reserved as Julie Hollstrom, not shout the news to the world?

"I imagine we can make a fairly accurate guess about your mother's progress by then, but I can't promise anything at this point."

"No, of course not. Anyway, I wanted to tell you about this before I started asking questions you might think improper for a single woman."

"Nothing is improper except ignorance, Julie." Against his better judgment, Morgan left his post by the cupboard and came to sit with her. "I don't suppose your mother ever told you what we euphemistically call 'the facts of life.' It's nothing to be ashamed of, or frightened of."

It's beautiful, it's sweet, it's wonderful, it's glorious, he wanted to tell her as all the old feelings rushed back at him. When it's right, when a man and a woman love each other, there is nothing more exquisitely delightful in the whole world.

But that wasn't the kind of answer he could give Julie Hollstrom. He had the feeling it wasn't the kind of answer she wanted to hear.

"Oh, I know the mechanics of it." Her hands found the corner of the tablecloth to twist. "Rinton, Indiana, was a farming town, so I kind of grew up knowing 'the facts of life.' "

She tossed the wrinkled corner of checkered cloth away and swallowed her shyness.

"I want the truth, Dr. Morgan," she said quietly. "I saw Hans and that girl from Nellie's Saturday night. He slapped her and dragged her down the alley. No, don't try to tell me I was mistaken. I confronted him yesterday after church, and he didn't deny it, so don't you."

That surprised Morgan almost as much as Julie's stern defiance. He hadn't expected Wallenmund to own up to his sins so readily. Only maybe Hans didn't consider his actions very sinful.

"He said that what he did with that girl was something he needed to be a man. Is that true? Do men really *need* women that way?"

Of all the questions he had expected her to ask, this was not among them.

She looked so innocent, waiting for his reply, and yet when he searched her eyes he found the fear that still lurked. He was certain, however, that at least at this moment she was not afraid of *him*. She did indeed trust him, and he felt a stir of pride at that. He had done little enough to deserve it, but he would do his best to keep it.

He also knew that what he was about to tell her could not help but hurt. If she had come for reassurance, she would not get it from him, for he could not give it. He was going to call the man she had agreed to marry ignorant at best, a liar at worst.

The truth hurts, he had been told so many times, but lies destroy. He would not see Julie Hollstrom destroyed.

"Some men do have needs, Julie, just the way Hans told you. But some of us consider what we have with a woman to be a very special thing." Strange phrases started into his head even as he tried to keep his concentration on a calm, sane, respectable answer to her question. "Men sometimes get this proprietary feeling about their women, and you know as well as I that an adulterous woman is rarely tolerated by her husband, while a woman is expected to ignore her husband's indiscretions.''

He was off on a tangent, expressing what he thought must be Julie's feelings, though she didn't seem at all hurt that Hans had strayed. Maybe she just thought that, as a still-unmarried man, he was free to indulge his lusts any way he chose. Morgan chided himself for putting his own opinion into the picture when he had only been asked for facts.

"I'm sorry, Julie, I didn't mean to rant and rave that way.''

"But what you said is true. Women do accept their husbands' infidelities. What choice do they have?''

Julie Hollstrom still had a choice. She was not yet bound to this man she had promised to marry. Morgan, shaking his head to silence the insanities of dreams he could never realize, determined to make her aware of that choice.

Don't let her marry the bastard, insisted one of those crazy little insanities, one that wouldn't be shaken loose.

"Not all men are like that, Julie. From the day I met Amy, I never touched another woman. I never wanted to. I waited three years before we were married, and I never regretted it.''

"Hans has waited six.''

No, he hasn't, Morgan wanted to spit out. Hans has just been biding his time, entertaining himself with the whores. And I'll bet he never gives you a second's thought while he's lying with another woman.

But when Morgan tried to phrase that vicious answer in more suitable terms, he looked at Julie and knew he didn't need to. She understood completely.

"You loved Amy very much, didn't you? More than you think Hans loves me."

He felt awkward. He'd let himself get caught up in his old feelings again and said things he shouldn't have. He lifted his coffee cup to give himself a chance to think, but the cup was empty. Even the dregs had dried, leaving only a dark ring on the bottom of the cup.

"I can't judge his feelings, Julie. I shouldn't have said what I did, and I'm sorry for that. You asked me a simple question and I've made a real muddle of things. I should have said, yes, some men need sex on a regular basis and others do quite well without it. Some don't seem to care who they have it with, others abhor the thought of touching a woman they don't truly love."

"Like you and Amy."

"What Amy and I had was very rare. I don't expect to see the like of it again. I never touched another woman. When Amy was pregnant and very, very ill, I didn't ask her to submit to my attentions. I didn't even have any desires then, because I knew she wouldn't respond. Without that, it would have been nothing. That was the beauty of it, the sharing, the joy we had together."

She had never seen him like this and knew that it was the thoughts of Amy that lit his eyes with that golden emerald brightness. He loved his wife as much now, six years in her grave, as he had the day she died. No mortal woman could hope to compete with a memory like the one captured in Amy's wedding portrait, much less the one that lived in Morgan's heart.

Julie, accustomed to disguising her emotions, carefully hid her disappointment. Some of it escaped, however, and Morgan did not miss the dimming of the hopeful spark in her eyes. Where there had before been a dream of a smile on her lips, now there was only patient resignation.

He was about to apologize, for he had not realized how deeply his words wounded. He had given her a glimpse of the unattainable, a peek into a paradise she could never enter, and now she faced her marriage—which even earlier he honestly doubted she anticipated with any great joy—with a sense of loss, for it could never be what he and Amy had had.

But the man who had come Saturday with the boil on his face came again, knocking on the closed front door. Julie went to answer the summons, glad of the diversion that kept her from confessing all that was in her heart.

Morgan watched her walk from the kitchen through the parlor and to the door. Her shoulders didn't bow under the weight of her acceptance. As though she defied disappointment, she faced her future with a kind of pride. It made her all the more pitiable, all the more desirable.

* * *

Morgan ran his fingers through his hair, squeezing the water until it trickled down his wet back. The breeze chilled him, warm as it was, for the water had been warmer, here on the roof all day.

Throughout the long day he had tried to find the words to explain to Julie that he had made a mistake. Whenever he had finally put together a speech that expressed his feelings accurately but stayed within the bounds of propriety, then another patient walked through the office door. As soon as each crisis—and there were a dozen of them—had passed, then the words were gone, too.

She made him feel so damn clumsy. When they worked, he moved with the old confidence, as though he had never been away from his work. And Julie fit in so well that he was hardly aware of her except as an extension of himself. All of that changed the instant he tried to talk to her as a human being rather than as his nurse.

He was too tired to lie out here long. He wanted to curl up and go to sleep after a long day, something he could not do comfortably on the roof tiles.

Inside, where the dim starlight did not reach, he groped his way to the bedroom. Everything was as it should be, he noted: the single bed, the little table, the photograph. He sat on the edge of the bed and reached for the portrait.

"It never gets any easier." He sighed. He touched the roses lying on her lap, remembering how she had pressed them in the Bible.

He stretched out on the bed, propping a pillow behind his head and standing the picture on his chest. He stared at the sepia portrait, searching for answers to unasked questions. The longer he looked at Amy, the more he thought of Julie. She was a puzzle he couldn't figure out. He didn't think she loved Hans, yet she seemed determined to go through with the marriage.

"And what the *hell* does she feel so damn guilty about?" Morgan asked the night's silence.

He received no answer. Exhausted and frustrated because that and so many other questions would not let him sleep, he got out of bed and stumbled down to the kitchen, which was dark as a cave.

In the pantry, behind a sack of cornmeal, lay the other bottle of Horace's scotch. Morgan closed his fingers securely around the neck. It was cold comfort clutched to his naked chest. As he sat down at the table and reached for the cork, he realized with a sardonic laugh that he couldn't indulge in his old vices the way he used to. Someone might come pounding on the door at any moment, and how would it look if the doctor answered that summons drunk and buck naked?

"Three, four weeks ago it wouldn't have mattered," he told the dark house as he mounted the stairs again. "No one bothered drunk Del Morgan. He could sleep naked in his kitchen any time he wanted to, and sometimes did. Now he has to put his pants on. He has to be *respectable*, and respectable doctors don't sit naked in their kitchens with a bottle of fine whiskey."

He had to set the bottle down to pull his trousers up, button the fly, and tighten the belt, but as soon as he was decent, he picked up the bottle and walked out onto the roof.

Stars dazzled him in a moonless sky. He picked out the summer constellations: Scorpio, Libra, the Great Bear as constant as ever. Cold, distant little lights always out of reach.

He went back into the house and dragged the mattress to the roof. Respectable or not, he wasn't stupid enough to do without some comfort. He lay down on the bare mattress and cradled the back of his head on his cupped palms.

He needed answers. Julie Hollstrom had brought him back from one corner of hell, but the torment hadn't ended.

He reached for the bottle of scotch and wrestled the cork from it. Some of it spilled out onto his hand; he wiped it on the seat of his pants. The smell almost sickened him.

No amount of liquor could bring Amy back, and Morgan discovered suddenly that he no longer wanted the empty oblivion. He wanted Julie, and whiskey wouldn't pry her loose from Hans Wallenmund.

What would? he wondered as he yawned and stretched and finally closed his eyes. Money? Was it paying off that mysterious debt to her father that kept Julie tied to the farmer she didn't love? Morgan rolled over in anger and knocked the whiskey bottle on its side. He grabbed it and as he set it safely away from his impromptu bed he remembered something Julie had told him just that morning.

Her father had worked in a bank. In Rinton, Indiana. Adam St. Rogers was practically right next door in Ohio. If anyone could find out the truth about Wilhelm Hollstrom and his family, it was Adam St. Rogers.

Julie called his name twice, then climbed the stairs with a heavy heart. The doorway to the rooftop stood open, and Julie saw the bare mattress with the whiskey bottle not far away.

Morgan stood by the wall, facing the backyard and the rising sun. Bare-chested, barefoot, unshaven, he turned and greeted her quietly.

"Good morning, Julie. I'm late again, aren't I."

She nodded, unable to speak, then quickly averted her eyes. She had been devouring him unashamedly with her gaze.

"Have I embarrassed you, Julie?"

"Yes—no. I mean, I wasn't expecting . . ."

Her voice trailed off even as he watched her. In the morning light she looked fresh and innocent, though her green skirt showed signs of mending and her yellow blouse, clean from yesterday's laundry, was worn thin at the elbows. He knew her hair was long in that tightly coiled bun, but even the severe style couldn't dim the shimmer of summer sun on spun silver. It glowed like a halo above her bowed head.

She's beautiful, he thought, more beautiful than I ever imagined.

He walked to the bottle and leaned over to pick it up. Julie watched, trying to hide her disappointment.

"Here, take it," he ordered. "Look at it."

"No, I don't even want to touch it."

"But I want you to. See?" He pointed to the level of liquid inside. "It's full."

Finally, slowly, she looked up.

He gave her a grin that crinkled his eyes, that glittered in those gold-green depths.

"You didn't drink it?"

"Not a drop."

She hesitated a moment before mirroring his smile, and when his arms opened, she went into them just as reluctantly. It wasn't proper, not at all. He was practically naked, and she was more than practically engaged. Worse yet, she understood the danger far better than he, because if Morgan was merely seeking congratulations on his victory, Julie found much more.

Chapter Eighteen
✦✦✦✦✦

JULY SIZZLED ITS way toward August, one busy day at a time. Thaddeus Burton left Plato the Thursday after his arrival, taking the stage to Prescott. He managed his crutches well, and left behind his horse at the livery to ensure his return, though by then no one doubted the big man's honesty.

His absence from the doctor's office was keenly felt, however. With Burton gone, Julie found herself slipping into her old shyness again. She had been able to laugh with him, and with Morgan sometimes, too, but in the house alone with the doctor, she retreated into herself.

Morgan noticed it and had no trouble locating the cause. It didn't matter that, as the days and weeks went by, neither Julie nor her parents formally announced her engagement. With or without a firm date set for the wedding, she considered herself betrothed, and she had betrayed her promise when she let Morgan wrap her in his arms that Monday morning. More guilt, and he felt it too, because he blamed himself. He swore there would be no repetition.

He also swore to find the cause of her other guilts. Promptly after sending her on her way that morning, he sat down and wrote to Adam St. Rogers. A telegram would have been faster, but Morgan could not avail himself of that convenience with the object of his investigation manning the telegraph office. So the letter was long, containing confessions and apologies as well as questions. When Morgan had written it over several times to make certain he had left out nothing, he carried it to the post office before opening the clinic for the day.

Some of his patients, like the McCrorys, paid him cash which, after paying his bills, he faithfully deposited in a growing account in the bank. His longstanding debt at the general store was soon erased, and by the time Burton had been gone a week, Morgan decided to spend some of his hard-earned riches on himself.

He let Ezra Farnum fit him for a new coat, silk-lined. The old one needed alterations, and it was worn enough that it wouldn't last much longer anyway, so buying a new one, Morgan told himself, made perfect sense.

He did not tell Julie about it.

The more skilled she became at her work, the more he fought against taking her for granted. It wasn't easy. She learned quickly, more quickly than he had ever imagined she would. When he caught her reading his medical books and discovered she had no course of study, he made a list for her. Every night she took books home, and he knew she read while fixing supper because he had picked up one of the volumes and found a page spattered with cooking grease.

He didn't dare wonder what he'd do without her.

He could only wait, and hope for a reply to his letter to Adam St. Rogers that would tell him something, anything. He didn't even know what.

Two weeks after Burton left for Prescott, Morgan was making his Thursday morning errands in the sweltering heat, and he couldn't get that long-awaited reply out of his mind. When he stopped at the post office, he crossed his fingers for an instant before pulling the door open.

"Hey, g'mornin', Doc!" Mr. Nisely called over the counter. "Been waitin' fer ya. Got a letter fer ya t'day. Mebbe it's the one ya bin waitin' fer."

But by the time the elderly postmaster had finished all that, Morgan had the envelope in his hand and could see for himself that it wasn't. The postmark was Prescott.

Inside the envelope was a folded sheet of paper, but when Morgan opened it, another smaller sheet fell out, almost dropping to the floor before he caught it. It was a cashier's check in the sum of one hundred dollars made out to Dr. Morgan.

He let out another low whistle but did not say anything in front of the postmaster, who had never been accused of keeping a secret.

Outside in the late morning sun, Morgan squinted to read the note while he walked to the bank, the only detached building between the post office and the boardwalked shops.

"*Dear Doc,*" the slightly scrawled letter read,

> *I made it to Prescott and got my claim filed all nice and legal. Found out too that my partner*

Jim Spense, r.i.p., had stashed some money in a bank here in the mine's name. Damn fool place for money, if you ask me, but he didn't. Anyway, I figger a chunk of it belongs to you and Miss Julie. Don't you go paying none of my bills in Plato with this. I'm spending part of the loot on myself, resting up here at the hotel like you told me to. But soon's I get solid on my feet again I'll be back to pay all my bills. I kinda miss that old strawberry horse anyway.

Morgan laughed, remembering the detailed instructions Burton had left for Gus at the livery.
He had reached the bank but didn't immediately go in. He leaned against the brick wall in the last sliver of shade before noon and continued reading.

I know I don't have to worry about you cheating Miss Julie outa her share, so I won't tell you how to split this. But just don't go getting married to her until I get back to Plato. I just love weddings and will be very hurt if I don't get a invite to yours.

Morgan coughed, folded the letter quickly, and put it in his pocket. He'd have to make sure Julie didn't see it.
He put half the hundred dollars into his account and took the other fifty in cash, including the shiniest double eagle Dan Kincheloe had in his drawer. Dan said nothing about the gold coin, but Morgan suspected the teller had sus-

picions of his own. Still, neither man said a word, and Morgan walked back outside to finish his errands. He tucked the gold piece in a pocket separate from the rest of his money.

Next stop was Farnum's for the final fitting on that new coat. Morgan pushed the door open and the bell hung above it tinkled, bringing Ezra from his workroom.

"Ah, good day, good day, Dr. Morgan," he greeted around a mouthful of pins. "Here, let me help you off with that coat and we'll get the new one on right away, right away."

The tailor reached up to remove the garment and deftly hung it on the coat tree by the door. Taking his tape measure from around his neck, he led the way to the back of the shop and there took the new coat from a hanger.

"It looks done to me," Morgan said, shrugging into it. The silk slid easily over his arms with a soft rustle.

"Not quite, sir, not quite." Ezra smoothed the black fabric over the broad shoulders. "I got the sleeves a wee bit too long, just a wee bit, but it's no trouble to shorten them." He fussed with the cuffs, inserting pins into them so that Morgan had to move carefully to avoid pricking his wrists. "What it really needs, sir, is a new waist-coat. A fine new waistcoat to show off that gold watch chain of yours. No sense having a new coat and wearing it over an old waistcoat, sir, no sense at all."

Morgan was about to protest that he couldn't

afford it, but then he remembered the money from Burton. It was found money, the kind to be spent on luxuries rather than necessities, and most of his necessities were taken care of anyway.

Still, he'd never been spendthrift and could see no reason to begin now simply because he had a bit of extra cash.

"No, Ezra, I don't think so. And don't try to sell me trousers. You made the mistake of telling me when I brought the others in for altering that you had made them out of your best material and that they had plenty of wear left in them."

The tailor came around to the front of him and flattened the lapels of the coat, then checked to make sure it hung evenly.

"It was the truth, sir, the God's own truth. Trousers take more wear than coats, you know, so I always use the best fabric possible. Now of course I used my best in this coat, too, sir, my very best, and I don't have much call to, except for special occasions. Very special occasions. And if you aren't going to be either married or buried in it, the least you could do is wear it over a new waistcoat and do it justice."

Ezra, being dead serious, jumped back a step or two in fright when Morgan began to laugh.

He was still laughing, partly at himself for having ordered the new waistcoat that he didn't need, when he walked into McCrory's. There he purchased only the items he did need: soap, coffee, salt, and a tablet of paper to use when drawing diagrams for Julie. He had just paid and was on his way out the door when Katharine Hollstrom walked in.

"Good morning, Dr. Morgan," she sang.

He tipped his hat politely.

"How are you feeling this morning?" he asked her.

"Quite well, thank you, though I'm sure I'll feel even better next week when you finally take this thing off." She lifted the splinted arm and gave it a disgusted look.

"Don't expect too much right away," he warned. "It's been idle a long time and the muscles will be rather weak. It may take several weeks for you to regain full use of the arm."

She made no attempt to hide her disappointment, and in fact seemed to play on it, pouting almost like a spoiled child.

"And I did so look forward to being able to help Julie."

"I'm sure if you take things slowly and don't try to do too much the first day, you should have no trouble," Morgan encouraged. He tried to make a graceful exit then, but Katharine, who was no less plump than she had been six weeks ago, effectively blocked his retreat.

"At least it will be more use than it is now, and so will I. You can't imagine what a trial it has been for me to sit by and watch her work so hard. Especially now that this new treatment of yours has me feeling so much better than I did."

Katharine's sincerity was tinged with such

drama that Morgan immediately dismissed it. He found himself caught in the old dilemma again. He could wish Katharine a speedy recovery, which would free Julie to spend more time with him, or he could continue the charade of invalidism and delay the wedding. For the sooner Katharine regained her health, the sooner Hans would demand his bride.

And that thought brought back Ezra Farnum's words.

That Thursday was busier than some, but still there were quiet periods between patients. During any one of those moments, Morgan could have given Julie the gold piece, but he waited until he knew they would not be interrupted. Finally, when the last patient had left, Morgan closed and locked the door.

"Please, Julie, sit down and relax for a few minutes."

She did as he asked, seating herself on one of the plain wooden chairs along the wall. Morgan pulled up another and straddled it backwards to face her. He reached into a pocket and took the coin in his hand, enjoying the secure heaviness of it.

"I got a letter from Mr. Burton today."

"Oh? Is he well?"

"He's fine. He's spending some time in Prescott recuperating."

"I'm glad. I won't worry about him so much now. He really was a very nice man."

"Yes, he was, despite coming in here looking like an outlaw."

It was easy to talk about Burton, and for those few moments of almost idle conversation Morgan thought he had lost his nervousness. But the instant silence descended, he felt eighteen years old again.

He coughed.

"Mr. Burton sent me a check to pay for his care while he was here. It was a substantial amount, more than I would have asked from him."

"Well, you did save his life."

She left him a convenient opening; he took it.

"With considerable help from you. Mr. Burton also recognized your contribution, so he wanted you to have this."

He held out his palm with the gold coin lying on it. Julie stared, disbelieving.

"Go on, it's yours. You earned it."

"Twenty dollars? No, I can't take that much. You did so much more than I."

She hid her hands under her apron.

"He sent me a hundred dollars, Julie. Surely twenty at least is yours. Put it away if you like; stick it in your hope chest or something."

At that remark, she did turn away.

"No. I don't want it," she insisted with strange fervor.

"Why not? You earned it honestly, Julie. You worked as hard as I did that night he came in here, and you really did more afterward. You fixed his meals, you saw to his personal needs, you sat up nights and watched him."

But thinking of Thaddeus Burton reminded Julie of a kiss in a stifling hot surgery and an embrace in the cool of a summer morning. She looked again at the money Morgan offered her and saw it for what it really was.

Or was it? Had the letter from Burton reminded the doctor, too, of those minor but still significant transgressions and urged him to ease his conscience with purchased forgiveness? He had had money before and never felt the need to give any more of it to her than her weekly salary. Perhaps Burton had indeed insisted that part of his payment go to her. She could not refuse the man's generosity, but neither did she wish to give Morgan the notion that she could be bought.

"Please, Julie, take the money," he begged gently. "Consider it a gift, the kind you never expected. Spend it lavishly. Buy yourself a new dress, a new pair of shoes, maybe a frilly hat. You deserve that much, at least."

And you deserve so much more, he added in his thoughts.

Slowly, she brought one hand out from under her apron and extended it toward his. She took the coin from his palm, taking great care not to touch him more than absolutely necessary. Care was not enough. Her fingertips came alive in that fraction of a second, and she quickly hid them again, now clutching the heavy coin.

Morgan breathed a sigh of relief. He had been afraid for a minute there that she wouldn't take it after all; now at least he could refuse if she tried to give it back. He hoped that would not be the case, since she seemed to have taken secure possession of the coin, and he further hoped he could prevail upon her to accept a bit more.

He took his billfold from his coat pocket and slid a five-dollar bill from it without looking at Julie. As he put the billfold away, he began to speak.

"This isn't a gift, Julie," he told her, forcing his voice to a sternness he couldn't feel. "It's an investment of mine, one you aren't allowed to argue with."

"No, I can't take any more—"

"I said you aren't allowed to argue, so be quiet and don't interrupt me again. I want you to buy material to make yourself some extra aprons, just like the one you've got on. The new ones will be strictly for working here. You're ruining all your clothes with bloodstains and extra scrubbing, and there's no reason why you should sacrifice your own possessions. Also, I owe you for the dress I tore a couple of weeks ago."

Slightly panicked because she didn't know what he was talking about, she asked, "What dress?"

"The one that caught on the cabinet."

"But that wasn't your fault," she answered with a sigh of relief now that she recalled the incident. "I snagged it on the nail."

Though it wouldn't have happened if you

hadn't been standing so close to me, she also remembered with a little shiver.

"Still, it was a result of your working here, and that makes it my responsibility. I don't know much about yard goods, so if this isn't enough for five or six aprons and a dress, just put the rest on my bill at McCrory's."

He met her eyes evenly, without any of his own shyness, because he had reminded himself over and over and over and over that this was strictly business. Aprons could not by any stretch of propriety be considered a gift, especially when she clearly needed them. The dress was, perhaps, a little different, and he could almost read her thoughts as she prepared to refuse that part of the offer.

"If you think it would appear improper, use this money to buy the dress and charge the fabric for the aprons," he suggested, stretching his hand with the folded bill toward her.

She shook her head and kept her hands securely hidden.

"No, I can't accept it. I'll purchase the apron material and start on them right away, but not the dress. I . . . just couldn't."

"Why, Julie? Are you afraid of what people will think?" He leaned forward, his elbows on his knees, the money still held out to her. "No one need know where this money came from. You can tell them it's from your earnings, which in a sense it is. I can give you smaller bills, if you prefer, to make it look like you've saved up for it. Why must you refuse everything I offer you?"

"I don't. I took the gold piece, didn't I?"

"Only because I insisted and because it wasn't from me. Look at you now. You're as far back on that chair as you can get, and I'll bet your knuckles are white under that apron because you've got your hands clasped so tight together." He watched her eyes drop at once and saw the pink come to her cheeks. "Julie, the last thing I want is for you to be afraid of me," he said softly.

"I'm not afraid of you!" she insisted.

"Yes, you are. Your eyes are all wide and glittery, as though you were ready to cry, and your lips are trembling, too. When I handed you that double eagle, you jerked your hand away as though my fingers were red-hot metal. If it's something I've done, if it's because of those kisses, then tell me. But tell me the truth, Julie."

The truth? How could she tell him the truth?

She couldn't tell him anything. She couldn't speak at all. When she tried to open her mouth and once again deny her fear, not a single word came out. The searing fire of his green gaze evaporated the lie from her lips.

"Julie," he whispered softly, slowly, "tell me the truth, please? Is it because of Hans? Tell me it is, and I won't ask further. But only tell me if it's the truth. You don't lie very well, you know. Your mother is much better at hiding the truth than you, but I can see through her most of the time, too."

He studied her, from the nervous movements of her hands under the apron to the slight slump of her shoulders. She was fighting with herself now, debating whether to tell him what he wanted to know or to try to conceal the facts from him. She met his gaze, but this time there was something new in her eyes. Fear, yes, always the fear, and curiosity, too, for she clearly wondered why he wanted so badly to know her secrets; but now there was a pleading. For what? he wondered. To leave her alone? Or does she really, deep down, want to confess it all and only hesitates because I'm not urging her strongly enough?

He listened to the answer that came to mind but silently laughed it off.

"I'm waiting," he reminded her, and she did not seem startled, though they had sat in tense silence for several minutes. "And I'm not going to let you out of here until I get an answer, an honest one."

Somehow she must get the words out, must tell him something he would believe. But not the truth. He must not know the truth, not yet.

"I've never been around men very much," she finally forced herself to say. "I told you before that I've spent most of my time taking care of my mother and Willy. I didn't have any chance to—"

"Oh, stop it, Julie!" he shouted. "I warned you I'd see through your lies, and this is another one. It doesn't bother you to bandage old Gus Ernberg's smashed thumb or put salve on Simon McCrory's burn. Look at the way you tended Thaddeus when he was here, changing dressings on that leg wound and everything else you

did for him. You talked to him and laughed with
him and I never saw you afraid of him."

Now there was no pink blush on her cheeks,
only a pallor that emphasized the warm depth of
her wide eyes and the cherry temptation of her
fear-parted lips.

He apologized at once, realizing he had done
more harm than good.

"I'm sorry. I don't blame you for being afraid
of me right now. I shouldn't have hollered at
you like that. But damn it, Julie, you can be so
frustrating at times."

He got up from the chair and with one hand
set it back where it belonged. Then, with a
sweeping motion he deposited the five-dollar
bill on her lap. It didn't stay there, of course; it
drifted on the stirred air and finally fell to the
floor. Julie watched it for a moment, then, when
Morgan turned his back, she leaned down to
pick it up.

He shoved one hand into his pants pocket and
ran the other through his hair in a gesture of
perplexity.

"We can't continue like this, Julie," he said,
still facing the far wall. His voice had returned to
calm, though nothing else about him had. "If
you won't give me your complete cooperation,
then I'm afraid we will have to terminate this
arrangement."

Leaping to her feet, she cried, "No!"

"No?" he echoed. "And why not? I can't be
forever worrying about your—"

"I'll tell you the truth, I swear it," she told him

desperately. She wanted to take his hands in hers and cling to him, vowing anything, anything at all, so long as he did not send her away. Telling him the horrible truth might result in the same fate, but she had no choice unless she could somehow disguise it.

"All of the truth?"

"Yes," she whispered, more frightened than ever.

Looking at him, seeing into those clear dark eyes, she knew she could not lie. He would hate her, would cast her out with disgust, but she would tell him the truth.

"Then let's go in the other room where we can be comfortable at least. Is there some lemonade left? Or coffee?" he asked.

Morgan insisted Julie sit on the sofa while he brought the lemonade, which had grown warm since she made it at noon. Still, it was wet.

When he had sat down beside her, he said, "Well, I'm still waiting."

"I . . . I don't know where to begin."

"How about at the beginning?"

"That's just it. I don't know where the beginning is. No matter where I start, I'm going to end up making you hate me."

"Hate you? Oh, Julie, I would never hate you. Never. Whatever you've done, or has been done to you, I wouldn't hate you for it."

"But it isn't just that. It's what I *am*."

"You're kind, generous, hardworking, sensitive, intelligent." And beautiful, too, but he couldn't tell her that. Not when she was so close to him, and so close to telling him the truth. "Those aren't exactly the qualities a man hates to find in a woman."

"It's something else, and I wish I could find a way to tell you so that you won't think me wicked and—"

"You, wicked? Never. And if you tell me you are, I'll accuse you of lying again." He knew then that he had been right all along. She must be Willy's mother and felt the stigma of her sin. He had to reassure her that he, at least, did not hold her to blame and that long-ago event was nothing to continue being ashamed of.

"Julie, you're stalling. If no other place comes to mind, then why not tell me about Willy."

She looked at him with pure, unadulterated confusion knitting her brows and asked him, "What does Willy have to do with me?" No flush of embarrassment, no pale-faced admission of guilt.

Now it was Morgan's turn to stammer.

"I . . . I thought he was your . . . son."

He didn't know what to expect next. A slap for his insult at the very least, or even her immediate departure. But clearly he had made a mistake. That extra bit of logic that he had ignored had been correct: If Wilhelm hated Julie for her indiscretion, he would not have lavished such attention on her offspring. Yet despite the error, Morgan remained certain that the boy had something to do with Julie's burden of guilt.

She didn't slap him, nor did she get up to leave. She merely smoothed the loose strands of her hair back from her face, trying to tuck them into the net around her bun.

"No, Dr. Morgan, he's not. I suppose I should be angry for your assuming he was, since it assumes a great deal that is not kind about me, but the truth is not far from it. Willy is indeed my brother, born exactly as I told you. And, as I told you, I was not there when he was born. Neither was my father. He was out looking for me."

"You ran away from home?"

"In a manner of speaking. I eloped."

That came as a shock, but Morgan quickly recovered. She must not still be married, if she was now engaged to Wallenmund, but of course anything was possible when people came west.

"I wasn't allowed to socialize very much, even though I was at an age when it seemed every other girl was getting married. Papa said I was needed at home, because of Mama expecting the baby."

He tried to imagine her loneliness. Comparing it to the fun he and Amy had had, he could understand why Julie wanted to escape.

"I met Ted Sheen in the post office one day, and he offered me a ride home. I knew I shouldn't accept, but Ted was so handsome, and I had never had anyone offer me a ride before. Somehow, Papa didn't find out and Ted came to see me again, even though I told him not to."

A shudder swept through her, drawing her arms around herself as though a cold wind had chilled her to the bone. Morgan felt a chill himself, in the pit of his stomach. It was the same when he held the scalpel just before cutting into human flesh.

"We had a little barn behind our house, more like a shed because we didn't keep any livestock, and I met Ted there every night for a week, just after dark. I was so afraid I'd get caught, and so was he, but it seemed we just couldn't help it."

She paused and began that nervous twisting of a corner of her apron.

"Your father caught you, didn't he."

"Yes. There was a storm coming in, so I told Ted to spend the night in the barn until the storm was over. I was trying to close the door quietly, but the wind took it out of my hands and banged it against the side of the barn.

"Next thing I knew, Papa came screaming from the house in his nightshirt. He called me names, and when Ted tried to explain, Papa wouldn't listen. Then Mama came outside, too, crying and begging Papa not to do anything foolish. He wouldn't listen to her, either, and finally he pushed her away so hard that she fell. I went to help her, but Papa pushed me away, too."

"That's when your mother went into her labor, wasn't it."

Julie nodded. The apron corner twisted tighter.

"She yelled something about the baby and getting a doctor. I wanted to help her, I really did, and I tried, but Papa wouldn't let me near her. He said it was all my fault. Finally, Mama started screaming, and Ted told me to come with him. I was so frightened that I didn't know what else to do.

"We ran into town to get Ted's horse from the livery stable. He got one for me, too, and he told me he left money and a note for it so no one would think he stole it. He said we'd ride to the next town and get married that very night and then we could come back to Rinton and live like proper people so Papa couldn't ever say anything about me again."

Morgan wanted to interrupt her, to offer her some comfort, some strength, but he knew that she had to make this confession on her own. And she seemed to draw her own strength from the experience, as though this unburdening did indeed lighten her load.

"Ted found a minister who was willing to marry us, and I was so excited then that I almost forgot to be afraid. I was getting married. A man had wanted me enough to make me his wife. Me—skinny, ugly Julie Hollstrom who was taller than almost every boy in town."

"Julie, you aren't ugly. I can't imagine that you ever were."

"Well, I was, believe me. But it was nice for a while to think that I wasn't. And Ted really had married me. We were going to go back and tell my parents, but we never made it."

Her voice dropped and she shivered again, so violently that Morgan slid closer to her and put his arm around her to warm her, even in the hot afternoon. She had comforted him when he poured out the black bitterness from his heart; now he did the same for her.

"It was raining and a long time until morning when Papa and the men from town found us. They said Ted had stolen the horse from the livery stable, that he was a horse thief and should be hung. They said they hadn't found any money or note in the stable, and I hadn't actually seen him do it. I should have lied, I should have told them I saw the note and the money, but maybe even that wouldn't have done any good. Papa was an important man in Rinton, and the others all believed him."

She took a deep breath before continuing, and her voice dropped even lower, but Morgan had no difficulty hearing her. In a way he wished he had, but then again, once he knew the truth, he could not bear the thought of asking her to repeat it.

"When they found us, we were resting under an old oak tree by the side of the road. Papa said Ted was guilty, so they hanged him from the tree right there."

Chapter Nineteen

✦✦✦✦✦

THE LONG LASHES descended, closing her eyes to remembered sights, but that could not stop the flood of hot tears. Nor could the tears halt the words.

"I begged and I screamed and I cried, not just trying to stop them but to cover up the sound of what they did. I shut my eyes, but nothing drowned out the sounds. And nothing stopped him. My father killed my husband."

She wiped the back of her hand across her eyes, then took the handkerchief Morgan offered her. He said nothing. Anger left him speechless.

Wilhelm Hollstrom was a monster beyond comprehension.

"It was morning when we got back to the house," Julie went on in a frozen, numb little voice. "Willy had been born during the night, and the doctor didn't expect either him or Mama to live."

"And of course your father blamed you," Morgan said stiffly, biting down the anger, the hatred, the nausea. "Oh, God, Julie, how could he? That's cold-blooded murder!"

"No, no. He believed he was right. He was protecting me. And later on a man came to town who said Ted had stolen a horse from him, too. Papa told me all about it."

"Then he lied."

"You don't know that. You weren't there."

Yet he did know it, as surely as he knew the sun would come up in the east tomorrow, as surely as he knew Julie was entirely blameless. Gentle, trusting, lonely Julie. To think of her witnessing a man's death, a brutal, horrible, senseless—he failed to find sufficient words to describe her nightmarish ordeal. And in the grief and shock that followed, she had believed anything her sadistic father told her.

Morgan curbed his anger with effort, because he knew it would do Julie no good.

"I think it's time to clean up around here so you can get home," he said quietly.

"Not yet. I'm not finished."

"Oh, yes, you are." He moved his arm to get up, but Julie's hand went to his knee, innocently and yet insistently, and he was paralyzed.

"You said you felt better when you had told me about Amy," Julie reminded him. "Please, give me the same chance."

He could not refuse her, not when her eyes as well as her voice pleaded with him. Replacing his arm around her, he pulled her closer. Very gently, he stroked those fine, loose hairs at her temple, smoothing them back with a rhythmic caress. Nothing, he knew, could soothe or ease the pain, but perhaps this gesture would mean something.

Julie sniffled and blew her nose on his handkerchief.

He listened, and he saw. Her descriptions were brief, but her voice, the tense shivering of her body within the semicircle of his arm, filled in the details.

It began with Katharine's slow recovery, compounding the guilt Wilhelm had already piled on his daughter. And later, he claimed that her behavior had shamed and humiliated his family so much that they had to leave Indiana.

"I met Hans shortly after we settled in Minnesota. He wanted to get married right away, but Mama needed me at home, and there was no room to take Hans in, too. He had no job and all he knew was farming, so six years ago he set out for Arizona, where he said he would get rich and send for me.

"He hadn't been gone but a few months when I met Stephen. He was a salesman, with dark hair, bright blue eyes . . ."

"A real talker, too, I'll bet."

"Yes, he was," she added ruefully.

"You were young, Julie. You had no one to tell you traveling salesmen have the morals of a jackrabbit."

"But decent men never so much as looked at me!" she exclaimed. "Mama said I should try not to look so nice, that that was what attracted the wrong men. I started wearing the spectacles then, but it didn't help."

Though he wanted to comfort her, Morgan realized there was nothing he could say until she had told him everything. It was, after all, exactly what he had asked for.

"Mama couldn't take the cold winters in Minnesota, so we moved to Kansas City. There I met a cavalry officer, Lieutenant Andrew McWilliams, just like every girl dreams of. Except that he

already had a girl. A wife, in fact, in St. Louis."
Now a new element crept into her voice—a sarcasm, a bitterness turned inward. She believed in her guilt, and that was the worst of it all.

"Julie, I'm sorry," he said quietly, disgusted at how lame the words sounded.

"Sorry? Why? It was my own fault for flaunting myself at him."

"You? Flaunt yourself?" Morgan snorted a bitter laugh. "Good God, Julie, you don't even know how to flaunt yourself. Amy used to tease and flirt ten—no, a hundred times more than you could ever do, and she was no more wicked than a newborn babe."

"But she didn't attract married soldiers and horse thieves and itinerant peddlars the way I did. They were wicked, and I had to be wicked, too, if they wanted me."

Her head had been resting on his shoulder; now she let it slip and hang in shame, away from the steady caress of his fingers.

"Hans is the only one who treated me like a . . . like a good woman. He respects me and he will make a good husband for me."

The lack of emotion in her statement told Morgan that she had memorized the words, words her father had probably taught her, to make her believe in her guilt and shame. Morgan did not believe any of it.

"That still doesn't explain why you're so afraid of me. Do you think I'm one of those wicked men?"

What a stupid, stupid question! Of course she

does! he told himself angrily. You were the town drunk, you threw up in her flowers, you didn't mind letting her see you half naked, and more than once you managed to kiss her. Why wouldn't she think you wicked?

But she didn't answer him right away. Slowly, she got to her feet and walked away from him, twisting the handkerchief around her fingers. Her hair had come loose, the long braid swinging down the middle of her back with each step.

Did she dare confess to him what she felt? He seemed more inclined to pity her than hate her. If she revealed her feelings, he might maintain his present opinion, or he might change his mind and think her wanton and shameless. She had, after all, let him kiss her, and this afternoon, she had permitted him to lock the door and hold her almost intimately on the sofa for a very long time. Hadn't Mama always said no decent woman let a man touch her?

"Julie, you are not wicked." When she didn't turn around and he wasn't sure she had heard him, Morgan stood and walked a step or two toward her. "Men like to make conquests of innocent girls like you, and if you had no one to teach you how to handle them, it is hardly your fault if sometimes there was a little trouble. And you can't take the blame for everything else, either."

As though they had minds of their own, his fingers reached for her, clasping her thin shoulders to turn her around, then drawing her closer.

"How can I explain away the mistakes of half

a lifetime in just a few minutes?'' Morgan whispered. "How can I make you see that you were never to blame? Your father pushed your mother to the ground and it was the fall that brought on her labor, not your actions. Even in his anger at what you were doing, no decent man would have done that to his wife. And your mother has been lying to you all this time.''

He had thought carefully about telling her; it was not something he let slip because of his emotional reaction to her story. She needed to hear the truth, just as she had needed to tell the truth. There was no reason to hide anything anymore.

Julie said nothing, though he felt her stiffen slightly in his arms. He held her exactly as he had held her before, but somehow the feeling was different, stronger, deeper, warmer inside him. He had to let her go, for more reasons than one.

Leaving one arm loosely around her waist, he guided her back to the sofa and gently pushed her down, though he did not join her. Nearness to her was doing strange things to him that he was in no condition to deal with now. Her problems had to come first; he would handle his own later.

"I don't think your mother was ever very sick,'' he began, feeling his way across uncharted ground. "Maybe it took her a little longer to recover from Willy's birth than normal, but I'm quite sure she recovered fully.''

Julie searched for the handkerchief she had

dropped earlier. Morgan picked it up and handed it to her, then thrust his hands into his pockets.

"I don't understand," Julie replied. "I saw her, I watched her every day. She could hardly walk, and you know how terrible her headaches were."

"No, I don't. I only know what she *told* me. And you've seen how much better she is now. Do you think a concoction of sugar and vinegar and a little bit of whiskey is enough to make that dramatic a change in her health if she were really sick?"

Julie seemed to believe him, or at least if she had any serious doubts about his claims, she hid them well.

"I haven't the faintest idea why she'd want to put on such a monstrous act for nine years, Julie, but she has; and for some reason now she's trying to cast off the role. She apparently played it quite well; she had your father completely fooled. She said he hadn't touched her since Willy was born."

"But he was afraid another baby would kill her. I knew that."

"It was an excuse. She's perfectly capable, even at her age, of having another baby, and nine years ago she was no different. But I don't care about her; I care about you. I can't stand seeing you hurt the way you do all the time. And I think too much of you to let you go through the rest of your life thinking you were to blame for something that had nothing to do with you."

It was all very logical and made perfect sense. His charges had the ring of truth.

"Oh, it's all so confusing!" she cried suddenly, startling them both. "And why would Mama lie to me? If I didn't cause Willy's birth and she wasn't really ill, then why did I—no, it isn't true. It can't be."

She was thinking aloud, not speaking to him, Morgan realized, and he felt more uncomfortable than when she had poured out her pain to him. He could comfort her, but he could not think for her.

"They hate me," she said quietly, coming to a clear revelation. "If I am innocent and they hate me, then they are monsters and I am no better, for I am their child."

"No, that's wrong!" Morgan insisted, but he had the feeling she never heard him. He could stand it no longer. He jerked her to her feet and shook her, like a rag doll or a sleepy child, to bring her to her senses. Willingly, as though she deserved the punishment, Julie accepted the shock. Her acquiescence infuriated him even more, because he felt so powerless against the evil that had been done. And if he told her the one thing that might make a difference, she would only classify him with the other bastards who had used her.

"Stop it!" he ordered. "For God's sake, how can you give in to it so easily? Do I have to beat you to a pulp to knock some sense into you? Your mother is a vain, lazy, petty woman who cares for nothing but herself. Not even you. It didn't enter her mind that she might be hurting you when she played the invalid. She only cared about keeping a husband whom she hates out of her bed. I told you before that it was your father's temper and his violence that brought on Katharine's labor, *not* anything you did. I'm a doctor, Julie; don't you believe me?''

Hungry, hot, and bone-weary, Morgan climbed the stairs to his bedroom. Johnny Cole's timely knock on the office door had put an end to the scene in the infirmary that afternoon, though it was hardly the end Morgan wished for. Julie composed herself quickly, as he supposed she had done many, many times in the past. It almost frightened him how easily she hid her feelings, and he wondered just how much more she had buried within.

Johnny's grandmother, old Mrs. Westerman, had had another attack, and Morgan grabbed his bag and followed the boy to the house on the other side of the Castle. He ordered Julie home, insisting there was nothing she could do to help. The truth was that he feared he'd be too distracted by her presence to render the elderly woman any assistance at all. As it was, he could barely keep his mind on his work, though there was little he could do anyway.

Ev Cole's mother-in-law lingered through the early evening and into the night. The old woman's daughter, Ev's wife Laura, had to be sedated and was snoring peacefully when her mother died shortly after midnight. Morgan couldn't help thinking how much stronger and more serenely beautiful Julie would have been helping him instead of the hysterical Laura.

The thought stayed with him while he walked home, glancing toward Julie's house, dark now and silent. His own was no different, and twice as lonely. He peeled off sweaty clothes and dropped them to the floor carelessly, his mind still tangled. He opened the window shutters to let in the breeze, but even the fresh scent of the night air and the innocent calls of nocturnal beasts did not penetrate the clouded barrier to his soul.

He didn't light the lamp, for he knew what he would see. Amy. Memory of her was the only thing to get through the silent wall, and he could not bear to look at her when thoughts of another woman tormented him. As he lay on the bed, a sheet drawn over him against the chill of the breeze, he tried to force the pain away. The bottle of scotch was still in the kitchen pantry, and he did not delude himself that he didn't consider getting it. But after tonight it offered insufficient solace.

Exhaustion brought some relief, though the unconscious knowledge that he had only a few hours left in which to sleep seemed to keep his rest light and troubled. He never lost all touch with the reality of the darkened bedroom, the tangled sheets, the window open above his head, but wisps and fragments of fantasy joined him.

A vision of Julie, as he had never seen her and wished to see her, glided to his bedside. Though there was no moon, only stars, he could see her plainly. Her eyes, soft and warm and pleading. Her lips, which he had tasted so briefly, smiling and parted with a hunger he ached to appease.

He blinked, not to stop tears, for there were none, but to clear his head of the dream. The image had been almost too real, and yet he knew it was only a phantom of his weary brain.

The hot pain, however, was very real. The joy of rediscovered desire terrified him, because he wanted Julie, no one else, and he dared not have her.

Chapter Twenty

✦✦✦✦

THE ALARM WAKENED him to a glaringly bright morning. The sun through the open shutters already heated the room uncomfortably. After silencing the metallic nuisance beside his head, Morgan stretched and yawned and wished he could have lain abed another four or five hours at least. Friday, however, was invariably busy, and any delay on his part in getting the office open only meant Julie would be stuck with the burden of explaining his tardiness.

Julie. The very thought of her brought back the dreams—the nightmares—of yesterday and the night. Sitting on the edge of the bed with the cold tiles on his bare feet to chase the last streamers of sleep from his groggy brain, Morgan held his head between his hands and tried to sort the real from the imaginary, the remembered from the dreamed. Unfortunately, all the bad things were real, all the good things impossible.

He combed his fingers through his hair and then rubbed his unshaven chin while he yawned again. Of all the horrible things he had thought of Wilhelm Hollstrom, nothing had come close to the truth. Poor Julie, to have been forced to watch—to listen—while her father killed her husband. Morgan shivered again at the thought.

It was no wonder, he told himself as he stood and stretched, that she felt so little enthusiasm for her upcoming marriage. One wedding had ended in disaster, and she probably could not get that out of her mind as she prepared for a second.

He turned to close the shutters against the blinding sun and the day's heat. Then he straightened the bed and sighed before he gathered clean clothes and headed for the kitchen to shave and fortify himself with coffee.

Last night must have been a dream, all of it.

And it was just as well. He had allowed himself to be honest and open with Julie because he knew she was safe, whether she knew it or not.

He could not seduce her, though he admitted he was beginning to wish he could, but his disability gave him the opportunity to treat her much differently than most men would. If last night had been real, he might have lost that candor and changed his attitude.

But why not? a voice inside him asked. Staring at his face in the mirror, he listened to the voice repeat the question and he failed to come up with a suitable answer.

"I admit I don't want her to marry Wallenmund," he told his reflection as he slathered his cheeks and chin with shaving soap. "But that doesn't mean I have to offer to marry her myself. If I did try to court her, I'd have to be damn careful not to play into any of her fears." He let the warm lather soak his whiskers for a few moments and stropped the razor firmly, unemotionally. "I can't say I'd be unhappy if she accepted me. Whoever gets her ought to be damn thankful. Lord knows she can cook, and she's so good with children, even that brat Willy, that she'll make a wonderful mother someday. As far as helping me the way Amy did, I have a feeling, ashamed as I am to admit it, that Julie will be even better."

He scraped a cheek carefully, not forgetting the mornings his hand had been far from steady. He looked closely at his reflection and decided it was almost time for another haircut, too.

He finished the right cheek and went on to his chin and throat.

Amy helped me, he thought, not daring to

talk aloud for a few seconds, but Julie would take the work to herself. She'd be a full partner in everything. Amy used to listen to my gripes and my disappointments and she'd soothe them out of my system, but Julie would share them with me, and nothing would ever be as discouraging again if I had her to shoulder some of the burden with me.

"But could I ask her to do that?" he wondered, wiping the razor on the towel that hung around his neck. "I couldn't ask her to love me the way Amy did, and there'd never be any promise that I'd love her either. Maybe that would be best, too, for both of us. We could enter into a relationship with no emotional shackles to each other, a logical extension of what we already have."

The problem was that what he had with her right now wasn't enough. He rediscovered that every time he got close to her, emotionally or physically. Even in the bright light of day, when the phantasms of night were supposed to be vanquished, he felt that insane desire growing again. He lifted the corners of the towel to wipe off the last traces of lather, but there was nothing to wipe away the seductive dream-image of Julie that lingered in his mind.

He covered his face with the towel and struggled against the power of that image. He knew damn well what it was telling him, and he couldn't ignore what it was doing to his body. Not all the dreams had been dreams; part of them had been very, very real, as this was real now.

Julie smoothed the new apron over her second-best dress and stepped out the front door. She smothered a yawn and tried to stretch a kink out of her neck. Up half the night sewing the new apron and during the other half trying to sort out the incredible tangle of conflicting emotions her discussion with Morgan had aroused, she had had trouble staying awake while she fixed breakfast and now could think of almost nothing but going back to bed. But she had already seen Morgan walk up to the office, where a crowd had gathered early, so she had no choice but to persevere.

If he noticed the new apron, he had no time to comment on it, and within minutes of her arrival, Julie forgot about the garment anyway. It was one of those days when one absurdity seemed to lead right to another, and for that she was grateful. Had it been a day of crises and tragedies, she was certain she could not have withstood the strain. As it was, she actually found moments to smile.

When she first entered the surgery, she found Morgan already busy, peering into Lucas Carter's left eye from a distance of something less than two inches.

"That you, Julie? Hand me those tweezers over there." He pointed to the instrument just barely out of his reach. "I've found the offending eyelash and don't want to lose it."

When he had the pale, curved hair out, he held it up for Lucas to examine.

Lucas returned the favor by squinting the other eye closed and aiming a stream of tobacco juice accurately at the brass spittoon.

"Amazin', ain't it, how a little whisker like that can hurt so damn much," Lucas said. "I couldn't hardly see straight enough to spit."

No sooner had Lucas left and had Julie been about to call the next patient in than Ada McCrory came screaming up the front stairs with her youngest child, two-year-old Bridget, in her arms. The child, crying nearly as hysterically as her mother, wore a pair of sewing shears around her chubby little wrist.

"I can't get 'em off!" Ada wailed. Julie led her into the surgery, where Morgan waited, a picture of masculine fortitude and patience. "I was mending when a customer came in, and I set all the needles and the scissors up where I didn't think she could reach anything. When I come back, she was puttin' her hand through the handle, and now I can't get it out!"

"Don't worry, Ada, everything'll be fine. What goes on will come off, believe me," Morgan assured her. "Here, Julie, you take Bridget and sit up on the table. Ada, help yourself to a shot of whiskey there. It's some of Horace's best imported stuff."

Julie took the child from her mother, which

seemed to calm Bridget. She really didn't seem bothered at all by her heavy bracelet and immediately began to investigate the long row of buttons down the front of Julie's blouse.

Morgan took a jar of petroleum jelly from the cabinet and opened it, then smeared a generous amount all over the adorned hand. In a matter of seconds, the shears slid off. Ada hadn't even swallowed her second whiskey.

But those few seconds were enough for Morgan to see again how natural Julie looked with a child on her lap.

From then on, the morning went more or less normally, although pulling a candle stub from Sid Ackerman's ear did provide mild amusement between extracting a couple of teeth and stitching a cut knee. Sid claimed it was an accident, but the smell of cheap whiskey was so strong on him even at ten o'clock in the morning that Morgan insisted afterwards that the candle had probably been put there on a dare or as a bet in a card game.

"Sid has bet crazier things," Morgan explained while they cleaned up after repairing a ranch-hand's knee. "Once, when I was more or less sober, I had a straight flush and there was a huge pot on the table. I was pretty sure Sid had a full house at least, but he was also out of cash and I didn't want him to fold. So he said he'd bet me a bald head. If he won, I had to shave my head. If I won, I got the pot and he'd shave his head."

"And you won?"

"Luckily, I won. If I'd been drunk, I wouldn't have."

A howling scream from some distance away cut through the conversation in the full waiting room.

"My God, what was that?" Morgan asked as he ran through the waiting room and out to the front porch with Julie right behind him.

Within seconds, young Skip Jenkins, the blacksmith's apprentice, came charging clumsily down the street. His hands were clasped behind him, and his frequent screams drew patrons from the Castle, the post office, and the shops to see what the commotion was about.

He bounded up the stairs of the physician's office, and the odor of scorched denim and burnt flesh that trailed him offered the explanation.

Facedown on the surgery table, he didn't need to say a word. The fabric of his trousers and underdrawers was crisply burned away, and the blistered red shape branded onto his buttock could not be mistaken.

"I sat on a horseshoe," he gasped.

"Better send someone for new pants," Morgan suggested to Julie. "This pair is going to need patching."

The burn wasn't as serious as it could have been, but Morgan ordered the youth to rest for a few days at least and to come back in a day or two to have the wound checked for infection.

Limping, and dressed in an old bathrobe to keep from chafing the injury, the boy walked out of the office with a face as red as the burn on his other end.

In between a smallpox vaccination and a woman with a chronic cough, Simon McCrory arrived to pay for his daughter's extrication and to let Morgan know another shipment had come for him on the noon stage.

"I took the liberty of bringin' one box over with me, but there's two more waitin'. You want me to have Ard bring 'em over from the depot, or you want to pick 'em up yourself?"

Glancing toward the still half-full waiting room, Morgan chose the former.

"I don't know when I'm going to get away from here, and you know how it is on Friday nights. We've gone too long without a shooting, and I have a feeling in my bones we're going to pay for it tonight." He tossed the half dollar to Julie, who took it to the desk and entered the fee in the ledger while the men talked.

But they talked much longer than it took her to write a few numbers and a name in the book, and she couldn't help enjoying the chance to sit down for a few minutes. She ached everywhere and her eyes would hardly stay open, and she couldn't believe how scribbled her writing looked compared to her normally neat penmanship. She was utterly exhausted, and she probably wasn't doing anyone any good by trying to work when she ought to be asleep. But all she had to do was look at Morgan and she knew she could not have left unless he commanded her to do so.

He doesn't hate me, she had told herself a thousand times since last night. I told him the truth, and he doesn't hate me.

Nothing else seemed important. It was too much to think that perhaps he felt something more than pity for her, but at least that was better than the disgust she had expected. Watching him talk with Simon McCrory, she let her mind—so busy all day with patients and instructions and medications—wander a bit, both back into the recent past and forward into the very near future.

She had liked the feeling of little Bridget McCrory on her lap. When Willy was a baby, she had enjoyed him, too, and she had looked forward to his growing up and being something of a companion to her. But holding Bridget had struck a strange chord in Julie, maybe because of the way Morgan had looked at her for a fleeting second. Was he contemplating the procedure ahead, or was he looking at Julie with a child on her lap and thinking what she was thinking? Because she couldn't help wondering what it would be like to hold her own child—*his* child—on her lap.

"Julie?"

The voice was muffled, as though from a great distance, but the hand on her shoulder was warm and very close. She opened her eyes, then raised her head.

She found herself looking right into those bottomless green-black eyes of his.

"You fell asleep," he scolded with a smile. "Have I been working you that hard today?"

She blushed and jumped to her feet.

"Oh, I'm sorry. Who's next?"

Morgan leaned back against the side of the desk and flipped the ledger closed, using a slip of paper with a multitude of scribblings on it for a marker.

"All gone."

"But the waiting room was full just before Mr. McCrory came."

"I know. In the past three hours I've pulled two teeth, set a broken arm, prescribed a strong dose of castor oil for Mrs. Lindner's stomachache, diagnosed mumps for Elias Stowe, and confirmed Mrs. Hildebrand's suspicions that she is pregnant again."

"And where was I all this time?"

"Sound asleep, right here at the desk. No, I didn't bring the patients in here; I used the other room and gave them a believable excuse."

She felt like an utter fool. Her blatant dereliction of duty was embarrassing enough, but worse was the feeling that Morgan's nearness sent through her. And the smile he gave her didn't help at all. It made her think maybe he *had* been reading her thoughts, though he certainly did not leer at her the way her father had said men leered at the women they wanted.

"If it weren't for your family," he said, "I'd offer to buy you supper at Daneggar's, but I know you have them to take care of. And frankly, Leif's cooking isn't all that great."

He laughed, and Julie managed to find a trace of humor, too.

"Why don't I invite you to dinner at the Hollstroms'?" she replied without really thinking. "It's just a pot roast I put on this morning that I hope Mama kept a fire under. It was a larger cut than I usually have and I put extra carrots and potatoes with it, so there's more than enough to go around."

Sunday dinner was one thing. Having guests on the Sabbath was a social ritual, one performed without comment necessary later. For all that had gone between them in the past few days, Morgan would have accepted an invitation to Sunday dinner with little hesitation, though some reservations. Friday night, however, was not so socially sterile. Gossip found fertile soil here and grew wilder than Cincinnati ragweed.

"Are you sure?" he asked, both of her and of himself.

"I told you I had plenty to go around. No applesauce cake, though."

"I'm not worried about dessert. I may have to leave abruptly, you know," he warned. "Friday night can be rather boisterous, and accidents have been known to happen."

He was going to accept. Julie's heart leaped to her throat, pounding so rapidly and so loudly that she doubted she could speak without a warbling tremolo. Even Hans had never come but on Sunday, and Julie knew very well the significance of having Morgan sit down with the family for Friday night supper. Surely he understood, too, didn't he?

He pulled out his watch and snapped it open.

"It's quarter past four now, and I have one call to make," he told her. "What time shall I come?"

"Six o'clock will be fine. Do you want me to stay and put these supplies away?"

He had almost forgotten the three large wooden crates from Denver. Even if they worked together, it would be an hour at least before they finished.

"No, let it go for now. We'll do it in the morning. Go on home, and I'll clean up here."

But Julie insisted she had shirked enough duty for one day and refused to leave before she had finished recording the day's business on the ledger and straightened up the surgery.

"It won't take long, and you can make your call while I'm here to watch the office."

She illustrated her determination by sitting back down at the desk and reopening the ledger. As she reached for the pen she had laid aside earlier, she asked, "Is this piece of paper supposed to be a record of the patients you saw today?"

The writing covered both sides from top to bottom and margin to margin, and some of the names were blurred to illegibility, to say nothing of the numerals.

"Can't you read my writing?" Morgan asked with friendly sarcasm. "Ansel Porter, two teeth pulled, two dollars paid. Harry Blum, set and splint arm, five dollars paid." He began to pull coins and a few bills from his various pockets and laid them on the desktop beside the ledger. "Hettie Lindner, consultation, one dollar not paid."

Julie scribbled as furiously as she could but still failed to keep up with him and finally gave up.

"You're doing that on purpose!" She laughed, setting the pen down and flexing cramped fingers. "All right, all right, I'll go home, but I just hope you can remember all this tomorrow, because I can't begin to decipher these chicken scratchings of yours."

"I'll remember, don't worry. Now, scoot, and I'll lock up after you. If anything comes up, I'll be at Nellie's. One of the girls has been running a fever, and I said I'd look in on her."

He spoke as casually of the girls in the brothel as he would of the McCrory children, and Julie knew the ailing prostitute would receive the same conscientious care. Was that why Morgan felt no animosity toward her despite her past, because he held nothing against anyone, even the whores who serviced the miners and ranchhands and drifters? Did he consider Julie Hollstrom no worse than they? She suddenly realized that considering her no worse was not enough. She wanted him to think her something—*someone*—special.

But she could not let her feelings show, not now. Whatever he thought of her, he had indeed consented to join her and her family for supper, and surely he would not do that if he did not think her respectable at the very least.

"For the last time, Papa, I assure you I meant nothing of the sort!"

With one hand on her hip and the other brandishing a long-handled wooden spoon, Julie confronted her father angrily.

"It is not proper!" Wilhelm repeated. "You are promised to Hans and should not be consorting with an unmarried man."

He kept his voice down, but the anger rang in the tightness of the words, the strangled sort of breathlessness at the end of each sharp sentence. Julie let her eyes stray from her father's furious countenance to the cowering shadow of her mother.

Katharine had, Julie admitted, warned that this would happen. Though she had agreed with her daughter that there was nothing essentially wrong with inviting the doctor to dinner—his patients did it frequently enough—there was the matter of Julie's reputation to think of. Hans would probably think the very worst of this episode.

But Katharine did not suggest that Julie cancel the invitation as a way of avoiding trouble. Instead she seemed quite content to leave the situation as it stood.

Wilhelm did not. As if echoing Katharine's earlier admonitions, he took a half step closer to

Julie and asked, "Just what do you think you will tell your fiancé? That you had dinner with another man? And what do you think he will say to that?"

"Must I tell him anything?" Surprised at her own defiance, Julie turned back to the gravy that was just beginning to thicken. "No, Papa, I'm not trying to keep anything from Hans, and of course I will tell him that we had Dr. Morgan for dinner. I have nothing to hide."

It was just as well she had turned around, because a guilty flush crept up to her cheeks. Those kisses loomed much greater, suddenly. And her feelings. Stirring the gravy slowly, she began to think about hiding those feelings, not just for a day or two or even a few weeks, but for the rest of her life.

"Papa, it's over and done with. I invited him, and whether it was a mistake or not, we can't turn him away. I promise not to do it again."

"You most certainly will not. And I think it is time to start thinking about a date for this wedding. Hans and I will discuss it Sunday."

The spoon nearly clattered to the floor, but Julie caught it just in time. When she looked around, Wilhelm had already retreated to the parlor.

Julie spoke very little through the meal; her mind was staggering under a weight of confusion. Seated across from her, Morgan rarely so much as glanced her way, but his manner suggested that he was more than just grateful for a decent meal. How much more? Enough to encourage her in the enterprise that little voice inside proposed to her?

A loud pounding on the front door brought her back to the present with a blink. She waited alertly while Wilhelm went to the door. Just a few seconds later, he returned.

"A patient for you, Doctor," he muttered, barely civil.

Morgan pushed his chair back and set his napkin beside his plate.

"Excuse me," he said quietly, his face a mask of concern.

At the door stood a boy of twelve or thirteen. Morgan could see the shadow of another person, perhaps a woman, seated on the top step of the porch.

"You the doc?" the boy asked.

"I am. What can I do for you?"

He pushed the screen door open and stepped outside.

"It's my ma. She's havin' a baby, only Pa says it's too early. She's in a awful bad way."

Before Morgan could say a word, he heard Julie's footsteps behind him.

"I'll come if you need me," she said.

Chapter Twenty-one
✦ ✦ ✦ ✦ ✦

THE LONG STRUGGLE was over. The surgery smelled of blood, sweat, tears, and pain. One lamp had guttered out, leaving the room bathed in sharp shadows.

Morgan dried his hands on a clean towel and stepped away from the table where Alice Elroy's body lay still.

"I did everything I could." He sighed. "Everything I knew how."

He dropped the towel to the floor with the dozens of others and then turned to Julie. She was bent over the makeshift crib on the counter. At first he thought she was just checking on the tiny infant nestled among the flour sacking in the hastily emptied packing crate, but when he saw her body shake and then stiffen, he knew she was desperately fighting tears.

"Go on home, Julie. I'll tell the boy and take care of things here."

She shook her head. Why did he always send her away? And why couldn't she tell him that no matter how difficult, how gruesome the tasks ahead, she would endure any and all of them if only she could stay with him? To go home and be alone while her mind relived the events of the evening would be far worse torture.

"I'm all right," she insisted, trying not to sniffle. "Besides, what are you going to do with the baby?"

"There's nothing I *can* do. You saw for yourself how weak he is."

She knew he was right. She knew that if she stayed she would only watch another human being die. Another shudder rippled through her like a blast of cold wind. Then warmth enveloped her as Morgan's hands on her shoulders gently turned her around and pulled her into his arms.

"I don't know what I'd do without you, Julie."

He had no intention of doing anything more to express his gratitude, yet he still felt somehow relieved when Ard Hammond, the stage agent and undertaker, arrived. Julie found a sheet to wrap the body in before Morgan lifted it onto Ard's stretcher.

"You want some help carrying her down to the shop?" the physician asked.

"Nope, I brought my boy with me," the grizzled, morbid-looking Ard replied. "Dave!" he called suddenly. "Git on in here and he'p me."

His son, who entered the room briskly and took up the other end of the stretcher, would no doubt eventually look just like Ard.

Julie watched the men and their burden leave, then she returned to her work. She walked wearily to the kitchen to fill a bucket with hot water from the stove and to get the mop. The mess had to be cleaned now, or it would be impossible to stand tomorrow.

When she returned to the surgery with her bucket and mop, she found Morgan already busy at the table. He had cleaned up the worst of the gore.

"What are you doing?" she asked.

"I thought I'd lend a hand. I figured you wouldn't leave until everything was done."

"You were right. By the way, have you got any spare clothes here you can change into? You ought to get that shirt soaking in cold water or the bloodstains will never come out."

He looked down at his ruined shirt. It was a good shirt, too, not one of his old ones. He had worn it to dinner, never expecting an emergency of quite this proportion. The pants, too, were stained, and with more than just blood.

"No extra shirts, but I think there's a pair of old denims upstairs."

"Then go put them on and I'll get these soaking."

The two rooms above were almost bare, except for Horace's bed and dresser in one and a stack of storage crates in another. In the second room Morgan found the old denims, folded more or less neatly on top of a crate. He set the lamp he had carried with him on the floor and shrugged out of his shirt. Next came the pants, which at least wouldn't show the stains. Quickly, knowing that Julie was working and waiting, he pulled the dungarees up over his hips and buttoned them.

Julie had hauled the galvanized washtub from the pantry and filled it half full of cold water.

When Morgan couldn't find her in the surgery, he went immediately to the kitchen, and there she was, wringing out the towels.

"Need some help?" he asked, dropping to his knees beside her.

She shook her head and turned slightly away from him.

He sensed the change instantly.

"Julie, what's wrong?"

A softly strangled sob burst from her like a soap bubble, and she dropped a wadded rag into the washtub with a mournful splash.

"The baby's gone, too," she said.

"Oh, God, no."

He told himself over and over again he had known it would happen, that there was no hope, but the reality, the finality, only now hit him.

"Don't cry, Julie, please, don't cry," he crooned, as he curled her into the embrace she fit so well. "There was nothing we could do, nothing at all. God, Julie, please." He kissed the top of her head and held her tightly. "Don't cry. I can't stand it when you cry."

She tried, as hard as she could, but the tears refused to come under her control. And the sobs shaking her whole body resisted all her attempts to still them, as though they had been too long imprisoned and now surged free. Clinging to him, she wept for the tiny life that had so briefly breathed, but also for other tragedies, both old and new.

For Ted Sheen and Amy Morgan. For Del Morgan, who had lost so much of himself when he lost his wife and son. And for herself. Never before had she cried out her own pain, her own sorrow. Always she had wept for someone else. But holding him, knowing at least at this particular moment he needed her as much as she needed him, she suffered the sharpest pain she had ever felt. The tears of self-pity obeyed no commands.

Morgan stood without losing his hold on Julie. He stumbled in the darkness, then found the sofa and sank onto it with a sigh. With one hand he reached behind him to open the window and let in the cooler evening air, and Julie, still crying softly on his chest, nestled close to him. He stroked her temple, the gesture familiar now. But as her hands moved on his body, the unfamiliar pain blossomed.

His skin was warm and slick with sweat under her trembling fingers. Trapped behind him, her hands became too aware of the texture of the man, but the act of freeing them only increased the awareness. From the almost satiny smooth skin of his back, under which she could feel the firm muscles glide easily, to the tight flesh over his ribs, she drew her hands slowly, exploringly, reluctantly. She tucked one arm between her body and his, feeling the sudden lurch of her own heart against the back of her wrist while the tips of her fingers encountered the coarse hairs on his chest.

He could hardly breathe. He must not let her continue this, but he could not find the words to make her stop. When the words came, he wondered who spoke, and could not believe it was he.

He captured her hand in his and squeezed it as he said, "No, Julie. Don't touch me like that. Just hold me, and let me hold you, and then we'll both feel better."

If he had thought to halt the rising of his desire by stilling her hand, he found only defeat. The fingers he clasped so tightly curled possessively around his and held his hand against the warmth of her body. Now he, too, felt the rapid pulse thudding against her ribs. When she turned her tear-wet face toward him and her lips moved in a tentative kiss just above his own heart, his sigh became a moan of agony.

"No, Julie, please, no," he gasped, though his body betrayed him and he could not stop her kisses or deny the effect they had on him. "This isn't right, Julie, not now, not here."

Though he continued to murmur against what was happening, he could not ignore the delightful rightness of his feelings. She felt good in his arms, as though she belonged there, belonged to him. But he knew she didn't. She belonged, of her own volition, to another man, and Del Morgan had no right to step between like this. He shivered against the cold of losing her embrace, but he found the strength to grasp her arms and set her away from him.

"No, Julie," he insisted firmly when she struggled briefly to free herself. He dared not take advantage of her the way others had.

She lifted a hand to touch his shadowed cheek.

"But I—"

"No arguments," he interrupted. "It's nothing to be ashamed of, but we have to forget it, all right?"

Though in the dark room he could not see the flush of humiliation that stained her cheeks, he knew it was there by the way she turned away. Still holding her arms, he felt the tensing of muscles that signaled she was ready to flee.

"Julie, we have to talk," he said earnestly. "For God's sake, will you look at me?"

"I can't. I just tried to tell you—"

"Listen to me first, all right?" He halted her confession before it started. "I know what you're thinking."

He talked, but she couldn't listen. His words could not penetrate the screaming echoes that rang between her ears. *I love him, but he'll never love me back. I love him, but if I tell him, I'll lose him.*

He stood and pulled her to her feet, and finally she forced herself to hear what he was saying. The echoes, though fainter now, remained, like a mournful chorus.

"Go home, Julie. Get some sleep. And don't show up here tomorrow, do you understand?"

Horrified, she lifted wide eyes to him. He was sending her away, not just for tonight but forever. Her heart stopped beating and her breath strangled in her throat.

"You've been working much too hard, and an extra day's rest is the least I can give you," he went on. "I'll stop by around noon, to see you and to take a look at your mother's arm, all right?"

With a gasp of relief, her lungs filled again, and the frantic pulse resumed its rhythm.

"I'm all right, really I am," she insisted. "I can stay and finish here. I don't want—"

"I said, no arguments." God, would she never leave? He was approaching the limits of whatever control he had, and he doubted he had much.

But I don't want to leave you, her throbbing heart ached to tell him, and I can't bear the thought of your being alone with what's in that other room. Let me stay. Please, God, let me stay. But she let him guide her to the door, first with his hand gently cupping her elbow, then without even that slight contact.

"Good night, Dr. Morgan," she said, not able to leave without some farewell. "And I'm sorry."

"I thought I told you, no apologies."

"I meant about Mrs. McElroy and . . . the baby."

Guilt knifed through him. He had been so thoroughly preoccupied by the living woman that he had forgotten the other. And the infant. Remembering them, he regretted the need to send Julie away. Now he wanted her with him, needed her desperately to share the burden of pain with him as he knew she would. At the same time, he knew even more certainly that he dared not let her stay.

"We did everything I knew how, and it just wasn't enough. Like I said, no apologies. We did our best. Good night, Julie."

He held the screen door open, though the moths flitted in, drawn by the lamps still burning in the parlor. As much as he hated to see her go, he breathed a long sigh of relief when she walked down those two steps. That last smile of hers almost made him take her in his arms again, and if he had, he would never have let her go. The surge of engorging blood to his loins was unmistakable and couldn't be ignored.

At the bottom of the stairs Julie turned, seeking one last glimpse.

She saw, clearly delineated by the lamplight, a man.

Chapter Twenty-two

✦✦✦✦

MORGAN HAD NOT been able to look at the tiny form inside the crate. He forced himself to reach under the single thin blanket and touch the baby to verify what Julie had told him, but once certain that the boy was dead, he could not look. With a heart as heavy as the hammer in his hand, he nailed the lid back on the box. Then he lifted the cradle-turned-coffin and began the short walk to the stage depot where Ard had his other business in the back room.

Relieved of his burden, Morgan walked slowly

home. Emptiness waited for him, an emptiness he was in no hurry to reach. Only his conscience resided there now, and he was too weary to face its accusations.

He brought warm water from the roof to the kitchen and washed there, then walked to the dark parlor. Winnie no longer left a light for him; she didn't worry about his tripping or stumbling in drunken blindness. Still wearing the old denims, he stretched out on the sofa, his feet hanging over the arm as he lay his head back and closed his eyes.

Guilt blanketed him, exactly as he had known it would, and he was too tired to fight it. He had seen the horror and humiliation in her eyes when he forced her to leave. But what else could he have done? If he had let her stay and had tried to explain, he would only have succumbed to his newfound weakness. He was damned if he did and damned if he didn't. Either way, he knew she would assume he thought the worst of her. If he rejected her, it was because he thought her wicked, and if he took advantage of her, it was because he thought her wicked.

And the irony, of course, was that he thought no such thing. Quite the opposite, in fact.

He could no longer avoid declaring his intentions to Julie, if she would even listen to him. Out of necessity—and he swore at Horace again for dying so precipitously—he had entered into this relationship without thinking. If indeed Julie loved that bastard Wallenmund and was determined to marry him, then Morgan need not go any further. He would merely suggest that she turn her attentions to her fiancé. Finding another nurse would be difficult, but he had warned himself not to take Julie for granted, and he would set about finding a replacement as soon as possible.

If, on the other hand, Julie had the slightest doubt, the barest hint of reluctance, perhaps another man stood a chance.

Try as he might, Morgan couldn't get comfortable on the sofa. It was too short and too narrow and too hard. The more he tossed and turned, the more he thought about Julie. Not the Julie of the medical books or the applesauce cake or the broken spectacles or the neatly embroidered sutures. The woman whose images filled his brain was the one who had curled against him and kissed his skin.

He twisted onto his back again, and one leg slipped off the sofa, his bare foot finding the tiled floor cold. A dip in the much colder water of the creek might wash this terrible wanting away, but he was too tired to get up, even though he knew he'd have a stiff neck from sleeping on the sofa. He was too tired to do anything but snore.

In the morning, when he was rested, he would face the rest of the problem. He would decide how to go about telling Julie of his feelings, and probably rehearse a speech as moronic as the one with which he had proposed to Amy. But it would have to wait until morning.

* * *

The storm that wakened Julie in the middle of the night, just in time to close the window before the rain soaked her, continued through late morning. Thunder rumbled and echoed off the mountains, lightning shattered the leaden clouds, and steaming rain poured in sheets.

She wandered down to the kitchen at the usual hour to prepare breakfast and found her mother already at work. Though still hampered with the broken arm, Katharine had managed to fry a dozen strips of bacon and was now stirring shredded potatoes in the skillet. Above all these scents, the aroma of hot, fresh coffee floated.

"I'll finish that, Mama," Julie offered, rushing to take the spatula from Katharine's hand.

"No, you won't. Dr. Morgan was just here and told me you're to rest all day. You get yourself right back up to bed and sleep."

Stunned, Julie put up no resistance when Katharine grabbed the spatula back and flipped the hash browns over quite neatly. Their underside was just perfectly golden brown.

"And no coffee for you, either," Katharine added. "You may have a glass of milk, but coffee will keep you awake, and he gave specific orders. Sleep is what you need, and I intend to see that you get it."

"May I have some toast at least?"

"Yes, but I'll bring it up to you after your father leaves for work. Now, do I have to chase you out of here?"

Katharine laughed lightly, a hauntingly familiar laugh that Julie remembered quite well, though it had been years since she had heard it. It was almost as though the last nine years had simply disappeared, and this was the mother she had known so long ago.

Confused and acknowledging that a few more hours of sleep wouldn't be unwelcome, Julie left the kitchen and slowly climbed the stairs. She heard her father moving in his room, smelled the tingling scent of shaving lather borne on steam, and knew that Katharine had brought him his shaving water. The morning became more perplexing than ever.

Though tired enough to lie back down on her bed, Julie could not shake the years of early rising quite so easily. She was yawning with her eyes closed but was still wide awake when Katharine arrived with a tray covered with dishes.

"Oh, Mama, I can't eat all that!" Julie exclaimed when she saw two eggs nestled on a mound of potatoes, golden toast dripping with sweet butter and strawberry preserves, four thick slices of bacon, and a tall glass of milk.

"Dr. Morgan told me I was to see you had a good breakfast, too, so that means I'm going to wait right here until it's all gone. You'd better start eating, young lady."

As stern as Katharine was, she continued to smile. Julie looked at her and wondered where the old sincerity had come from. Julie hadn't seen that smile on her mother's face since long before Willy was born.

Under her mother's unswerving eye Julie began to eat, and before very long she discovered she had eaten almost every bite. The food was delicious, and not only because she hadn't had to cook it. Not once during the entire meal had she been interrupted, and Katharine even asked her if she wanted more.

"I don't think so, Mama. I'm really very full."

"Good. You always sleep better on a full stomach."

Unfortunately, Julie was more wide awake than ever. Curiosity had roused her from the last hold of weariness.

"I slept well last night, Mama, and it wasn't that late when I got home, so maybe—"

"It was almost midnight when you walked in the door! Don't you call that very late?"

"Midnight? But you were still up and so I thought—"

"Of course I was. I was waiting to make sure you came home safely."

Julie was too accustomed to watching her words to blurt out the accusation that Katharine had never been so concerned before. Not only was Katharine's staying up late unusual, and her explanation, but Julie detected something like disappointment in her mother's last statement as though Katharine had almost hoped Julie would stay with Morgan.

"Well, I'm too awake to sleep now. I thought maybe I'd get some goods from McCrory's and do some sewing. I'm afraid I ruined my dress last night."

Katharine lifted the tray from her daughter's lap and paused as if lost in serious thought for a moment.

"It's raining, you know. You'll get soaked through to the skin and the doctor will have a fit if you take a chill and get sick and then can't work for him."

"I won't get sick, Mama." Julie threw the sheet back and swung her feet to the floor. "It's still awfully warm outside, and I won't be in the rain but a minute or two running across the street and back."

"I just hope the doctor doesn't see you and blame me for it."

When Julie went downstairs a few minutes later, she found Katharine in the parlor with several magazines, including the new *Godey's* and some back issues of *Frank Leslie's*. She motioned to Julie to join her.

"I think we could duplicate these waists quite easily, don't you?" she asked, showing Julie the drawings of several styles. "You'll want something relatively simple, with sleeves that can be rolled up like a man's. And none of these impossible collars! How could a woman work in weather like we have here and breathe with all that lace strangling her throat?"

"But then I'd need skirts, too. I only have two, and the green is—"

"That green is ready for the rag bin! Yes, you'd better have at least three or four more skirts. We'll purchase the material today, and then I can do the sewing while you're at work. Dr.

Morgan said I'll be at least able to do some chores when this *thing* comes off Monday."

"Monday?"

"Yes. Look, I think the rain is letting up a little, so why don't you run over to the store and buy what you need. I'll clean off the dining room table and we can begin cutting in there."

If the rain had let up when Katharine looked out the window, it had returned to a downpour by the time Julie stepped off the porch. She didn't dare run, because the muddy street was too slippery and dangerous. Besides, the sucking slime pulled at each step, forcing her to take extra care not to lose a shoe.

She climbed the stairs to the sidewalk and ducked under the dripping overhang, though she couldn't avoid a drenching stream down her back. It didn't matter: She was already soaked nearly through to the skin. While trying to stomp the worst of the mud off her shoes, Julie realized that she had no idea how to pay for the goods she intended to purchase. She had not brought a single penny with her.

Under no circumstances, despite the orders from Morgan regarding aprons, could she put the bill on his account.

Expecting Ada, who usually waited on customers, Julie was surprised when Simon strolled from behind the hardware counter at the back of the store.

"Mornin', Miss Julie," he greeted.

"Good morning, Mr. McCrory."

She nodded politely and smiled, and Simon

thought that, wet and bedraggled as she was, she certainly didn't look much like the girl he and Lucas used to watch carrying lunch to her father. She had lost that dreary, dusty, worn-out look.

"I came for some yard goods," she told him as she walked purposefully in that direction.

"Good day for sewin', ain't it."

"Yes, I suppose it is." She reached the sloppily piled stack of bolts and ran a finger down the edges. The calicos and ginghams were mixed right in with the denim and muslin and sturdy broadcloth, with nothing in any particular order. "I'll take four yards each of the black, blue, and brown broadcloth. No, not the brown. Make it this green instead."

Simon pulled the bolts from their places in the stacks, miraculously avoiding toppling the colorful ziggurat. While he unrolled and measured the fabrics, Julie studied the bright prints and checks. It was hard to make up her mind when faced with so many choices, especially after such a long time without the temptation. She particularly liked a soft lavender gingham but knew it wouldn't be suitable, nor would the bright red and yellow calico that sat on the top of the heap.

She had to be practical, she reminded herself. Plain and practical, just as she had always been.

"And three yards each of the blue and white muslins, plus this yellow."

Simon was panting by the time he had pulled those three bolts out, because the butter-yellow calico, printed with small blue flowers, was on the very bottom. But as he realigned the tottering stack, Julie caught sight of another bolt, so slim it had been hidden between the others. Once she had seen the clear cornflower color, however, she knew she could not leave the store without it.

"And this blue batiste: Is there enough left on the bolt, do you think, for a blouse?" she asked Simon.

Very carefully, he extracted the fabric from under the weight of those pressing down from above. The stack wobbled, prompting Julie to reach for and steady it with a gasp.

"Can't tell without measuring it."

This wasn't Simon's area of expertise, and he acted as though perhaps he felt foolish measuring out and cutting fabric for women's clothes.

"Then measure it," she ordered, surprising herself.

It came to four and one-quarter yards, more than enough, and Julie took it all. She had even thought of a way to pay for it.

"You can put this on my father's account," she told Simon calmly. After all, Katharine had suggested the purchases and had even offered to help with the sewing.

Why? Julie wondered quite suddenly.

Barely remembering to thank Mr. McCrory, Julie wandered slowly away from the counter and toward the door, her mind fully occupied with questions.

Katharine had looked remarkably fit this morning, standing over the kitchen range with a spatula in her hand. In the weeks since beginning the treatment Morgan had prescribed, Katharine had had other moments of seeming vigor, but they never lasted long enough for her to do anything useful. Her headaches came and went with puzzling irregularity, and her digestion seemed little improved at times. Yet today, as Julie had remarked to herself immediately upon the discovery, Katharine looked as though she had never been ill.

By the time Julie reached her own front porch again, drenched without having felt the rain, the curiosity had become an obsession.

"Oh, Julie, look at you!" Katharine exclaimed from her chair in the parlor. "Get right upstairs and out of those wet clothes! I'll put on some tea."

Julie set her package on the bottom stair and then proceeded up. In the privacy of her room, she dared to examine some of those questions individually, like a surgeon dissecting a cadaver.

Why, if Katharine had never been ill, had she pretended to be for so long? Two possibilities came to mind. Either she hated her daughter and had long ago decided to take revenge upon her by forcing her into this slavish existence, or she maintained an elaborate fiction simply to deny her husband his marital rights. Yet, if indeed Katharine were afraid of another pregnancy, she could merely have used that as an excuse. Couldn't she?

Julie peeled off her dripping dress and shivered until she found a towel to dry with.

On the other hand, if Katharine so disliked Julie all these years, why had she suddenly changed her tune to one of helpful kindness and affection?

And, Julie asked herself, why am I suddenly so suspicious?

She pulled on a dry blouse and stepped into the frayed green skirt, then padded down the stairs in her stockinged feet. When she arrived at the bottom of the stairs she looked into the parlor, expecting to find Katharine still lounging with her periodicals. Instead, the sound of rustling paper and light humming drew her eyes to the dining room.

"The tea is all ready, there on the sideboard," Katharine told her between snatches of melody. "I've been looking at your selections, and I can't say I entirely approve."

Julie felt her heart sink to her toes. The blue batiste. No doubt Mama felt it was impractical and extravagant. No doubt Mama would tell her to return it. Worse, perhaps Katharine would appropriate it for herself.

But before Julie had a chance to say a word in her defense, Katharine went on, "I like this blue very much, and it will make up beautifully, but the others are so plain. Did Mrs. McCrory have nothing else?"

"I . . . bought what I thought I would need for working, Mama," Julie stammered, confused and somehow embarrassed. The batiste, which she had thought would meet with disapproval, was the only thing Katharine did like. Just another source of confusion and curiosity.

"Well, while you were shopping, I sent Willy over to Donnie Kincheloe's so he'd be out of our hair. I suggest we use this opportunity to get as much done as possible. Shall we start with the blue batiste?"

Morgan stepped into McCrory's and waited patiently while Simon assisted a customer. Seeing that it was Julie and that she was buying several pieces of dress goods, he almost came out of his concealing shadow, but something held him back. He did not want to embarrass her if the fabric was not for the dress he owed her, nor could he even mention the gift itself.

And when he heard her tell Simon to put the materials on her father's account, he shrank back further into that gloom that was as much mental as physical. Only after she had left did he walk out from behind the lantern-festooned post and approach the counter.

"Sorry to keep you waitin', Del," Simon apologized while he took the requested cheroots from the humidor. "Miss Hollstrom must be gettin' her trousseau ready."

Black brows arched over the murky green eyes.

"Her trousseau?"

"Well, I can't imagine her buyin' fancy French

material for anything else. Not quite the stuff to wear workin' for you, anyway."

"Yeah, you're right, I guess," Morgan mumbled in return, wary against saying more. He nodded to Simon and walked on out into the rain.

Chapter Twenty-three

✦ ✦ ✦ ✦

MOTHER AND DAUGHTER worked until noon, when Julie took lunch to Wilhelm. The rain had stopped and a brilliant, clean-washed sun shimmered in the steam. Wilhelm grunted something about the meal being better than what he usually had, but he did not make it a compliment. Rather, his words hinted at adding to Julie's guilt for abandoning her family's welfare again. Julie was too confused and too preoccupied with new problems to worry about old ones.

She stopped for a few moments at McCrory's on the way home to buy a card of jet buttons. There were plenty of plain white pearl buttons in the sewing basket, but Katharine had insisted black would set off the blue batiste better. Julie had not been able to argue with that enthusiasm.

Katharine proved to be of much more help than Julie ever expected. Almost as though one arm weren't held captive, Katharine pinned and cut and measured with no sign of disability. Julie had to do all the sewing, but with Katharine to do the rest, she was able to spend almost all her time at the little sewing machine, until the constant treadling cramped her calf muscles.

The effort was, however, worth it. Long before Wilhelm was expected home, Julie and her mother had finished the blue batiste blouse and the black broadcloth skirt.

Julie put them on and was delightedly parading in front of the little mirror above Katharine's dresser when the front door banged open and then slammed shut.

"Juliet Rosalind!" Wilhelm's voice thundered louder than the morning's storm.

Katharine glanced at the clock on the dresser and then whispered, "What is he doing here? He shouldn't have been home for another hour!"

The abject terror in her mother's voice frightened Julie more than her father's unmistakable wrath.

She walked from the bedroom to the landing at the top of the stairs and called down, "We are here, Papa." She couldn't be sure if her voice trembled or not, but her knees threatened to collapse.

Wilhelm, standing at the foot of the stairs, spun around, his hands bent into fists at his waist. In one of them, Julie noticed, he held a small slip of white paper. For a moment, father and daughter stared at each other, unmoving, until Wilhelm brandished the paper and his fist at her.

"I have just been to the general store," he announced, almost stammering in his fury. His fleshy face had turned bright red, and his shouts vibrated the timbers of the house. "Mr. Simon McCrory gave *this* to me. He said you had forgotten it."

"Papa, I only—"

He would not let her speak.

"Three yards of this, four and a half yards of that, and all charged to my account. Do you not have money of your own?"

He seemed to wait for an answer, but Julie knew she would only be interrupted again. Besides, she could find nothing to say. She had known, when she told the storekeeper to put the purchases on Wilhelm's account, that her father would not allow it.

"*Slut!*" he screamed, taking one step upwards toward her. "Do you think that I am made out of money that you can squander it on fancy materials to parade in front of that man?"

Why did she have to be wearing the batiste blouse right now? It condemned her, just as she deserved to be condemned, for he was right. Nothing she could say would change Wilhelm's mind. The evidence was there for all to see.

He mounted the stairs slowly, his angry fist preceding him with undisguised menace.

"Over twelve dollars this extravagance has

cost me! How am I to clothe your brother when you spend so much on yourself?"

"Willy?" Julie gasped, feeling a now-familiar swell of anger. "Willy has more clothes than he can possibly wear in a year, and then he'll be too big for them."

Her defiance halted Wilhelm midstride, but only for a moment, not more than a matter of seconds at most. He had reached the halfway point on the stairs and was close enough for her to see the swollen veins on his forehead, the droplets of sweat sliding down his temples.

"How dare you talk back to me," he hissed, his voice low but more threatening than ever. "All these years I have fed and clothed you, saved your reputation for you, and this is how you repay me?"

Somehow, Julie's numbed legs carried her, by infinitesimal steps, backward in the direction of the door to her room. But she felt nothing except pure rage and hatred. For those few hours today, she had known the exquisite joy of living, of doing something for herself, and now he had turned it to guilt again. This time, however, she had the means to meet his challenge.

She backed through the open door and without taking her eyes from her father, Julie opened the small metal box on the top of her dresser. Inside it lay the heavy gold coin Morgan had forced on her. She had treasured it these past few days, dreaming of ways to spend it and yet knowing that she would never part with it, for it meant far more to her than just money.

She took it out and held it tightly, the sharp edges digging cruelly into her palm and clenched fingers. But it wasn't the pain in her hand that brought the tears hot and stinging to her eyes and the sobs that strangled her words as she flung them, with the coin, at her father's head.

"Take it!" she shrieked. "Take it as you've taken everything else from me! You leave me with nothing but what you give me: shame, guilt, unworthiness. You may as well have my money, too."

Missing its intended target, the double eagle bounced harmlessly off Wilhelm's shoulder and then clattered down the bare steps. When it came to rest by the front door, Julie had already shut herself in her room.

It was a tedious Saturday, made worse by the enervating heat and sticky humidity that followed the rain. Throughout the long afternoon Morgan struggled against inertia until finally, shortly after six, he had cleared the waiting room, had seen his last patient, and prepared to go home. The office smelled of sweat and snot-nosed children and colicky babies and all the other odors of summer discomforts, with not a breath of breeze to dissipate them. Morgan looked around at the mess he was leaving and walked out the door anyway.

He washed hurriedly in the kitchen, then changed his clothes for more comfortable denims and a wrinkled but clean cotton shirt before setting out for Daneggar's. Liza Tucker had invited him for supper in return for bandaging her son's sprained ankle, but he had turned her down. He wondered just how long the young widow had been looking in his direction that way.

He didn't want to be with a woman now, unless that woman was Julie Hollstrom. He had quite made up his mind to speak his piece this morning when he saw her go into McCrory's, but then had second thoughts. Lack of privacy was a good excuse at the time, he thought. And when Simon told him about her purchases, Morgan was doubly glad he'd held back. He'd only have made fool of himself, stumbling over a proposal he had rehearsed and rehearsed only to have her politely refuse him and remind him she already had a fiancé.

Daneggar's was crowded and noisy and smelled little better than the clinic. Leif's eldest daughter, Lorraine, made a buxom show of leading Morgan to a corner table and announcing that the evening's special was pork chops, mashed potatoes and gravy, and peas and carrots. He ordered the special, declined a drink, and slumped back into his corner.

He watched Lorraine weave between the tables toward the kitchen. Her hips swayed under a black skirt, enticing any and all who watched. He knew when she took his order that she had used the noise of the supper patrons as an excuse to lean over the table and give him a more-than-generous glimpse of the full mounds of her breasts beneath a low-cut white blouse. He hadn't turned away from the display, but neither had he felt any reaction.

She tossed her red hair back from her shoulders when she brought his meal. Her blue eyes fixed on him with undisguised seduction, and Morgan felt himself wanting to respond. He wanted to want her, he *tried* to want her, but there was nothing, so he politely thanked her and reached for the salt and pepper.

Lorraine bounced off.

The chops were dry and overdone, the gravy greasy, and the peas mushy, but he ate anyway. Leif's cooking left a great deal to be desired, but his wife made damned good apple pie, so Morgan had two pieces for dessert. He left a quarter on the table for Lorraine, and then headed for home again.

Eight o'clock and hot as hell. He was drenched in sweat before he walked into the parlor, all dark and cool from being shuttered all day. Maybe, just maybe, he'd have a quiet evening all to himself. He had seen, on the way back from the restaurant, that the Castle was almost deserted. A storm generally kept people home, and the ranchhands and farmers were sometimes prevented from coming to town by swollen creeks and washes. Of course, muggy, electric weather like this often brought out the worst in those who did get their hands on a bottle, so he wouldn't count on a lack of trouble.

Tired, his hunger satisfied, too lethargic with the heat even to get up and go to bed, Morgan dozed on the sofa, his feet propped on a table, his head lolled back uncomfortably. He fell asleep just barely deep enough to dream, yet not so far that he lost touch with reality. It was as though he watched himself dream from across the room.

He dreamt of Julie, of being with her day after day, of working with her, laughing with her, talking quietly with her, making love with her. And he watched it all with silent detachment, knowing none of it was real. When he wakened, stiff in the neck and with one leg gone to sleep, he felt no rush of confused reality, only a sense of impatient misery. If she was going to leave him, he wished she would do it quickly and get it the hell over with.

Thirsty after those dry, salty pork chops, he strolled through the kitchen and out the back door to the pump and a drink of cold water. The splash on his bare feet revived him in the muggy dark of the evening. Though some light lingered in the west, the sky above the creek and backyard was inky blue, with stars already brightening and blinking.

Stars. Brilliant and tantalizing and always out of reach. They taunted him tonight. Numbly, ignoring the prickles of returning circulation in his foot, he pulled on his boots and headed back through the house and out the front door.

The mud sucked at his feet, but he almost ran, taking long, hurried strides with enormous determination. The cemetery gate swung open with an agonized scream, then continued to squeak as it swayed back and forth. Morgan didn't close it behind him.

He stepped in puddles without feeling them, and when he came to the granite stone where the roses bloomed, he knelt on the raised grassy mound without heeding the wetness that soaked his jeans.

"God help me, Amy, but I love her," he whispered.

Julie had not left her room, nor had anyone sought admittance. For hours she lay on her bed and sobbed and wished she had the courage to get up and leave. Years of practicality, however, had left her too sensible of life's harsh realities. She had no money, not since throwing away her hard-earned twenty dollars, and she had no place to go. If she had thought—and she examined the issue carefully for any hint of hope—that Morgan cared for her in any particular way, she would have gone to him. But she had already shown him how foolish she could be where men were concerned, and she could not humiliate herself needlessly again. He respected her now, and that was worth a great deal more than a batiste blouse and a gold coin.

If only she hadn't been so impulsive about the money! She pounded her pillow angrily again. She had thrown away her freedom when she threw the coin. Now her only choices were to stay with her family and be miserable but at least be with Morgan a few hours out of the day, or to marry Hans and be away from it all.

She shuddered convulsively. The idea of lying with Hans, of letting him touch her and make love to her—but it wouldn't be making love. It would be mating, the way he bred his cows. It would be nothing like what Del had described between him and Amy.

She heard the sounds of Katharine preparing supper, but no one came upstairs, either to ask for help in the kitchen or to call Julie to the meal. So she went hungry. She had become more and more accustomed to regular meals, and now she felt the loss of this one more keenly than before. Her stomach rumbled loudly when the smell of fried beefsteak wafted through the house, but even hunger wasn't a strong enough incentive to brave her father's fury.

She changed her clothes, removing the precious blue blouse and new skirt and slipping on an old soft nightgown, then lay down on the bed. The time passed slowly until she heard Willy grumble his way to bed shortly after dark.

The argument started soon after. Wilhelm growled low and Katharine wailed softly, so that Julie could not understand what they fought about. For well over an hour, from the time the sun was a glowering red disk outside Julie's window until the last light faded over the mountains, her parents quarreled in the parlor.

Then, quite suddenly, Katharine's voice raised

to a shrill scream, broken by a loud slap and a heavy thud. Frightened, Julie sprang from her bed and staggered across the room. While she fumbled in the dense dark for the doorknob, she heard her mother, sobbing, run up the stairs, across the landing, and into her room, where she slammed the door hard enough to shake the entire house.

"Don't you *dare*, Wilhelm Hollstrom!" Katharine shouted above the sound of furniture being pushed against the door. "Don't you dare!"

But a few seconds later, both she and her daughter knew that her threats went unheard, for the front door opened and then banged shut, and Wilhelm's footsteps pounded down the porch stairs.

Julie waited, her heart thudding, her breath held burning in her lungs. She hadn't been so terrified since the night Willy was born. And for some reason, she worried now about Morgan. Would her father try the same sort of thing with him? At the very idea, a wave of nausea slithered through her.

She had to tell him. She had to risk everything on the slim chance that he cared, even a little. She turned the knob and opened the door, then waited, counting to a hundred very slowly, to be sure Wilhelm was not going to return.

The landing was dim, lit only by the lights below, but it was not empty. His face nearly as white as his nightshirt, Willy stood in the doorway to his room.

"It's all right, Willy," Julie told him, settling her own shaky voice. "Go on back to bed."

"But I'm scared," he whined. "What's wrong, Julie? Are you in trouble again?"

"Yes," she answered truthfully. "And it's none of your business. Get back to bed. I have to see Mama."

But Willy refused to be placated, and after several failed attempts to get him into his bed again, Julie gave up and let him tag along as she went to see her mother.

She knocked tentatively on the closed door. When there was no response, she tried the handle. It turned, and the latch clicked free, but the door refused to yield.

"Move the chair, Mama," Julie ordered. "I want to talk to you."

"Go away," Katharine whined, sounding exactly like Willy.

"No, Mama. I need to see you. Are you all right? Did Papa hurt you?"

To her surprise, Julie discovered that she felt real concern for her mother, not just the obligatory worry. Had those few hours of comradeship this afternoon restored all that nine years of slavery had destroyed? Or was it something else?

"I'll break the door down if I have to, Mama."

At that, there was a creak of bedsprings and the tapping of high heels on the floor before Katharine slid the chair out from under the doorknob and the door swung inward.

Katharine's hair hung loosely tangled about her shoulders, as though someone had grabbed it and pulled it free of its pins in a single swipe. Her eyes looked larger than usual in the gloomy light as she peered hesitantly around the door.

"Is he gone?" she whispered.

Julie nodded. "But I don't know for how long."

Katharine's eyes darted about nervously, from Julie to Willy to the descending staircase and the door at its foot.

"Julie, go get Dr. Morgan, right away," she ordered in that same desperate whisper.

"Are you hurt? Did Papa hurt you?"

"I . . . I don't think so, but I'm not sure. Please, just go get the doctor."

"All right, Mama, I'll try to find him. Just let me put some clothes on and—"

"No, Julie, please go now. Your father may be back any second. Here, take my robe and put it on." She handed the long velvet garment to Julie, who didn't take it right away. "Hurry, please, Julie, *please!*"

Again Julie heard terror in her mother's voice. Ignoring Willy, who shouted behind her, Julie raced barefoot down the stairs and opened the door. She stopped on the porch only long enough to fit her arms into the sleeves of her mother's robe, which was inches too short, and to decide where to begin her search.

The office was dark; he wasn't there. Ignoring the mud that clung to her feet and spattered her nightgown, Julie ran across the street and down the lane toward the adobe house. It, too, was dark, and something about the place suggested stark emptiness. Worried, Julie raced back toward the main street, though she had no idea where she would go next.

Lucas Carter sat on the porch in front of McCrory's. Julie called to him.

"Mr. Carter, have you seen Dr. Morgan this evening?"

He shot a long stream of tobacco in her general direction.

"I seen him at Leif's havin' supper, but not since. I know he ain't at the Castle, though, Miss Julie. Mebbe he got called out o' town on a 'mergency."

"Yes, thank you, Mr. Carter, that must be it."

She turned to head home, disappointed and afraid, because she knew there had been no emergency. There was no sign tacked to the office door, and Morgan was always careful to leave word when he was called away.

And where had her father gone? Should she go looking for him? Would she find him with Morgan? She shivered. That nightmare could not possibly come again.

She didn't realize, walking in the dark, that she had passed the gate to her front yard and was nearly to the edge of town. What brought her back to reality was the sound of crying, or maybe it was laughter, from the churchyard. Now that her eyes had become accustomed to the near-total darkness, Julie could see that the gate hung open, though there was no breeze to stir its rusty hinges.

Her feet found the same puddles Morgan's

had, and she walked just as unerringly to the rose-garlanded grave where he knelt.

He had been talking, but at the sound of Julie's sloshy footsteps on the path, he stopped and held his breath.

"Dr. Morgan?"

"Julie?"

She halted a step or two from him.

"I've just been talking to Amy about you."

She retreated another step. Was he drunk again?

He got to his feet and reached a hand out to her. When she didn't take it, he let it fall slowly to his side.

"I'm not crazy, Julie," he told her. "And I'm not drunk, if you thought that. But sometimes I like to come and talk to her, you know?"

She nodded and hugged the loose robe tighter around her. She fumbled for the belt but it was gone, or perhaps she had never had it.

"Please, Dr. Morgan, it's very late," Julie dared to say when he paused for a moment. "I only came here because my mother's been hurt and she wants you."

"In a minute, Julie, in a minute. It's taken me all day to get up the nerve for this; don't interrupt me."

Now she was frightened, but she could not leave him.

His voice, which had been a little shaky and almost dreamy, firmed and settled into a strong timbre that sent a queer thrill down Julie's spine.

"Amy was my life, everything I lived for, Ju-

lie. The sun, the moon, the very earth I walked
on. When she died, it was though all the light
turned dark. I couldn't find my way through it
without her. I stumbled, I fell, I banged into
things and got hurt."

Her right hand still held the edges of Katharine's robe together, but Morgan had wrapped
both his around her left. Warmth enveloped her,
spreading upward from that tiny portion of an
embrace.

"Do you see those stars up there, Julie? Amy
and I used to try to count them. But they don't
hold still, and you can't reach out and pick them
the way you would berries in a basket. They just
sit up there and tease with their sparkle. They
don't light up anything bright enough to see,
and yet we know the night would be unbearable
without them.

"But then there's the firefly," he said.

He let go her hand long enough to pluck one
of the glimmering beetles from Julie's hair. It
crawled along his finger awhile before winging
off into the sultry night.

"It brightens the night no more than a star,
and only for a brief second, while the stars shine
steadily," he whispered. "But it will light on
your hand and let you hold it for a while, and
somehow the dark isn't so dark."

He caught another of the little creatures and
imprisoned it in a loose fist. As it lit up, the glow
seeped out through his fingers. When he flattened his palm, the firefly didn't leave, as though

it were content to rest there and shimmer captively until he blew gently, and, like its companion, it flew off.

"You've been like the firefly to me, Julie. My life has been one long night since I lost Amy. Finally you came along and lit that night with a brilliance I could hardly remember. Unlike the frozen, distant, teasing stars, you were right here where I could touch you and hold you . . . and let you go, if I wanted to."

"And if I didn't want to go?"

She could scarcely believe she had said those words, and yet they seemed the most natural reply to all he had told her. No, he hadn't said a single word about love. She kept that fact quite clear in her reeling mind. And not a word about marriage, either. Still, she didn't think he would resort to such poetic comparisons if he merely wanted her to stay on as his nurse.

"You are free to do as you wish, Julie. I can't and won't hold you against your will."

It was torment to say those words, when what he really wanted to do was beg her to stay. He struggled against that stubborn pride, but he knew he did the right thing. Pleading would only embarrass them both, more so if she turned him down.

He touched her chin and tilted it up until her eyes met his. His kiss was soft, giving and not taking even what she offered.

And then she remembered her mother.

She pulled away from him roughly, clumsily, and turned her back to him.

"Please, Dr. Morgan, my mother needs you. She sent me to find you right away."

And I can't stand kissing you like this when I know you're still thinking about Amy, she thought. If you want me at all, it's because you think I can take her place, and I can't. I won't.

Not waiting to see if he followed, Julie splashed through the puddles and the mud back to her house. Through sheer effort of will she kept from crying, though her eyes blurred and she saw nothing.

Hans Wallenmund walked up to the door of the Olympia House after leaving Nellie's. He was wiping the worst of the mud from his boots when he heard the squeal and clang of the cemetery gate. Though it was difficult to see anything in the darkness shortly before midnight, he made out the vague figure of a woman. He almost thought her an apparition from beyond the grave, for the white of her gown glowed eerily where the darker robe parted to reveal it. But when she stood in the doorway of her house and the light hit her fully, Hans knew it was Julie. Surprised that she would be out at such an hour and in such scant attire, he waited and watched.

Less than five minutes later, his vigil was re-

warded. Del Morgan lazily crossed the muddy
street and mounted the Hollstroms' steps.

It was exactly as Hans had expected. Wilhelm
had told him to be careful, to give the girl no
opportunity, but Hans had not counted on the
physician's rehabilitation over so short a period
of time. And he had believed the man when he
said he had no use for women. Obviously, Morgan had lied.

Hans had nothing better to do than wait. His
evening at Nellie's had been satisfactory, though
it had cost him more than usual, and he was in
a relaxed mood. He found a chair on the porch
and sat down, then lit a fat cigar.

When Morgan left the Hollstrom house only a
few minutes later, Hans jumped to his feet and
in seconds had positioned himself at the corner
of the hotel where the lane back to the adobe
house began.

"Halt, Herr Doktor Morgan," he ordered.

Morgan froze, blind in the dark after leaving
the well-lit house.

"What do you want, Hans?"

"Only that you keep your promise."

"I made you no promises."

"No? Then you will now. You will leave Julie
alone, or I will kill you. She is mine—all mine—
and no one is going to take her away from me. If
you touch her again, I will see you dead."

Chapter Twenty-four

✦ ✦ ✦ ✦

KATHARINE TOOK TO her bed immediately after Julie went in search of the doctor, and she did not leave it. When Morgan came, he prescribed a glass of sherry as a sedative and waited only until Willy, still awake, brought the bottle and Katharine gulped down the required dose. Without another word to any of them, Morgan left.

In time, Katharine dozed off and Julie got Willy back to bed. Then Julie helped herself to a glass of the wine and eventually fell asleep, still in her soiled nightdress and borrowed robe. She did not hear her father come home.

But Wilhelm had obviously come home sometime before morning, for he appeared in the kitchen shortly after Julie put water on the stove for coffee. She prepared his breakfast without a word and he ate it in similar silence before announcing that he would meet her in church. With no other explanation, he left his dirty dishes on the dining room table and then walked out the front door.

Julie watched as he crossed the street and strode in the general direction of the hotel and stores, but a sharp cry from Katharine demanded Julie's attention before she saw her father's ultimate destination.

For the first time since she could remember, Julie missed Sunday morning church service. She sent Willy off by himself with orders to join the McCrorys if Wilhelm couldn't be found, but Julie stayed home at her mother's frantic insistence.

The Katharine of yesterday afternoon who had resembled so much the Katharine of more than nine years ago had once again become the whining, petulant invalid. She demanded a thousand tiny favors that Julie rushed to satisfy, always falling a tiny bit short. The tea Katharine begged for was first too hot, then too cool, then, when it had been warmed again with more hot water, was too weak and had to be brewed from scratch.

After finally drinking a cup of tea that suited her, she decided she felt much better and asked Julie to help her dress for church.

"Don't you think you'd be better off resting, Mama?" Julie asked. "It's unbearably hot out there today."

"But your father will expect us, Julie," Katharine sighed. "Here, help me out of bed and over to the chair. I think if I can sit up for a while I'll feel much better."

The exertion, she then claimed, made her thirsty again. She wanted cold water, which Julie dutifully brought. Katharine selected a crisp peach-colored muslin dress and actually showed signs of recovering her enthusiasm when Julie got her laced into her stays. But when she had the dress slipped over her head and was standing at the foot of the bed while Julie did up the row of buttons down the back, Katharine slumped to her knees. She complained of a splitting headache, shortness of breath, dizziness, and a host of other ailments. The dress and corset came off, and Katharine was helped back into bed.

Julie had no time to think. She raced from Katharine's bedroom to the kitchen and back again, bringing tea, water, toast, jam, honey, a clean spoon to replace the one Katharine dropped on the floor. Somehow, between all these mad dashes, Julie managed to cut slices from the ham she had bought yesterday and shred potatoes to fry in the skillet for dinner. There would be no dessert; she couldn't find time for that.

When Katharine ran out of physical needs, she turned to emotional ones. She begged Julie to stay with her, even to hold her hand for a while, until Julie insisted that she had to leave to tend the meal. Katharine gave her just long enough to flip the potatoes over, then she called for further assistance.

Open the window. Draw the drapes. An extra pillow. Comb her hair. Another cool drink. Perfume on her throat. A fresh nightgown. Close the window. What was that noise? Another headache powder.

The frenzy didn't diminish when Wilhelm and Hans, with Willy in tow, returned from church. Now Julie had three more "patients" demanding her attention. Willy, unaccustomed to being told to wait, pouted on the stairs and twice tripped Julie as she raced to answer her mother's whined summons.

With dinner on the table at last, Julie hoped her father and Hans would stop expecting her to wait on them. She had put the food in front of them and could think of nothing else they needed. She did not bother to serve herself; she knew no one would let her eat.

But Hans quickly consumed all the ham and Wilhelm and Willy both wanted more, so she had to slice additional meat and fry it for them. Katharine asked for a tray, but then didn't like anything on it. She decided she wanted more toast.

At three o'clock, precisely three o'clock, Hans and Wilhelm rose from the table. The once-spotless cloth was stained in a hundred places where they had spilled things while trying to pass dishes. Willy's glass of milk had been tipped over, leaving the cloth stuck to the table. Julie would have to spend hours repairing the damage to the finish. She stood in the doorway between kitchen and dining room and stared at the disaster—and the mound of dirty dishes awaiting her.

"We are going out, Julie," her father announced in a tight voice. "You will stay here and take care of your mama."

What else? She sighed to herself.

When, as soon as the adult males had departed, Willy began tormenting Julie even further, she sent him on his way as well. The sun was out, the mud had nearly dried, and she could not stand him underfoot another second. She ordered him to find Clancy or someone else and play. Otherwise he would have to help her with the dishes.

Willy, still wearing his good clothes, left without another word.

Julie trudged upstairs to fetch the tray from Katharine's room and there found her mother had fallen quite fast asleep. Breathing a sigh of relief and exhaustion, Julie tiptoed out and mumbled a prayer that at least she would get through the chore of dishes without interruption.

She did. And she used the time alone and undisturbed to sort out the thoughts so jumbled since last night.

She knew she had made a terrible mistake. Overwrought and wrapped in her own insecurities, she hadn't realized that Morgan might have his own fears. If she had been afraid to make her feelings plain, wasn't it just possible that he hesitated to reveal his as well? She thought him still in love with his wife and unable to turn to anyone else in the same way; hadn't she, after all, given him every indication that she was going to marry Hans?

It was a hopeless muddle. She knew, with her hands sunk in hot soapy water, that they had both made the same error. She now saw Morgan's poetry last night for what it really was: a painful declaration of his deepest emotions. And she, fool that she was, had turned away from him. He had understood her own fears, her unsureness, and had given her the opportunity to make known her feelings without embarrassment to either of them. In her ignorance and guilty pride, she had rejected him.

Suddenly, that feeling that she had only allowed to exist as a vague sort of hope sprang to full strength. Scrubbing at the skillet where bits of ham had stuck and burned fast to the cast iron, she let the knowledge flood from her heart through her whole body. Each pulsebeat reminded her that he loved her, just as she loved him. She could go to him now, unafraid, unhesitant.

The note tacked to the front door of the office said that there had been an emergency and the doctor would be back by evening if possible. Disappointed, Julie turned away and returned home. She had already been to the adobe house and found it as empty as the office.

Katharine had slept all the while Julie washed dishes and was still asleep when she left to find Morgan. Returning from that failed mission, Julie hoped her mother would waken soon, for such a long nap during the day presaged a sleepless night, and Julie didn't want that. She planned to be well rested before going to the office first thing in the morning and declaring herself as soon as the doctor arrived. The anticipation alone kept the smile from fading when she entered the unfriendly dimness of her father's house.

When Julie heard her father and Hans enter the house, she stood at the top of the stairs and raised a finger to her lips when Wilhelm looked her way.

"Ssshhh. Mama is asleep."

"Then wake her," Wilhelm growled. "Tell her to come down here now."

Something was up, something Julie knew she should be prepared for and wasn't. Though a few minutes ago she had been confident of the future she was going to make for herself, a tiny niggling doubt had remained. She could not count her single chicken before it was hatched and peeping in her hand.

"Yes, Papa."

"And be quick about it."

"I'll tell Mama to hurry."

Katharine, of course, did not hurry.

"Oh, Julie, please, let me sleep longer," she begged first. "My head hurts so bad."

"Please, Mama, I don't want Papa angry again like he was last night. And Hans is here, too. It would be embarrassing if there was another scene."

Katharine managed to drag herself out of the bed with a profusion of groans and moans and long, weary, overly dramatic sighs. She refused, however, to go downstairs until her hair was combed and pinned into a neat chignon—and it had to be done three times before it suited her—and she changed her choice of dress twice before she settled on the peach muslin. In the midst of all this primping, Julie suddenly realized she still wore the shabbiest of her clothes and that the faded brown gingham was now speckled with food and soap stains. Her hair hadn't been properly combed since last night, and she felt sticky all over with sweat.

She laughed, thinking that she had actually gone to find Morgan and declare him her heart's desire looking like this.

"Is something wrong, dear?" Katharine queried, giving her daughter a strange look.

"No, Mama. I'm just tired, that's all."

"Well, so am I. Let's go downstairs and see what it is your father wants now and then I simply must get back to sleep. I can hardly hold my eyes open as it is."

She yawned delicately to punctuate that claim, then got up from her chair and headed for the landing.

Julie followed her and didn't bother even to smooth her hair back from her face. She didn't care what she looked like and almost wished she had her spectacles back.

Hans got clumsily to his feet from the sofa when Katharine entered the parlor, but he was seated already when Julie walked in just a moment later. He slouched forward on the center cushion of the sofa, leaving Julie only a place on one side of him or the other, unless she wished to stand. As little as she liked the thought of being so close to him, her legs demanded that she sit. The sofa enfolded her; she could not avoid leaning back and actually relaxing for the first time all day. If Wilhelm had not immediately begun his speech, she probably would have fallen asleep very quickly.

"Hans and I have reached an agreement," he said with no preamble. "You will marry him next Sunday."

"*What?*"

With total disregard for grace, propriety, or even decent manners, Julie struggled to a more upright position while her father went on.

"I find it necessary for the sake of the family that something be done about your conduct."

"My conduct? But, Papa, what have I done?"

She glanced at her mother, fully expecting Katharine to swoon, but Katharine merely wiped the back of her hand across her brow and yawned again.

"I saw you last night with him," Hans blurted out. "You were in your . . . your nightdress."

"It was an emergency! What else was I to do?"

As though her explanation were so worthless that it need not even be argued, Hans went off on a different tack.

"People are talking about you. They say you go to his house early in the morning."

She blushed, for she had not thought anyone knew of the two times she had indeed wakened Morgan, but even that did not quell her indignation. She was innocent of any wrongdoing and would not let them make her guilty.

"He was needed to tend to other patients and it was—it *is*—my job to find him." She wished there were some way to get away from Hans, for arguing at this close range was very uncomfortable. But she did not want to stand and have all their accusing eyes on her. And it would be too easy then to flee. For the moment, she must bear the burden and wait. Later she would have someone to run to.

"Nevertheless," Wilhelm resumed, "people are talking. I will not have it, Julie, not again. So I have decided. The wedding will be next Sunday."

"But what about Mama? She's not well enough to take care of the household alone."

As if to underscore that statement, Katharine sighed and pressed her fingertips to her temples.

"Please, Wilhelm, I must get back to bed," she whined. "Let us hurry this up."

"You see!" her husband verbally pounced. "That doctor's treatment has worked no better than any other."

"But, Papa, she has been getting better."

"Oh, yes, for a day or two, and then she goes right back to being as sick as ever. She is never going to recover, and there is no sense waiting for a miracle. I will have to engage a nurse to take care of her."

Julie glanced at her mother then and noted a slight frown pucker Katharine's brow.

"And where do you think you will find a nurse out here?" Julie asked.

"There is that Tucker woman, the widow with the young boys. I think she would be grateful for a small salary."

Wilhelm's attention to details served to discourage Julie slightly, but only for a moment. She knew Liza Tucker.

"And what if Mrs. Tucker finds herself another husband? There aren't many single women around Plato, Papa, and a lot of single men." Not very many, but at least one or two.

"Then let it be my worry. You always complain of the work anyway. You act as though your mother's care is too much a burden on you, though it is all your own fault. Even last night was your fault."

Wilhelm continued with cold calm. "Hans and I have compromised on the matter of your dowry. I have said that I must be compensated for the loss of your services tending your mother, but he insists your reputation is now such that he needs additional payment to make you his wife. I tell you this only so you will be aware of the generosity we are both showing you."

"Generosity? You call bargaining over me generosity?"

Katharine forestalled Wilhelm's next argument.

"Sit down, Julie. Your shouting makes my head ache even more," she begged. Something hard and insistent, not weak and whining, in that plea made Julie obey.

"It is settled, Daughter. You will be married next Sunday, as Hans and I have agreed. You will spend this week preparing to become his wife. There will be no more working for the doctor. I will so inform him as soon as we finish here."

"*No!*" Julie screamed.

Her single cry echoed and re-echoed, then all was silent for a moment.

"Do you dare defy me?" Wilhelm whispered. "Your insolence deserves a beating."

He had hit her before in fits of anger, but he had never actually beaten her. Yet Julie was not certain he would refrain this time, with Hans there to help him. She was outnumbered and forced herself to accept. There was always tomorrow.

She took several deep breaths, conscious that both Hans and her father stared malevolently at her. She felt a strange prickling along her spine.

"I want to tell him myself," she said calmly.

Now it was Hans's turn to shout.

"No! I don't want you going near him again. I swore to him I would kill him if he touched you again."

"You did what?"

His blue eyes were pleading, but the desperation in them frightened Julie. His hands grabbed for hers and she reacted too slowly to prevent his clasping them tightly.

"I have wanted you for so long, Julie. You know that. When I saw you with him last night, I swore I would kill him. And I meant it. You are promised to me, and I will hold you to that promise."

She recovered from this shock and pulled her hands free. They felt bruised and sore and dirtied.

Julie knew begging would accomplish nothing. Gathering all her faltering courage, Julie made a threat of her own.

"And I swear to you, you will let me tell him myself or I will never marry you. I would sooner die."

Chapter Twenty-five

+ + + + +

JULIE BATHED IN the cool of the predawn. She had slept very little, and the bath served to refresh and waken her as well as cleanse. She wrapped her hair in a towel and dried her body quickly, knowing it would be less than half an hour before Wilhelm wakened. She had slipped out of the house twice during the night to check for Morgan, but by one o'clock in the morning he had not returned. She had gone home to bed then, for she had to be at the clinic as early as possible to speak to him.

She slipped her arms into the sleeves of Katharine's robe and then walked out onto the back porch to brush her hair dry. The humidity that had followed Saturday's storm had disappeared; the dry heat of the desert returned with a vengeance on this last day of July. Julie smiled to herself. Today was her birthday, and she intended to give herself a gift.

She finished with her hair and began to braid it as she usually did, but then she decided to leave it loose. Ted had liked it that way, and maybe Del Morgan would, too. It was longer now than nine years ago, and the soft straight strands fell almost to her knees. She could not remember the last time she had cut it, for she always wore it carefully plaited and coiled. Surely, though, she hadn't cut it since . . . since Ted admired it.

The blue batiste blouse replaced the robe, the black buttons shiny even in the half-light of early morning. Julie fastened the new skirt around her waist next, then sat down on the bench at the kitchen table to pull on her stockings and shoes. She would have liked a mirror, but there was none here.

After checking the fire in the stove to be sure it wouldn't go out before she returned, Julie quietly opened the back door and stepped outside. Though it was doubtful Morgan would be at the office this early, she had to see for herself. He had been gone a good portion of the night and might have brought back a patient. She dared not go to his house, but there was nothing to stop her checking for him at the office. Nothing.

The house between Julie's and the clinic belonged to the schoolmaster and was vacant a good part of the summer. Julie had no worries about being seen, therefore, when she cut across the backyards and walked up to the rear entrance to the clinic. The pale glimmer of a lamp in the kitchen sent her heart to her throat. Morgan was there.

She knocked tentatively.

He answered the summons almost at once. The sudden sight of him when he had opened the door and stood on the other side of the screen from her sent Julie jumping backwards a step or two.

He looked like hell. And he smelled of whiskey. His clothes were filthy, his shirt torn almost to rags. The darker stains could only be blood, though they were hard to distinguish from the other smears and splotches. The left knee of his denims flapped a three-cornered tear, and the skin showing through was scraped raw. A small cut over his eye had scabbed, but the streaks of blood he had wiped away still marked the side of his face.

He looked at her, all fresh and lovely in that twilight before sunrise, and the bitterness flooded back. Her trousseau blouse, as blue as the sky would be this evening, clung to the body he would never know, could only dream about. The tiny waist—he had never noticed how tiny before this moment—and softly curved hips draped the new skirt gracefully. And the hair. God, he had never seen hair like that before. Pale as platinum, it crowned her like a wedding veil without a single wave or curl. A man could run his fingers through it for miles.

"I know it's awfully early, but I had something

I wanted to tell you," she said before he even had a chance to greet her. "May I come in?"

Her smile was a knife, sparkling and deadly, but he could not resist it. He pushed the screen door open and held it while she walked past.

She was radiant, glowing, lit from within by some secret fire, and he knew he had never seen a woman more beautiful. Those enormous eyes captivated him with their glitter of happiness, but the delicious curve of her lips taunted too painfully for him to look at her.

He held out his hand stiffly.

"May I be the first to congratulate you?"

He was smiling. She went numb.

"I met your fiancé on my way home last night. He told me the date is set for next Sunday. I perfectly understand your not coming to work anymore, with all the plans you must have. Don't worry about me; I'll manage somehow until I find someone else."

He was actually happy for her! A knife turned in her heart when she realized how deluded she had been by her hopes. He didn't love her; he was merely grateful to her for bringing him back from the depths of despair. She had given him new life, but he was not going to give her love.

"I'm sure you two will be very happy," she heard him say and wondered how much she had missed. She couldn't listen to any more of his platitudes. Sick to her stomach, she ran from the kitchen and back to her own house.

*   *   *

After Julie's abrupt departure, Morgan sat down at the kitchen table with the bottle of whiskey in front of him, uncorked. Twice in the last few minutes he had actually raised it to his lips. After yesterday and last night, he needed something. But after seeing Julie, he knew nothing, not all the whiskey west of the Mississippi, would drown his agony.

He had spent twelve hours trying to save the victims of a landslide brought on by the storm. One man had been buried up to his chest and had died in excruciating pain when a broken rib finally pierced his heart before anyone could dig him free. Another had been saved only by amputating his arm and leaving it under the pile of rocks and mud. Three companions who had taken shelter under a rocky ledge were buried alive. The two who had come for the doctor suffered relatively minor injuries in their abortive rescue attempts, including a broken finger, a severely lacerated and bruised shoulder, and a probable concussion. To say nothing of the hangovers they'd have from the whiskey they had fortified themselves with throughout the long night.

Then the shock of Wallenmund's announcement. He had met the farmer on the road home, well after midnight, and he had truly had a difficult time being civil. Hans, on the other hand, addressed him like an old friend. Morgan's stomach turned at the hypocrisy.

"The wedding will be Sunday," Hans trilled. "You will come, won't you? I might even let you kiss the bride."

"What, and shoot me afterwards? No, thanks, I think I'll pass. Give my regards to her, though."

And then he had kicked poor Sam as hard as he could and sent the gelding off at an exhausted gallop.

Angry at himself, he wandered up to the office after depositing the rented horse back at the livery. He should never have let Julie leave him Saturday night. He should have come right out and told her.

"Hell, I shoulda told her I loved her a dozen times," he mumbled as he got to his feet and went to answer the knocking at the door. "I'm comin', I'm comin'!"

It was Boone Walsh, all six-foot-eight of him, standing on the porch, hat in hand. Like all the Walsh boys, Boone was shy. Morgan knew he wouldn't speak until spoken to.

"What is it, Boone?"

"Hi, Doc. It's Mama. She's havin' another baby. Miz Fulton said it's twins again and to come get her the minute anything started. But road's closed on account o' that landslide, and I get lost goin' the other way. Barney and Banner's cuttin' timber and I already sent Brian and Bart out to the cows, so I had to leave Bruce with Ma and come myself."

"And your daddy's drunk, I suppose."

Morgan grabbed for his bag and hat, which he

had dropped on the parlor floor when he returned earlier, and now he ushered the gangly Boone back outside.

"Well, he's gettin' that way. I brung a horse for you. Save gettin' Gus up."

Gus was crotchety enough late at night, so Morgan didn't argue when Boone showed him the leggy skewbald. He'd seen worse. With Sam worn out from the night before, the skew might be an improvement. As he mounted and hung his bag over the saddle horn, Morgan glanced back at the house. The note he had tacked to the door yesterday was still there.

Wash clothes. Bake bread. Iron shirts. Scrub floors. Change linens. Wait on Katharine. The routine started the instant Wilhelm left for work. And at nine-thirty, Liza Tucker showed up. Furious, Julie sent her home. She simply did not have the time—or the inclination—to begin training the new "help."

Katharine's condition deteriorated throughout the day. She ate some lunch; then, while Julie took Wilhelm's meal to him, Katharine claimed she went to the outhouse and threw up the entire meal. Julie berated her for attempting to walk any distance at all in the noon sun, but Katharine shrugged weakly and let herself be half-carried back to bed.

When Julie tried sewing, Katharine complained about the noise. The scrape of the shears set her teeth on edge. The whir of the sewing machine treadle upset her stomach. Around three o'clock she suddenly remembered that this was the day she was to have the splint Horace Opper had put on her arm six weeks ago removed. She nagged and nagged at Julie to get Morgan, but Julie refused.

"If he said he'd be here, Mama, he will be here. Don't worry."

"But perhaps I was mistaken. Perhaps he meant for me to come to the office. Please, dear, do go and check for me."

"I can't, Mama. I have too much work here to do."

"Oh, leave it for a little while. I do so want this thing off my arm!" she cried, threatening to burst into childish tears.

"Let's just wait a while longer and see if he comes. Half an hour, all right?"

And in half an hour, Julie prayed, I will come up with another excuse. Please, don't make me go to him, not now. I swear it will kill me if I ever see him again.

Slightly more than half an hour later, while Katharine was still whining about the doctor, Hans walked through the front door without so much as a knock and announced that he had come for supper.

Melissa Walsh delivered her ninth and tenth children with no complications. Morgan marveled, as he had when Brian and his twin brother Bart were born, that the slender, small-boned

Melissa carried her babies so easily and brought them into the world with so little apparent effort. Even this third set of twins posed no trouble for her. She named them Bonnie and Barbara, the first girls of her brood, and smiled cheerfully at Morgan when it was over.

Brendan Walsh lay stone drunk on the sofa in the sprawling cabin's living room when Morgan left shortly before noon. Brendan never knew how Melissa did it, either.

Boone accompanied the doctor back to Plato, partly to bring the horse back and partly to get some supplies. Morgan hadn't really wanted the company, but he was soon glad to have someone to talk to rather than sit alone with his thoughts.

The road from the Walsh ranch back to town curved south along the course of a wash. The stones were dry now, but here and there a puddle remained of the torrent that had scoured this bed so very recently. A narrow track crossed the wash at one point, and Morgan noticed recent wheel marks in the stiff but pliable mud. Following them with his eyes, he saw a cluster of buildings a quarter mile or so beyond the far bank. He did not recognize them nor remember their being there before, though they looked old and weathered.

"Whose place is that?" he asked Boone.

"Oh, that's where that German fella started a farm."

"German?" Morgan's brows arched quizzically. This wasn't the sort of place he had imag-

ined the prosperous Wallenmund to be taking
Julie to as his bride.

"Yeah. I can't say his last name, but his first is
Hans. He's got a couple of cows, some chickens,
not much. When he first come here, oh, 'bout
five, mebbe six years ago, he built a great big
barn." Boone's gargantuan arms spread wide to
demonstrate. "I bet he coulda put a hunderd
cows in that thing."

"What happened to it?"

"Oh, nothin'. It's still there, fallin' to pieces
like everything else." Boone turned slightly sideways in the saddle and shaded his eyes with a
broad hand. "See, that's him there, hitchin' up
his wagon."

Morgan swore quietly, fiercely. Wallenmund
was a liar as well as a brute. Julie honestly believed she was going to a prosperous farm, with
a white clapboard house, a spacious dairy barn,
and probably a picket fence with a rose-arched
gate.

He kicked the borrowed horse to a lope and
clamped his own teeth together as though he
were running with the bit.

He left the borrowed horse with Boone, then
headed for the post office. It was habit now to
check for a letter from Adam, though at this
point Morgan wasn't sure what difference it
would make. Still, he opened the door and
walked toward Mr. Nisely's window.

"Well, there ya are, Del. I been wonderin'
when you'd show up. Yer letter from Cincinnati
come this noon. Big fat one, too."

"Thanks," Morgan mumbled, snatching the envelope from the old man's hand.

He knew he was supposed to have the office open, but somehow nothing, not even sick or hurt people, demanded his attention the way this letter did. Ignoring greetings from friends and neighbors, he hurried down the street toward the lane. He opened the letter and tried to read, but the sun was just too damn bright and Adam's handwriting too damn spidery.

Adam St. Rogers, methodical as always, detailed everything. There were nine closely written pages, but two paragraphs near the end of the sixth gave Morgan all the information he needed.

> I had one helluva hard time finding out about your Mr. Hollstrom. The only bank in Rinton, Indiana, nine years ago went bankrupt in '81 and most of the people who had worked there left town. I did locate a Howard Irvine, however, who is now a teller at the new bank and whose father worked at the old one. The senior Mr. Irvine remembered this Hollstrom very well.
>
> Wilhelm Hollstrom worked in the Rinton Bank for twelve years. In the summer of '75, a serious shortage of funds appeared, and Wilhelm was suspected of embezzlement. An investigation proved little, and when later he left town following the lynching of a young drifter, the bank's owner considered the matter closed. It was discovered some months afterward that the young drifter was actually an agent for another

*bank, one in New York City, where Hollstrom
had worked before coming to Indiana. I investi-
gated a little further myself and discovered that
after the Hollstroms moved to Minnesota, Wilhelm was suspected there in a similar disappear-
ance of funds from a store where he worked. He
also left behind a mountain of unpaid debts, exactly as he had in Indiana. I traced him from
Minnesota to Kansas City and discovered the
same pattern. Unpaid bills, and suspicious circumstances upon his leave-taking.*

No, Adam had gone on to say, there was no
warrant out for Wilhelm Hollstrom, not after all
these years. Morgan was sorry for that. Apparently Wilhelm's pride was his greatest possession, after his greed and cruelty, and Morgan
would have enjoyed humiliating the man. He
intended to find much greater satisfaction, however, in saving Julie from a far worse fate. If he
could.

"Yoo, hoo, Dr. Morgan!"

"Come in, Winnie," he called. When he heard
her coming through the parlor, he folded the
letter and slipped it back in its envelope. "I've
been out to Walsh's delivering twins."

She set a tray on the table in front of him; he
could smell fried ham and hash browns.

"I know. Lucas saw Boone riding in this morning and told me you left together. I figured Miz
Walsh was about due—again. My goodness,
how many does that make now? Nine? No, if it
was twins then she's got ten now. Were they

boys again, or did she finally have some girls?"
Winnie lifted the cover from the plate that contained an enormous ham omelet and a pile of golden potatoes. "I left coffee here for you. Do you want some or should I go back and get some lemonade? I made it fresh this morning for the boys and believe it or not there's still some left."

"No, thanks, Winnie. Coffee's all I really want. Did you happen to notice if there's anyone waiting at the office?" He got up and walked to the stove where the coffeepot stayed warm and took a cup down from the shelf.

"What do you mean all you want is coffee?" she scolded, ignoring his question. "You were out all last night without supper and no breakfast either, because I checked with Leif to see if you ate there and he said you didn't. Now you just sit yourself back down there and eat your lunch."

"Look, Winnie, if I have patients—"

"Well, sir, I don't have any patience," she interrupted brusquely. "As a matter of fact, there are a couple of folks waitin' on the porch over there, but they can go right on waitin'. I told 'em so. I told 'em you'd been out on errands of mercy and would get to them as soon as you had your lunch. Now, eat.

"And while you're eating, I have a few things to say to you. I heard that mean old Mr. Hollstrom talkin' in church about his daughter yesterday. Now everybody in this town knows there ain't nothin' between you and Miss Julie, and I think anyone here would tell you she's done a fine job helpin' you and gettin' you to lay off the booze. Lord knows I do my share of talkin', but I listen once in a while, too, and I have never ever heard one single word against her. Not one. But her father seems to be spreading all kinds of stories, kinda like he was repeatin' things he had heard other folks say only I know nobody did. It's all him, and it's all lies."

Morgan chewed thoughtfully, digesting every word of Winnie's exactly as he did the food. She rambled and sometimes got her thoughts out of order so that he had to re-sort them in his own mind, but he got the gist of her speech and was suddenly too hungry to interrupt her.

"I don't rightly know if I should say this, but I never kept my mouth shut when I should've before, so this is no time to start." Winnie plopped herself down on the chair across from him and propped her double chins on her fists. "Miss Julie has been damn good for you, Del Morgan. In more ways'n one. She ain't Miss Amy and never will be, and no one can ever change that. But you gotta do something to make that man stop talkin' about her that way. You might even have to marry her, and that might not be such a bad idea. There, I said it and you can kick me back home if you want, but I'm not sorry a bit."

He swallowed, and without looking up, said flatly, "She's going to be married, to that Hans Wallenmund."

God, the words stuck in his throat like one of Winnie's unfortunate biscuits. She had made cornbread today, and it wasn't so bad, but the biscuits she usually made were the next best thing to inedible.

Winnie screwed up her face and tried to hold the word in, but it exploded from her anyway.

"*Bullshit!*"

Her face turned beet red, and Morgan couldn't hide a smile.

He was, however, too busy eating to keep her from picking up the thread of her filibuster.

"Well, that's what it is," she stammered defensively as her blush slowly subsided. "You ask Gus down at the livery what he thinks of Mr. Wallenmund."

"What's Gus got to do with it?"

"Well, last spring, Mr. Wallenmund came into town and asked to rent a horse. Said he needed to ride to Prescott and wanted a nice strong riding horse, 'cause he didn't need to take his wagon and his horse was only good for pullin', not ridin'. Gus gave him Sam, seein' as how Sam is about the best distance horse he's got. Well, 'bout a week later, Mr. Wallenmund"—she was spitting out the name now, not just speaking it—"drives back into town in his wagon with Sam tied to the rear. That horse looked like he was run to death, only he wasn't sweatin' or nothing. Just tuckered out, not like he would be after a ride even to Prescott. Gus takes one look at Sam and starts swearin' a blue streak o' Swedish, 'cause Mr. Wallenmund had used Sam as a plowhorse. Sam! Can you imagine?"

"And of course Hans denied it."

"Oh, of course. Just like he denies beatin' up Maude over at Nellie's. Nellie warned him again Saturday night about roughin' up her girls. She charges him double 'cause of all the extra expenses he puts her to."

He lifted the last forkful of potatoes to his mouth and cocked his head at Winnie. "How do you know so much about what goes on at Nellie's?"

She blushed all over again.

"I visit with Nellie sometimes in McCrory's. Did you know she was married once and her husband left her with five kids? She even taught school for a while, back in Iowa. And Iris's grandpa was a preacher. And—"

"All right, all right! I don't need a life history of all the soiled doves in Nellie's house. But you're sure about Hans roughing up Maude, and abusing Sam?"

Winnie drew herself up proudly and crossed her heart.

"I saw Sam when Mr. Wallenmund brought him in. And you know Nellie even better'n I do; she's a madam, not a liar."

He knew Nellie well enough to know she had told a few tales in her time, but he believed what she had told Winnie was true. The marks on Maude proved it.

He took out his watch and snapped it open.

"Quarter to two. Look, Winnie, do me a favor." He swallowed the last mouthful of coffee with a sigh of satisfaction. "I'm going to get cleaned up before I go to the office. Will you hold the fort there for me? Give me half, three-quarters of an hour."

"What about Miss Julie? Where's she?"

He stood and pushed his chair back. Somehow, telling Winnie wasn't quite as difficult as he had expected, but he couldn't control the anger that slipped out in his voice.

"They've set a date for the wedding and Hans won't let her work anymore. As soon as I get done with today's patients, I'm going to see what I can do about changing that situation."

In the parlor, Julie picked up the mending she had laid aside earlier. She knew Hans was perturbed that she had not chosen to sit beside him on the sofa, but with her parents upstairs, she had her choice of seats. And though she had been frantically busy all day, she had no intention of sitting idle now. With three more stockings to darn, she would at least have something on which to focus her attention other than Hans.

Why, for heaven's sake, hadn't he left? Supper was over, the dishes were washed, and it was nearly dark. Outside, Plato had settled into that soft silence that precedes sunset, when the shadows are long and indistinct and the light is so clear as to be almost tangible. After a harried day that differed from Sunday only in that Julie had even more work, she would have liked to walk in that evening calm, even though there was no cooling breeze. She could not bear the thought, however, of sharing it with Hans.

Nor would she give Morgan the chance to see them together. He must have seen Hans arrive, or at least have known by the wagon's presence that her fiancé was in town. She could do nothing about that. But she could prevent any further public evidence of her engagement. She refused to be seen with him. So she sat, quietly intent on her darning, while Hans watched her from across the room.

She felt his gaze, the heat of that unveiled stare, and though it repulsed her, she found herself able to resist the desire to escape. He had never stopped looking at her since the instant he had arrived. He sat at the kitchen table and watched her while she prepared supper, then fixed his eyes on her throughout the meal itself. Though he did not offer to help her with the dishes, he remained seated at the dining room table where he had a clear view to the kitchen. Her spine prickled and her hands felt chilled even in the hot soapy water because she knew her every movement was carefully observed.

But none of it mattered. He did not make any move to touch her, and as long as he kept his hands to himself, she would tolerate his stares. If he touched her, or tried to kiss her as he had before, she wasn't sure she could maintain her calm. She hoped she would not have to find out.

"Your papa gave us one hour," he said suddenly, so suddenly that Julie started. She hadn't realized she was that lost in her thoughts. "Ten minutes is gone already. Put down that sewing and come here."

"I can't. I must have all the chores done before—"

"I said come here," Hans commanded. He kept his voice low, a fact that in itself set Julie on her guard. "You must learn to obey me, Julie. When I am your husband, I will not stand for disobedience."

"You are not my husband yet, Hans, and I am not yours to command. I may never be."

She had said the wrong thing. In an instant, he was on his feet. He tore the sock from her hand and threw it toward the foyer, where it landed with a heavy thud of the darning egg inside it. Startled, she had no time to defend herself against his next assault. This time the little sewing basket, filled with pins and spools of thread and loose buttons, went flying through the air along the same course as the sock. Instinct pulled Julie out of her chair before she could stop herself, and of course Hans was right there.

His large, hard hands grabbed her arms painfully and pulled her against him.

She could not raise her hand to slap him, for he held her arms too tightly, but she could and did turn her face away from his kiss. He would have to let go her arm in order to hold her head, and then she would strike.

But he did not let her go. He lowered his face to her neck, to the extended corner where it joined her shoulder and the skin and tendons were pulled taut. Lips hot and wet, he mouthed the cool flesh before running the edges of his

teeth threateningly along a pulsebeat. Julie
moaned and twisted away from him.

Hans laughed, but there was no humor in that
low snarl.

"So, this is how you like it? That is good, very
good. I like it too, when there is some pain."

"I don't like it at all," Julie corrected, her voice
low with a snakelike hiss of anger. "I loathe it, as
I loathe you. Let go of me."

He laughed again, completely undaunted by
her denial.

"But I have no intention of letting go of you. In
just six more days you will be my wife and—"

"No! I won't marry you. I would rather slave
for my mother and put up with my father for the
rest of my life than marry you. If you drag me to
the church, I will refuse the vows. You can't
make me marry you."

She tossed her head defiantly and then gazed
into Hans's eyes. They were on a level with hers,
not above hers as Morgan's were. Once she had
thought Hans's eyes were the prettiest, clearest
shade of blue; now she saw nothing but icy cold
in them, no depth, no soul. She was not afraid of
him.

"Your papa wants to be rid of you. You shame
him. He will not let you stay here, even if you
wish to. So where would you go? To the doctor
who isn't even a man? Did you know that, Julie?
Your precious surgeon is a gelding, not a proud
stallion like your salesman or that drifter your
papa took care of."

Julie bit her tongue. Something warned her

not to reveal the truth, not yet and not to Hans. Neither would she show him any shock or shame.

"He is still twice the man you would ever be," she spat.

He hit her then, releasing her arm and slapping her cheek so quickly that she could neither react to avoid the blow nor counter with one of her own before he had thrown her to the floor.

"I will show you what is a real man."

He placed one booted foot on her skirt, high enough to hold her down, while he began slowly to unbuckle his belt. Next, instead of unbuttoning his trousers, he pulled the long leather band free from his waistband and wrapped the buckle end of it around his fist. Now, despite her effort at control, Julie knew fear.

"Your papa did not beat you, and that was a mistake. He should have taught you obedience."

"As I suppose you plan to do now?"

"Exactly."

He snapped the belt sharply so that the tip just flicked her thigh, where he had pulled the skirt fabric taut. Julie flinched at the pain, but made no outcry. She reached for the buttons on the skirt and quickly undid them. Before she could scramble out of the garment, Hans had snaked his weapon again, this time catching the back of her shoulder. There would be a welt, she suspected, from that lash, but no permanent injury. And the pain was bearable.

Another blow landed on her buttocks as she got to her feet and ran for the stairs, and this time she could not suppress a short, sharp wail of pain. Stumbling in her haste, she felt an iron grip on her arm as she tried to clasp the banister and maintain her balance.

She saw bloodlust in those blue eyes, then a sound above drew both his attention and hers.

"You fool!" Wilhelm whispered from the landing. "People don't mind when the whores scream, but they will come running if you start the same thing here. Wait until you have her in your own house."

Wilhelm's scolding shocked Hans into loosening his hold on Julie's wrist, and she took the opportunity to race up the stairs. Shoving her father aside, she frantically sought the refuge of her room.

Breathless, she leaned against the door and waited for the summons that never came. Angry whispers floated up from the foyer, but she did not listen to them, did not care to listen to them.

She wasn't certain how long she stood there. The last light faded outside her window, and the night sounds drifted in. Hans might have left immediately after the argument with Wilhelm or might have stayed much longer.

She wasn't even positive he had gone at all.

She shivered, and a yawn escaped her. She wanted sleep, days of it, and yet when she looked at her bed, she knew somehow that she could not lie upon it.

She went to the narrow wardrobe and fumbled in the dark for the clothes she wanted. Her searching fingers encountered the soft batiste of her new blouse and lingered there, but she knew that was not the garment she wanted. The light blue would be too easily seen. She finally found the dark blue calico, recognizable by its relatively unworn texture and the long sleeves. She took it out and pulled it on.

Not for a second did she take all her attention away from the hallway outside her door, for she listened for footsteps, voices, even snores that might have told her anything, but she heard not a sound. It was almost as though she were the only person left in the house.

She did not unpin her hair. It was more easily concealed when coiled at her neck this way than loose. With no mirror to examine her appearance, Julie trusted to her imagination to tell her how she looked, and then she went to the dresser.

In the box that had held her gold piece lay a small collection of lesser coins, and some greenbacks. She had counted them often enough to know that she had almost ten dollars—hardly a princely sum, but it was all she had. It would at least buy her a ticket out of Plato, and perhaps she could make a new life somewhere else. Hadn't her father done it often enough?

She stuffed the money into a pocket and then placed her ear against the door.

She heard nothing, and opened the door. The one advantage to having no lock was that though she could not lock anyone out, neither could they lock her in.

Now the sounds came to her. Willy thrashed

in his sleep and mumbled something from a dream. When she whispered his name, he did not answer; she knew he was sound asleep. From the slightly ajar door to her parents' room filtered Wilhelm's snores and, barely audible, little whimpers from Katharine, as though her headache invaded even her sleep.

Julie slipped silently down the stairs. She waited again in the foyer, listening for any sound from the rooms above, but the family slumbered on as though they had no cares, no worries, no guilts.

The front door had a tiny squeak on occasion, so Julie padded through the dining room and kitchen to the back door. It opened without a whisper, and she closed it carefully.

Chapter Twenty-six

✦✦✦✦

TIRED FINGERS CURLED into a loose fist at Julie's side, but she couldn't raise them to the door yet. The fist, indeed her whole arm, quivered with nerves stretched like the strings of a harp. She inhaled deeply, smelling the tang of chili that must have been Morgan's supper.

She had seen no lights in any of the windows when she walked down the lane and then around to the back of the adobe house. No doubt Morgan was already in bed and asleep, as anyone in his right mind should be. And he probably wouldn't hear her even if she did knock. So she tapped softly, as though to fulfill her own prophecy.

There was no reply. Julie waited, knowing she could not return home and yet not daring to knock again. With her knuckles still poised an inch or two from the door, she held her breath.

Then a light flared above her, a brief glow that illuminated a thin cigar and a man's dark, brooding face. He had been on the rooftop patio, probably watching her all the while. Embarrassed by her own boldness and his observance of it, Julie turned to leave before he could reach the stairs and climb down them.

"Wait."

It was a command so soft and gentle that she wouldn't have heard it by daylight, but in the night's quiet, his voice rang clear.

So she waited, as he had asked, and in a matter of seconds he was beside her. His breathing was only slightly hurried, whether from the quick dash from the roof or from something else wasn't readily discernible. He took the cheroot from between his teeth and held it in his fingers. The smoke curled up between them, pungent and warm. The glowing red ash shed no light.

"Julie."

The word caressed her, though he had not touched her, and she felt the brazen warmth of desire surge through her.

"Were you waiting for me?" she dared to ask.

"No." He could barely see her in the moonless dark. "Yes. Yes, I was waiting, or at least hoping."

His voice rose slowly, then sank again on that last word. He felt as if his breath had been sucked right out of his lungs and his heart had somehow leaped from his chest to his throat. He wanted to touch her, not as he had so often when they worked together, but as they had touched when they were not working.

"Let's go inside," he whispered.

She wanted him to take her hand or clasp her elbow, but he didn't. Instead he reached for the door handle, then kicked the unlatched oak panel inward, opening the way into the kitchen. Julie walked ahead of him, pausing after three or four blind steps. A match scraped on a boot sole, and then Morgan walked past her to light the lamp on the table.

She almost gasped at what the kerosene glow revealed. Morgan looked awful, almost like the derelict she had stumbled across in front of Mc-Crory's store all those long weeks ago. Though his face was clean-shaven, his cheeks looked sunken. Lines etched sharp hollows around his mouth, and exhaustion had painted dark shadows under eyes that never left her for an instant.

"I'm glad you came."

Those green eyes took in every detail of her face, the high cheekbones flushed with nervous pink, the brown eyes wide and lustrous, the lips he had kissed so preciously few times now parted just enough for her tongue to slip out and moisten them. His own mouth was dry, inside and out.

"I wanted to see you," she managed to reply.

Searching for words and tripping over every one he wanted to use, he stumbled until he found level ground.

"I meant to come see your mother today. How is she?"

"She stayed in bed most of the day. Papa removed the splint." Feelings she couldn't hide surfaced, and she turned away from him.

He moved behind her, placing one hand on her shoulder as though to turn her around, but he exerted no force. He didn't need to. Just his touch seemed to be enough. She faced him again, her eyes lifting to his. Now no words were necessary.

His hand slipped from her shoulder to her neck, sliding under a single strand of loose hair. As his thumb caressed her temple and felt the racing pulse, his fingers cupped the back of her head. She let his hand take the weight, and his clasp tightened.

"I want to kiss you, Julie, but I'm afraid."

"Afraid?"

"Afraid that it isn't what you want."

She had seen pain in his eyes before, and she had seen him cry, but the agony in his confession struck her with its intensity. Yet when he tipped her face upward to meet his, his mouth was gentle, softly touching just the fullest part of her lips. Warm breaths mingled in a single sigh.

His fingers fumbled with the knot of her hair and sought the pins that held all that silver silk imprisoned. One by one the tiny shackles clattered to the floor, and one by one the shining strands twisted free.

"So beautiful," he murmured, clasping a long length of hair to press a kiss upon it. A breath of rainwater and Pears soap filled his nostrils. "Oh, Julie, you shouldn't be here, but I'm so glad you are."

He filled his arms with her, curled a hand to hold her head against his shoulder. It fit so well there, as though it had been made expressly to lie in the hollow above his breast. No doubt she heard his heart pounding, her ear pressed so tightly to him that he could feel the delicate whorls through his shirt.

She closed her eyes to hold in the tears. She felt so safe. No one could hurt her, neither Wilhelm with his threats and reminders, nor Hans with his hard hands and stinging belt. If only it could always be this way.

"Are you crying?" he asked.

"Yes."

"Why?"

She tasted the words of her answer on the tip of her tongue, but they never went any further, for when she looked up again he was waiting with an answer of his own.

This time his mouth covered hers possessively, driving all thought from her reeling brain.

When she reached her tongue out in tentative greeting to his, she felt his surprise and immediately withdrew.

"I . . . I'm sorry," she stammered. "I thought . . ."

"You thought exactly right. Exactly."

He ran his fingers into her hair to loosen it further and to hold her head while he kissed her a third time. When she responded, more hesitantly even than before, he welcomed her, gently pulling her tongue into his mouth to taste and discover.

Now he could feel her body heat through the soft fabric of her dress. As he slid his hand down her back, his sensitive fingertips distinguished the upper edge of a camisole, then the drawstring of her pantalets under the waistband of a petticoat. And beneath all that, Julie herself. A Julie who would be warm and passionate and giving, as she always had been.

The hunger grew in him. Now he tasted fully of her, sliding his tongue past hers to the edge of her teeth and beyond. Thirstily he drank of the sweetness and craved more. Her mouth open to him and her body clutched tightly to his were no longer enough to satisfy the long famine. Starvation flooded his loins with familiar urgency.

He had wanted her before, but never like this. The wanting was a pain, a fire, a screaming that filled him with emptiness. Had she stood passive in his embrace, the fire might have remained controllable, but he knew there was frenzy in the way her arms encircled his waist and her fingers clutched at his shirt. Frenzy, yes, but also fear.

Now it was Morgan who withdrew, though he carefully eased himself just far enough away to break the bond of that kiss. Her eyes widened, and the tears spilled freely from them. Tenderly he touched his lips to a salty ribbon on her cheek.

"Please, Julie, tell me why you're crying," he begged. He had to know if she had come just for comfort or for another reason. Did she know what she was doing to him? He could not take advantage of her if she did not, and yet he hoped—almost prayed—that she did.

"No, I won't let you go," he reassured her when she clung even more tightly to him. "Let's sit down and talk for a minute, all right?"

She nodded and sniffled and finally loosened her hold on his shirt long enough for him to lead her into the parlor, where some light from the kitchen filtered to cast soft shadows.

"If I were still a drinking man, I'd offer you some brandy or even a shot of whiskey," he began, once he had her seated on the sofa. "I don't even have any coffee left from supper."

"It's all right. I don't need anything."

There, she was calmer now. She displayed lingering agitation by twisting a fold of her skirt around her finger and by lowering her eyes, but the desperation seemed to have left her.

"Good. Now, will you tell me why you came to see me this morning looking happier than I've ever seen you and now tonight you act as though the world has come to an end?"

"Because it has!" she wailed suddenly, and

the words came in a rush. "When I came to you this morning it was because I wanted to tell you I would refuse to marry Hans if you didn't want me to marry him. I was hoping you'd say something to put a halt to all the plans, but instead all you did was congratulate me. That was the *last* thing I wanted!"

"Why didn't you say so?"

"Because you never gave me the chance!"

"But you looked so . . . happy! Damn it, Julie, what was I supposed to do? A couple hours after Hans confronted me with the fact of your engagement, you came traipsing up to my back door dressed in that gorgeous blue blouse that Simon had told me was part of your trousseau. You were positively radiant, Julie, the way any woman should be when she's going to marry a man she loves. And that was exactly what I thought was going on!"

They were shouting at each other in whispers, yet still Julie paused before replying. If she were discovered here—but she could not dwell on that. Not now.

"I don't love him. I hate him. He beats the girls at Nellie's and he tried to beat me."

Morgan was on his feet at once, his hands clenching into fists held tightly to his sides.

"I'll kill him if he laid a hand on you, Julie. I swear it."

She could still feel the welts and yet denied them.

"No, he didn't touch me," she whispered

softly and extended a supplicating hand to bring Morgan beside her again.

They sat in silence for a moment or two, Morgan's arm finding its niche around Julie's shoulders and pulling her close.

"Then why did you buy all the dress material?" he asked, resting his cheek against her hair. "Simon said it was for your trousseau."

"How did you know about that?"

"I was in the store. But that doesn't answer my question."

Julie calmed herself and tried to explain without losing her temper.

"My mother told me to do it. She even helped me with the sewing. But I didn't buy it for a trousseau. I just wanted to . . . to look nice for you."

"But Simon said you charged it all to your father's account."

"I paid him back. With Mr. Burton's gold piece."

"*What?*"

"It was all I had! Or almost all. The rest of it is here in my pocket. Nine dollars and seventy-six cents. Enough to get me to Mesa, maybe."

"Mesa! What the hell do you want to go to Mesa for?" Morgan thundered.

"Well, what am I supposed to do? Go ahead and marry Hans? My father certainly won't let me stay at home if I refuse to marry Hans, and even if I did, I'd spend the rest of my life waiting on my mother. She's taken to her bed again, and

I don't think she's ever going to get well. Whatever medicine you gave her worked for a while, but after the other night, she's just as sick as she was when we came here."

Morgan lowered his voice again, but with an effort he wasn't sure he could maintain.

"I told you your mother isn't sick. She's putting on an act. And you said yourself she helped you with the sewing Saturday." Then, remembering her intention to leave Plato, he pressed the topic again. "You still haven't told me what you plan to do in Mesa."

"Does it matter?"

"Yes, damn it, it matters! *You* matter!"

"But I didn't matter enough this morning. You were going to let me marry Hans." She regretted the childish petulance in that statement, but she meant it anyway.

"Only because I thought it was what *you* wanted. *I* didn't want it, and if I had known then that you were against it, too, I'd have helped you stop it. Just as I intend to stop you from leaving."

In the breathless pause that followed, he understood what she had so far left unsaid. Perhaps it was just her presence in his house at this ungodly hour that explained her desperation.

"Will you stay if I ask you to?" he asked quietly. "I need you, Julie. Don't leave me, please."

If she answered, he didn't hear. The throbbing of his own pulse drowned out any other sound as he gathered her once more into his arms and crushed her to him. Now the desperation was his. He tried to communicate it to her in the way he held her.

Mouths met hungrily, then parted to gasp for life-giving air. Morgan's hands found themselves seeking the fine silken tangle of her hair and then he buried his face in it. The fragrance intoxicated him, but unlike the whiskey that had deadened his senses for so long, this gentle liqueur aroused him to a feverish delirium of desire. Only one thing was missing, and he knew he could add the single ingredient needed to make the most potent ambrosia in existence.

He kissed her ear, letting his lips tug softly on the lobe until she sighed with mounting passion. He could tell she fought it. There was no reason to delay, to tease, to torment. One more kiss, this time to her jaw, and then he told her.

"I love you, Julie."

She stiffened in disbelief. He had to believe that, refused to accept any other possible explanation.

"I love you, Julie," he repeated, no louder, no more insistently.

She opened her eyes and discovered the room had gone dark. Morgan laughed quietly, his breath warm against her neck.

"I was going to fill that lamp. That's why it was sitting on the table. I think it's completely empty now, don't you?"

She shivered.

"Are you afraid?" he asked.

"Yes."

"Of me?"

"Yes, and of myself."

"Why? Because other men have claimed to love you and didn't mean it?"

She blushed in the dark at his accurate assessment. He knew her so well.

"Then tell me how I can prove it. Shall I give you the money to get to Mesa? Or anywhere else you'd like to go?" He kissed her again, close to the base of her throat just above the collar of her dress. "You name it, Julie, and I will do it, if it is in my power."

She took a deep breath, and he was not unaware of the way her breasts pressed against him.

"Del?"

It was the first time she had used his name. She found the sensation queerly exhilarating.

"Yes?"

"Make love to me."

He must have misunderstood her. Of all the things she could have demanded as proof of his declaration, this was one he had never expected. Never. He had to be sure.

"What?"

"I knew it." She sighed, fighting tears of unspeakable humiliation. If Morgan hadn't been sitting on her skirt, she would have escaped, though she couldn't have gotten far in the dark without falling over or into something. And if he hadn't been taken so completely by surprise, he might have let her go.

"Knew what?" he asked, taking hold of her arm.

"You're still in love with Amy, so much that you won't break your marriage vows with her even now. I . . . I don't know what made me ask that. Please, I'm terribly sorry."

"Oh, Julie, Julie, Julie. Nothing would make me happier than to make love with you, right now," he crooned when he had her once again within his embrace. "I just can't quite believe that's what *you* want. Are you sure?"

"More sure than I've ever been of anything in my life."

His hands encircled her face and tilted it slightly upward, and though she couldn't see his eyes, she felt him studying her, searching her soul for something.

"Do you love me, Julie?"

The words seemed confused, like birds that have been caged so long they become afraid to fly. She had to nudge them past the open door, off the end of her tongue until they spread their wings and soared.

"Yes, I love you," she whispered joyously.

As he led her through the dark to the stairs and up to the second-floor hallway, Morgan wondered, and almost voiced his thoughts aloud, why he was going through with it. If he had any sense at all, especially a sense of decency, he would not take advantage of her while she was in this kind of emotional state. God knew he wanted her badly enough, but that was hardly a good reason. And though she had

begged him, he was sure she would regret her
wanton behavior soon enough. Yet he was
equally sure that he could not deny her.

He held her hand and guided her into the
bedroom—not the one he normally occupied,
but the one that contained the beautifully carved
bed he had shared with his wife. He searched
his heart for feelings of guilt and found none.

"Would you like me to light the lamp?" he
asked. "Or do you prefer darkness?"

"I . . . I don't know. Which do you prefer?"

"This time I'd like to be able to see, but if you
think you'll be too embarrassed, I won't mind."

It was a shrewd calculation intended to assure
her of his desire for her and her alone. In the
dark, she might have convinced herself that he
was pretending she was someone else. But calculated or not, he meant what he said. He
wanted to make love to Julie Hollstrom, not
some invisible being, no matter how willing and
passionate and responsive.

"Then light the lamp."

He turned the flame as low as he dared before
replacing the chimney and then turned to face
Julie. In the weak light, she looked exceptionally
fragile, exceptionally beautiful. He touched her
hair first, sliding his fingers into it and combing
out the little tangles.

"I never imagined you had all this tucked into
that little knot on the back of your head," he said
with a smile. "But you were right to hide it. Hair
like this is enough to drive a man wild."

He liked the way she blushed and tried to hide a smile of her own.

"Shall I leave the room and let you, uh, get comfortable in the bed?" he asked.

She blushed again, deeper this time.

"I don't know. Is that the way it's done?"

"Sometimes. Some people leave their clothes on, too." Her helpless confusion touched him then, and he gently turned her around so he had access to the buttons down her back. "But I like it better this way, with just us and no clothes to get in the way. Is it all right if I undress you, Julie?"

She could only nod her head. The touch of his fingers at the back of her neck sent shivers down her skin and fire through her veins. Perhaps he would find her undesirable, but she had to know. There may never come another chance.

With every button, he planted a kiss down her back, even when he came to the two just above her waist that were left undone because she hadn't been able to reach them herself. On the bare skin above her camisole, his lips left little tingles; through the thin cotton of the undergarment his kisses were gently warm.

When he had finished with the fastenings, he did not immediately slide the dress off, but took his time. He bared first one shoulder to lavish it with kisses, letting his tongue taste her skin and make it quiver with strange, delightful new sensations. Then he lifted her hair and draped it over his head as he pushed the dark, unbecoming calico off her other shoulder. Now his kisses drew little sounds from her throat, nothing more than soft sighs yet, but still the beginnings of passion.

He tugged the cuffs of the sleeves over her hands and then let the dress slither its own way to the floor. When it lay in a dark blue heap around the hem of her petticoat, Morgan moved to stand in front of her. He curled an index finger under her chin and tilted it up a fraction of an inch.

"Aren't you going to look at me?" he asked. "If you're afraid, or just want to change your mind and stop, say so. I won't force you, Julie. Not ever."

She couldn't speak, so she answered him by lifting her eyes to his and then reaching to unbutton his shirt. If her hands were not as steady and sure as his had been, she still managed to accomplish the same feat, including the trail of kisses in the wake of the opened buttons. Down the shallow valley of his sternum to the carved hollow where his ribs met, she pressed her lips to his chest and gloried in the way his breath caught and held.

The hair on the taut skin of his chest and belly tickled her nose. Her nostrils flared and drank the scent of him in massive gulps. While her hands clutched the front edges of his shirt, she buried her face against him, her lips murmuring some quivering silence against his flesh.

"Don't be ashamed," he chided quietly as she sank to the floor between his slightly spraddled feet and hung her head. "You've asked me to prove my love, and I will, but only if you are not afraid of showing yours. Let this be between us a thing shared, not merely given or taken."

He pulled her to her feet once more and lifted her shy hands to the collar of his open shirt. Where he had rolled up the sleeves, she had some difficulty sliding them down his arms; but soon, with no more encouragement, she had the garment off him and on the floor.

There was no spare fat on Morgan's torso, from the broad shoulders to the flat-muscled abdomen she had so hungrily tasted. Though Julie felt a flush of innocent shyness creep up her throat to her cheeks, she could not turn her admiring eyes from him. Why did the sight of his naked chest, with its dark, shiny hairs and puckered nipples, stir her to a smile? She had seen many male bodies in the past few weeks, and a few of them might even have been called attractive. But she had not wanted to be held tightly to any of them. Her fingertips had never ached to touch the little nubbins of darker flesh on a man's breast. It was only Del Morgan's body that she wanted to know so completely.

Her eyes moved to his hands as he lifted the hem of her camisole. With the same sureness of purpose he showed in surgery, he raised the flimsy garment over her head. The soft friction of cotton fabric sent an electric charge through her own nipples, and she looked down to find them crinkled and hard.

Still steady, Morgan's hands molded them-

selves around the creamy flesh. One by one his
thumbs touched the miniature erections, elon-
gating them and drawing Julie's passion closer
to the surface.

"How long," he wondered aloud as he let the
current sing along his nerves, "have we tormented ourselves? Why did we deny this when
we both wanted it so badly?"

Julie heard him, and her brain registered his
question, but she had no control over her answer. Like molten honey, the words oozed from
her slowly, matching the flow of warmth that
spread outward from his touch.

"I didn't know," she sighed. "So many things
that I didn't know. Ah, God, Del, please."

Her head fell back limply, yet her hands found
sudden strength. They tugged blindly at his belt,
undeterred even when his lips and tongue and
teeth made a fresh assault on her throat. He
could feel the vibrations of her moans, the tensing of tendons in the throes of delightful new
experiences, as clearly as he felt the searching of
her fingers for buttons and buttonholes.

He had wanted every single detail perfect,
from that first instant when he saw her approaching his house to the imagined conclusion
of this first physical celebration. But perfection
required time, more time than either of them
wanted to spend. As he pulled loose the knots
that held the last of Julie's underclothes and
kicked himself free of his own, Morgan regretted
the spoiling of his dream. Yet slightly flawed
reality was still better than unattainable perfec-

tion. He slid one arm behind her knees and lifted her naked into his arms to carry her to the bed.

And he was pleased to note that when she lay there, with her hair fanned out behind her head in a silver shower, she smiled at him.

There was time yet. If not for the perfect fulfillment of all his dreams, at least enough to satisfy the most urgent. Even before he lay beside her on the wide, comfortable bed, he began a slow exploration of her body. Her breasts were high and full, the engorged nipples dark against ivory skin. At his touch, she shivered and sighed and her eyelids fluttered down involuntarily, only to open quickly.

"You aren't afraid to look?" he asked.

"I'm more afraid that when I open my eyes you'll be gone, and this will all be some dream I'm waking from." His hand slid lower, from her breast to the wavelets of her ribs and on to the flat stomach. "I want to see and to remember everything."

"Then I must give you plenty to remember."

It wasn't enough that his hand moved lower still, his fingers combing into the curls of richly golden hair shrouding her femininity. That alone sent such a ripple of shock through her that her back arched up from the mattress and a slow wail fluttered tremulously from her throat. But that combined with the wet warmth of his tongue on a swollen breast drove her almost to tears. The wail became a series of cries as frayed and soft as an old satin ribbon. He suckled one tumescent peak, drawing his teeth gently along its length, while his finger found another, warmer, wetter, more secret place.

Words, singly and in short, incoherent phrases, mingled with the moans. Julie's fingers threaded themselves of their own volition into the dark curls on Morgan's head, but she could not tell if she wanted to pull him up so that she could kiss him or if she wanted to hold him to her breast where his mouth was doing such incredible things to her body. Nothing seemed real, nothing seemed controllable, though part of her remained fully and clearly conscious. The man she loved was loving her, driving her insane with passion she had never known and did not understand.

She sensed that she was ready for him. She felt the ease with which he slid one finger inside her willing body. The sensation did not startle her, nor did she shy away from his careful, gentle probing. When had her legs parted to allow him such entrance? She did not know. But she did know that when he settled his long length between her limbs, she felt somehow secure.

"Del, please," she begged, her body seeking his instinctively. At the very threshold he waited. "I can't bear it any longer."

Why did he hesitate? She could feel the hard length of him throbbing against her. Afraid that he might leave, she wrapped her legs around his, curling her toes under his ankles to hold him fast.

"Are you sure? Once it's done, it's done."

"I'm sure. Oh, God, I was never more sure of

anything in my life! Love me, please, Del, love me."

At first there was just the fullness of his flesh entering hers, easily, warmly. When he withdrew slightly, she rose with him to keep him within her. The next thrust slid deeper, opening her wider, but still filling her gently. Julie lifted herself to him, seeking the ultimate joining, and it was then that she felt the first twinge.

"No, Julie, don't hurry it." Morgan's voice steadied her. "Slowly, slowly, love, so it doesn't hurt. I don't want to hurt you, love. Not even a little. Never, never, not even a tiny bit."

The rhythm of his words matched the easy persistence of his body. He would not hurt her, not if he could help it. Though he had not really expected to find her intact and regretted the necessity of pain to mar this night, he felt a new surge of emotion at the discovery. Slowly, with each increasingly forceful thrust, he felt the membrane begin to give. And he knew not all the tension of her inner body came from the pain. If somehow he could bring her to her pleasure before his own demanded the satisfaction of full penetration, he might save her the worst.

"Relax, love . . . relax. . . . It's all right. I won't hurt you."

She was crying, sobbing at the pressure building inside that screamed for release she could not find because she did not know it existed.

"Easy, love, easy. Let me show you, let me love you."

With a tortured scream, she grabbed for the

elusive ecstasy. Arms, fingers, legs, and womb clutched at him, seeking it. Unable to wait any longer, Del plunged through the last resistance and let the rapture take them both together.

Chapter Twenty-seven
✦✦✦✦

"AH, FIREFLY," MORGAN sighed.

He breathed deeply but easily. It had taken no great physical exertion to achieve this most marvelously satisfying pleasure, and now he lay peacefully content. Holding most of his weight on his elbows to avoid crushing the woman beneath him, he watched while she surrendered to replete exhaustion.

"Can you breathe?" he asked after bestowing a kiss on her sweat-dampened temple.

"Yes. Oh, Del, don't move." She flung a limp arm across his shoulders and clasped him tightly with her legs still wrapped around his. "Don't leave me. Not yet."

He chuckled.

"I can't stay there forever."

She acknowledged that truth only reluctantly. Using muscles she never knew existed until just moments ago, she clung to his relaxing organ even while she wished she could draw a full, deep breath. She wanted to cry, to spill out all the suppressed emotions, and yet she had never in her life experienced such utter contentment. And though she gloried in the passion she had seen satisfied in his green eyes, she worried about the price her own wanton desire must cost.

"If you could, would you?"

"Would I what?"

"Stay there? Forever?"

He laughed, and that did it. Though Julie strained her hips upward, she lost him and cried out at his leaving.

"Yes, I would." He kissed the side of her neck, just below her ear. "Forever and ever." She shivered when his lips moved lower, to her shoulder and then her collarbone. "Marry me, Julie, and I'll prove it." His teeth grazed the bone beneath the pale skin, and his breath warmed her throat.

"Marry you?" she whispered.

Could he feel her heart leap, then stop, then jump again with a surge of new life? He must have felt it, for he had slid his entire body down the length of hers so that his mouth now rested just between her breasts. As he cupped the satiny mounds closer to his face, Julie felt his lashes flutter on her skin.

"Marry me," he repeated. Now his tongue flicked sideways, up toward a nipple that had gone as soft as his penis.

"When? How? Oh, Del, stop that, please."

He trailed the tip of his tongue to the other side, again reaching no more than halfway to the peak. He riffled the tips of his fingers over the little nubbins softly, drawing a moan but no answer from her. He slid farther down her length until his chin rested in her navel. He looked up at her, saw her watching him between the firm globes of her breasts.

"Well? Will you marry me? Tomorrow? We can get Wintergarden, I suppose. I confess I don't know a damn thing about the legal aspects of getting married in the Arizona Territory, but I'm sure the preacher can handle the details."

While she watched, he dipped his tongue into the shallow depression of her navel.

"Yes, yes, I'll marry you," she whispered. "Now, this minute, if you want."

But when she extended her arms to draw him to her, she found him sliding farther out of her reach. She gasped and tried to squirm away, but his weight held her fast.

"What are you doing?"

"Making love to you," he added quietly, calmly. His hands still curved comfortably around the outer swells of her breasts, but his lips were level with the upper edge of the golden curls between her thighs. "I hurt you a little while ago. Now I want to kiss it and make it feel better."

Again she tried to pull away from him.

"No, Del, don't. It isn't—"

"What isn't it? Right? Decent? Normal? It's beautiful, Julie. It's a way of showing love, and that's what I want to do for you, show you how much I love you."

So he did, despite her efforts to wriggle free. He plundered her body as he had her mouth, seeking the most sensitive places with his tongue and lips and teeth. He trailed his hands down her sides and around her hips to her buttocks to still her struggles.

He found the source of her passion and touched it, feeling the shudder of sheer pleasure ripple outward from that core to the ends of every nerve in her body. She no longer fought to escape him, but to achieve that soul-splitting ecstasy she had so recently discovered.

"No, Del," she gasped. "Not like this." She raised her back and shoulders from the mattress and reached hungry hands to him. Her fingers twined in his hair and tugged the soft dark curls. "Like before . . . inside me. Please, Del, please . . ."

He knew when he poised his body over hers that he had brought her close to the precipice. If he took her too soon, she would plunge over the edge almost instantly, and he didn't want that. He wanted to draw the pleasure out, extend it to its fullest and then savor the culmination at length.

He licked a nipple, hard now as an unopened rosebud.

"Slowly, love. We have all night."

He raked his teeth over the other peak.

"All night and all of forever."

Then her hands, sliding frantically between close-pressed bodies, found him and tightened around him. The groan that embrace dragged from him died only when his lips found hers. He devoured her. His tongue slithered to the far corners of her mouth, stroking along the inner surfaces in anticipation of another invasion. Julie met and engaged him in this frenzied duel, all the while seeking impalement on that other sword.

He sheathed himself in her warmth to the hilt with a single thrust. No maidenhead barred him, no pain hindered her, as they joined again. He drove home, and she held him there.

The frenzy, but not the desire, waned. Julie sighed a kind of lazy fulfillment. With his tumescence securely ensconced, Morgan raised his head and opened his eyes.

"You're beautiful," he told her. "Inside and out." When she reddened and tried to turn away from his slightly lascivious smile, he laughed and kissed her nose. "I didn't mean it that way. Well, yes, I guess I did. You *are* beautiful inside, like warm satin all wrapped around me. But I also mean the Julie inside the body. Here." He pressed his lips to the sun-gilded line along which her hair parted. "And here." Now they came to rest just above the shadowed valley between her breasts.

Holding him, she could not hold back the tears. As though the love he offered her refused to dwell in a heart filled with pain and sadness, she let it all spew forth.

"Don't ever let me go," she wept. "I love you so much, so very much."

It seemed to take hours to climb that torturous mountain again, yet they treasured every step. Sometimes Julie moved with him, raising her hips when he came close to complete withdrawal. Other times she let him pull away and then met his return with her own. Like ballet dancers, they moved in perfect harmony, not always matching steps identically, but preserving the synchronicity. Parting, meeting, circling, pausing, they built toward the swirl of the crescendo.

He plunged deeper because she drove him to it and gave back to him every ounce of wild pleasure. He knew she was closer to this climax than he. He would have let her slake her sexual thirst fully, undisturbed, but he could not, for by the time he felt the tightening that precedes release, he was too near his own to hold back.

The sudden convulsions wracked her whole body, not just the fevered center of her. She cried out with the wondrous delight that seemed unending, as each of Morgan's final thrusts multiplied the ecstasy. Just when it seemed she could bear no more, he reached the summit. She felt then what she had not felt that first time, the explosion of his body within hers, the pumping of his seed into her womb.

As before, he waited until their bodies were no longer joined, then lifted himself on shaky arms and legs and eased gently away. Lying on his back beside her, he clasped her hand.

"I love you." Julie sighed raggedly.
"I love you, too."

Julie wakened to darkness. Vaguely aware that
it was too early to get up, she sighed and rolled
over. She felt uncomfortably cool and groped
blindly for a sheet. Finding a loose corner, she
tugged until she got enough free to cover herself, but in doing so she discovered two very
surprising facts. She was stark naked, and every
muscle in her body ached.

With a lazy smile that quickly became an even
lazier yawn, she remembered. She tucked the
sheet under her chin and reached her other hand
out for Del.

He was gone, though the space beside her
retained a slight warmth. Ignoring the soreness
that seemed worse the more she moved, Julie
rolled from the bed and shuffled her feet along
the floor until she encountered bits and pieces of
clothing. She identified her petticoat and dress,
but rejected them both and finally found just the
camisole and pantalets. Pulling them on in the
dark, she stretched luxuriously and yawned
again.

She ran her fingers through her hair to comb
out the worst of the tangles while she oriented
herself to the room again. She looked to the
shuttered window but could see no light even
around the edges. Had Del extinguished the
lamp, or had it, like the one in the kitchen,

burned itself out while they slept? And how long had they slept?

Cautiously avoiding any obstacles in her path, Julie made her way in the general direction of the door. She encountered another garment, which she identified as his shirt, and slipped her arms into it. It was cool from lying on the floor, but soon her body would warm it, and she found a special comfort wrapping herself in something he had worn. Listening at the door, she heard the sounds of something moving around in the kitchen.

On silent feet she wandered down the stairs and through the parlor, aware now that Morgan was busy starting a fire in the stove. When she entered the kitchen she found him on his knees, blowing gently on the kindling, his own bare feet curled beneath the seat of his dungarees. He wore no shirt, and his hair looked as though he had combed it backwards with a pine cone.

He was absolutely the most beautiful creature she had ever seen.

Not knowing if he had heard her approach or was merely ignoring her while he built the fire, Julie stole up behind him and, dropping to her knees, wrapped her arms around his waist. She kissed the smooth cool skin of his shoulder and whispered, "Good morning."

"Good morning," he greeted in the same quiet kind of voice. "Want some coffee?"

He got to his feet, bringing her with him, and then turned in her loose embrace to face her. A light kiss seemed inevitable.

"I suppose so. What time is it?"

"About quarter to four. Did I wake you? I didn't mean to let the door slam when I filled the coffeepot."

"It doesn't matter. Something woke me, but I don't know what. And I needed to get up anyway."

She rested her cheek against his chest and closed her eyes. Never in her life had she felt so perfectly at home as in this man's arms. He held her gently, comfortably, and propped his chin on the top of her head.

"You don't need to do any such thing," he scolded lightly. "Today's your wedding day."

Now she tilted her head to look at him, to study the green eyes closely. He didn't blink under her scrutiny.

"You meant it?"

"Of course I did. I don't make marriage proposals I don't mean." Seeing the beginning of a tear in the corner of her eye, he squeezed her a little more tightly. "Did you think I was the type who made promises in order to seduce innocent maidens?"

"No, I would never think that of you," she confessed honestly. "I just thought maybe I had dreamt it. I still can't quite believe it's true."

"You do still want to marry me, don't you?"

"Of course I do!"

"Good. As soon as it's relatively decent to do so, I'll go wake up Reverend Wintergarden and find out just exactly what formalities we have to go through. By the time I open the office this afternoon, I expect to have our relationship fully legal."

She clung to him, her arms tight around his waist. He turned her face up for another kiss, softer than any other he had given her and yet more filled with his love.

"Now, let's have some coffee, all right?" he suggested.

He had brought the lamp from the bedroom and set it on the end of the table, and while Julie made the coffee, Morgan refilled the empty lamp and lit it, too. Then, sitting opposite each other, they sipped scalding black coffee and munched on slightly stale bread.

"My shirt looks much better on you," Del teased, blowing on the coffee to cool it a little. "Every time you lean over it gapes open and I can see all the way down to your belly button."

She blushed and clutched the garment more tightly around her.

"Now, Julie, you know you could have gotten dressed before you came down here and you didn't. I think you like letting me see you."

"I do. I mean, I did," she admitted shyly, "but when you talk about it so easily over a cup of coffee, well, it isn't quite the same as . . . as last night."

"Then let's finish the damn coffee and go back upstairs. Wintergarden won't be awake for hours yet."

"No, Del, I can't. I have to go home."

"Home?" he snorted. "What the hell for? This is your home now. There's nothing over there you need that I can't give you. You even told me you brought all your money."

"It isn't that. Oh, I have a few things, like my new clothes, and the aprons I made for work, and some other small personal things, but I need to go tell them."

"I can do that. Julie. I don't want you going there anymore. Not alone, at any rate."

She shook her head, and he saw a strange determination stamp itself firmly on her features.

"I can't explain it, but I need to go there and tell them. I . . . I won't tell them everything, though I doubt I'd even need to, but I want to do it on my own."

It was more than determination. Pride lifted her chin and made her cheeks glow. It straightened her shoulders under the loose-fitting shirt. After all the years of shame, she felt pride again, and he knew he had to let her do this her way. The fact that she took her pride from him sent a fresh thrill of love through him. She had brought him back from a living hell, but she took no credit for herself. She was proud of him, and that meant everything.

"All right," he consented. "But I'm going to watch you. I'll wait on the hotel porch, and if I hear one little scream, I'll be there in a second. Do you understand?"

"Yes. Thank you. For everything."

* * *

They kissed good-bye at the gate to the Hollstroms' yard, and then Julie watched Morgan walk away. She could barely make out the bulk of the Olympia House across the street, but the light would grow quickly. Birds twittered noisily and a few dogs had started barking. Roosters crowed nearby and in the distance.

Julie walked slowly around the house to the back door. Though the front was unlocked, as always, she felt more secure entering as silently as she had left. No one should be awake yet, and she planned to make her announcement during breakfast.

The kitchen was still dark and silent. Julie took a match from the box on the wall and struck it on the side of the stove to light a lamp. Though she was starting a bit earlier than usual, she set about her regular chores as though this morning were no different from any other.

Morgan settled himself on one of the old chairs on the hotel porch and pulled out a cheroot. He could see glimmers of light in the Hollstrom house now. He imagined Julie going about her tasks, lighting the stove, fixing breakfast, waking her father and mother and brother. He watched for lights in the upstairs windows, but they remained dark. He sighed, sending a puff of fragrant smoke spiraling into the morning stillness.

* * *

Julie climbed the stairs and went into her own room first. Now there was some light, enough to see to collect the few things she intended to keep. She still had her money in her pocket, and added to it a brush and comb, her hairpins, and the tissue-wrapped bar of Pears soap she had splurged on. From the wardrobe she took only the blue blouse and the new skirt, folding them over her arm while she took the aprons and her few undergarments from the drawer.

She carried her belongings down the stairs and placed them in a neat pile on the dining room table. When her parents came down for breakfast, they would see the clothes and that would give Julie the opportunity to break the news to them. She would be close to the door, too.

After making a final check in the kitchen to see that the water was ready for coffee, that the bacon was starting to sizzle and the toast wasn't burning, she made the last climb up those stairs.

Katharine stood in the doorway to her room, yawning groggily and looking extremely disheveled, even for a woman just out of bed.

"Is Papa up?" Julie asked, surprised to see her mother awake this early.

"Isn't he downstairs?" Katharine countered.

"No."

"Well, he isn't here either. And from the looks of the bed, I'd say he's been up at least an hour. I took all the blankets."

Julie scowled and tried not to let herself worry.

Perhaps Wilhelm had got up while she was busy in her room and had gone out to the privy. Surely there was no way he could guess where she had been all night. There was no reason for him even to suspect she had been anywhere but asleep in her room.

Morgan put out the stub of cigar on the sole of his boot and shifted uncomfortably on the chair. He hadn't brought his watch and could only estimate that at least an hour had passed. There were still no lights at the Hollstrom house.

He turned at the sound of footsteps approaching. Of the two figures descending the steps in front of McCrory's and heading for the hotel, Morgan recognized Ted Phillips's silhouette instantly. The other man seemed to hang back, almost walking behind the marshal's bulk, and Morgan couldn't see plainly in the uneven light.

"Morning, Ted," he called pleasantly. "You're up early."

"Yeah, you too, Del."

What was Wilhelm Hollstrom doing out with Ted Phillips at this hour of the day? Morgan hadn't seen Julie's father leave the house, and he hadn't taken his eyes off the place since she walked up to it. He tensed as though for a fight.

"What's up?" he asked quietly.

"Look, Del, I don't like this any more'n you, but I ain't got a choice," Phillips began apologetically. "This guy here has swore out a warrant and I gotta arrest you."

"Arrest me? What the hell for?"

Wilhelm walked out from his hiding place and looked down at the man in the chair, but he said nothing. Morgan, afraid of his own reaction to the man who was soon to be his father-in-law, gripped the cracked arms of the chair and held himself in it.

"Mr. Hollstrom here says you did somethin' to his daughter. He's chargin' you with rape."

Chapter Twenty-eight

✦✦✦✦✦

JULIE STARED OUT the window to the sullen heat lines that radiated from the barren ground. The sun stood directly overhead to cast sharp, short shadows that did not move. No breeze, no breath of air stirred the ungodly heat. The parlor clock chimed a dozen times. Noon.

She had not cried, nor even screamed when her father came triumphantly into the dining room and made his vicious announcement to Julie and Katharine. Shock seemed to numb them both, though Julie recalled that Katharine hadn't gone into either hysterics or a fainting fit. She had given in with her usual resignation to Wilhelm's orders and dutifully shut Julie in her room, but she hadn't resorted to the familiar tactics of evasion.

Julie sat on the bed for a while, right after she heard Hans help Wilhelm fashion a bolt on the outside of her door. But she soon drifted to the window and there watched the western mountains come to life with the sunrise. No one had said a word to her all morning, not even to offer her breakfast or, now that it was noon, lunch. She could not have swallowed food anyway.

She did not waste time wondering how Wilhelm had found out. She didn't care, and it didn't matter. What mattered was rectifying the situation. She never for a moment thought that Del would hold her responsible for it, but she knew she was the only one who could set him free. She just had to think of the right way to do it.

Wilhelm had made it quite clear to her that escape from her temporary prison would do no good. To begin with, the drop from her window to the rocky yard below would almost certainly injure her. And the marshal had already been warned that she was in no condition after her "ordeal" to be trusted in anything she might say. As insurance, Wilhelm had taken her clothes, her few dresses as well as the skirt and blouse left in the dining room. She was cooler in just a simple shift, but she could not go outside practically nude.

So she waited, and thought, and listened. She had no trouble hearing the loud voices from the parlor, but they argued in the more comfortable German they had grown up with, and Julie couldn't understand a word they said. Once in a while Wilhelm muttered something to Katharine, whose higher tones and trembling whine carried almost too clearly up the stairs, but she said nothing to give Julie a clue as to the nature of the men's argument.

What facts Julie had were few, and she knew enough not to believe everything her father had told her. Morgan was in jail—she believed that much, as well as that he had been charged with rape. Julie had almost laughed at that, but she knew she did not dare enrage Wilhelm further. He told her there would be a trial, that he had sent the marshal's telegraph to the circuit judge. The Honorable Mr. Booth was expected to arrive Wednesday morning. With any luck, the sentence would be handed down and carried out before the end of the week, in plenty of time, Wilhelm implied, for the wedding to take place as scheduled.

Julie had no idea what laws in the Arizona Territory governed those convicted of rape, but she fully expected her father to demand the same sentence he had pronounced on Ted Sheen.

Winnie Upshaw brought Del a cloth-covered tray with his lunch and a pitcher of lemonade, but she wasn't allowed any time alone with him. Ted Phillips stood less than ten feet away, doing his sworn duty even if the scowl on his face clearly showed his disgust. He checked the tray for weapons when Winnie brought it and checked it again when Morgan handed it back to her, then he ushered her to the door.

"Damn it, Del, I feel like a real ogre, keepin' you locked up in here like this. No visitors, no nothin'. What the hell's the matter with that guy?"

Morgan shook his head and sat back down on the bunk.

"I don't know, Ted, but I'm sure as hell gonna find out. As soon as Simon gets Leo sober, I want to see him. If I fall asleep, you wake me up, okay?"

"Yeah, I will. But I still don't know what you want with that old drunk. He's no more good as a lawyer than you was as a doctor when you was drinkin'."

"Just let me worry about that. Bring Leo to me, and I'll take care of the rest."

"Okay. Look, do you mind if I go over to Daneggar's and get me some lunch? You won't go tryin' to bust out, will ya?"

Morgan shook his head again. He could do with a little privacy for a while.

"Go ahead. And don't worry; I won't go anywhere."

Not while Julie's still in that monster's hands.

He had seen, through the front window of the marshal's office, when the wagon came to town. No doubt Wilhelm had sent word to Hans the instant the deed was accomplished. Had they cooked up the scheme together? No, Morgan doubted Wallenmund had the brains to concoct a rabbit stew, much less this sort of plot. And it had to be a plot. There was something too clever about everything to be spontaneous.

And what about Julie? Was she, perhaps, somehow connected? No, he dismissed that thought the instant it came to him. What in God's name did she have to gain by it? He had seen the bruises on her arm, knew the way she was treated. Besides, he knew the truth about her father.

He was tired. And hot. The worst feature of the little two-cell jail was that it generally baked its occupants into confession long before they came to trial. Winnie's lemonade helped some, but its effect was only temporary. Sleep, at least until Leo Woode sobered up, offered some escape from the heat, so Morgan stretched out on the thin mattress and closed his eyes. He fell asleep almost immediately.

Wilhelm brought Julie's supper and then watched while she toyed with it. After ten minutes, he announced her time was up and removed the plate from her lap. Then he locked her in again. She got up from the bed and returned to the window. At least now it was cooler. Her skin felt burnt from standing in the sunlight all afternoon.

"I should have been married today," she whispered to the sunset. "I should have had my supper with my husband. We'd be sitting up on the rooftop now, maybe reading a book or a magazine or talking about the patients we treated today. And then when it got dark, we'd go to bed and—"

Her musings, undistorted by tears, stopped when a scream from the kitchen brought Julie out of her thoughts of Morgan. There was a moment of silence, then another scream, clearly Katharine's.

When Julie heard the thump of heavy footsteps up the stairs, she turned warily away from the window to watch her door. The bolt lifted, and the door shot open. Wilhelm, his face red and dripping with sweat, held Katharine in his arms. She looked limp, and there was a streak of red across her cheek.

"Take care of your mother," Wilhelm spat as he deposited his wife on Julie's bed. "If you haven't forgotten how."

He slammed the door so hard the whole house rattled, then he threw the bolt back into place with a jolt. Terrified, Julie stared at the shut door for a moment before she slowly turned her gaze to her mother's crumpled body on the bed.

Katharine rolled over and opened her eyes.

"My God, I thought he'd never get me up those stairs!" she breathed. "Apparently Dr. Morgan was right about my being overweight."

No sign of hysteria, no grogginess as after a faint. Julie continued to stare, totally perplexed.

"I also thought I'd never find a knife sharp

enough to cut myself," Katharine went on. "I'll have to remind Willy to sharpen them more often."

Julie finally found her voice, but something kept her from approaching any nearer the bed. The window, even with its long drop, offered at least a chance of escape.

"Mama," she asked suspiciously, "what is the matter?"

"I cut my thumb. See?" Katharine held up the bloodied appendage.

Without moving a step away from the window, Julie commented, "It doesn't look like the sort of thing one screams like a banshee about."

"Well, it was the best I could do with those damned dull knives." She sat up and smoothed her rumpled dress, noticing a few bloodstains but shrugging unconcernedly.

"Why would you want to cut yourself?"

Katharine got to her feet with no sign whatsoever of her earlier collapse. Her smile gave way to a serious frown as she walked steady toward her daughter.

"How else was I going to get your father to let me see you? I had to find out just what's to be done about this predicament, and that meant talking to either you or Dr. Morgan. A cut thumb seemed the easiest way. We don't have a great deal of time, so I suggest we not waste any more of it."

"Wait, Mama. I don't understand this at all. Are you telling me that you want to help me?"

"Of course I do! Oh, Julie, what else would I do? Haven't I always helped you?"

Julie remembered just barely in time to keep herself from laughing out loud. Had her mother gone mad? Katharine was so totally unlike her usual self that Julie imagined her mind had finally snapped under this latest stress.

"I don't consider making me wait on you hand and foot for the past nine years helping me at all," Julie spat, refusing to disguise her anger. "You used me like a slave, Mama."

"Oh, dear."

Katharine stumbled backwards to the bed and sat down again heavily. She said nothing for a few seconds and just stared at the rather nasty laceration on the ball of her left thumb. It continued to bleed steadily.

Julie, still cautious, walked to the dresser and took out a handkerchief.

"Here, Mama, use this. You're going to ruin your dress."

Like an automaton, Katharine wound the corner of the linen square around her injury and tucked the leftover fabric into her hand. But she seemed to have no real interest in the bandaging and frequently glanced up from it to watch as Julie returned to her post at the window.

"Do you really think I care about a stupid dress at a time like this?"

There were tears in Katharine's eyes when she whispered that question. Over the years she had often turned to weepy histrionics to get her way, but this time Julie suspected there was a difference. At least there were no histrionics.

"Mama, I don't know what to think!" Julie whispered exasperatedly. "Papa has Del in jail for something he didn't do, I'm locked in my room with no clothes, Hans is shouting in the parlor, and you come up here grinning like a canary-eating cat because you cut your thumb on a dull knife! And then you try to tell me you only want to help. To tell the truth, Mama, I think you're a little insane."

With a wry smile, Katharine answered, "Maybe I am. Twenty-seven years with Wilhelm Hollstrom would be enough to drive anyone insane." Then she looked up at Julie and the smile faded. "And if I thought it was all a mistake, I know I would go insane. Oh, Julie, did I do wrong? I only wanted to make sure you'd be happy and wouldn't make the same mistake I did."

Something cold ran down Julie's spine. Fascinated and terrified at the same time, she leaned against the windowsill and listened, and she could not believe her mother lied.

"I married your father because I had to, not because I wanted to. I was fifteen years old, and the only way I knew to earn a living was on a music hall stage. My father—your grandfather—was a fairly well known actor, but like most men in that profession, he was inclined to drink and chase women and indulge in every bad habit known to man. My mother, unfortunately, loved him dearly and stayed with him, dragging me with her. You have no idea what it's like worrying where your next meal will come from, or whether you'll have a bed to sleep in. Once, in Pennsylvania, we slept in a train station for three nights, and Papa begged from the passengers passing through."

"What does this have to do with Del and me?" Julie demanded to know. "You're the one who's wasting time, Mama, with all this family history."

"Because I want you to understand. Anyway, after fifteen years I decided I had had enough. There was a young man in New York, a lawyer's son, who took a fancy to me. I had grown up around adults, not children, so I was able to pass for twenty when I was barely twelve. David was five years older than I and yet he seemed so much younger." She sighed with memories but quickly cleared her thoughts. Julie was right; there was no time to waste.

"I don't know why David stopped seeing me. Perhaps his parents found out he had been spending time with an actress, which was tantamount to falling in love with a woman of the streets. But one night when I was supposed to meet him, he didn't come. I waited and waited, and came back the next night, but I never saw David again. Some years later, when you were still a child, I read in the newspaper that he had been killed during the war."

"Oh, Mama, I'm so sorry. Why didn't you ever tell me?"

"Maybe I should have, a long time ago,

because—well, never mind the becauses now. David Anderson was killed and there was no bringing him back. I was married to Wilhelm by then anyway and had you, so there was no sense in my mourning him. Wilhelm had given me the security that I wanted, and I had decided that that was far more desirable than the effervescent wine of romance. I was never hungry, never cold, never alone, and I had a father for my baby. There was nothing more I could ask for then."

It took a moment for Katharine's statement to make full sense to Julie. She hesitated to ask the question, but then realized she had to have confirmation of such a suspicion.

"Are you saying I'm not really Papa's daughter? Does he know?"

"I'm sure he suspects. I didn't know for certain myself when I met and married him. He had just arrived from Berlin and had been offered a position with a bank in New York. They would only hire him on the condition that he had a wife. I was desperate to avoid going back on stage after—after David, so I married him. Some weeks later, I discovered I was expecting you. I wasn't positive that David was your father until you were born too early to have been Wilhelm's. Fortunately, he had gone to Philadelphia on business for several weeks, so when he came home I just told him you were six weeks younger than you really were."

"My birthday wasn't yesterday?"

"No, it isn't. You were born on the first day of summer, June twenty-first."

It was not easy to comprehend all this startling information. Julie found herself struggling more to accept her mother's love than to believe any of the other things she had been told. She had resented Wilhelm for so long that she had never realized how much she hated him. She accepted his treatment of her because she had believed herself responsible. Now she knew the truth: He would have hated her no matter what she did.

Julie digested all these revelations for a moment, then realized the room had grown dark. She had a lamp but no matches. Not that the lack of light mattered particularly, but she became more aware of the passage of time. Wilhelm might return at any moment.

"Mama, hurry up. What does this have to do with the way you've treated me all these years?"

"I'll try to hurry, dear, but it isn't easy condensing so much into a few minutes, I hope you know." She took a deep breath and plunged into the tale again. "I didn't want you to make the same mistake, choosing security over love. Within a few years of our marriage, I knew I was never going to be happy with Wilhelm. And yet, I knew I could never go back to what I had had. So I decided, I think right around the time I learned of David's death, that I would make sure you knew enough not to settle for anything less than the best. I wanted you educated and accomplished to the best of my ability, no matter what Wilhelm said. And when he got it into his head that he didn't want you consorting with the common yokels in that little Indiana village, I didn't disagree. I wanted something better than that for you, too. I'm still not sure why he was against it, but I never argued with him."

"Is that why you didn't try to stop him when he went after Ted?"

"Didn't try? Oh, Julie, I almost killed myself trying to stop him!"

Julie had to put her finger to her lips and shush her mother because Katharine's voice had risen almost to hysteria.

"I followed him that night. I tried to walk into town to get a horse and ride after him, but when he knocked me to the ground in the yard, he started my labor. I had gone through so much false labor with you that I thought it was the same thing. I expected it to stop soon so I could go on, but it didn't. I practically had to crawl back to the house, and I thought that damned son of his would be born in the road for sure. I didn't care. I fully intended to play the role of an invalid after the baby was born anyway, so this only added evidence. Unfortunately, it also prevented my saving that poor young man's life."

At that, Julie's knees turned to water. Shaking uncontrollably, she slid to the floor, her back still against the wall for support. She blinked, and tears rolled down her cheeks.

"When Wilhelm brought you home and told me what he had done, I threatened to kill him, or worse, kill Willy. I was, however, in no condition to do harm to either of them, and by the time I recovered, I also realized that Willy hadn't done anything. It wasn't his fault he was born. And then Wilhelm reminded me that if I killed Willy I'd end up dead myself, hanged just the way Ted was, and that would leave Wilhelm to raise you alone, with a memory of me as a murderer. That was something I couldn't face."

"So you put up with him rather than leave me alone." It all seemed quite logical now, though still a rather difficult concept to adjust to.

"What else could I do? You were my daughter and I loved you."

"But why make me do all the work? And why did you force me to wear those ridiculous spectacles? And old clothes? And all the other things?"

"Because I didn't want you to attract the wrong man. When a man sees a beautiful woman, he ignores everything else about her. He doesn't care if she is as stupid as a mushroom or as cruel as a badger, so long as she is pretty. And I wanted you to have all the skills a woman needs, whether you ever had to use them or not."

"That still doesn't explain why Willy had everything handed to him on a silver platter and I had to make do with almost nothing."

"I couldn't do anything about that. There simply wasn't the money for me to equalize the material considerations. I told myself that it was all to the good. If you looked too prosperous, you would attract a man too interested in your money. Also, you needed to appreciate what possessions you had and not squander them. No man worth his money wants it squandered by a spendthrift wife."

Julie couldn't help but think of the way Del had tried to give her money, and her extreme frugality almost made her laugh. Her mother had taught her well.

She struggled to her feet and walked toward Katharine, hands outstretched. Together, hands clasped tightly, they sat beside each other on the bed.

"There were times, Julie, when I wanted to tell you everything. It was so hard to keep it all a secret."

"But you thought that if I knew, I wouldn't be able to play the part convincingly enough. Oh, Mama, why didn't you give me the chance? At least you could have let me try!"

"I couldn't risk it. If you had known I wasn't sick, you'd have run off with the first man who came your way. The cavalry officer in Kansas City, for instance. Even if he hadn't been married, he wasn't good enough for you."

"Couldn't you have let me choose for myself?" Julie asked, growing angry again. "Is that what you've done again, removed another undesirable suitor? Good God, Mama, what do you want? Del's a good man. He's not wealthy, but he can give me a nice home and take care of my needs. He's respected in this town and so am I.

Or at least we were until you started your infernal meddling."

Katharine shook a stern finger at Julie and just barely remembered to keep her voice down.

"My infernal meddling, if you'll remember, is what got the two of you together in the first place. And even when I wasn't meddling, if it hadn't been for my broken arm, you would never have met him."

"Don't be ridiculous, Mama. You had nothing to do with it. First it was your arm and then it was Willy's cut, and you couldn't have caused that."

"No, I didn't, but who told you to pull that poor man onto the porch and fix him some breakfast? And who kept sending you to find him for my medicine? Who begged Wilhelm to let you go work for him? Who invited the doctor for lunch?"

Katharine paused, as though to let these thoughts sink in and stir other memories of other instances, but when she began to continue, the sound of Wilhelm's heavy tread on the stairs kept her silent. Julie held her breath, and her astonishment.

Wilhelm did not knock, but the slice of light under the door indicated he carried a lamp or lantern and had only one hand to slip the bolt. Two seconds, maybe three, were all Julie had. A gesture from her had Katharine scrambling to sprawl exhaustedly on the bed, while Julie returned to the window to stare stoically at the desert night.

"She's asleep," she whispered to Wilhelm when the door opened. She did not turn to look at him.

"Good. Let her sleep." He muttered, "Clumsy woman," as he backed out the door again and would have locked Julie in for the night if she hadn't stopped him.

"What about me, Papa?"

"You?"

"Yes. Where am I to sleep?"

Now she turned, slowly pivoting on the balls of her feet until her eyes met the almost blinding light of the lamp. He held it off slightly to one side to avoid the worst of the glare himself, and in doing so gave Julie a clear view over his shoulder to the man behind him. Hans squinted against the flame, but nothing could hide the naked emotion that manifested in a flaring of broad nostrils and furtive lick of his lips.

Wilhelm ground out a guttural order in German that sent Hans into another room.

"You can sleep on the floor, like the bitch you are," Wilhelm then said coldly to Julie.

She said nothing, displayed no reaction at all. When Hans returned and threw a heavy quilt at her, she did not bend to pick it up. She lifted her chin a trifle higher and turned back to the window.

Let them leave, she prayed silently. And for once her prayer was answered. With a curse that needed no translation, Wilhelm slammed the door shut. He did not forget the bolt; Julie jumped when it slid home.

Only when the two men's voices settled in the parlor did Katharine move. She sat up and propped her back against the wall and Julie's thin pillow.

"That was clever, dear. I would never have thought about the sleeping arrangements. The quilt will be quieter and easier to handle than the mattress."

"Now what are you talking about?"

"Why, getting out of this house, of course. You have to escape somehow, you know."

"I hadn't really thought about it."

"Well, I have." Katharine tossed the sheet back and as she swung her feet to the floor began to pull the bedclothes free. "You can't just jump out the window, and you have nothing to anchor a rope to. But with a little luck, I ought to be able to hold these sheets long enough for you to reach the ground. I had thought to throw the mattress out first in case you fell, but—"

"No, Mama," Julie interrupted quietly. She faced her mother in the almost impenetrable darkness and put all her determination into her voice. "I'm not leaving this room."

"Good heavens, why not?"

"Because I think it's exactly what Papa wants."

Leo Woode's law books were stacked neatly under the bunk. A lantern in the corridor separating the cells from the office afforded Morgan plenty of light for reading, but Morgan hadn't yet looked at the books. He lay quietly, not terribly uncomfortable, with his fingers laced together behind his head while he contemplated the one question for which all the legal treatises in the world had no answer.

Should he deny his love for Julie and hers for him by pleading innocent to the charge? To do so he would have to risk the shame and humiliation the whole town would heap on her if he admitted the truth, that she had come to him willingly. He could not do that to her, even if the only alternative was to admit to his own guilt.

Damn Hollstrom to hell! he thought viciously as he pulled off one boot and let it clunk to the floor. Why is he so willing to let Julie marry that bastard Wallenmund and even more willing to brand me a rapist? What the hell makes Hans a more suitable son-in-law than me?

Then, quietly aloud, he voiced another perplexing but strangely significant query.

"And why is Hans still playing the role of fiancé if he considers Julie the 'damaged goods' her father called her?"

He kicked off the other boot and readjusted the lumpy pillow beneath his knuckles. And then he began talking.

Staring at the mottled ceiling, he asked, "Why would a man want his daughter to marry a dirt-poor farmer when she could have a relatively respectable and at least financially solvent physician? He's got to know Julie would tell him the truth about us, so how can he expect Hans to accept her? And why would Hans be willing to go ahead with it? None of it makes sense at all."

He rolled onto his side and reached under the bunk for one of Leo's books. Medical texts were dull, but they couldn't hold a candle to these boring volumes of precedents and statutes and court cases. Maybe half an hour's reading would put him to sleep. He could use it. Then maybe in the morning, when he was rested and his anger had cooled a little more, he'd have some answers.

He cocked one knee and propped the heavy tome on his thigh. Leo had stuck bits of paper among the pages, but they marked nothing of interest. As Morgan flipped through the book, he shifted slightly onto his side, to put the light more directly on the page.

A clatter on the adobe floor startled him, but he immediately recognized the sound. He set the book down and leaned over the edge of the bunk to search for the coin that had fallen from his pocket.

He couldn't see it at first, in the shadow under the narrow bed, and almost gave up. A nickel or even a half dollar wasn't worth hanging upside down for. But as though the rush of blood to his head had increased his powers of reasoning, he suddenly had the key to the whole puzzle. In retrospect, he wondered why he hadn't seen it sooner; it was so absurdly simple.

Some men would do anything for money.

Chapter Twenty-nine

✦✦✦✦✦

THE SPACIOUS, OAK-PANELED ballroom of the Olympia House had never overflowed with people the way it did the morning of the second day of August.

Judge Booth wasted little time selecting a jury; the twelve good men and true were seated before nine-thirty. Then Ted Phillips brought Morgan over from the jail and read the charges.

"Yer Honor, Mr. Wilhelm Hollstrom charges that Mr. Morgan did seduce his daughter and—"

"Whose daughter, Mr. Phillips?" the judge asked. "Mr. Hollstrom's or Mr. Morgan's?"

"Oh, Mr. Hollstrom's, sir. Miss Julie. She works for Del. Mr. Morgan, that is. Er, Dr. Morgan. Yer Honor."

"Proceed, Mr. Phillips."

Morgan sat quietly, not listening to Ted's confused rendition. Instead, he scanned the crowd for some sight of Julie. Her father, the bastard, was there and Wallenmund, right in the front row. But there was no sign of Julie.

He turned his attention then to the jury, the twelve men seated on painted gilt chairs to the judge's left, at the front of the ballroom. Six of them, including Ard Hammond, were friends or neighbors from Morgan's early days in Plato. The other six were newcomers, men who had known him mostly as a drunken bum and who probably still weren't sure of his reputation. Something in the way Ard Hammond lounged on his chair assured Morgan he could count on at least one vote of not guilty, regardless what evidence was presented, but he warned himself not to count on eleven others as loyal as the mortician.

"I said, Mr. Morgan, how do you plead?"

The judge's voice, as stern as his white-bearded visage, cut into Morgan's thoughts.

"Not guilty, Your Honor."

"Very well. Mr. Hollstrom, you may present your case."

"No, wait," Morgan interrupted, getting to his feet. He wished he had listened to Ted's advice to have Winnie bring him some decent clothes, but Morgan had been more concerned with an early-morning conference with Simon McCrory. "I have a request to make, Your Honor."

Booth looked down a long, hooked nose at the accused.

"A request? For what?"

"I wish to be confronted by my accuser. Surely no one in this courtroom is going to believe that the crimes I'm accused of were perpetrated against Mr. Hollstrom himself."

"No!" Wilhelm protested, coming to his feet, too. "I have made the charges, so now he must answer to me."

Morgan held his temper in check, but only

barely. His fingers itched to curl around the man's throat and stop his vilifications once and for all. But that would not do Julie any good.

"A crime, Your Honor, must have a victim. If Mr. Hollstrom is not the victim, then I say he must produce one or there is no crime."

Ted Phillips gave a thumbs-up to that. The agreement from the crowd was enthusiastic, forcing the judge to pound his ivory gavel and call for order. Then he tugged at his beard a moment and trained his bright black eyes first on one man, then the other.

"Then I order Mr. Hollstrom to bring his daughter to the courtroom. Will thirty minutes be enough time?"

Wilhelm's anger was almost a tangible essence, a smoldering heat ready to explode. As though the gathered citizens of Plato felt it, too, they waited quietly under the crystal chandeliers for Wilhelm's answer.

"Half an hour will be sufficient," he grumbled.

"Fine. Mr. Phillips, you and a deputy will accompany Mr. Hollstrom. Court is recessed until ten-twenty-five."

Katharine lamented her appearance in Julie's tiny hand mirror but wasted no real time bemoaning the absence of brush and comb.

"All right, Julie, now will you go out the window? At least then you can open the back door and let me out of this room. We'll get your

clothes so you'll be properly dressed when you
march into that courtroom and tell them the
truth."

Julie, stiff from sleeping on the floor, shook
her head slowly.

"No, Mama, I'm going to wait right here."

"But don't you see? You could be here forever!
He may *never* let you out! How can you save Dr.
Morgan unless you tell the judge what really
happened? You love the man, don't you?"

"Yes, I think so."

"And he loves you?"

"He told me he did."

"Then you had better help me with these
sheets and get downstairs before it's too late."

But they were already too late, as the sound of
masculine voices and heavy footsteps told them.
Julie sighed, relieved she had not had to argue
further. She did not want to be forced to tell her
mother the true reason behind her decision. One
night of confession might have been good for
Katharine's soul, but it was not enough to make
up for nine years of mistrust. Julie would keep
her own counsel at least a little longer.

When Wilhelm unbolted and opened the door,
Julie experienced a small flush of satisfaction.
Her tactic had worked, at least in part. Ted Phillips, standing just behind Wilhelm, wore a look
of shocked disapproval when he saw Julie wearing just the thin shift. He turned his head away
politely.

"You have fifteen minutes," Wilhelm told her.
"Dress or I'll—"

The marshal's voice interrupted.

"The judge says you gotta come, Miss Julie," he said, keeping his eyes averted. "Del—Dr. Morgan—says he wants to be confronted by his accuser."

"I've accused him of nothing," she answered. "It is my father who made the charges, not I."

"Well, it's got somethin' to do with producin' a victim. Anyway, the judge says you gotta come."

Katharine, still facing Julie and with her back to the door, silently reiterated her plea.

Go, she mouthed sternly. *Tell them the truth.*

Julie thought for a moment, then walked toward the marshal, who had somehow eased his bulk between the door and Wilhelm.

"All right, I'll go. But I expect you to testify, Mr. Phillips, that I do so under duress."

"Okay, Miss Julie. Mr. Hollstrom, you give her them clothes and then we'll go downstairs. If it takes her a little longer, then we'll just let the judge wait."

In maneuvering himself past Wilhelm again, Phillips pushed the door farther open and revealed to Julie the other two men who had accompanied him. One she vaguely recognized as a local man, though she couldn't recall his name. The other was Hans, his face a mask of fury. He waited until the others had left and then spoke to Julie in a low, heated whisper.

"He is guilty, Julie," he warned in such a way that she could not mistake his meaning. "If you want him alive, you will accuse him just like your papa said. Otherwise I will kill him. I swear it."

Then he pulled the door shut and followed the others down the stairs.

Julie walked to the clothes Wilhelm had laid on the dresser. To her relief he had brought the blue calico, not the batiste blouse. Her shoes and stockings were there as well as her comb and brush.

"Mama, I want you to listen to me." She pulled on pantalets, then wriggled out of the shift before slipping a camisole over her head. "I'm going to tell them the truth, all of it."

"But you heard what Hans just said. Oh, damn him! If it weren't for him, I'd agree with you, but now, under the circumstances . . ."

"No, Mama, I have to do it." She tucked her petticoat into the dress and then slipped her arms into the sleeves. "Here, can you get these buttons?"

"Well, I was wrong. Oh, dear, my fingers won't hold still." Katharine fumbled with the buttons. "Don't you think it's better to keep Dr. Morgan alive? Hans meant what he said."

"I'm sure he did, Mama, but I don't intend to let him get away with his threats anymore."

"And just how are you going to stop him? He hasn't left you much of a choice."

"Actually, he hasn't left me any choice at all. That's why I have to do this."

She tied her shoes firmly and then stood up. "Are you ready, Mama?"

*　　*　　*

The courtroom buzzed with muted conversation that subsided the instant Ted Phillips strode through the open door from the hotel lobby. Aware that every eye was on her, Julie hung back for a brief second, but she regained her courage even before Lucas Carter prodded her with a bony finger in the small of her back.

"You can't get out, Miss Julie," he drawled. "Me'n Skip's gonna be sittin' on the porch, and no prisoners leaves without the marshal's say-so." He patted the gun at his hip for emphasis. "Now, you just walk up there where the marshal's waitin'."

She moved, slowly at first, then more determinedly, past all those leering, accusing eyes. Not a whisper reached her ears, but she knew the words were in their minds. Harlot. Wanton. Fallen woman. Somehow she didn't care. All that mattered was the man she had spent one wonderful night of her life with. It would not, she vowed, be the last.

Yet she did not look at Morgan when she reached the front of the room. She kept her eyes on the judge. The man's eyes, narrowed under black brows, fastened brutally on her as she approached the banquet table behind which he sat.

"Swear the witness in, Mr. Phillips," he ordered.

Ted took the worn Bible from the table and held it in front of Julie. She lifted her hands almost mechanically, placing her left on the cracked leather cover of the Bible and raising her right palm to face the marshal.

Tears welled in her eyes as she murmured "I do" when Phillips had muttered the familiar oath. She couldn't help but think of other vows to which the same two words could have and should have been replied.

"Please be seated, Miss Hollstrom."

She let Phillips lead her to the chair provided for witnesses and sat down slowly.

Then she saw Morgan for the first time since kissing him good-bye in the freshness of dawn after their night together. She could read nothing in his expression; even his green eyes seemed black and lifeless. He betrayed no emotion and gave her no hint of what he expected from her in return.

"Miss Hollstrom," the judge began in a gentle voice that did not fit his image. "I am not going to question you now. I merely want to clarify the charges against the accused. And please speak loudly enough for the jury to hear you. I don't care if the rabble in the back row can hear or not, but it is important that those men over there hear every word clearly."

"Yes, Your Honor."

Despite her resolve, Julie could not hide her nervousness. Her lips were dry; she kept licking them with the tip of her tongue. Her hands perspired so that she had to wipe them repeatedly on her skirt. Though the crowded ballroom was hot, it was not the August heat that brought beads of sweat to her forehead.

"Then we'll begin. Do you confirm the charges brought against Delbert R. Morgan, M.D., by

Wilhelm Hollstrom, that Dr. Morgan had unlaw-
ful and forcible sexual congress with you on the
night of July thirty-first?"

She glanced only briefly at the judge, then
turned her attention fully to Morgan. He sat
without moving a muscle, not looking at her.
She struggled by sheer force of will to draw his
gaze, needing his encouragement, some sign of
his love, but he continued to stare to her left, at
the velvet-curtained window that faced the alley
between the hotel and the general store.

How beautiful that night had been! she recalled in the split second before giving her answer. How beautiful she had felt, letting him
love her until they slept in satiated exhaustion.
He had even told her she was beautiful. And he
had told her he loved her. He had asked her to
marry him. She could not deny that love. If it
had been hers only for a brief moment, for a
single precious night, she cold not now deny it.
Though it branded her for life, she would pro-
claim it loudly.

"No, Your Honor, it is not true at all."

At last Morgan looked at her, and his eyes
were clear now, brilliantly sparkling as he tried
to hide a smile.

He couldn't believe his ears.

It was not what he had expected at all. For the
past nine years Julie had believed the worst of
herself; Morgan hoped one night might have
changed that, but he hadn't dared to count on it.
God only knew what Wallenmund and her father had done to her to try to persuade her to

their way of thinking. She didn't look physically abused, but Morgan knew a lot of bruises might be hidden under that dress. Besides, Julie was the type to suffer more from the mental torment Wilhelm Hollstrom practiced to perfection.

Whatever he had done, however, wasn't enough to destroy her this time.

"She's lying!" Wilhelm stormed, jumping to his feet. He very likely would have attacked Julie, had Ted Phillips not blocked the way. "She's lying! I saw them together!"

There was such an uproar from the crowd that Booth had to rap repeatedly with the gavel before silence returned.

"Mr. Hollstrom, this is my courtroom and I am asking the questions!" The judge shouted with every bit as much fury as the man being hustled back to his chair. When Wilhelm was once again seated, Booth turned his attention back to Julie.

"Miss Hollstrom, are you or are you not charging that man"—he pointed with the gavel at Morgan—"with rape? Remember, you are under oath to tell the truth."

"I remember."

"Well, then, did he or did he not rape you?"

Another murmur rose from the crowd, perhaps startled at Booth's bluntness, but it died quickly. Julie stammered a bit as she overcame her own embarrassment, but when she spoke, her voice held steady with the strength of her convictions.

"No, Your Honor, he did not."

"Then he seduced her!" Wilhelm screamed, stirring the crowd again.

This time Booth had to wait until the commotion died of its own accord. No one could have heard the gavel.

"You, sir," the judge threatened Wilhelm, "will confine yourself to speaking when requested to do so. Another outburst and I will have you removed from the courtroom." Chastened, Wilhelm slumped in his chair.

"Someone is lying," Booth announced in a tone worthy of a revival preacher. "I rode sixty miles to try this man, and his alleged victim now says nothing happened to her. I do not like my time to be wasted."

He raised his gavel, but before he could bring it down, Morgan jumped up quickly.

"Wait another minute, Your Honor."

"What is it now? I am prepared to dismiss the charges against you."

Morgan breathed a sigh of relief, then chuckled quietly to himself. He wondered if he was putting his head right back in the noose Julie had rescued him from. But he knew he had to go through with this madness.

"I don't want the charges dropped," he insisted. "I want my name cleared completely, and Miss Hollstrom's, too."

Booth favored the audience with a biblical glare, and not a whisper was heard.

"All right, Dr. Morgan. I've been called to this godforsaken corner of Arizona to hear a case and hear one I will. Miss Hollstrom, you are excused for the time being, but remember that you are still under oath."

Ted Phillips escorted Julie to the chair between her father and mother. She made herself meet the stare of the man who sat immediately behind the chair left vacant for her. She would not give Hans the satisfaction of seeing her cower. Demonstrating her own innocence and hoping that she thereby proved Morgan's, she held her head high.

The judge, after he had assured himself with a sweeping glance that his courtroom was in order, called Wilhelm Hollstrom to the stand. Julie watched with a silent prayer as Ted Phillips held the Bible and Wilhelm solemnly swore to tell the truth. She wondered if he would honor that oath.

Hans leaned forward and put his mouth so close to Julie's ear that when he licked his lips, she felt the wetness of his tongue graze her skin. She shuddered, then his words made her stiffen.

"He will not leave this room alive, Julie," he hissed, barely audible even so close. "You are promised to me, and I will not let you break that promise. I warned you what would happen, and I swear to you, I do not break my promises."

A cold lump in the pit of her stomach spread a chill through her. Had she done the wrong thing in declaring Morgan innocent despite Hans's threat? her terrified heart asked her.

She had no answer. More afraid and yet more

determined than she had been before, Julie cleared her head of all such thoughts and focused her attention entirely on the present.

The judge had finished his preliminary examination and had gone on to the details, for Wilhelm was speaking, venom in his every word.

"I saw them, Your Honor," he insisted. "It was five o'clock in the morning, and they were walking together from his house."

"Did you actually see them leave his house?"

Undaunted, Wilhelm did not stammer or even hesitate in his reply.

"They came down the lane, and there are only four houses there. I do not think they had been anywhere else but his house at that hour."

"Are you sure you can correctly identify the people you saw? Can you be positive it was Miss Hollstrom and Dr. Morgan, not someone else?"

"She is my daughter! Would you not know your own daughter? She was wearing the same dress she has on now. He walked her to the gate in front of my house and after she went inside, he walked over to the porch of this hotel. He was there when the marshal arrested him."

Morgan listened, knowing the man spoke the truth, for once. He had hoped for lies, even little ones, but it didn't really matter. Wilhelm had told enough lies already.

The judge continued, "What made you think that anything untoward had happened between Dr. Morgan and your daughter?"

Julie held her breath and found a warm hand clutching hers under a fold of her skirt. Something of the bond between her and her mother had survived; they clasped hands for strength.

When Wilhelm spoke, Julie's reaction was a pale echo of the outrage that shook the entire ballroom.

"Morgan had shown improper attention to her on other occasions. He seduced her away from her family and her betrothed, using his medical practice as an excuse to keep her out all night. I was forced to stop her working for him because her reputation was becoming tarnished."

The gavel pounded loudly as shouts rose to screams. A dozen people leaped to their feet, their cries denouncing Wilhelm in an unintelligible jumble of epithets and oaths. Julie heard more than one voice urge that her father be tarred and feathered for even suggesting that Morgan was anything less than honorable. Winnie Upshaw's voice was among the most strident.

"Now, look, folks!" Ted Phillips shouted with a voice that matched his physical proportions. "Judge Booth is just doin' his job. Every man's got a right to his opinion; we ain't a state yet, but we abide by the Constitution anyway, so Mr. Hollstrom here's got the right to his say. Sooner we all shut up and let the judge get on with things, the sooner we can all go home and get back to work. Dr. Morgan, too."

The scuffling of chairs and mutterings settled once again, but Phillips nodded to the two deputies who had come in from their post on the porch at the sound of the disturbance. Lucas and

Skip Jenkins brought their chairs into the lobby, where they would be just that much more convenient if another disturbance erupted.

Morgan, following the marshal's gesture, watched the two men take their places just outside the double doors to the ballroom. It was near noon now, and they were probably glad to get in out of the sun anyway. Warm as it was in the hotel, the porch would soon be as hot as the surface of a griddle.

Judge Booth rapped once for attention and then addressed the crowd.

"I have had just about all the interruptions my limited patience can stand. I warn you all. One more interruption of this sort and I will clear you all out. Is that understood?"

Like a penitent classroom, the assembled townspeople mumbled their agreement, and silence reigned once more. Morgan wondered with a wry smile just how long they would remember the judge's warning.

"Once again, Mr. Hollstrom. Can you recall any particular incidents?"

Wilhelm, too, seemed subdued, as though determined not to let his anger control him and distract the judge. "Once she came home with her dress torn. And Morgan is known to be a drunkard and spends much of his time at the house operated by the woman called Nellie."

"And who is Nellie?"

Ted Phillips answered quickly, before Wilhelm had a chance.

"Nellie's a madam, Your Honor. Runs a little

whorehouse down the alley behind the general store. Nellie don't bother nobody, and if it wasn't fer her profession, I'd say she was a right decent person."

"Thank you, marshal, for the information and your testimonial."

Phillips reddened a little and retreated to his post between the jury and the witness.

"One last question, Mr. Hollstrom. Did your daugher ever complain to you about Dr. Morgan's actions? Did she ever mention any acts of violence or threats of harm to her?"

For the first time, Wilhelm faltered. His eyes darted from his daughter to the physician who sat so calm and confident on the other side of the room. Morgan, knowing Wilhelm had to answer the question, smiled.

This is a farce, he laughed to himself. If it weren't for Julie, I would make this scheming snake crawl on his miserable belly.

Finally, Wilhelm found his tongue and words for it to speak.

"No, she did not complain of his actions. He seduced her, I told you. She was such a good daughter, so loyal, so hardworking, until he came along. Now she behaves like a common slut, and it is all because of *him*."

Another ripple of conversation began to run through the crowd, but a single tap of Booth's ivory gavel silenced it.

"All right, Dr. Morgan. I am finished with this witness for now, but I may wish to question him further, if you don't mind, after you."

Morgan nodded his assent politely and then got to his feet. He scraped the chair back quietly and gathered into his hand a pile of small slips of paper. Holding them but calling no attention to them, he approached his adversary.

"I'm a doctor, not a lawyer," Morgan told the judge by way of excuse. "We've only got one lawyer here in Plato, and he drinks. I didn't practice medicine when I drank, so I don't think I should expect him to practice law when he's three sheets to the wind either."

He did not look at Booth while he said this but kept his eyes on Wilhelm. He would give the man credit; Hollstrom never batted an eye or showed the least sign of nervousness. It didn't matter.

"I'll see to it, Dr. Morgan, that you keep within the boundaries of the law," Booth replied.

"Thanks. I figured you would." He paused, and for a moment all the regrets, all the hesitations came back. No matter what he did, Julie would be hurt, humiliated, and he had no way to warn or console her. He could only hope and pray that her show of defiance earlier would see her through the worst that was yet to come.

"I don't have too many questions for you, Mr. Hollstrom. I can't deny that I was walking with your daughter the other morning. I'll just ask you if you don't think there might be another reason why the two of us were together early in the morning. Isn't it possible that I was called on an emergency and needed her help?"

"No," Wilhelm answered firmly, without hesitation. "She no longer works for you. She told you that herself Monday morning."

Morgan ignored the fact that it was Hans who told him of their wedding date, not Julie, and said, "But in an emergency, I would certainly have called on her, nevertheless."

"She would not have gone."

"Wouldn't she? How can you be so sure?"

"I forbade her to work for you! She is to marry Hans, and it is not right for her to work for another man!"

While Wilhelm regained his composure, Morgan smiled knowingly at the jury. Ard Hammond smiled back.

"Hans?" Morgan asked. "Perhaps you should tell us a little about this Hans, the man you consented for your daughter to marry. Is he a wealthy man?"

Wilhelm drew himself up proudly.

"Hans is prosperous, yes. He has a farm not far from here and raises Holstein cows."

"I see. And you would not object to having a prosperous son-in-law."

"Hans is a good man; he will make a good husband. Julie should be thankful she is getting him, after the way she has disgraced herself."

"Disgraced herself? But I thought you blamed me for her downfall." He hadn't worded it as a question and therefore did not to wait for any response from Wilhelm. If the jury noticed it, so much the better. "Or is there another problem with the intended son-in-law?"

"What kind of problem could there be?"

"Well, it would be a problem, wouldn't it, if the prospective groom decided he didn't want damaged merchandise? How much have you promised to pay him to take your daughter off your hands? Did his price go up when he found out his bride might be slightly less than perfect?"

Oh, God, how he hated to say that! How he wanted to turn and face Julie and let her know how he hated it.

"I agreed, when Hans first expressed his wish to marry Julie, to settle a certain amount of money on her. This is the custom in the old country, you know."

Morgan breathed a sigh of relief. At least he hadn't been wrong.

"But I did not pay Hans to marry her."

"And what was he to give you in return? Isn't it also custom for the groom to give a bride-price, to compensate the family for the loss of their daughter? In your case I would imagine the price would be quite high, seeing as how Julie did all the cooking, the laundry, the cleaning, while your wife sat around and read the *Saturday Evening Post* all day."

Julie felt the blue eyes behind her harden into narrow slits of hatred. Hans's threat echoed more and more loudly through her brain, almost shutting out the bitter feud fought in front of her. Her fingers tightened around Katharine's until neither woman could feel a thing.

"Yes." Wilhelm was answering when she

turned her attention to the trial once more. "I am not a young man. My son is weak and in poor health; I cannot count on him to help me when I grow too old to provide for myself. I spent everything I had to bring my family west, and Hans has put all his money into his farm. Now he has nothing to make a good home for his bride. So we make a deal, all right? Is there something wrong about that? I give him some money to buy furniture for his house and he gives me an interest in his farm."

Morgan understood the murmur of the crowd. They saw nothing wrong with Hollstrom's explanation. He knew they would not agree with the man for long.

"I don't know how you can expect Mr. Wallenmund to give you anything when he doesn't have anything to give."

"What are you talking about? He has a fine farm, a new house, a big new—"

Morgan interrupted quietly, "Hans has nothing. I saw his farm the other day. Have you ever seen it? A ramshackle house, a couple of sheds that may or may not house some cows, maybe a few chickens, and a pig or two. If he offered you an interest in that, you got the raw end of the deal."

A good portion of the audience ignored the judge's threat of expulsion and gave vent to some laughter, but even that didn't last long. The judge intervened, but he addressed his remarks to Morgan, not the crowd.

"I really fail to see where this line of questioning is leading, Dr. Morgan," he said.

"If you'll just let me continue a few minutes longer, I believe you'll understand."

Booth leaned back in his chair and wiped a handkerchief across his forehead.

"All right, proceed. But it's past noon already, and I believe we could all do with some refreshment. Do you wish to finish your questioning now, or shall we recess for luncheon first and continue when we return?"

Morgan had to think for a moment. He had planned to strike now, when Hollstrom was already weakened by this unexpected revelation, but perhaps the anticipation would do the man some good. Besides, Morgan suspected that Julie had had little to eat or drink in the past twenty-four hours, and at least he could assure her of a decent meal. Somehow, he'd get word to Ted to see to it.

"I could use a bit of refreshment myself, Your Honor."

"Then court is in recess until two o'clock. Marshal, you will see that the accused is kept under guard?"

"I will, sir."

Chapter Thirty

✦ ✦ ✦ ✦ ✦

THE NOON STAGE was late and didn't pull into Plato until almost half past one. A single passenger stepped out of the dusty coach, to be greeted by Ard Hammond's son. The driver tossed down a faded, well-worn carpetbag and a packet marked "U.S. Mail"; then, there being no passengers or parcels to take on, he slapped the reins and the horses lurched to a reluctant trot northward through the town.

Thaddeus Burton leaned on his cane and rubbed the sore spot on his leg. The ache came more from the cramped quarters the big man had had to endure than the wound itself, though he knew it would be a long time before he was completely recovered.

"Town's awful quiet," he commented to the Hammond boy. "Doc Morgan got his office open today? I want to settle up with him and then go get that strawberry horse o' mine."

Dave Hammond shook his head with the morbid sagacity of his father's profession.

"Dr. Morgan is at the hotel, like just about everyone else. They got a trial goin' on there."

Burton took the carpetbag from the boy and shifted his weight to ease the bum leg a little more.

"Trial? Who done what?"

"I don't rightly know. Pa told me I wasn't old enough to hear about it."

Guessing the tall, gawky youngster to be at least fifteen, Burton wondered what crime could possibly be so horrendous.

"I s'pose Doc's gotta testify about the body and so on," he mused out loud.

"I don't know about that, seein's how he's the one on trial."

"Doc Morgan?"

"Yep. Had him in jail overnight, too," the boy added.

"Well, I guess I better hightail it over to that hotel then an' let 'em know what I think of the doc. You don't suppose they're all done, do you?"

The Hammond boy lifted his thin shoulders.

"Ma just came home a little while ago to fix us lunch and said it looked like it was gonna be a while 'fore Pa got done. He's on the jury, see. But Ma didn't say much. If I didn't have to stay here and watch the place for Pa, I'd be over there myself, even just listenin' by the window."

Burton tucked the carpetbag under his other arm for a minute to fish a coin from his pocket and flip it to the boy, who grinned gratefully. Then the big man limped off. He headed first for the hotel but changed his mind after a few steps and turned in the direction of the livery stable.

* * *

Hans Wallenmund had been caught in the crowd rushing back into the courtroom. A dusty-faced rancher took the chair directly behind Julie. Though he was angry, Hans knew he did not dare insist on what he considered his rightful place. He had been publicly humiliated and would only be laughed at if he made a scene.

He waited impatiently in the lobby until the judge called the court to order again. Hans watched as Wilhelm returned to the witness stand and was reminded that he was still under oath. It made no difference now what either of them said. Whether Morgan was found guilty or not, Wilhelm would never consent to the wedding. Hans knew that.

If he could not have Julie and the money he had been promised as her dowry, he would see to it that Morgan did not have her either. That, too, had been a promise.

Hans walked up to Lucas Carter, who had taken his post just outside the courtroom door.

"I would like to have my rifle back now," he told the temporary deputy.

"Leavin' so soon?"

"I must get back to my farm," Hans answered, bracing himself for a sarcastic reply.

"Me, I wouldn't miss this fer nuthin'," Lucas drawled. He sorted through the weapons stacked against the wall behind him and found the battered Winchester Hans had duly checked earlier. "Ain't been nuthin' this excitin' since Walt Noomer kilt his old man back in 'seventy-nine. Plenty o' witnesses that time; trial lasted damn near two weeks.''

But Hans didn't wait around to hear that last sentence, nor the questions about the infamous Noomer trial that young Jenkins began to fire at Lucas. Hans was already out the door and standing on the sun-blasted porch.

He thanked God for that ungodly sun. Carter and the blacksmith's apprentice should by rights have been stationed outside, but the west-facing porch was an inferno once the sun passed its zenith. That as much as the threat of a riot in the courtroom had brought them indoors. Hans took a handkerchief from his hip pocket and wiped it across his forehead.

He scanned the single street, and saw no sign of life. There were sounds coming from the Castle, but not a single living creature ventured out in the sun. He regretted leaving his horse and wagon at the livery, but there was no time now for such thoughts. Pushing that and a few other thoughts out of his mind, Hans descended the steps and walked around the corner of the hotel into the alley. Here was some shade at least, but with no breeze to stir the sultry air he felt no relief. That would come later. He had no intention of remaining very long in the alley anyway.

"*Ja*, he iss a very good horse," the gnarled Swede agreed with Thaddeus Burton when the big man had paid the bill and had taken possession of his strawberry roan again.

Burton patted the animal's shoulder affection-
ately.

"Berry'n me's been through a lot, ain't we, old
boy. Looks like you took good care of him for
me, too. I figger that's worth at least fifty bucks
to me."

Gus's old eyes brightened and his well-
wrinkled face split with a wide, toothless grin.

"*Ja*, I figger so, too!" He laughed.

"Now, I'd be happy to take him off your hands
right now, but I heard from the boy down at the
depot that the Doc's in some kind o' trouble.
You got any idea what's goin' on? I can't believe
Doc Morgan'd do anything to anybody."

Gus rubbed his chin.

"No, it don't seem right. He iss a good man,
yust like your horse."

"Then what're they sayin' he done?"

"That fella who works at the telegraph, you
know, with the daughter that's the doctor's
nurse? Well, that fella, he says the doctor raped
the daughter."

"Miss Julie? No, you gotta be kiddin' me. He
wouldn't do nothin' like that, not to her."

He paused a moment, letting the severity of
the situation sink in, for Gus quite plainly was
not kidding.

"Okay, look. You keep Berry here for me for a
while longer." Burton slid a well-cared-for rifle
from the scabbard on the saddle that hadn't been
cinched tightly yet. He took one look at the
weapon and grinned again. "I see you took care
of more'n just my horse."

Gus shrugged. "No sense letting it get ruined."

Burton laughed out loud and dug a five-dollar gold piece from his pocket. When he flipped it, Gus stretched out a leathery hand and caught the coin easily.

"Thanks," Burton then said quietly. "I may just need this little popgun. Now, tell me where I kin find this kangaroo court."

Julie's lunch sat like a lump of misery in her stomach. She had eaten because she was famished and because she could not bear the stares of her father and of Hans through the meal, but she felt no better for it. Katharine, she had noticed, seemed to feel the same way.

The only bright spot of the afternoon was that she no longer had Hans behind her. She had no idea where he was, and though that worried her, she knew he could not harm anyone in the courtroom. Lucas and Skip kept a tight guard over all the firearms. Only Ted Phillips and the deputies themselves wore guns.

Morgan himself seemed little concerned. He held that same bundle of little pieces of paper as he walked slowly toward Wilhelm. Julie wasted no time wondering what might be written on those notes; she could only pray this whole drama played itself out quickly and that there were no encores.

"If I may," Morgan began, addressing the entire court, not just Wilhelm, "I'd like to answer the question Judge Booth posed just before lunch. I think he'll agree that this whole thing has come down to a matter of which witness is going to be believed. Since both Mr. Hollstrom and I have said rather opposite things, one of us must, apparently, be lying. He, and his daughter before him, were sworn to tell the truth, but that doesn't mean a tinker's damn if you don't believe them."

He riffled the papers in his hand slowly and stared at them for a moment or two. The courtroom lapsed into anxious silence, disturbed only by the fluttering of fans and the rustle of drapes at the open windows where a slight breeze had finally come up.

"Mr. Hollstrom, you told the court this morning that you made a financial settlement with Hans Wallenmund in exchange for your daughter. I've already told you that Mr. Wallenmund had nothing to offer you. But what about your end of the bargain? You did say that you agreed to give him cash as a dowry for your daughter, correct?"

"I did. This is customary."

"And just where did you plan to get the money? It seems you don't even have enough to pay the local merchants. Or did you plan to cheat them until you could get enough money from Mr. Wallenmund's farm?"

Wilhelm's face turned an angry red, and the way he gripped the arms of the chair was enough to make Ted Phillips lower his hand a few inches toward the Colt revolver on his hip.

"I do not know what you are talking about," Wilhelm hissed in a voice quaking with fury.

"I am talking about these," Morgan answered, waving the fistful of papers. "When Simon McCrory mentioned to me that you had a sizable account at his store, I wondered if you owed anyone else in Plato. I found out that you did."

One by one he laid the slips on the table in front of the judge, who could see that each was written in a different hand and signed by the proprietors of nearly every retail business in Plato.

"To Ezra Farnum you owe eight dollars and forty cents. To Gus's livery, five dollars even. To Taft's Butcher Shop, six dollars twenty-five cents. To McCrory's General Store, forty-two dollars and eighty-seven cents, and you haven't even paid them for the dress material Julie bought and which she then repaid you for. In fact, Mr. Hollstrom, you never paid for the telegram to bring the judge here!"

Booth resorted to the gavel once more, but the crowd was more interested in hearing what else Morgan had to say, and what explanation Hollstrom would come up with. Silence returned almost instantly.

But Hollstrom said nothing.

"You're a miser, aren't you?" Morgan accused quietly. "You never part with a cent. You didn't leave Minnesota because of your daughter's reputation; you left because you owed everybody money. That's why you embezzled from the bank in Rinton, Indiana." It was a guess, a wild yet calculated guess, but when Wilhelm's face went from red to purple and he made no reply, Morgan knew he had hit upon the truth. Even a denial at this point would be too incriminating.

"Thank you, Mr. Hollstrom. I have no other questions."

"But you don't understand!" Wilhelm wailed as Morgan turned his back to walk away. "I had no choice."

"No choice?" Morgan echoed. He spun on the balls of his feet and glared once more at the man he hated so much he could almost wish to kill him. "You were ready to sell your daughter! You would have sent me to prison, or worse, just so she would marry the man who had promised you part of his 'fortune.' Ha! Both of you trying to defraud the other. How appropriate, how *just*, except that she got caught in the middle."

Every eye, every ear, was trained on Morgan. He had their complete attention. Realizing somehow that his acquittal was practically guaranteed, Julie let the tears that welled up in her eyes overflow.

Perhaps it was a trick of the light filtered through those tears that made her notice the shadow at the window. Or perhaps when she raised her hand to wipe them away she turned just enough and caught sight of the gun barrel resting on the windowsill. She never had enough time to wonder what brought that horrible image into her line of vision; she only had time to react.

She screamed and leaped from her chair, ignoring Katharine's hand on her arm to restrain her. Julie could not even think of a coherent warning, knew only that she had to draw someone's attention to the man at the window who leveled the barrel of his rifle on the sill.

"Julie, for God's sake—" Morgan gasped, and if he said any more, it was lost in the explosion of the gun.

Julie heard nothing at all. Deafened by her own cry, she now saw only one man, and the red that stained the front of his faded blue shirt. She ran to him.

Pandemonium reigned all around them. Ted Phillips shouted orders above the general hysteria.

"Nobody leaves this here courtroom!" the marshal bellowed, brandishing his revolver. Then, calling to his deputies, "Lucas, you see nobody gets out, hear? Skip, find out who the hell was in that alley. Where the hell is Clark?"

A ruddy-faced man in white shirt and gray trousers held up with plaid suspenders pushed his way to the front of the crowd.

"I'm here, Marshal. What can I do?"

"Go get a room ready for Del," Phillips ordered the owner of the Olympia House. "And find some . . . some stuff to make bandages out of, I guess."

He looked at Julie, who had helped Morgan, despite his protests, to the nearest chair, the one she herself had left.

"It's only a flesh wound," he was telling her. She had already torn the sleeve off to reveal the single jagged wound from which bright blood gushed in a steady river down his arm. Remembering the night Thaddeus Burton had been brought to surgery, she quickly wrapped the bloody cloth around Del's arm just above the wound and tied it as tightly as she could. She had to keep him from bleeding to death first.

Clark Garroway had run from the room and now returned with a chambermaid and an armload of hotel towels. The girl immediately dropped the towels and fled, her face pale, but Julie paid her no attention. She grabbed a towel and began to clean away as much of the blood as she could.

"When I saw you," she whispered, "all I saw was the blood on the front of your shirt. I thought you'd been shot in the chest and were dead."

He lifted his good right arm and touched her cheek, wet with her tears.

"I almost thought so, too," he said, managing a laugh, though the pain, dulled by the first shock, was becoming almost more than he could bear. "Pull that tourniquet tighter," he ordered, "and let's get this damn trial over with."

"You can't be serious! Del, this isn't a splinter in your thumb or an eyelash in your eye."

"No, I know it isn't. But it won't take more than a few minutes to wind this up, and I'd just as soon finish what I've started."

Grace Fulton shouldered her way through the crowd with a basin of water and set it on the chair beside Morgan.

"I figgered no one'd think to get any water," the midwife said, "so I went to the kitchen."

Julie nodded her thanks and dipped another towel in the water. Once again she tried to talk Morgan into letting her, with Grace Fulton's assistance, take decent care of the injury, but he adamantly refused. Pushing both women aside, he got to his feet and started toward a white-faced Wilhelm Hollstrom, who hadn't budged from the witness stand.

He could feel the warm blood seeping through the towel wrapped around the wound and knew that the blood loss was making him dizzy. He didn't know how much longer he could stay on his feet with the pain washing over him like the Ohio River in spring flood, but he had to end this whole mess once and for all, bullet or no bullet.

"Dr. Morgan, let me explain," Wilhelm begged, his face as pale as though it was he who had been shot.

But before Morgan could begin the oration that he hoped would bring Wilhelm Hollstrom to his knees, an enormous voice interrupted from the rear of the courtroom.

"Hey, kin somebody help me? I got a guy here with a couple of fingers shot off."

Julie recognized Thaddeus Burton at once. And the man draped over his shoulder had to be Hans.

* * *

Judge Booth took advantage of what he knew was only a temporary calm to order the courtroom cleared. Almost as fast as people left the hotel, they gathered outside in little knots and the more curious scurried down the alley to peer in the windows until Garroway drew the curtains. When the onlookers protested, he closed the windows, too, to shut out their squawks.

In the gloomy ballroom, an eerie silence descended. Ted Phillips went to Burton's aid and the two of them carried the unconscious Hans to the front of the room, where they laid him out on the floor. His nose, as well as his hand, was bloodied.

"Did I interrupt somethin'?" Burton asked softly—or as softly as he could.

"Yes, thank God." Morgan laughed. "A murder, I think."

"Well, I was comin' to find out what this here trial was all about, and I seen him pointin' that rifle in the window. I didn't figger that was quite the thing to be doin', so I hollered at him."

"Please, Mr. Burton," Julie interrupted. "Let Dr. Morgan finish his speech and you can give us your explanation later."

She tossed another of the towels to Grace Fulton, who knelt beside Hans and lifted the mangled hand.

Morgan turned to the judge, but Ard Hammond spoke first.

"I don't think Del needs to say another word," the mortician intoned. He turned to his fellow

jurors and asked, "Any o' you gentlemen have
any objections to a verdict of not guilty?"

Eleven heads shook the unanimous answer.
"Then, Your Honor, we find the defendant
innocent."

There was no rejoicing. Morgan had already
succumbed enough that he did not protest when
Ard Hammond slipped a supporting arm around
his waist. With Phillips's help, the undertaker
steered Morgan toward the table in front of the
judge. Booth, seemingly unperturbed by this
highly unorthodox turn of events, cleared his
own papers out of the way. Clark Garroway
brought two lamps and lit them to dispel the
shadows.

"Wouldn't it be better to take him to the
surgery?" Julie asked of no one in particular.

Morgan answered her. "No, just send someone for my bag. I'm afraid I'll pass out if you try
to get me that far."

He was in considerable pain, his eyes tightly
closed against it. He sat down on the table and
then lay back slowly with a soft gasping cry of
agony that he couldn't halt. Julie took the hand
he reached up to her and squeezed it reassur-
ingly.

"You can do it, Firefly. I know you can."

Grace Fulton, anticipating correctly, had already gone to the doctor's office and brought
back the satchel with his instruments—and a full
bottle of scotch.

"You know what you're doin'?" she asked Julie.

"I think so."

The jurors filed out with Booth behind them like a shepherd guiding his flock, and then Ted Phillips quietly hustled Wilhelm and Katharine out the door as well. Only Thaddeus Burton remained, and his size told the marshal not to waste time trying to evict him.

While Grace laid out the instruments on a towel within Julie's reach, Morgan kept up a steady stream of instructions and conversation in an effort to hold on to consciousness.

"The bullet must have ricocheted," he said. "Even a twenty-two should have done more damage fired at that close range." He tried to open his eyes but couldn't. Or maybe he did and everything was black anyway. "I don't think there's any nerve damage; I can still move my fingers. Just check to see if the bone's chipped or maybe broken."

Swallowing a rising nausea, Julie took a deep breath and then ventured to examine the wound while he continued to talk. When she probed with a slender finger, he winced and jerked convulsively, his back arching off the table, and sweat poured from him. Julie withdrew and wiped her own forehead on her sleeve.

She whispered, "The bone's not broken, and I didn't feel any chips."

"Good job, love. Now get me sewn back together and we'll take a look at Mr. Wallenmund," he told her when he found his voice again. "And don't worry about the embroidery."

"You take your time with him," Grace Fulton

countered. "I can take care of Mr. Wallenmund.
I've stitched up shot-off fingers before and I can
do it again." When Morgan tried to argue, she
shushed him and went on. "I'm gonna send this
big galoot that brought Hans in back over to
your place for a stretcher and then him and the
marshal are gonna tote you home. You ain't
doin' no more doctorin' today. You ain't doin'
nothin' but restin'."

Grace picked up a needle and threaded it with
a length of catgut and then handed it to Julie.

"I hear you're quite a seamstress, Miss Hollstrom. Mebbe you could give me a few point-
ers."

Morgan lay still, only his clenched teeth indi-
cating he felt the jabs of the needle and the pulling of the thread through muscle and then skin.
When Julie had finished and removed the tourniquet, she was pleased to notice that there was
very little bleeding. And the bloodless hand that
had grown so blue and cold now flushed with a
healthy pink and warmed in her own grasp.

Though he argued that he was perfectly capable of helping Grace with Hans, Morgan did not
get up from the table when Julie placed a hand
on his chest and ordered him to remain right
where he was.

"Mrs. Fulton is right. You need your rest,"
she told him.

Thaddeus Burton hesitantly approached and
added his own insistence.

"You do like Miss Julie says, Doc, or I'll flatten
you just like I flattened that fella what shot you."

Morgan laughed.

"I expect you would at that. But I thought you shot Hans."

"Oh, I shot him all right. I walked all the way from the livery, though, and my leg was achin' pretty bad. I guess that's what threw my aim off. When I saw him standin' there at the window, I just pulled up the gun and fired. I meant to hit the barrel, so just in case he got his shot off, it'd go sideways or somethin'. I hit his hand instead."

"That's enough, you two," Julie cut in. "Mr. Burton, I think the doctor needs to rest now."

Hans moaned. Grace was closing the skin over the two stumps on his right hand, where Burton's shot had done its damage.

"I could use some help," the older woman called quietly. "I think he's comin' around."

Julie and Burton knelt and held Hans still while Grace finished her own stitchery. She worked quickly, if not as artistically as Julie; but even so, Hans rapidly became aware of his situation.

"Did I kill her?" he asked in a hoarse, terrified whisper.

"Her?" Grace echoed. "No, you shot Dr. Morgan, but he ain't even close to bein' dead."

"It was Julie I wanted to kill. I knew she would never have me after he made a fool of me in there, in front of them all. She was promised to me, and I could not let him have her."

He yelped when Grace plunged the needle into his flesh again, and then he fell silent.

"Wish I'da aimed at his head," Burton muttered angrily.

Exhausted, Julie slumped on the chair someone had pulled up beside the table for her. It might have been Grace or Thaddeus or one of the deputies who came for Hans. Clark Garroway and the same chambermaid who had brought the towels now bustled around the ballroom cleaning up the mess. Clark brought a pillow that Julie placed under Morgan's head, but he still complained about the hardness of the tabletop.

"As soon as Marshal Phillips gets back, we'll get you home," Julie promised. "I can't believe Hans wanted to kill me."

"Don't worry about it, Firefly. It's all over. He just got his pride hurt pretty bad. The way he was blubbering when Ted took him out of here, I don't think we have to worry about him coming after you again."

"Are you sure?"

"Sure I'm sure. Maybe this whole thing will wake him up and he'll start *working* on his farm. I won't even press charges against him, but I do need to see the judge before he leaves town. Do you know where he went?"

"No, I don't, but what do you need him for if you're not going to press charges against Hans?"

"Oh, several things. For one, Ted told me your father had you locked in your room. That's false imprisonment, or something. And selling you to

Hans is slavery, or 'involuntary servitude,' as the Constitution puts it. We fought a war in this country over it, and I don't intend to let anyone get away with something a couple of million good men died to see abolished."

Later, perhaps, she would tell him that her own father, whom she had never known, was one of those millions. But for now there was only the future to consider, not the past. She laid a tired hand on his forehead.

"Are you serious?" she asked. "Or just a bit feverish?"

"If there's any fever in my blood, it's because of you, Firefly. And that's another thing I need to see the judge about. You and I have some unfinished business. We were supposed to get married yesterday."

Julie tried to stammer a reply, but no words came out.

"Wintergarden's off to Staynes Junction to dedicate their new church, so I thought maybe I could prevail upon Judge Booth to make this legal between us."

"Now? Today?"

"Why not? Yesterday was good enough."

"But look at me! Look at you! We're both covered with blood, and you can't even stand up."

"I can and I will, if I have to lean on my best man. I'm sure Mr. Burton won't let me fall."

"Mr. Burton?"

"Who else? You remember that letter he wrote to me, when he sent the check."

"How could I forget."

"Well, he told me then that he wanted an invitation to our wedding."

Julie could hardly believe her ears, and yet she knew she wasn't dreaming. Nightmares like the one she had been through these past few hours were something you woke up from; they didn't fade into gloriously happy reality like this.

"You *are* serious, aren't you."

"Damn right, I'm serious. Do you think I'm going to let you go, after what we've been through today? As soon as Ted and Mr. Burton get back here, I'm going to have them escort you home so you can clean up and pack your things, and then they are going to escort you right back to my house, where we are going to be married, today."

She knew he meant exactly what he said. She knew, too, that more than anything else she wanted the same thing. Seeing him shot, thinking even for a tiny second that he was dead, had been the worst part of the nightmare. The prospect of life without him was unbearable, and she had seen how very precious each second of that life could be.

She got to her feet and leaned down to kiss him softly, withdrawing before he could free her hand and put his good arm around her for an embrace.

"I love you," she whispered, just as Ted Phillips and Thaddeus Burton re-entered the silent ballroom.

Chapter Thirty-one

✦✦✦✦✦

Julie tried to convince her escorts they weren't necessary, that she could find her way home without any assistance, but neither Phillips nor Burton paid any attention to her. With one on either side, she continued her protests across the now-deserted hotel lobby.

"Really, gentlemen, I appreciate your concern, but it isn't far at all," she insisted. The doors were closed; Phillips, without a game leg, jumped to open them. "I can't imagine—oh, my God!"

She gasped at the sight of the crowd that formed an almost solid barrier. Lucas Carter and Skip Jenkins had kept most of the gawkers off the porch, though a few youngsters dangled from the railing.

"How's Doc Morgan?" a dozen or more voices chorused the instant Julie appeared in the doorway.

Surprised as much by the gathered populace as by the blast of heat and afternoon sunlight, Julie took several seconds to find an answer.

"He's . . . he's just fine. Recovering nicely." She blinked and shaded her eyes. The crowd stretched nearly all the way across the street, almost to the fence surrounding Wilhelm Hollstrom's front yard. Julie tried to recall the times she had heard Morgan advise friends and family of a patient's condition following surgery. "I'm sure he'll be good as new in a week or so."

A cheer rose from the several hundred townspeople gathered in this, the worst heat of the afternoon. And somehow Julie knew part of the cheer belonged to her.

They were still cheering when Phillips and Burton began to clear a path through them. Julie smiled her gratitude now and received a friendly wink from Thaddeus Burton as he waved his cane to make slow-movers hurry. He knew as well as she that she could never have made it alone.

But at the gate, aware of the still-curious crowd slowly dispersing behind her, Julie stopped and turned to her escorts once more. What lay ahead was something she had to face on her own. She could not rely on borrowed courage.

"Marshal, please," she insisted again, more firmly than before. "I think you ought to go back and help Dr. Morgan. I'll be all right, and none of us wants Del trying to do too much in his condition."

Burton gave her a slightly worried frown.

"You sure, Miss Julie?"

"Positive, Mr. Burton. I won't be long; if I'm not at the doctor's house in an hour, then you can come and get me. Break down the door, the walls if you have to," she compromised.

"Well, all right, but not a minute more." He touched the brim of his hat and opened the gate for her. "And if anything happens in there in the meantime, you just holler."

"I will. And thank you. Thank you both."

She turned then, feeling a sudden chill inside, and lifted her chin proudly as she walked to the house without a single backward glance. No guilt, no shame now. It was as though she, not Morgan, had been declared innocent in that impromptu courtroom. Freed at last of her burden, Julie entered the front door with calm determination. Wilhelm no longer had the power to frighten her.

Something intangible hung in the air of the parlor, as though an argument had just ceased, interrupted by Julie's arrival. She saw Katharine in her chair by the window as usual, Wilhelm standing nearby with his hands clasped behind his back, his gaze fastened on the closed curtains.

"You will start packing now, Julie," he said without looking at her. "You have made it impossible for us to stay here any longer. We will go to Mexico, I think. We will leave tonight."

Julie laughed loudly, almost hysterically, and she knew it was partly with relief.

"I'm going to pack all right, Papa, and I'm going to leave. But I'm not going to Mexico. You can go if you like, but I'm staying right here in Plato."

Before Wilhelm had a chance to argue, Katharine cut him off.

"I told you she couldn't be bullied anymore, you fool," she said. "And neither can I."

He turned then, to his wife, not to Julie; but Julie remained where she was, standing in the archway between foyer and parlor as though she sensed a threat in Wilhelm's anger.

"You must go with me!" he shouted, but with a frantic pleading in his voice. "You have no choice!"

"Oh, yes, I do," Katharine chortled. "You made a very big mistake telling me about Clara, Wilhelm, and I intend to do exactly what she did: blackmail you."

"Who is Clara?" Julie asked, confused.

"Wilhelm's wife. His first wife, that is, the one he left behind in Berlin when he came to New York. They've been married for thirty-three years, and for the last twenty-seven she's been blackmailing him."

"No, that's not true! I sent her the money willingly because she was my wife. Only when she came to America and found out about . . . about you, then she blackmailed me." His voice dropped to a defeated whine at the end. "I had no choice then but to pay her. I had Willy to think of."

Willy. Always Willy.

"He was my son, and I could not let him grow up a bastard like me."

Katharine craned her neck to look around him at Julie.

"Did you want something, dear? You needn't stay and listen to us wash our dirty linen. Wilhelm has just been telling me he married me under false pretenses, and I've just told him he isn't your father."

She seemed quite casual about it, and Julie suspected her mother was truly enjoying all these revelations. Or rather, she was enjoying a kind of revenge on the man who had been her bigamist husband all these years.

Wilhelm, determined not to be defeated again today, insisted, "I don't care what she wants! She has shamed me again, carrying on with this doctor and then lying when she has sworn to tell the truth. She will come with us!"

"No, I won't, Papa. Del and I are going to be married in about an hour, which is what we were going to do yesterday, until you shoved your nose where it didn't belong."

Now it was Katharine who laughed, with sheer joy.

"Oh, this is choice!" she crowed. "Every day you will rub his nose in it, too. Wilhelm, we are staying, right here, in Plato, with Julie and Willy and Dr. Morgan and Clara, too, if she wants to join us."

"No! If Julie wishes to stay, I will let her. But you are my wife and I—"

"Ah, but I'm not your wife," Katharine slyly reminded him. "I'm your mistress or concubine or something like that, which makes your precious son a bastard."

Julie could see Wilhelm slump. His pride in his son was something too deep not to be wounded easily. He turned away from Katharine and would have walked out of the room rather than let anyone observe his shame, but Julie's presence in the doorway blocked his departure.

"It's all your fault," he hissed at her. "You slut, you have destroyed my son's future."

She drew herself up defiantly until she felt as though she towered over him, his petty spirit making him shrink in her eyes.

"You can't do that to me anymore. It's your fault, not mine."

"Isn't that what I told you she'd say?" Katharine called. "I hoped I had raised Julie to find a good man to marry, but I must have done a better job than I thought. My dear, you have a veritable prince in your Dr. Morgan. Go get your things and don't be late for the wedding."

The wedding. The very word loosed a thousand butterflies in the pit of Julie's stomach. She had so little time and so much to do, but she had to take a few minutes of that time to say what she had come back to this house to say, and a few other things as well.

"I won't be late, Mama, don't worry. Will you come?"

"Oh, I'd love to! And Willy, too. He's still over at McCrory's, but I expect him home any minute. I don't suppose you want Wilhelm here to play the father of the bride and give you away."

Julie shook her head.

"I'm not going to be a hypocrite, not in this town." She looked at Wilhelm and uttered words she never thought she would. "The people here trust me, far more than I trusted myself. They stood up for me today when I almost wouldn't stand up for myself. They love Del, and I know they would have protested if he had chosen a woman who didn't measure up against their standards. I heard them when I came back to this house a few minutes ago, and they actually compared me to his first wife. They didn't find me lacking in any way.

"Do you have any idea how that made me feel? These were strangers and yet they believed in me. You made me feel worthless; they made me proud."

Katharine's applause broke the strained atmosphere as she walked from her corner to the foyer.

"I couldn't have said it better myself. You see, Wilhelm, it's exactly as I told you it would be. I'm not going to go with you to Mexico, Julie's not, and I seriously doubt if you can make Willy go either. Will you leave without him?"

Wilhelm had no answer except the defeat in his eyes.

Katharine continued, "You can't run forever, you know. So what if Clara writes to the marshal or the territorial governor or even the president? What proof does she have? Haven't you and I been living together as man and wife for the past twenty-eight years? Who's going to dispute that?"

"But, Mama, if—"

"You had your say, Julie. You have your own life to lead, and I suggest you get yourself ready for it. I've already made my bed and I fully intend to keep lying in it." Katharine smiled confidently. "I married this man because I wanted security, and I don't intend to give that up. It's a bit late for me to start thinking about romance and all that poppycock now, so I'll settle for what I've had all along. Wilhelm and Willy and I are going to stay right here in Plato. There will be a nice public apology for all the trouble Wilhelm caused the doctor, and of course all the debts will be paid. Including the bill for the dress goods at McCrory's," she emphasized. "It's the least this dummkopf can do to make amends."

Though Morgan's parlor was small, it easily accommodated the few guests: Simon and Ada McCrory, Ted Phillips and Winnie Upshaw, and best man Thaddeus Burton. Judge Booth had already taken his place in front of the white-washed beehive fireplace when Katharine and Willy knocked at the front door. Julie, waiting at the top of the stairs, nodded her consent to Burton or he probably would not have admitted the latecomers.

The ceremony was brief, lasting something under ten minutes, yet even that seemed a small eternity to Morgan. He didn't feel the nagging throb in his arm, only the exquisite pain of impatience. As he slipped the simple gold band on Julie's finger, he couldn't contain a sigh of monumental relief.

Winnie had brought a cake, and Ted Phillips contributed a bottle of champagne with which to toast the newlyweds. Willy whined because Katharine wouldn't allow him even a taste of the bubbly wine, but her stern rebuke, the first she had ever given him, shocked him into sullen silence. Tipsy more from an overabundance of emotion than from a single glass of champagne, Julie couldn't stifle a little giggle at her brother's discomfiture and had to promise Del a complete explanation later. Perhaps much later.

He could not take his eyes from her, and though he had dutifully followed her instructions to put his arm back in a sling after the ceremony, his other hand kept straying to touch her: her cheek, her hand where the ring from McCrory's store shone brightly, her hair that had served as a bridal veil, all shimmery and silky down her back. She wore no satin and white lace, just the blue blouse and black skirt she had made with her own hands. Yet she was so beautiful. And she was his.

It was Thaddeus Burton who finally shooed the guests home. He complained that if his leg, injured a month ago, still hurt, then Morgan's arm must be that much worse and he ought to get his rest. The McCrorys left first, followed almost immediately by Ted Phillips. Winnie stayed just long enough to clean the dishes and then she, too, departed.

"I'd like to talk to Julie alone for a few minutes," Katharine told Thaddeus when he gave her a look that hinted she was overstaying her welcome. "I won't be long."

Again Julie had to assure him it was all right, and then she led her mother into the empty dining room. Willy, still pouting, remained in the parlor to smother his pique with another piece of cake.

"Oh, Julie, you look so lovely!" Katharine breathed happily. "And so happy. It's all going to work out the way it should, I just know it now. And to start it out right, I have something to return to you."

She held out her hand, closed in a loose fist, and dropped its contents onto Julie's upturned palm. Julie didn't have to see to know that it was a certain gold double eagle.

"Wilhelm had it hidden, along with some other money, in the privy, of all places," Katharine explained. "When I asked him just how he was planning to finance a journey to Mexico, he finally confessed he had been saving all along. He said it was for Clara, but I told him that Clara had already got more than her share and I was taking charge of the rest."

"And he let you?"

Katharine laughed. "For once he's right: He really doesn't have any other choice this time. He either does what I say or I will tell everyone the whole truth about him."

"But wouldn't that ruin your reputation as well?"

"Mine? Oh, no, dear, because I would be the wronged woman, married under false pretenses, and so on. I've thought it all out very carefully, and frankly, I think I'm too clever for him." She curled both hands around Julie's and leaned forward to kiss her daughter's cheek. "Do come and visit me now and then, dear. I would like a chance to really make up for the past nine years, if it's at all possible.''

"Oh, Mama, I don't know what to say. Yes, I'll visit, though you know I'll be busy helping Del with his practice, just like before.''

"Of course. But maybe a cup of tea on Tuesday morning?''

Julie smiled and wrapped her arms around her mother.

"I promise.''

Katharine sighed deeply and said, "I was so afraid you wouldn't. I was so afraid that after all this you would hate me as you hate Wilhelm, and with good reason.''

"No, I don't hate you, and I don't think I even hate him. I won't dismiss his actions by saying that the end justifies the means, but in a way I wouldn't have Del if it hadn't been for all the trouble Papa caused. I won't thank him for it, but I won't hate him, either.''

Katharine embraced her daughter once more, then collected her son and left. Willy started to throw a tantrum on the porch and received a sound whack on his unsuspecting bottom.

"Would you really have left Plato the other night?'' Del asked, carefully shrugging out of his coat. Julie took it from him and hung it in the wardrobe.

"Does it matter now?''

The green eyes with their broad streaks of black and fine dusting of gold shimmered in the lamplight as she turned to him. Julie remembered them as the first thing she had noticed about the man that afternoon last June. They would be with her always.

"Hell, yes," he whispered. "It matters."

She walked to him and pushed his hand away from the buttons he was struggling to undo one-handed.

"If you had sent me home, if you hadn't—if we hadn't done what we did, then yes, I would have left. I could not have stayed here knowing you didn't want me."

Her fingers brushed his skin, sending little shocks along each nerve.

"Even though Hans had threatened to kill me if I touched you? He would have assumed that I did."

A shudder went through her and she lay one hand flat on his chest, on the hard, untouched muscle beneath the curling dark hair. He quivered slightly at her touch and covered the hand with his, then gently pushed it down toward his waist, then lower still.

"I didn't mean to risk your life," she whispered as tears came to her eyes. "I wasn't even thinking about that. All I knew was that I loved you and I had to know if you loved me, too."

"Oh, Julie, don't cry. Do you think I didn't know all that? But I never once forgot his damned promise."

She looked up at him, her hand still resting on the throbbing warmth, and he smiled.

"You didn't? And you went ahead anyway? But why?"

"You mean it isn't obvious? Because I loved you, Firefly. More than anything."

He could use both hands to unbutton her blouse, and he did. Even through the soft blue fabric his touch aroused her and made her breath rasp in her throat.

"I had known love, Julie," he explained. "I had parents who loved me and never hesitated to show it. My sister took in laundry to put me through school and almost lost her fiancé because of it. And Amy followed me joyfully from the comfort of a wealthy home in Cincinnati to this dusty furnace and never once complained, all because she loved me." He couldn't wipe away the tears that squeezed from his own eyes at the memory. "You had never known love like that, and I think it frightened you. I know it scared me to death."

"You?"

"Hell, yes, me. Especially when it hit me the first time."

"With Amy?"

"No, I mean the first time I realized I loved you."

"Don't go giving me any love-at-first-sight nonsense."

He laughed, then finished unbuttoning her blouse and pulled it free from her waistband.

"The first time I saw you, on the porch in front of McCrory's, you were a scrawny, dusty stick in

clothes too big for you, with spectacles sliding
off the end of your nose. All that hair was tied
up on top of your head and you almost looked
bald. And I was a pickled mackerel, too drunk to
see straight anyway." He paused only long
enough to help her pull her arms from the
sleeves of the blouse. Then she took it to hang it
in the wardrobe, too.

"But a few weeks later, when you'd got me
sobered up a little and I was coming back to
life, I woke up one night from a dream about
you, and I was in a state I hadn't been able to
achieve in years. I had thought I was beyond
that forever, emasculated by my grief, yes, and
my guilt in Amy's death. But it had all made
me think it was for the best, that you were safe
from me, and I from you, even though I had
already started feeling things for you I knew I
shouldn't."

She took his shirt from him and tossed it carelessly onto the chair. Then her hands went to his
belt, drawing a groan from him that closed her
eyes for a moment.

"Oh, God, Julie, don't do that." But when she
tried to pull her hand away, he clasped it to him
once more. "No, don't stop, either."

Long, deep breaths of enjoyment settled him
so he could continue, but his voice was more
ragged, his words slower.

"And then one night I went to Leif's for supper and Lorraine waited on my table."

"Lorraine? The redhead with the big—?" She

made a descriptive gesture with one hand in front of her own chest.

"Yeah, that's Lorraine." He laughed at Julie's blush. "I stared at her, Julie, and I tried to conjure up the same reaction, but I couldn't. And there was another time when I wanted you so badly I couldn't stand it and I even thought of going over to Nellie's. But I knew that wouldn't work either. I didn't just want a woman; I wanted you."

There were no more words for a while. Julie fumbled with the trouser buttons while Del untied the strings of her camisole, but then they reached an impasse. He had to sit down on the bed to let her pull off his boots, and then he stepped out of the trousers. When he tried to draw the almost sheer undergarment over Julie's head, a sharp pain shot through his arm, too sharp and to sudden to ignore.

"Damn it," he swore. "A man should undress his wife properly on their wedding night."

"There will be other nights," Julie said comfortingly as she pulled back the sheets and silently ordered him to lie down. He crooked his good arm behind his head and watched her.

If he couldn't undress her, he could at least enjoy watching her do it herself.

Perched on the edge of the bed beside him, Julie pulled the camisole up and over her head. As she raised her arms, her breasts lifted and the tight nipples caught the lamplight in sharp relief. Del reached to touch one, but she evaded him and stood to remove the rest of her clothes. The black skirt fell to the floor, and she did not pick it up. Soon the muslin petticoat and underdrawers, too, lay where they fell.

"Is there a graceful way to take off shoes and stockings?" she asked uncertainly.

"I don't care if you pull them off with your teeth."

He watched every movement, not just of her fingers with the shoelaces, but the play of muscles in her shoulders, revealed between strands of hair that would not stay where she tossed them down her back. And the way her head twisted on the smooth column of her neck so that the lamplight cast changing shadows on her face. He felt his desire grow just watching her bend her knee and stretch her ankle to remove a black cotton stocking.

She stood, her feet still warm and the floor cool.

"Where are you going?" he asked.

Julie didn't answer. She walked to the lamp by the door and blew it out, leaving only the one by the bed lit. Then, knowing Del's gaze followed her naked body with loving adoration, she returned to the bedside and snuffed the other flame.

It would be a minute or two before his eyes fully adjusted to the dark, but he didn't need to see to know that she walked to the dresser, where she picked up a brush and began to pull it through the long strands of her hair.

"Come here," he whispered. "I need you."

"Oh, Del, what about your arm?"

"Damn my arm. Tonight is our wedding night, even if it isn't much of a honeymoon."

"But how can you—"

"I can't. So you'll have to make love to me."

He couldn't quite reach her until she turned to face him, and then, by stretching his good right arm as far as it would go, he caught her hand and dragged her closer. She stumbled and almost fell onto the bed, her hands landing on his chest. Laughter and desire rumbled from him, and he pushed one of those hands down under the sheet. When her fingers found him, he couldn't control the surge of need that arched his back and made him clasp her whole body to his.

He could see now, though only through the bridal veil of spun platinum that cascaded over both of them.

"Ah, Firefly, light of my nights." He sighed, combing his fingers through the shimmering strands. "Make love to me, Julie. Now."

He threw back the sheet, revealing the strength of his ardor, and wordlessly he guided his bride atop his hungry body. Then that instinct he had earlier aroused in her took over. She found him, covered him, took him inside her with a delicious sigh of pleasure.

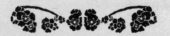

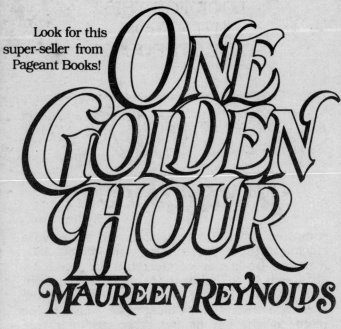